FALLING FOR HER FAKE FIANCÉ

BY
SUE MacKAY

THE FAMILY SHE'S LONGED FOR

BY
LUCY CLARK

MILLS & BOON

Sue MacKay lives with her husband in New Zealand's beautiful Marlborough Sounds, with the water on her doorstep and the birds and the trees at her back door. It is the perfect setting to indulge her passions of entertaining friends by cooking them sumptuous meals, drinking fabulous wine, going for hill walks or kayaking around the bay—and, of course, writing stories.

Lucy Clark loves movies. She loves binge-watching box-sets of TV shows. She loves reading and she loves to bake. Writing is such an integral part of Lucy's inner being that she often dreams in Technicolor®, waking up in the morning and frantically trying to write down as much as she can remember. You can find Lucy on Facebook and Twitter. Stop by and say g'day!

FALLING FOR HER
FAKE FIANCÉ

BY
SUE MacKAY

MILLS &
BOON

Published in Great Britain 2017
By Mills & Boon, an imprint of HarperCollins*Publishers*
1 London Bridge Street, London, SE1 9GF

© 2017 Sue MacKay

ISBN: 978-0-263-92673-6

Printed and bound in Spain
by CPI, Barcelona

Dear Reader,

At the end of writing *Pregnant with the Boss's Baby* I wanted to write Mac and Kelli's story—so here it is.

In their backstory, they've had a close encounter of the sexual kind after their friends' wedding. Back at work, they find it hard to focus on patients and not each other. So when Kelli needs a partner for her brother's wedding Mac puts his hand up—and then the fun really starts!

Weddings have become a bit of a theme for these stories, and I've loved writing them. And I haven't finished. Michael and Stephanie have been nagging me to write their story, and I'm not good at ignoring a good nag. So watch out for that book, which is going to come after a duet I am writing with the lovely Louisa George.

I love hearing from my readers at sue.mackay56@yahoo.com or drop by my webpage suemackay.nz

Cheers!

Sue MacKay

Books by Sue MacKay

Mills & Boon Medical Romance

Reunited...in Paris!
A December to Remember
Breaking All Their Rules
Dr White's Baby Wish
The Army Doc's Baby Bombshell
Resisting Her Army Doc Rival
Pregnant with the Boss's Baby

Visit the Author Profile page
at millsandboon.co.uk for more titles.

CHAPTER ONE

KELLI BARNETT PULLED a face, even though her bestie at the other end of the phone couldn't see her. 'I am not going with him, stand-up citizen or not.'

'Who *are* you going to take to Billy's wedding, then? You've got to find someone pronto.' Tamara's frustration was obvious. But then her family were equally frustrated with her at the moment so the tone was overly familiar.

Her brother's wedding was turning into a nightmare. 'No one.' If only it were that easy.

'You know your mother's going to sit Jason beside you if there's no one else to take that place.'

Oh, yeah. 'Maybe I'll pull a sickie, say I've caught some severe gastro bug that I can't share with the wedding guests.' Maybe she could take a flying leap off the end of the jetty and swim all the way back to Auckland city from the island where the wedding celebrations were going to take place in less than a week's time. But no, she would never jeopardise her brother's big day.

'Are you being obtuse? Like this guy's awesome, and you don't want to admit it.'

She hated the smug laughter Tamara was indulging in. 'You've met Jason. What do you think?'

'He's doing well as a lawyer, owns his house and drives

a top-of-the-range car that goes too fast. He'll make the perfect husband for someone.'

'Not for me.'

'Just checking here. You're turning him down at every opportunity because?' Persistent was Tamara's middle name since she'd found the love of her life and thought Kelli should do the same.

Kelli snapped, 'He's dull as dishwater.'

'Doesn't light your fire, huh?'

'A wet blanket would ignite that faster.'

'And Mac Taylor would set your whole world alight.'

The phone dropped out of Kelli's suddenly lifeless fingers. 'Damn you, Tamara,' she growled, but not loud enough for the words to carry to the phone now lying on the footpath outside Auckland Central Hospital. Tam was her best friend but sometimes… Bending to pick it up, she glanced at her watch. 'Got to go,' she told Tamara in her top don't-fool-with-me voice. 'I'm going in to sign my next contract with Personnel and then get to work. Bye.' She hung up before there was any more nonsense from her pal.

But moments later the phone rang and she didn't have the heart to send the call to voicemail. 'You'd better have something sensible to say or I'll hang up again.'

Tamara just laughed. Again. 'Ask Mac to partner you to the wedding. And before you cut off our friendship for life, think about it. You two were hot for each other at my wedding. The way you danced with him said more than I know you're ever going to admit.'

Kelli jerked to a stop in the middle of the hospital entrance, yelling, 'Are you out of your mind?' She'd just spent six weeks working in Fiji on an exchange with Suva Hospital and if that hadn't put Mac on the back burner then she was in trouble. Especially now she'd been bumped from day to night shift—Mac's shift—all because another nurse had taken early maternity leave due to high blood pressure.

'Only looking out for you, Kells, like you did for me.' Tears pricked her eyes.

Thanks, girlfriend. Appreciate it. Would love some of what you've got but it isn't going to happen. Not while I'm still afraid to reach out for it.

A quick slash across her face with her palm, a deep sniff, and, 'Why is it when someone falls in love he or she wants the same thing for everyone else?' People were bumping and nudging her as they streamed past. She was getting later by the minute. There was the meeting with Personnel—might be less complicated if she headed to the local supermarket and asked for a checkout job where she'd never see Mac—before her shift in the emergency department started at three. Very soon. It had been a full-on day, avoiding her mother and finishing unpacking from her time away.

'Because love's so good. Crazy good, wonderful. The sun shines even when it's raining. Of course I want that for you.' Tamara sang happiness.

'You think I'll get that with Mac?' She'd like to. No, she wouldn't. This was Tamara rubbing her up the wrong way causing these pointless ideas to surface. 'Don't answer that. I am not going to ask Dr Taylor to partner me to tea break, let alone anything else.'

Kelli's heart stuttered as she strode into the ED. Shoulders back, hands forced to hang loose at her sides, butterflies under her ribs.

Where was he? Looking around, she tried to calm the churning going on in her belly. Mac would be somewhere in here. He never ran late for a shift, and now that he was head of department he probably arrived extra early.

She shouldn't have come back. Doing a runner while she had the chance would've been the better option. The hospital board had sent her to Fiji to cover for a nurse coming here to upskill in emergency treatments, but no one on that board would've gone out of their way to track her down and haul her back if she'd done a bunk.

Too late, Sunshine. You're back, with another contract covering the next twelve months all signed and kicking off right now.

Where was he?

'Hello, Kelli.'

Bang. Right on cue. Slap between her ribs. That low, raspy voice raised images of a hot night in Sydney after Tamara and Conor's wedding. Without any effort or cohesive thought, she usually felt Mac on her skin, *under* her skin. But her radar must've been temporarily turned off because she hadn't noticed any change in the atmosphere until he'd spoken. Bracing herself, Kelli turned to face her heartache eye to eye. 'Hi, Mac. How's things?'

Mac was striding towards her, head up, back straight. 'Oh, you know. Same old, same old.' He shrugged as though life was a bit of a bore really. At least, she thought he was aiming for a casual movement to underline his comfort levels around her, but those muscles under his shirt were tight, tension rippling off them. 'Except it's not for you, is it? Shift change is at three, not fifteen minutes past.'

'Sorry, but I didn't ask to be bumped to the night shift,' she growled. Two could play this game. He might be setting the tone but she could just as easily keep up with the play.

His head jerked up a notch. 'I know.' A conciliatory note creeping in? Better if it didn't. Aggro would keep them apart, which was all she required of him. Unfortunately he hadn't finished. 'We had no choice but to bring you on board.' Perhaps not conciliatory, more annoyed. 'None of the other nurses would change and your return from Suva fitted in perfectly with our most experienced nurse having to take urgent leave.'

'So they told me over the phone on Friday.' Kelli didn't blame Mac for the change in her working times. Despite being Specialist in Charge his hands would've been tied, and by the looks of him he was no happier about it than she was.

'You only found out on Friday?' He sounded appalled, which won him a point or two. 'I told Personnel to get in touch with you more than a week ago.'

'You didn't think to phone me yourself?'

He swallowed hard. 'Yes. I did.'

'Yet you didn't.' Good one, Mac. Not a great start to their working relationship if he couldn't even do that. Really went to show how little he thought about those kisses.

Mac had kissed her in ways that tricked her heart into thinking he might've found her attractive in some small way. But deep down she'd known all along she was blowing in the wind. Gorgeous, sexy hunks didn't fall for her.

According to the school bullies, she had a lot in common with elephants, and not their phenomenal memories. When plastic surgeon Steve, now ex-fiancé, first came on the scene she was long past those jibes, until he offered to do breast and butt reductions free of charge.

And now there was Mac, a man who kept himself aloof from people all the time. A man who when asked if he was single by one of the nurses had replied tightly, 'Yes, I am,' and gone on with his work. His tone had been so raw no one had dared ask another thing. Yet for one night, away from home and work, sharing their closest friends' special day, he'd been different. Funny, fun, relaxed. She'd been hypnotised and felt close to him. Far too easily, considering her heart had been on lockdown since the humiliation Steve had caused her.

Which was why she and Mac had to remain totally professional on the job. She was not going through that again. Rolling her shoulders, she muttered, 'Guess we'll do our best to knock along.' And she'd do her darnedest not to remember that hot night in Sydney every time she came within breathing distance of him.

'Kelli.' Mac tapped her shoulder lightly. 'I apologise. I should've been the one to tell you about the changes, even if it was the personnel department's place to get in touch with you.'

She gave a tight smile. 'Yes, you should've. We're better than that.'

Mac scowled at her reproach, and she instantly worked to loosen the tightness in her neck and shoulders, and took a step back. No loosening the cramp in her belly while standing close to him. But keeping him onside was important. Working in Auckland Central's emergency department was her dream job and she'd do anything to keep it.

Anything? Avoid Mac as much as possible? After they'd shared kisses that had tricked her alter ego into sneaking out and letting her hair down—literally. And into having the most amazing time with a man she'd ever experienced, and that was without sex.

Her shoulders slumped. Mac had walked away when they stood outside her hotel room, key at the ready, leaving her wondering what had caused his abrupt change of mind when his desire for her had been plenty evident. A part of her had been relieved. Everything had happened so fast, those kisses so explosive, she hadn't had a moment to consider the consequences. Not least what he'd think after seeing her naked.

But since then there'd been no putting alter ego back in the box. It was up and fighting. Instead of her usual placatory persona being in charge there'd been nudges and changes going on inside that messed with her mind.

Working in Suva had given her time to take a long look at herself. Getting away from Mac and his inscrutable face after Sydney had been a priority. It had been as though he regretted their night of dancing and kissing. Which hurt bad. She hadn't been able to forget one touch, one kiss. Nor the gut-twisting moment he'd walked away from her outside her hotel room when she'd believed they were heading inside to the king-sized bed. That should've shut down all these hot, needy sensations that slammed through her whenever he came close. Should've. Didn't.

Might explain why she found it hard to return to being the woman who played safe in order to keep people on side so they couldn't find anything to pick at her about. It hadn't been about that with Mac and yet she'd still been rejected. So why wasn't she angry with him? Ignoring him? Why the heat and need for him?

In Fiji she'd figured it was time to dump the past. To stand tall and stare down anyone not accepting her as she was. To stop feeling sorry for herself and start taking some risks, get hurt maybe, loved, but most of all live. Had that night with Mac brought this on? Or was it because he'd shown her something she wanted? Excitement and maybe something more, something deeper?

Despite her new approach to life—still in training—Tamara's insane suggestion had blindsided her.

Ask Mac to partner you to Billy's wedding.

If only she could, and feel blasé about it. What if he laughed at her? Made her feel small? On the inside only; she'd never been small physically. 'Elephant, elephant.'

Those taunts had returned with a vengeance after Steve did his number on her.

So much for looking life in the eye, Kelli.

'You okay?' the man wrecking her new purpose asked.

She stared at him. 'I guess.' Her belly tightened painfully while her heart went on a rampage, beating up a storm behind her ribs. Mac was sexier than she'd remembered. How did that work? That chest stretching the top of his scrubs turned her toes upward, and made her fingers itch to slip across the expanse of warm skin covering it. That was how.

She raised her eyes to his inscrutable face, despair trickling out on a sigh. He was better looking than her brain had allowed. Definitely sexier now she'd felt his strength under her palms. A lot more serious too, if that was possible. Selective memories here. She should be thinking only of watching him walk away from her that night and the twinge of relief that nudged her, nothing else. But some things were downright impossible.

Her tongue stuck to the roof of her mouth as moisture dried up.

I can do this. I can do this. I have to do this.

The next phase of her career was going to be an absolute blast. 'Right, we'd better get on with the show. Any changes in staff since I've been away?' Apart from the nurse she was now filling in for, that was.

'Michael's swapped to our shift, having decided day shift without Conor around wasn't so much fun,' Mac told her as they began walking towards the hub of the department. 'Otherwise all's normal.'

'Cool. I like working with Michael.' Kelli looked around at the familiar territory, and tried to feel at home again. But it was impossible when Mac was within reaching distance. The Mac she'd got close to, not the Mac she'd wondered what it would be like to make love to. There was a difference between wondering and knowing. A huge, belly-tightening, heart-shaking difference, and she didn't have the answer. Her fingertips tingled with memories of him; warm skin, rippling muscles. And that was only his back, his arms. She gasped.

Stop it.

So much for putting that night behind her and getting on with her life. Kisses had never wrecked such havoc on her equilibrium before.

'Everyone likes working with Michael,' growled Mac.

Her head flipped up. Jealous? But the burnished green eyes that met hers said no, instead warning she was not special around here. Definitely not special to him. Anywhere. 'I'm sure they do,' she muttered as something sharp lanced her heart. 'How did my swap from Fiji work out?'

Relief filled those thoughtful eyes. 'She was overwhelmed for the first few days but once she got the hang of the continuous stream of patients she found her stride. Talk about soaking up knowledge faster than a sponge takes in water. She thrived, and didn't want to go home at the end of her stint.'

'I can understand that.' Perhaps she could swap permanently with the Fijian nurse.

'You didn't want to come back to Auckland?' Mac asked, his voice now grave. 'Or to ED and working on night shift?' He mightn't have asked 'Or working with me?' but the question hung between them.

She avoided the hot topic. Hot? She was standing by Mac, right? Scorching. 'Bit hard to give up those beaches and the warm water and return to Auckland in autumn.'

Did you miss me at all while I was away, Mac?

'Talked to Tamara lately?' he asked. Guess that meant no.

'Less than an hour ago.' The friend whose wedding had

started the inferno between her and Mac. 'She's sick of being pregnant, says her belly feels like it will pop open any minute.' She'd been full of unwanted advice.

'Conor told me she's as restless as a hive of bees.'

Definitely not going to talk about themselves. She could run with that. Safer, if not sad considering how well they got on in Sydney. *I missed you so much it kept me awake most nights, Mac.* But playing safe was her way and she'd grab this with both hands. Best way to put the whole caboodle behind her.

Then the phone in her pocket vibrated with an incoming text. Probably her mother, in which case she'd not even look, definitely wouldn't answer. She was not going to the wedding with Jason; nice, successful, upright citizen that he was. Today was Monday. She had until lift-off on Friday to find someone to go with her.

Ask Mac to partner you to the wedding.

Go away, Tam. *Go away.* He wouldn't want to attend a wedding where he knew no one but her.

You both only knew the bride and groom at my wedding.

Yeah, well, that was different. It had been small, and while Conor's Irish family were full on, they'd been convivial, not loaded with awkward questions about her and Mac. Unlike her mother if Mac partnered her to Billy's.

'Hey, Kelli, welcome back.' Stephanie, the head nurse on night shift, appeared before her, a genuine friendly smile lighting up her face. 'Great to have you working with us.'

Now that was a better welcome. 'Glad to be here.' Put some effort into it. 'Truly.' If not for working alongside Mac, that was. 'I'll have all those mornings to do other things.'

'Like?' Stephanie grinned. 'Sleep in?'

'More dress designing.' Her passion outside nursing. Why did her gaze slide sideways towards Mac? He was not one of her passions. He couldn't be. Dress designing. Mac. Her mind flipped back and forth. Passion.

'I'd forgotten you made those amazing dresses.' Stephanie was prattling on, oblivious to the fact Kelli was distracted by their boss. 'You ever try selling them to the fashion shops?'

Dragging her focus back to Stephanie, she nodded. 'I've sold a few that way.'

'We'd better keep you happy working with us or we'll lose you to a new career.' Stephanie reached over to the counter and picked up a file.

'Nope. Nursing's my first love. Designing's a hobby.' She held her hand out for the file. 'What've we got?'

'A lad of seven, fell off his skateboard, probable fracture of the left ulna. He's all yours.' Stephanie didn't let go of the file. 'For now I'm doing triage, but that could change. Letting you know in case you're interested.'

'Thanks.' Kelli headed for the waiting room and her first patient of the day. Of the shift, of the night roster. Of working with Mac. Her feet tripped over each other. This should be easy-peasy. It wasn't. Mac had dominated her thoughts since Sydney. Honestly? He'd started sneaking under her radar months earlier when he'd first arrived in Auckland Central's emergency department. The volume had been turned up by those kisses they'd shared, had her hormones in a right tizz.

Concentrate on work. Sure. 'Davy Roughton?' she called, scoping the room.

'That's us.' A young, distressed woman stood up and helped a boy off his seat.

Kelli crossed to them, bent down to the boy's level.

'Hello, I'm Kelli, your nurse. I hear you had an accident with your skateboard.'

His top teeth dug deep in his bottom lip as he nodded slowly. He held his left arm awkwardly against his chest. 'It went too fast.'

She grinned. 'They do that sometimes, don't they? Like they're trying to trick you into thinking you can do anything.'

Another nod, this time more relaxed. 'I can do jumps and things. But the board went over the step too fast and tipped me off.'

'You'll have to train your board to behave.' She straightened up. 'Come on. Let's get you fixed up.'

The mother said, 'The triage nurse suspects he's broken his arm.'

'We'll have Davy taken to Radiology for an X-ray to verify that. Then it will be a case of applying a cast and sending your young man home with painkillers.' She looked down at the lad. 'He's a brave soul. Not a lot of tears.'

'There were a few initially but Davy's usually fairly stoic. Like his dad.' Mum sounded closer to tears than her boy.

'Let's get this sorted. Would you like a coffee or tea? There's going to be a bit of hanging around.'

'Love a tea, thanks. Milk and one.'

Kelli ushered them into a cubicle and helped the boy up onto the bed. After settling him in comfortably she checked his temperature. 'All good there. I'll get our patient carer to make that tea, and tell the doctor you're here.'

Mac was at the bedside when she returned minutes later. 'We need an orderly to take Davy to X-ray, Nurse.'

'Yes, Doctor.' She gritted her teeth.

Since when did they go all formal? Got it. Mac was no

more comfortable with her being here than she was having to stand within metres of him, seeing, hearing him, breathing in that tantalising male scent mixed with a pine aftershave. Her blood thickened just thinking about him.

He shot her a glare. 'Now, Nurse?'

Of course. An orderly. Nothing to do with male scent and heat. Kelli phoned the orderly room, then headed to the desk for another patient file. The boy was being cared for and there were more patients needing her attention.

'Something bothering you, Kelli? You seem distracted.' Mr Distraction himself stood on the other side of the desk.

Shaking her head at him, she muttered, 'Not at all. Just getting back in the groove.' Guilt prodded at her though. She *was* concentrating more on Mac than work. After six weeks away and no contact with him, she should be over him. Her body wasn't listening, craving for more—more tender, yet igniting touches, more bone-melting kisses, more of those hands, his hard, muscular body against hers as they moved to the band's music.

'When did you get back from Fiji?' The unexpected question cut through the daydream.

'Saturday night. A tropical storm on Friday closed Suva Airport for twenty-four hours so I couldn't get out.' Couldn't drive to the airport in Nadi for the same reason.

'So you've only had a day and a half to unpack and get back into your routine?'

'More than enough.' If you didn't count the family dinner on Sunday and being pestered about going to the wedding with Jason. 'I got the groceries in, did the washing, and generally got settled. My flatmates didn't go off the rails and trash the place while I was away. It's not like I was gone for a year.' Now there was a thought. Twelve months away would take care of what ailed her. But it wouldn't solve her immediate plan of who to take to the wedding to avoid her mother's choice.

If only her family didn't worry about her so much. Sure, her engagement to Steve had been a hellish mess, sending her into a funk ever since, but now she was ready to get out in the dating world, she wanted to do it her way.

On her hip the phone vibrated. Again. Only her mother could be so persistent. Her friends didn't bother texting while she was at work, knowing she wouldn't answer. Using personal phones on duty was a no-no. Of course Mum ignored that.

Careful. Mac was watching her closely, too closely, and she didn't trust that he couldn't mind-read. He could do pretty much everything else. 'What?'

'Nothing.' He turned away.

'Good. I'll get the next patient.'

He came back, looking as though he couldn't fathom what he was about to say. 'What is it that you're not going to ask me to partner you to?'

'How—?' The floor tilted. She made a grab for the desk. Drew a breath. Tried to unscramble the words in her head. 'Has Tamara been talking to you?' Kelli knew the moment the question was out she was wrong. Tam might poke her with thoughts on Mac but she'd never go behind her back and talk to him about them. Shaking her head, she added, 'No. She hasn't. So I don't understand…'

'That was who you were talking to as you stood in the middle of the entrance causing people to duck and dive around you?' His smile was bleak. Not heart-warming at all.

At least her heart didn't think so. But she needed an answer to his question. It was none of his business, even if his name had been mentioned, but she hated hearing someone talk about her and then look away when they realised she'd heard. It started all sorts of doubts and worries.

So. Go for nonchalant. For cruisy. For this is unimportant. For my mother's already got me a date so you're off the hook.

'I need someone to go with to my brother's wedding this weekend.'

But... Come on. Add, But it's all right. I've got it sorted. The words just wouldn't form.

'You thought you'd ask me?'

No, I didn't. Tamara did. But if I'd had the courage to put myself on the line I might have. 'Just an idea. But I know you're busy, and it would be boring 'cos you won't know anyone, and weddings can be tedious unless you're involved.' Gulp. 'Sorry you overheard. It wasn't meant to be put out there. Girl talk, you know?'

'I'll accompany you.' He sounded as if he'd prefer to be pig-hunting in the mountains.

'You don't have to.' She hadn't actually asked him. Didn't want him feeling sorry for her single status. 'You haven't thought it through.'

'Are you stuck for a partner or not?'

'One of my own choosing, yes.'

'There's someone who could go with you?'

'He's not an option as far as I'm concerned.' She shuddered. Whereas this man standing before her shaking his head in bewilderment was the best option ever. Which was why she should take up the Jason offer.

Hello? Thought you'd stopped playing safe.

'Then you've got me.' Mac watched her, bewilderment giving way to amusement. 'Cutting it fine, weren't you?'

'I have been out of the country for six weeks.' *In case you hadn't noticed.*

'Don't I know it.' Shock removed the amusement. 'I mean, I… I don't know what I mean.'

Or what you want me to think you mean. He'd missed her. Not necessarily something to get excited about with that denial hanging between them. 'You can pull out. I won't rant and rave all shift.' Not aloud anyway.

'You don't know me very well, Kelli.' He leaned one delectable hip against the desk and folded his arms across that spread of chest filling his scrubs so well. 'Saturday it is, then. What time's the wedding?'

Slowly, slowly, her stomach started heading down towards her knees while her fingers began trembling. As for her brain? It was on lockdown, couldn't put the words in order, let alone utter them.

Mac's eyes were fixed on her, waiting. 'Kelli?'

Gulp. 'The wedding's at four.' As he relaxed her stomach dropped further. 'At a resort on Waiheke Island. The celebrations are taking place all weekend, starting Friday night with dinner for the two families.' She'd arranged to have Friday off months ago.

His hands gripped his crossed upper arms. 'I see.'

Ah, no, you don't. 'My parents have booked me a suite at the resort. If you're my partner…'

'I'll have to share it with you,' Mac finished for her after a hiatus in the conversation. 'You're meant to be sharing it with this other guy?' His face was bleak.

'No. He's got his own room.'

'I could get a room too.'

She shook her head. 'The resort's booked out.'

'So being in the same suite as you will make this other man believe you're not interested in him.' Then his gaze darkened. 'You're not, are you?'

CHAPTER TWO

As Kelli's face paled and her expression became stunned, Mac felt nothing but relief. He'd wager his brand-new, top-of-the-range four-wheel drive that she was not the slightest bit interested in this other man and was not using him to make the guy jealous. 'Why don't you just tell him you don't want to go with him?'

'I've tried heaps of times, but with my parents backing him he thinks I'll see I'm wrong.'

'Tricky.'

'Very.' Her face tightened, her eyes anxious. 'You won't be able to swap your Friday shift at such short notice.' Then the caution deepened. 'Will you?'

Seemed having a partner was important to Kelli. Deep despair had dulled her eyes earlier when she'd been on the phone presumably talking to Tamara. He'd been within touching distance and yet she hadn't noticed him or any of the people pushing past. It was that despair that had him offering to help her out because he'd been there, knew how hard it was to face demons alone. Not the sanest offer he'd ever made when he was meant to be trying to put distance between them, but would he retract it? No way. Even if that was where he might be headed this weekend. 'I'll pull in a favour. You going to tell me what this is about?'

Her eyes widened as she looked beyond him. 'Later,' she murmured.

'Kelli, can you meet the ambulance due any minute?' Stephanie was upon them. 'We've got an eighteen-year-old male, drowned while surfing at Piha. He was revived, but secondary drowning is now a concern. You want this one, Mac?'

No, I want a case three floors up where I don't have to see Kelli, hear her voice, or be reminded what a total pushover I've been. Partner Kelli to her brother's wedding? I can't believe I offered to do that. Talk about a stupid idea.

It wasn't as if Kelli had begged him. She'd been shocked by his offer. Mac tapped his head with a clenched hand. 'I'll see him. Michael might like to join us since secondary drowning doesn't occur every day.' Then the atmosphere around Kelli and himself would be diluted somewhat.

'I'll go tell him.'

The bell from the ambulance bay was loud in the sudden silence between him and Kelli. Then she shook her head and rushed off to collect their patient, those endless, shapely legs eating up the distance with haste.

Mac watched her go. Waited for her to return. One hour working with her and he knew he'd made a big mistake filling the vacancy with Kelli. Not that he'd had any choice. She was distraction personified, made it impossible to think logically. Hence putting his hand up for that wedding position. What other reckless suggestions would he be making after a whole shift? A week? He'd be better off spending the coming weekend at Piha Beach where he could dig a large hole in the black sand dunes and bury himself, not spending the days on Waiheke with Kelli, mixing and mingling with her family, and no doubt being given a thorough look over.

No, mate, that's not your problem. The real problem here is that hotel suite. Double beds are a given in these places.

All he could hope for was that there were two. But something deep in his gut told him what fate thought of that idea.

Two nights sharing a room with Kelli would test him beyond measure. Hell, one night dancing with her in Sydney had burned him deep. Deep enough to bring up all the walls to keep from getting close when they were outside her hotel room and the enormity of what they'd been about to do hit home. Even casual sex with Kelli would've exposed more of himself than he had since his beloved Cherie. Mac grimaced. No pun intended. He hadn't been ready to let his emotions out of the box when they were still tender and bruised. The weeks Kelli'd been in Fiji had been a relief. Had given him time to put that escapade into perspective. He'd been determined that Kelli was not going to become a part of his life outside work. Yet one hour in and already that was a total screw up.

They were going to spend a whole weekend together. All because of his big gob.

Over the past six weeks he'd missed her more than he'd believed possible. But he wasn't ready. Doubted he ever would be. Not even a short fling with no strings. Doubted Kelli was a casual fling kind of girl given the intensity she approached people, work, pretty much everything, with. Unfortunately for her, for him, he'd given his heart to Cherie, and didn't have a second one beating in his chest. Moving beyond the dark that had resided in there since—since the day his life had blown apart and grief became his norm—wasn't possible.

Yet whenever an email from Kelli had come in on the department site during the past weeks he'd read it avidly to see what she was up to. Her account of fishing far out from land in a tiny canoe with the locals had had his heart racing, even though she'd obviously returned safely. There'd been a photo of a grinning Kelli holding up a trevally she'd caught. That grin had got to him, tightened his gut and other parts of his anatomy, but, worse, it had started gnawing away as if he was missing the point somehow.

He'd wake up in the middle of the night in a cold sweat only to lie staring at the ceiling, his heart pounding while images of Kelli paraded through his skull. Kelli in that figure-defining bridesmaid dress, Kelli dancing at Tamara and Conor's wedding celebrations, Kelli strolling down Darling Harbour pier afterwards in six-inch-high green shoes as if she were in sneakers. In his arms, reminding him of what he'd lost and couldn't contemplate opening up for again. In case he…

'Mac?' Stephanie waved a hand in front of him. 'Your patient's in cubicle two.'

Truly? How had he missed the stretcher being pushed past? Was it possible that Fiji Hospital ED needed to swap out a doctor requiring to upgrade his or her skills? Could it be a twelve-month exchange? Because he was available, as of right now. 'I'll just grab Michael.'

'He's already there.'

If he didn't know better he'd believe Stephanie was laughing at him. So he didn't answer, didn't give her anything else to be amused about. Pushing through the curtain into cubicle two, he introduced himself to the young man. 'Beau, I'm Mac, a doctor. I hear you got into some trouble surfing this afternoon.'

'The ambo guy said I drowned. But that was ages ago. Why am I in here? The surf club guys brought me round.' His hands were picking at the bedcover. Grumpy and twitchy.

'Drowning's no picnic. We need to monitor you for a while. Also I want to see if there's any water still in your lungs.'

'I reckon I coughed it all up. A little bit can't hurt, can it?' The words were snapped out. Aftershock from drowning, or his normal mannerism? He did appear a little bewildered.

'Do you remember much about things before the helicopter picked you up off Piha Beach?'

'Lots of people hanging around, talking at me.'

Kelli already had the pulse oximeter on his finger to keep tabs on his oxygen saturation. She was focused on their patient.

As he should be.

'Can you sit still for me, mate?' Michael asked. 'I can't listen to your lungs while you're moving so much.'

Beau scowled but sat stiffly, only moving to breathe deep when Michael asked.

Mac explained. 'You drowned, and had to be resuscitated. We need to keep an eye on you for a while yet in case there are any complications.' Mac glanced at Kelli. 'Heart rate?'

'Sixty-nine.'

Near to normal. Moving in beside her, Mac said quietly, 'Watch for mood swings. Beau seems edgy, but that might be his personality.' He tried not to breathe in that scent of flowers, but his lungs couldn't hold out until he'd moved away. Roses. Red ones. Like the ones in his mother's garden when he was growing up. But this scent was beguiling and tempting and—unwelcome. He bit down on the groan of longing building in the back of his throat. The night ahead stretched out interminably.

A bell sounded from the ambulance bay. Relieved to have an excuse to get out of this airless cubicle, Mac turned to head away. Drawn back to Kelli, he coughed. *Let it go, man.* But he just couldn't. 'It's good to have you back. The place's been dull lately.' It had? She hadn't even worked the same shift as him until today.

'I'm not noisy.' The tone might've been sharp but her mouth twisted in that adorable way he'd begun noticing at the wedding dinner.

'I always know when you're around.' *Talking too much, Mac Taylor.* There were hours to get through yet. *And* this was only day one of three hundred and sixty-five minus weekends. All those days to get to know Kelli and maybe understand why he felt different around her, if there was some hope for his future.

Kelli's head shot up. Despair and puzzlement shone out of her cobalt eyes. A faint pink blush stained her cheeks. 'Just as well I've been away then, isn't it?'

Mac forced his mouth shut and made for the curtain again, his stomach in a knot. He didn't trust himself not to come out with something equally stupid as that last little nugget. Before she'd taken the job in Fiji he'd only ever seen her as her shift was finishing and his beginning. Yes, and he'd always noticed her. Now he'd gone and told her much the same. Didn't make sense. It wasn't as though he was interested in her outside work.

Then why had he taken her to that Sydney night club after Conor and Tamara's wedding? How could he not, when she'd been beautiful in her emerald-coloured fitted gown and those shoes that weren't made for walking? Yet Kelli had walked the length of the pier and back in them. She had to be some kind of acrobat to be able to do that without falling off the heels and breaking her long neck. A delectable, beautiful, annoying acrobat whom he'd kissed—a lot. And ever since then, he'd not been able to forget any moment of that night. Was that why he'd agreed to go to this next wedding with her? Because after the last ceremony they'd made out together, and might repeat the scenario? He needed his head read—by an expert in craziness.

Behind the curtain he heard Beau ask in a wavering voice, 'Can I phone my mum?'

'Of course,' Kelli answered. 'Here's your daypack. Will your phone be in there somewhere?'

'I hope so.' The guy suddenly sounded much younger and vulnerable.

'I'll leave you alone to call her, but I won't go far in case you're worried something might happen. Want a coffee?'

Mac made a beeline for Resus and the patient being wheeled through from the ambulance. Having Kelli find him hanging around outside the cubicle was not an option. He might feel like a seventeen-year-old in lust but for Kelli to recognise that would blow the lid on any hope of working together with some semblance of normality. As for what spending the weekend in close proximity of each other would do to him, he couldn't begin to imagine.

The paramedic greeted him with, 'Mac, this is George Falkiner, fifty-one, a digger driver. The ground gave way under his three-ton machine and he was tossed out and then hit by the bucket. He's stat one, hasn't regained consciousness in the time we've been with him. Multiple fractures to both arms and the right leg. Suspected internal injuries around the spleen and liver.'

'I'm surprised he's still breathing. Let's get him onto a bed and hooked up to our gear. On the count, everyone.' Their patient was quickly transferred from the stretcher to the bed, and Mac began an examination. 'Stephanie, I need blood bank on the line yesterday.' The guy was losing blood from a torn artery in his groin faster than water leaving a bath. Those internal injuries would be bleeding too. 'Get some group O sent down and a tech to take a crossmatch sample for further transfusions.'

'Onto it.'

'Then call Radiology.' Mac had started at the man's skull, gently probing for crushed bones and bleeds. He did not like the guy's chances, but that wouldn't stop him doing everything within his power to save him. Including putting all thoughts of Kelli aside.

Around him nurses and another doctor worked quietly and efficiently stemming blood flows, monitoring heart rate and blood pressure, examining limbs and probing for other injuries. A lab tech arrived with blood and a test kit to take a sample for blood grouping. George Falkiner had a damned good team on his side.

The cardiac monitor emitted the flat sound of no heartbeat. Mac snatched up the paddles. 'Stand back.' With a check that everyone had done as ordered he applied the electric jolt needed to restart the man's heart. It worked. 'Now there's a wonder. He's lost so much blood I didn't expect to bring him back.' But for how long? Sometimes things worked right, and sometimes: well, Mac wasn't going there. His patient didn't need the negative vibes. He'd managed to score enough on his own.

Mac was completely unaware of anything going on outside Resus. His focus was entirely on his patient, and it wasn't until they'd finally stopped the bleeding except for some internal strife, that he began to think there was a chance this man might make it. Radiology took their pictures, Theatre was on standby, and a general surgeon and orthopaedic surgeon were up to speed on what was required for their patient.

When George was finally wheeled away to Theatre Mac straightened his aching back and rolled his neck to loosen the muscles that were sporadically cramping. 'Glad that's over.'

'Grab a break while you can.' Michael spoke from the desk. 'The numbers are starting to crank up out in the waiting room but nothing urgent. I'll go after you get back.'

'Think I will.' A cold drink and something to eat would do wonders for the weariness gripping him now that the urgency of that case had gone. Tossing his scrubs into the laundry bin and pulling on clean ones, he headed for his office and the snack he'd put together earlier at home.

Once at his office desk he decided to stay put and do a bit of paperwork while he chewed on sandwiches. Even signing off a single document was one less to worry about. Not mentioning that in this airless pokey room he was safe from Kelli scent, Kelli comments, and definitely the wariness in those blue eyes that had appeared from the moment he'd agreed to be her partner this coming weekend.

Knock, knock. A head popped around his door. Kelli. Of course. So much for a few minutes' escape.

'Hi, everything okay?'

She stayed in the doorway. 'Just giving you the heads up. A nine-year-old girl fell ten metres off the family deck onto a fence post. Stat one. The chopper's bringing her in from Waitakere, ETA approximately ten minutes.'

Mac winced. 'Nine, eh? That's a small body to land on a solid object from that high.'

'The mother's with her.' Kelli stared at her hands. 'A parent's nightmare really.'

'How do parents cope with not always being able to keep their kids safe? It would drive me crazy.' Keeping those he loved or cared about safe was as ingrained as taking a shower every day. Not that he always did well at saving people. He looked at his bare ring finger as if he needed reminding.

'I guess they can only set the boundaries, keep a vigilant eye out, and cross their fingers.'

That didn't stop bad things happening. He'd done all of that and yet his wife had died. In bed. Beside him. While he slept. He was a doctor, and that had meant absolutely nothing when he was most needed. He should've sensed something was wrong with Cherie even in his comatose state brought on by exhaustion after too many sixteen-hour shifts in ED. But he hadn't. The aneurysm had been a silent killer, stealing the love of his life and their unborn infant.

Pushing down on the flare of pain and distress, he growled, 'Let me know when the helicopter's landed.'

'Yes, Doctor.' The door closed with a small bang.

Fair cop. It wasn't Kelli's fault he was flawed, hadn't been able to save Cherie. No, that was his to own. But it didn't give him licence to be surly with Kelli. Yet how to keep her away? How to stop the fissures she was opening within him from spreading throughout his soul just by being around her? She had hang-ups aplenty. Was always trying to appease people and keep the department happy and relaxed—except when it came to him. Then she could be lippy as all hell. Lippy. Lips. Oh, hell.

Those lips, that mouth. Soft while demanding, hot and giving, made to bring a man to his knees. How he'd walked away that night was beyond him. Showed the strength of his fear of opening up to another woman, because, as far as he could work out, that was the only reason he'd hightailed it away from her.

Hopefully his abrupt dismissal might keep her distant for the rest of the shift. By tomorrow he'd be over whatever was tying him in knots every time Kelli came near, and remember only that she was an exceptional nurse who always went the extra distance for her patients.

An attractive nurse with a body that filled scrubs in a tantalising way they weren't designed for.

A woman with shiny dark blonde hair piled on top of her head and kept in place with carefully positioned decorative combs. And when those combs came out, the thick locks had been satin in his fingers.

He wouldn't think of the smile that warmed him right down to his toes, and the laugh that lodged in his chest when he wasn't on guard.

All of that was before Sydney, buster. Not only since then.

Mac threw his pen at the far wall. Ping. Didn't underline his feelings. The water bottle followed. Bigger ping. Just as well he'd already drunk the contents.

Not feeling any better here. Cherie had been the love of his life. Had been? Still was. There wasn't room for another one. He'd never recover if something went wrong a second time. He was still recovering from losing Cherie.

Where was that chopper?

Ten minutes could whizz past in seconds, or it could drag out into an hour. Today was the drawn-out version. Mac chewed and chewed on his tasteless sandwich: cold beef with zucchini pickle care of his mother. She sent him a package about once a month, filled with jars of homemade jams and pickles, a fruit cake, and sometimes in winter homemade chocolates, which he gave to the kid next door. Comfort food that he enjoyed but wouldn't admit to in case it made him look like a spoiled brat.

His mother had been the cushion in his life growing up with a tyrannical father who believed his way was the only way for just about everything. Make that *absolutely everything.* So the packages were warmly accepted as a reminder of his mother's unconditional love and how not everyone was hard on others. They'd stopped when Mac married, but about a month after Cherie died there'd been one on the doorstep when he'd got home from work, and they hadn't stopped since.

Stephanie waltzed through the door without any pre-amble. 'Our girl's being brought down from the landing pad now.'

Instantly on his feet, Mac tossed the remainder of his snack in the bin. 'Let's go.'

'If it's okay, I've put Kelli on this one. She's good with the littlies.'

So were other nurses, and they weren't distracting. But, 'Why wouldn't it be all right?'

Stephanie watched him, her head on a slight angle. 'I think you can probably answer that better than me, but it seems she's got you rattled.'

Fortunately Stephanie headed out of the room so he didn't have to come up with some unlikely reply, denial being at the top of the list. And if he denied what she was implying, he'd be lying.

His gut had been in turmoil from the moment he'd seen Kelli on the sidewalk outside the hospital on the phone to Tamara, and didn't feel as if it intended settling down any time soon.

Time to focus on the job, starting with the young girl now arriving in ED.

Izzie had been given morphine making her barely coma-tose, which was a good thing, Mac decided as they worked to find the extent of her injuries. She'd hit the post with her thigh, fracturing the bone in three places. Her pelvis hadn't come off any better.

'Thankfully none of her organs were damaged,' Mac informed the girl's mother as they waited for the orderly to take the child to Theatre to have those bones seen to. 'Nor is there any head injury apart from the cut above her eye, though there's a severe whiplash to her neck, which will cause ongoing issues with headaches and muscle tension. Izzie will be referred to a neurologist for help with that.'

Tears poured down the young mother's face as she gripped her unconscious daughter's hand. 'But she will be all right? Won't she? Please say yes.'

He wanted to. He *really* wanted to. It was inherent in him to make people feel better, or safe, or at least able to function normally. It was something that had started the day he saw his father kicking the family dog for being sick on the kitchen floor. Mac had snatched Pippy away and run for the garden shed, only to be followed and given a lesson in not letting animals or people turn him into a miserable excuse for a man.

But being honest was right up there too. 'Izzie may always walk with a limp. Whiplash can also be hard to completely put right.'

The tears became a torrent. 'My poor little girl. It's not fair. She's always been such a monkey, climbing trees and ladders and getting into places no one would've thought possible. She terrifies me at times, but there's no stopping her. She thinks she's bulletproof.'

'She's probably had the biggest wake-up call possible.' *Or she'll take it on the chin and carry on being a monkey.* 'Parenting, eh? Who said it was easy?'

'You got kids, Doctor?'

Cherie had been four months pregnant when she died. 'No.' The word spat out, so he added with more restraint, 'Not yet.' Never. Unless... Unless he could talk about the past, undo those crippling fears enough to let the sun shine in—as in Kelli sunshine.

Right that moment Kelli walked past, helping her next patient, an elderly man with what appeared to be severe arthritis in his leg. She did not acknowledge him. Had been distant in the room with Izzie. Had been distant ever since leaving his office an hour ago.

Hopefully she'd find him a smile before the end of the week or it was going to be a long, awkward weekend on Waiheke Island. It was already a long, awkward shift.

Bring on eleven p.m.

That time did eventually tick over. Monday's were never frantic but this one seemed quieter than usual. In other ways Mac's mind was constantly on alert, Kelli alert. Her laughter, her voice, scent, the way the air cracked like an approaching storm. For eight hours he'd been put through the wringer, his body tense and filled with need. Immediately after completing handover he grabbed his bag and headed to the staff gym in the hospital basement. A hard workout would fix what ailed him.

In shorts and sleeveless sports top Mac strode into the workout room and slammed to a halt. He wasn't alone. Nothing new in that. But never before had Kelli Barnett been here at the same time. Then again, she worked night shift now. He hadn't known she worked out. Memories of firm muscles and a flat abdomen, a stunning figure accentuated by that dress, waved at him, reminding him of how his groin had tightened. Was tightening now. Went to show he hadn't really thought about it.

As he watched those long legs running on the treadmill his heart rate was increasing exponentially. Endless legs wound around his waist as they— Gulp. Out of here, now.

She hadn't seen him. He'd be gone before that changed. No way was he working out in the same room as Kelli.

'Hey, Mac, how's things?'

Spinning around, he came face to face with the surgeon who'd operated on young Izzie. 'Andrew, haven't seen you in here for a while.' *And I'm not about to, considering I'm on my way out.*

The pounding of feet on that treadmill was increasing in speed and noise. If Kelli was working up to a top speed she wouldn't be looking around the gym to see who else was here. He might still get away.

'Want to lift some weights?' Andrew asked.

'Not tonight.' He stepped aside, intent on leaving, but couldn't resist glancing across to the treadmills.

Caught. Kelli was holding onto the handlebar with one hand and staring at him as though she was oblivious to what her legs were doing. Her face a picture of surprise and—and annoyance? Either way, she definitely wasn't happy to see him.

She stumbled. Grabbed at the bar with her free hand, tried to get back to the measured, fast steps required to keep up with the machine's set speed. She kept tripping, as if she couldn't quite get it right.

Mac was already halfway to her. 'Hit the slow button,' he called as worry thickened his throat. Fall and chances were she'd twist an ankle or sprain a wrist.

The treadmill stopped. Instantly. Kelli lurched forward, banging into the control panel.

'The slow button, not the off one.' But he was too late telling her that.

Kelli remained upright, her breasts rising and falling fast, her hands at her sides. But man, could she curse.

Mac stopped beside the treadmill and watched her, his worry backing off, replaced with silent laughter as she gave herself a right lecture. 'Come on. You're not that bad,' he intervened at last.

Then she removed earplugs and glanced at him. 'Did you say something?'

'Nothing as potent as that diatribe I just heard.'

Heat seared her cheeks, turning them a sharp shade of crimson. 'Ouch. Did anyone else hear me?'

'I doubt it. You're a quiet banshee.'

'I'm stupid, is what I am. Losing focus and nearly falling flat on my backside. I can see the photos now. All dressed up for the wedding and sporting bruises up and down my thighs.'

That brought up a mental picture Mac couldn't contain. His gaze dropped to her thighs. Under Lycra they were toned, smooth, mouth-watering. The skin he could see was tanned, probably the result of time spent in the tropical sun. Then he heard the rest of her sentence. 'Is your dress very short?'

'It's ankle length.' Kelli looked away. 'With splits up both sides.'

'How high do these splits go?' He wasn't going to survive if they reached higher than her shins.

'Umm, to the top of my thighs.' She still didn't look at him.

'Oh, man.' Survival was out. His heart was already practising speed-dialling and another part of his anatomy was doing a sit-up. 'I see.' Unfortunately he could. His imagination was particularly overactive tonight. Pumping a few weights wouldn't have helped at all. He'd probably pull a muscle. *Don't go there,* his mind shouted.

'You getting on a treadmill?' his tormentor asked.

'I'll hit the rowing machine first.' Instantly he wanted to snatch the words back. What was wrong with one of the cycle machines? They weren't directly in front of the treadmills.

'Right,' Kelli muttered and punched some buttons to start the conveyor beneath her feet moving. 'Right,' a little louder as she slipped her earplugs back in place, pressed the gradient mode and began pounding uphill.

CHAPTER THREE

KELLI RAN UP and down hills on the same spot until the distance monitor came up with five kilometres.

Mac was still in front of her, sweat pouring off him as he worked those pecs and shoulder muscles, rowing his heart out.

While *her* heart was racing with exertion, and disconcerting need for the man in front of her.

She ran another two kilometres. Her legs might be getting tired, but her brain was still tripping around fast as though it had received a sugar bomb. Not lust, or desire, or anything to do with Mac. Couldn't be. Those emotions were on lockdown, afraid to surface in case she got sucked in and her heart torn out again when she was only just getting it back in shape after the last time. Now that they were spending the weekend together she had to be more vigilant about keeping hot thoughts about him under wraps. She couldn't have him looking at her and reading her emotions and needs. Nor could she deal with him kissing her senseless then turning away. Not a second time.

Did she mention desire? Hot and expanding throughout her weary body, her sluggish muscles; livening her up, not preparing her for sleep when she got home.

Time to stop the machine. Nothing was going to shut her brain up. Not in here anyway. Not with Mac wearing the sleeveless top that showed sweat-slicked, tanned skin, and muscles that reminded her how hard that body had felt under her palms.

Slowing the treadmill at a sensible pace this time, Kelli dragged in lungfuls of air and gave up trying to ignore the beautiful sight before her. Mightn't get another opportunity.

Those broad shoulders tapering down to a trim waist and flat belly made for a perfect package. That night dancing in Sydney he'd made her feel small and dainty. Enough so she'd let her hair down and enjoyed being with Mac on the dance floor, letting loose in a way that had made her briefly forget all her insecurities about her size.

'You going to stand there all night? Or are you going to do some more exercise?' Mac called over his glistening shoulder.

'You got eyes in the back of that shaggy head?' His thick, dark blond hair had lost all semblance of the usual clean-cut style, instead stuck to his scalp with small curls appearing at the edges. Cute. As in man cute, not baby cute.

'Something like that.' The rowing machine was slowing, Mac relaxing and letting his arms drop. When he stood up he scrubbed his face with his hand towel. 'I'm starving. Feel like hitting The Grafton All-Nighter for something to eat?'

Kelli would've said no, she didn't need food; but her stomach had other ideas, announcing with a loud rumble that some grub was the best idea all night. She bit back a curse. Already she doubted she'd get any sleep tonight, and spending the next hour with him would cancel tomorrow night's quota of zeds as well. 'Thanks, but I'll head home and see what's in the fridge.' Yoghurt, tomatoes, lettuce, a cucumber and a loaf of bread. Yesterday's shopping hadn't been extravagant or expansive.

'You want to avoid me?' Mac asked softly.

'Yes.'

'When I'm officially your partner for the weekend?' he added in that soft voice that lifted bumps on her skin.

'Isn't that enough?'

A spark of hurt flicked across his face.

Got that wrong, hadn't she? 'I thought it'd be enough with you meeting me on Friday and going from there. I didn't want to take up any more of your time than I'm already doing.' He hadn't exactly rushed to welcome her when she'd turned up for work that afternoon after a six-week absence, so he wasn't likely to want to hang with her much now. Yet he had volunteered for the weekend. Nothing made sense when it came to her and Mac.

His hurt remained. Who'd have known he was so sensitive? Not her. Which only added to the guilt starting to crowd her mind.

'I need to be brought up to speed on a few things,' he admonished, still softly, but there was no denying the grit behind his words. 'I can't put my foot in it when it comes to your family. They'll expect me to know something about them. Then there's the other guy.'

Fair enough. 'Five minutes for a shower?'

'You sure you're female?' Mac started to smile, then stopped. 'See you shortly.' He was off, striding across the room, putting distance between them quick fast.

Sharing a meal at The Grafton All-Nighter was going to be a *load* of fun.

'I've got Friday off,' Mac told Kelli after they'd placed orders for bacon and eggs, and lots of tea.

'That was quick.' Keen? Nah, determined, more like.

He was known for his take-no-prisoners approach to getting things done.

'It comes with having done many favours over the past year.' He sculled some water. 'What time do you intend catching the ferry to Waiheke on Friday?'

'How about four-thirty at the heliport downtown?'

His eyes widened, but all he said was, 'Fine.'

Kelli felt driven to explain. 'It's my dad's way. Ever since he became successful and the business grew so huge he's enjoyed sharing it round, feels he owes it to those who knew and helped him back in the dirt-poor days.' Her father was kind, generous to a fault, not a show-off.

'What's he in?'

'Civil engineering.'

'With the growth going on in Auckland I can see how he's done well.'

'The harder he worked, the luckier he became,' Kelli quipped, but couldn't deny her pride. 'My brothers, all three of them, work in the business. An engineer, a lawyer and an accountant slash business consultant.'

'You stepped outside the square.' Something passed through that intense gaze, something she couldn't name. Admiration? For her? Not likely. Probably a question about why she hadn't gone into the family business that he was coming up with a load of incorrect answers to.

'After growing up hearing about the company day in, day out, I wanted something different, something that was about me. Choosing a career where I could help people, make them feel better, was it.'

'We're on the same page there. Primarily I did medicine to help others. Plus being good at science and maths made it a no-brainer.' Mac leaned back in his chair, stretched those long legs to the side of the small table. 'Why is helping others so important to you?'

Eek. This was getting serious. Trying for nonchalance, she told him, 'I can't explain it. It's just who I am.' There was truth in that, possibly brought about from the hurt she'd dealt with, hurt she hoped others didn't suffer. 'I could ask the same of you.'

'I hate seeing people in pain.' Short, snappy words, with a dirty great stop sign behind them. Followed by, 'Which brother is getting married?'

Back on track, off taboo terrain. 'Billy, the engineer. His fiancé, Leanne, works in the accounts department of the firm. My other brothers are married and their wives also work there. I'm definitely the odd one out.'

'That bother you?' His mouth did that delectable lift at the corner, and naturally her stomach got all hot and stroppy. Nothing compared to how the rest of her body was reacting.

'It's nothing new. When I was twelve I was sent to a private school where many of the wealthy send their kids. I didn't fit in. Dad hadn't quite made the big league then but he wanted me to have the best. I was smart, but not filthy rich. Some of the girls were horrid to me.' Understatement. 'So I stopped going to school, hid out at the mall or the library.'

'Tell me more.'

She'd not be mentioning that they called her 'elephant'. 'When my parents found out I demanded to be sent to a public school, and not the one down the road from the private school but the one in another suburb where the chances of running into any of those awful girls were remote.'

'You got your way.' He wasn't asking.

'I was desperate. When they backed me I became determined to prove they'd made the right choice. In some ways it was harder to get ahead in the lower decile school, in others downright easy because no one wanted to knock me down all the time.' *Because on day one I arrived with a friendly smile and a willingness to fit in by keeping others happy. Three strapping brothers at my back didn't go astray either.*

'You were bullied at that private school?' His mouth tightened even before she answered.

'All the time by a roving pack of brainless bitches.' She was surprised by the strength of emotion overwhelming her as she remembered being taunted constantly, punished for things that happened, even when she hadn't been there. 'But I've moved on, grown a backbone, and become the person I want to be.' Would he believe that little white lie? Because it was a work in progress. She'd thought she'd got past those girls until Steve had undermined her confidence, resurrected her flaws. Now she knew from the bottom of her battered heart there'd be no leaping into commitment until she trusted herself to be true to Kelli, no matter what any man threw at her.

'I imagine you always had a backbone.'

'You do? Thanks.' File that one with the good stuff that came her way. Not that it was strictly correct.

The waitress arrived with their meals and cutlery, banging the plates down and shifting water glasses too hard so the contents slopped on the table.

When she'd wiped up and gone Mac asked, 'So who's the man you're avoiding by taking me to the wedding?'

'Jason Alexander. A lawyer. A friend of my brothers' from years back.'

'What's wrong with him?'

'Nothing really. He's friendly, kind, hard-working, caring. Fits in with my lot all too easily.'

Mac's eyes narrowed. 'What aren't you telling me?'

'He's too nice.'

'In other words, boring?'

'He doesn't tickle my keys.' Eek. Just the thought of Jason tickling any part of her turned her cold. 'My mother thinks he'd be *right* for me—you know, as in settle-down-with-him right.' She shuddered. 'I'm being unfair. He really is a great guy, but he doesn't do it for me.'

'How come your parents don't accept that?'

Because her ex had been cruel, selfish, and devastating in a nasty way. And because she'd been blind to his faults until he'd cut her down so painfully. 'Sometimes they're overprotective. I'm twenty-eight, but being the daughter after three sons comes with complications.'

'Am I going to be seen as the intruder?' There. A wee smile.

Might be wee, but it was powerful, switching on all her hot spots. 'Absolutely. You'll be quizzed on your intentions, asked about your favourite sport and car, and my brothers will challenge you to anything they can find, tiddlywinks if that's all there is.' Suddenly this was fun. As if Mac and she were good together. *Steady.* Getting ahead of herself. 'You're still on?'

'It's not only your brothers who put out a challenge,' he grumped. But there was laughter in his eyes. Warm and generous laughter. Rare indeed.

She melted some more. 'Where do you think I learned it from?'

The eggs were delicious, the bacon crisp and yummy. They ate in silence, Mac chewing thoughtfully. What was going on in that sharp mind? He hadn't missed a point about her family and herself, had caught on about the bullying quickly.

'Once the weekend's over and everyone's back to normal, won't the attempts to get you to date Jason resume? I won't be there to deflect them.'

'Probably, but I'll manage. I don't live at home, so it'll only be at family dinners that I'll have to confront Jason. Whereas a whole weekend is too much. I'd probably lose my rag and say something I'd regret. Jason had a bad home life and somehow became a part of our lot,' she added.

'You said you've often told Jason how you feel.'

'Yes. He just shrugs off my refusal.'

Mac went back to being quiet, finishing his meal and ordering an ice cream.

She declined one, thinking of her hips and that skin-tight sheath she'd be wearing at the wedding. That reminded her. 'We need to set some ground rules for the weekend.'

'Wondered when we'd have this conversation.'

'We can't have a rerun of Sydney.' *No kisses that make me boneless. Unless we follow through and don't stop at the door.*

'Which part? The ceremony? The dinner?' His smile widened, was wicked.

'Never knew you did cheeky.' He was leaving it all up to her, not making it easy. 'We have to act like a couple without getting too close, if you know what I mean.'

'I know exactly what you mean. No kissing, making out in that double bed, gazing into each other's eyes.'

'Mac!' He'd listed everything she wanted to do with him. 'Try to avoid deep and meaningful conversations with my family.'

'We've got to look believable. I'm a doctor, not an actor.' Still smiling.

She gave him one back. 'Me either. My family know me too well.'

'We'll be fine. I can be my normal aloof self and let

your family think I'm a stuck up prude who wants only to be seen and not heard.'

Laughter spluttered across her lips and she raised her hands in surrender. 'Whatever.' The weekend was looking better and better.

When Mac paid for their meals Kelli got cross. 'I pay my own way.'

'I'm your partner in crime. I don't let any woman I'm out with pay her own way.'

'We're not partners tonight,' she snapped.

'Get over yourself, because next I'm driving you home. If you're not happy about that then think of it like this. I'm getting into the role for the weekend.' No smile now.

'What? A bossy role?' She half meant it.

'That'll give you reason to dump me afterwards.'

Apart from the one about them not being compatible. *We were very compatible in Sydney.* But a string of hot kisses was not grounds for a relationship.

'Ready to go?' That exasperating smile just got more exasperating.

Kelli wanted to argue, insist she get a taxi to keep some space between them outside work until Friday, but that smile bowled over all her resolve, what little there was, and she gave up. It would be nice to be run around after by a hunk just once.

Her car was in the garage after refusing to turn over, having been untouched for six weeks. It hadn't been a flat battery so she'd had to wait until that morning to get a mechanic to come take a look. Some electrical fault that needed lots of work, and money, but she'd been offered a cut on the price if she waited until tomorrow. Seemed they were very busy, and since catching a bus to work was no big deal she'd agreed. Probably been sucked in big time, but cars were an enigma when their engines didn't turn over instantly. She'd make sure it was ready to pick up on her way to work tomorrow. Couldn't have Mac thinking he had the upper hand in case he hadn't been joking about being bossy.

After giving Mac her address Kelli sat waiting for more questions, but none came. He was too quiet. So quiet she thought she could hear his mind clicking over. Tick, tick, tick.

As her street appeared ahead she couldn't take it any more. 'What are you thinking? And don't say nothing, because I won't believe you.'

He turned the corner, parked with precision outside the house she shared with two other nurses and hauled the handbrake on before switching off the ignition.

Now the silence was deafening and Kelli's teeth were grinding while her hands were tight balls on her thighs. Somehow she managed not to yell at this infuriating man.

Shuffling that butt around on his seat, he leaned into the corner and eyeballed her. 'I want you to hear me out before shouting me down, okay?'

Her heart stuttered. 'I'll do my best.' Was this where he explained that he'd had time to think about the weekend and all the ramifications and he wanted to renege on agreeing to partner her? From what she'd observed at work Mac didn't do rushed decisions, but he had this time, so it wouldn't be a total surprise if he pulled out. There wasn't much for him in going to a stranger's wedding.

'Just checking first. How much do you want Jason What's His Name out of the picture?' Steely eyes were watching her so closely they wouldn't miss if her toes curled in her shoes.

Didn't Mac believe anything she'd said? 'Totally.' She held up her hand before he could go on. 'He's so involved with my family, whatever I do tell him is tempered with trying to be kind, yet firm.' Because her parents backed his attempts to woo her. Without their support he'd probably have found someone else by now. 'Almost like an ingrained habit.'

Mac was still watching her with that disturbing intensity.

'What?' she demanded.

He pulled further back into the corner, as though putting space between them before lobbing a bomb. 'If we pretended to be engaged, would that solve the problem?'

'Pardon?' Her ears were ringing, her head filled with strange jolts of words that weren't forming into sentences. 'Did you just say engaged? You and me?'

'I did.'

'To keep Jason out of the picture?' She wasn't buying it.

'That's the plan.'

'You don't think us sharing a room will give him pause for thought?'

'I don't know,' Mac said in that reasoned tone that irked. 'Do you?'

'Until we're back in the city and carrying on as per normal, maybe.' And, 'An engagement for the weekend isn't going to change that.'

'We could continue it for a week or two. Then when we—' he flicked his forefingers in the air '—*break up* you'll need time to get over it before you can talk to him.'

She probably would and all. 'It's a lie. I can't do that to my family.' They only wanted the best for her. That they thought Jason was the best was unfair, but not a crime. Mum was the worst offender, but the brothers didn't hold back from teasing her for letting her past get in the way of giving a good bloke a chance. Yeah, an engagement did have one or two merits. Lots of them if she thought of that blah kiss Jason had once given her, and his weak hands holding hers as he'd invited her to go to the cricket with him. She'd rather watch paint dry than watch cricket, even with a man she fancied. Mac.

No, I don't.

'Do you watch cricket?'

'There's a random question. Yes, as a matter of fact, I do. One-day games in particular.'

Still preferred the paint option. But while watching it dry she could fantasise about Mac. 'Going to a game with you wouldn't be a condition of being engaged, would it?' She watched him back as closely as he was her. Yes. There. Those lips didn't do serious nearly as often as she'd thought.

'Could be. Are you considering my suggestion?'

Suggestion? Well, it wasn't a proposal, was it? Not when there was no love involved, or just about anything else. Only a means to an end. 'We could say we haven't set a wedding date—that's the truth—and aren't in a hurry. Another truth.' Another lie. If she and Mac were engaged she'd be racing him to the altar.

'Sure. If we have to say anything at all. Won't your family be too tied up with the current wedding to be thinking ahead to another?'

'Mac, you have no idea what you've let yourself in for.' She shook her head at him. 'Mum will start planning the moment I mention an engagement.'

'Maybe we shouldn't, then. Just look so lovey-dovey that they'll be nudging each other and asking when we might be wanting to tie the knot.'

'Do you have to look ill when you say that?' For some inexplicable reason that stung, badly. Was she so unattractive he couldn't imagine being lovey-dovey around her again?

Suddenly her hands were being lifted from her thighs

and strong fingers wrapped around her fists. 'You're so lovely I want…' Mac gasped, swallowed. 'It's the reality of what we're doing hitting home. I'm not changing my mind. But it isn't going to be as easy as I'd first thought. My suggestion just made it harder.'

'It was never going to be straightforward, but then I know my family. They want so much for me to be happy, they don't see that I can be that without settling down.' She'd thought she'd found Mr Right once, truly believed he loved her for who she was, what she was, hadn't seen the disdain coming when she ate a cake or took a day off from the gym. Apparently she needed to watch her figure with the intensity a native falcon would prowl the vine-yards for birds. And he'd expected her to be glamorous when they socialised with his colleagues.

'You don't ever want to get married?' Mac's fingers tightened, loosened again.

'It would take some convincing from a very deter-mined man.' She gazed into the eyes of the man she was learning didn't give up easily. She might be ready to get a life but Mac seemed to have issues he wasn't letting go in a hurry.

Doubts pushed forward. 'Mac.' She sucked in a breath. 'I need to know more about why you're doing this for me.'

He sighed. 'I've kind of been waiting for that.'

Well? Was he going to tell her? Because if not then she had to think seriously about her stance. Patience wasn't her strong point, but somehow she found some and waited quietly, her gut churning.

'Someone once helped me when I was in a bad place and I've never forgotten it.'

'You're saying I'm in a bad place?'

'Not bad, but you need help to extricate yourself from

a tricky situation, and I want to be the guy to see you through it.'

Her heart was turning mushy. 'What can I say?'

He smiled. 'Thanks would work.'

She started leaning forward with the intention of kissing him thank you, and stopped. Kisses were incendiary between them and now was not the time for an inferno. 'Thanks.' But she still wasn't satisfied he'd told her everything behind his generous offer.

'Hopefully I can give you time to sort yourself out, get rid of that despair that sneaks into your eyes when you think no one's looking.'

'What?' She stared at him. He was too astute for her good.

'Something's worrying you and I don't think it's all about Jason.' He held up a hand. 'It's all right. I'm not asking you to talk about things you'd rather not, just letting you know I'm here for you any time you want to unload.'

Run, Kelli, run. Now, while you can. Before your heart decides he's the one for you.

She didn't know how to answer, couldn't tell him her hang-ups, her need to find her own way before joining up with someone for life.

The silence grew between them, not uncomfortable, but not endearing either. Finally Mac gave her a lopsided smile. 'So are we engaged or not?'

No. He read her too easily. Forewarned was forearmed, wasn't it? There was something warm and comforting about being with a man who understood her. She could enjoy the fantasy and relax over the weekend knowing she was safe from the digs about Jason. Tempting. Too tempting. 'Yes,' she answered before she allowed all those pesky doubts and honesty factors to change her mind.

Mac straightened up, giving a tight little laugh as he

reached to pull on his seat belt. 'That's that, then. I've just got engaged and I don't know what to say.'

'Hardly how I imagined it to go either.' Nothing like when Steve proposed. Roses, champagne, a rock on a ring. Clichés in hindsight. Kelli elbowed the door open. 'But thank you for offering to be my partner, engaged or otherwise. I'm starting to look forward to the weekend. I adore my brothers and this is a special occasion.' She sighed at the imagined sight of the guys all dressed up in their tuxes and Billy's eyes filled with love for his lady, his second chance at happiness. 'I promise to make sure you have a great time.'

'As long as they don't want to draw pistols at dawn I'm sure I can get through without too much stress.' This time the smile was soft and genuine, and for her.

Too many of those and she would be in trouble. Mac's smiles, gentle and warm, were hidden treasure. They wound around her, bolstered her courage to do the things she wanted for herself. Including going to the wedding with him. Come next Monday she'd probably be regretting this, but, hey, she could make the most of what Mac was giving her.

'The guys aren't monsters, just overprotective of me.' They'd been the ones to take retribution on the bullies at the private school. They'd also dropped by the new school to show solidarity if anyone was thinking she might be a pushover—which she was. But instead of their getting people's backs up the girls in her class had become firm friends so that they'd get invited home and could spend time hanging with her brothers.

'Glad to hear it,' Mac growled. 'One more thing. I don't have your phone number. Nor you mine. Fiancés probably should be able to get in touch with each other.'

'Fair enough.' She rattled off her number then waited

for Mac to text so she had his. 'Done.' Slipping out of the vehicle, she smothered a yawn. It had been a huge day. 'See you at work.' A great way for a newly engaged woman to say goodnight to her fiancé.

'Goodnight, Kelli.'

The engine started but Mac didn't pull away until she'd let herself in the front door of the house. Admirable, but a hot kiss would've gone a lot further.

'Bleeding heck, what have I done?' she whispered, her shoulder hard against the doorframe as she watched the tail-lights of Mac's four-wheel drive disappear around the corner. Jumped in the deep end of a monster pool with weights on her feet, that was what.

Mac concentrated on driving, nothing else. He couldn't let anything into his mind or he'd lose focus and go through a red light or cross the middle line or something equally dangerous.

Dangerous? That was exactly where he was at with Kelli. With her warmth, and sense of fun, and stunning looks, and, damn it, everything about her, she threatened all his barriers, undermined his need to stay self-contained, uninvolved, out of another relationship. He'd had the ultimate love with Cherie. A man didn't get that twice. And if by some twisted stroke of fate he did, he'd be on tenterhooks for the rest of his life waiting for the axe to fall again.

Focus, driving only, remember?

He'd smiled when Kelli had explained her brothers were protective of her. Because it was great there were people to guard her back. Not because he couldn't help himself and had to let those warm feelings out. Not that.

Relief rocked him. Kelli wasn't interested in this guy Jason. She hadn't run for the hills when *he'd* offered to be her partner. Was she keen on him? A little bit? Well, she'd stayed in the car when he'd suggested the engagement thing. Went to show she wasn't thinking straight because it really had been one of the wackiest ideas he'd ever come up with.

Toot, toot. A car sped past, the occupants waving fists at him.

He glanced around. So much for concentrating on driving. The four-wheel drive was stopped in the middle of an intersection, the indicator flashing for left when he needed to go right. Thankfully it was well beyond midnight and the traffic was light to non-existent now that those unhappy fist-wavers had gone past.

Do I tickle your keys, Kelli?

She hadn't been shy in coming forward that night in Sydney, had kissed him as fiercely as he'd kissed her. It had been a one-off night, brought on by too much champagne and watching their friends all gooey-eyed for each other. Had to have been, or his world was slowly tipping off its axis.

They were about to spend a weekend together at another wedding celebration, under the microscopic watch of people who cared for Kelli. Could they pull it off, or would it soon become obvious he was a fraud? All he asked was that if the family learned the truth they went easy on him because technically he was on their side.

That need to protect was alive and kicking, with Kelli in its sights, whatever the cost to himself.

CHAPTER FOUR

'LET'S GET YOU to X-ray,' Kelli told the middle-aged woman sitting awkwardly on the bed, grimacing with pain whenever she moved. 'You do need to breathe occasionally, you know,' she added gently.

'How can I, when it makes my ribs shift?' Holly muttered.

'Bit tricky, eh?'

'Stupid ram. What was his problem anyway?'

'You didn't see him coming?' Kelli waited for Holly to ease herself upright.

'Never had cause to worry with this ram before. Every now and then we get a bolshie one and know to stay well clear until we find a place for him on a farm somewhere, but Angus has always been so docile.'

'You should've brought him in here for a check-up too. Could be something's got him in a twist.' Kelli chuckled.

'My husband's taking him to the vet once he's got me back home. At least he put me first,' she joked. 'What happens if my ribs are broken?'

Kelli sucked air through her teeth. 'You're not going to like this but plenty of rest so as not to jar those ribs.'

'That's not happening.' They headed along the corridor to the elevator bank. 'Painkillers?'

'Absolutely.' Kelli punched the button for the second

floor. 'Do you have another job apart from looking after the sheep at Cornwall Park?'

'We spend a lot of time helping on our son's farm in Karaka. His wife is disabled and requires a lot of care. I'm more patient with the stock so I'm kept outside.'

'Families, eh?' Kelli had yet to break the news to her parents that she was 'engaged', and was wondering if it would be best to keep that gem on hold, only to be used in extreme circumstances. They now knew she was bringing Mac, but nothing more. Reluctance at fibbing railed against the need to be able to enjoy Billy's wedding.

There was a lot more to Mac than she knew about. Like what had caused him to fall into that dark place he'd mentioned? She was starting to see past that barrier he kept in place, especially at work. He'd obviously been hurt and naturally wanted to protect himself from it happening again. Had a woman he loved dumped him? Or did his pain go back further, to childhood or his teen years? He wasn't one for putting anything about himself out there, so to have told her as much as he had said that he trusted her. Which meant she couldn't press for more info, had to wait until he was ready to share. Another sigh. She'd take this one day at a time.

After the elevator whisked her patient away Kelli returned to the counter to see who was next. It was pointless spending time thinking about what made Mac tick. The answers weren't here, at work, or if they were she wasn't seeing anything other than his medical skills and caring nature. If she was going to learn more about her *fiancé* she'd have to ask him some pointed questions. Not that he'd likely answer them.

'Take a break,' Stephanie told her before she reached the counter.

'I'll be in the cafeteria, too,' Mac informed the head

nurse, who immediately locked her gaze on Kelli and gave an almost imperceptible nod.

Almost. Not quite. 'What was that about?' Mac asked.

'Ask Stephanie,' Kelli retorted and dived into her bag for the salad she'd put in there earlier.

'Best not.' Mac opened a bag of crisps as they walked out of the department and offered them to her.

'No, thanks.' That dress was so form-fitting one chip might make all the difference to how she looked on the day.

'Talked to your family today?'

Her cell phone had been remarkably quiet most of the day. Possibly too quiet. It wouldn't mean her mother had dropped the date issue even knowing it was solved. She'd want all the details on Mac. 'I phoned to tell them they could relax because I was bringing a wonderful man to the wedding who I couldn't wait for them to meet.'

'Wonderful, eh?'

Naturally he'd pick up on that. He was a man. 'Don't get carried away. I could hardly say you were an uptight, pompous type.'

'I'm surprised you didn't.' He actually laughed and held out a chair for her at a table in the cafeteria. 'Any mention of the other?'

As in engagement? 'I thought it could wait until the last minute. I already turned down an invitation to dinner tonight.' Thank goodness for night shifts.

'Do you want to wear a ring?' Mac was studying his crisps too intently. They were only potato chips.

'Are you serious? That would be going too far.' She was almost shouting, and at the shock on Mac's face she pulled on the brakes. 'I figured on saying we haven't had time to choose one yet.'

'That's fairly close to the truth, I guess.' Now he

seemed to be interested in watching her again. Which was more exciting? Her or the crisps? 'You'd better give me the lowdown on what I'm expected to wear to the wedding.'

'Do you own an evening suit?'

His eyes crinkled at the edges. 'Yes, mam. And a morning one, some business ones, and others.'

'You're a suit man.' There was something about a good-looking man dressed in a suit and tie that made her all gooey inside. Mac had looked awesome in the stylish one he'd worn as Conor's best man in Sydney. She blamed that suit for losing her composure with him. Along with the dancing, the atmosphere, her friend's happiness after a difficult few years. But the suit had been the start of her emotions and hormones spiralling out of control. Navy with a crisp white shirt and emerald-green tie to match her dress. Oh, yes.

'You're looking decidedly dreamy,' Mac noted. 'Care to share?'

No way this side of Christmas. Or any time after. Knowing he'd made her feel happy and safe and even okay-looking that night would be giving Mac ammunition to tell her the opposite. As Steve had done, time and time again. She shuddered. Mac wouldn't do that. He was too kind. Or was she once again being naïve? 'More likely that's tiredness. I was late to bed last night, and up early.'

Bed. Another loaded word. They were going to be sharing one for two whole nights. After another wedding, where Mac would wear a suit, and she would get all excited. 'You going to take your PJs?'

A bark of laughter cut across her musings. 'The last time I wore those I was ten.'

'They wouldn't fit.' A giggle was starting. The idea of Mac in pyjamas was so not turning her on. Exactly the point she'd been trying to make, but the image in her head of him was hilarious and the giggles won out. 'I can sort of picture you in striped pants and top.'

'Racing cars.'

'Truly?'

'Yep.' He grinned, a rare sight that zapped her in the tummy and woke up those butterflies behind her ribs. When Mac relaxed the grip on his emotions he was a sight dreams were made of. His handsome face became beyond wonderful, good-looking mixed with fun and care and enjoyment. And sex. His green eyes reminded her of spring fields, and that mouth... That mouth could be soft as cotton wool, as demanding as a hungry child, as heat provoking as a firelighter.

She wasn't going to survive the weekend. Not and come out sane at the other end. She was going to be in a constant state of terror in case she jumped his bones or fell under his spell and had, not one, but two sensual nights in bed.

Rules, Kells. You've got rules in place.

Rules were made to be broken.

Her phone vibrated. Tugging it free of her pocket, she answered, 'Hi, Mum.' For once her mother's timing was perfect. 'Did you get the florist sorted?' Her mother was chef de mission for the wedding since Billy's fiancée, Leanne, didn't have family in New Zealand to support her apart from some cousins who were keener on partying than preparing for the big day.

'Of course I did. Now, my girl, we're dying to meet Mac. What about lunch tomorrow before you both start work? Just your dad and I.'

Shouldn't have answered the phone. Once again out of the pan and into the heat. 'Not tomorrow, Mum. I've got to pick up my car, and get my dress from the dry-cleaner's.'

She'd finished the hem on Sunday and taken the dress in for a professional finish yesterday.

'You making excuses, by any chance, Kelli Barnett?'

Yes, Mum, and I've got more up my sleeve if I need them.

'This week is about Billy and Leanne, not Mac and I.'

Across the table Mac looked up from the crossword he'd begun filling in. His nod was in agreement.

'We were thinking if Mac met us before the weekend it would be easier for him on Friday night when he's amongst the whole tribe.'

Why did that have to sound so darned reasonable? 'Believe me, Mac won't have any problem fitting in.'

'Why are you hedging, my girl?'

Because she loved her mother to bits she gave in. 'Mac, have you got a spare hour tomorrow to have lunch with my parents?' *Say no, you're getting your hair done, or meeting with the Prime Minister about a dog, or you don't do lunch.*

'No problem. What time and where?'

Thanks a bundle. He looked so at ease she wanted to biff him upside of his head. The uptight version did have a place—like right about now. But what could she do? 'You hear that, Mum?'

'Twelve-thirty at Cardo's.' She'd heard all right. No doubt her ear was pressed so hard against the phone it hurt. 'Looking forward to meeting this man who's caught your interest.'

Kelli shuddered as she slipped her phone back into her pocket. 'Game on.'

'I can pull out if that'd make you happier,' Mac said in such a reasonable voice that she wanted to curl up and cry.

'What have I done? It's not as if Mum and Dad are bad people, yet I'm lying to them.'

'Remember why we're doing this.'

He'd said we. As in they were together in this pickle. 'Because I've run out of ways to deflect him without being a complete cow, and I can't do that.'

'So I'm the deflection.' Mac shook his head and smiled. 'Pleased to meet you. I'm Mr Deflection.'

'Stop it, you're making me feel better.'

'That's the whole idea, Kelli.' He glanced down at the crossword, filled in a word, then began tapping the pen on the page. 'Was there another man who caused you strife in the past for your family to be wanting to pair you off with the apparently very pleasant Jason?'

'Do you need to know this to be my fiancé?'

Mac locked his eyes on her. 'I think I do.'

That'd mean exposing her flaws—before the weekend.

Mac added, 'I'd like to know more about you.'

He sounded so genuine the words just spilled. 'Two years ago I was engaged to an up-and-coming plastic surgeon.' An ego with lots of ideas on how to improve her body and looks. 'No one in the family liked him. He was cold and calculating, but I was smitten and wouldn't hear a bad word about him.' Until the day he demanded she have breast reduction surgery and a butt tuck. He explained that if she refused he wouldn't take her to any of the swanky parties he liked to attend. An irrational fear of going under the knife had won out over her uncertainties about her appearance. By a very narrow margin. End of engagement.

'What changed your mind?' Mac asked softly, the crossword now lying on the table, forgotten.

'One day he was so insulting about my appearance and other attributes I had to take a long, hard look at him. Didn't like what I saw.' He'd made her feel worthless. 'I'd made a mistake and for a while doubted my ability to judge people.' That sounded easier than it had been. Still, some things were best kept under wraps, and lots of clever clothes.

'So your family want to protect you from that happening again?'

She nodded. 'When I broke it off with him, Steve was furious, humiliated me every which way he could. That upset my parents more than anything and is probably why I'm in this spot.'

'Well, we're going to prove you're up to making the right choices,' Mac concluded.

Knowing Mac was prepared to go in to bat for her was as if a huge weight had been lifted. 'You're saying you're right for me?' she asked cheekily. 'That no one can fault you as my partner?'

'Your words, not mine,' he laughed, then sobered. 'If you want to change your mind I won't stop you. It's your call.'

Not so together, then. At the same time Mac wasn't telling her what to do, which earned him points. 'We're still on. For the first time in months I'm excited about the wedding.' And not all that excitement was down to her brother's big day. Some of it came from the company she'd be keeping, however temporary.

Stephanie appeared beside them. 'Incoming chest pains, tachycardia. I've got no one else available.'

'Coming.' Mac stood and began heading for the department.

'You're not taking your mug up to the counter?' Kelli called all innocently.

'Thought you'd do it for me,' he shot over his shoulder. 'As forward payment.'

'I think I liked you better when you were serious and

proper.' But she smiled as she picked up his mug along with hers. Mac did that to her.

A little after eleven that night Kelli hit the gym. Running another seven Ks would counter the effects of last night's bacon and eggs. She shouldn't have had them, but she'd been hungry and had wanted comfort food to minimise the anxiety beginning to build up over Mac's role in the coming weekend.

All the treadmills were in use except for one. Right beside the one Mac was using. Kelli resisted the urge to curse. Hadn't he gone up to the surgical ward to talk to a patient they'd sent to Theatre earlier that night?

The treadmill was out. She needed space while she mulled over the dross banging around in her head. The rowing machines were right in his line of vision, a sight she understood too well after watching him last night. Mac was not getting an eyeful of her pulling on that equipment, sweating and puffing like him the night before.

The cycle machine was it. Her least favourite. The way those bike seats embedded themselves in her backside was horrid and always seemed to leave her feeling like tenderised meat. But sore backside, or ogled butt? She'd take the pain any day.

'The humidity isn't helping,' Mac gasped as she passed him.

'Eighty per cent last I heard.'

'You're not running tonight?' he asked when she didn't climb onto the adjacent treadmill.

'Thought I'd go for the cycles instead. Nothing like a good ride.'

Mac's eyes widened and he looked at her as he had that night in Sydney. As if he wanted her. Heat radiated off him. Flipping her head sideways, she tried to avoid his need, sure she was giving back an identical message. Her nipples were peaks pushing against her tee shirt, her sex hot and damp.

'Cycling it is,' Mac retorted, bringing her instantly out of her delirium.

Thank goodness. Something had to. She was standing in the gym, not outside a hotel bedroom. Right, on with the job. Anything to shut down her mind, put Mac on hold. Ah, put Mac aside for ever.

Earplugs in and the music loud. Deliberately setting a higher than her normal speed, Kelli shuffled her butt left and right on the seat to get as comfortable as possible and began to cycle, building up the speed slowly. It wasn't long before sweat ran down her spine, between her aching, thwarted breasts, and had her top clinging to her skin wherever it touched. Yuk.

Mac stopped running, headed over to the weights, and the air did not feel any lighter.

Puff, puff. This cycling was hard yakker tonight, for some reason. Glancing around to see if anyone was watching she pressed the button to lower the resistance by two notches. No point in killing herself before the weekend.

Sometimes she wished she had the strength to ignore the fact she was on the larger side and didn't have to put her body through all this trauma. Imagine not having to work herself into a sweat ball five days a week. But any time she even half-heartedly contemplated not going to the gym she'd think of Steve and his scalpel. Giving herself the weekends off was her treat, and definitely her favourite days of the week.

Thirty minutes later Mac tapped the back of her hand and waited until she'd cleared her ears of music. 'You going to be all night on that thing?'

'Nothing better to do.' Her thighs were aching and her glutes were so tenderised they were ready for the barbecue.

'You need a life, girl. How about another round at the All-Nighter?'

Then she'd have to row, cycle *and* run tomorrow. 'Best offer I've had all week. No, make that since you offered to be my partner.' Her legs were slowing. 'Are you finished here?'

He nodded and slashed at his moist cheeks. 'Can't get enthused.'

'Enthused? Over exercise? Are you nuts?'

Mac's eyes narrowed. 'If you feel like that why come here? It's not as though you're overweight or in need of a body makeover.'

Was the guy blind? Thoughtlessly she leaned in, brushed her lips against his, hesitated and began a full-on kiss. 'Thank you,' she murmured against him.

Firm hands were on her shoulders, gently pushing her back, away from that divine man with his lovely compliments. 'Much as I hate to stop you, we are in the middle of the hospital gym where colleagues are working out— with their eyes wide open.'

Oh. Right. Of course. 'Sorry.' *He doesn't want to be seen with me.*

'Kelli, stop saying sorry. You didn't do anything wrong. I'm thinking more that you won't like the gossip mill starting up about us.'

Mac was protecting her from the gossips?

Go, you, Mac Taylor. I could really get used to this.

No, she couldn't, shouldn't, wouldn't. Her family already tried to protect her and look how she objected when they stole some of her independence. 'Shower time.'

His mouth lifted. 'I suppose.'

'See you in ten.'

'Twice as long as last night?'

She was sweatier than last night. *And* she needed to give Mac time to forget asking why she might say sorry so often. If she even did.

She did.

Sorry appeased people, kept them from giving her a hard time. Sorry didn't always work. It most definitely was a habit she needed to break.

Starting now. Tonight. No more 'sorry' unless there was a very strong reason, and that didn't include trying to keep people onside.

Hey, didn't Mac say he'd hated stopping her kiss? Forget sorry, think about what that might mean. He wanted more kisses from her. Yes. Mentally punching the air, she headed for the showers.

Mac watched Kelli fork up her salad. 'Who eats lettuce at twelve-thirty in the morning?'

'Me.' Chew, chew. Add in a slice of tomato.

'You don't look half as happy as you did last night eating bacon and eggs.'

She swallowed and glared first at him and then at her plate. 'You're right. But last night was an indulgence. Tonight is reality.'

'There's not enough lettuce on your plate to keep a rabbit happy.' Was she a diet freak? 'You have a figure that'd send any man into raptures.'

'I like to keep on top of my weight.' Kelli looked everywhere but at him.

'Do me a favour and have something tasty and filling to go with that salad. I'd hate you to fade away to a stick insect.'

She blanched. 'Fat chance.'

'Kelli, girl, you're not fat. You're perfect. Tall and shapely, not thin and scrawny.'

She looked at him as though he'd lost his mind. 'Shapely is another word for plump.'

Reaching for Kelli's free hand, he wrapped it in his fingers, felt her tremble. 'Whoever told you that is an ass. Or worse. Personally, I don't want to feel bones when I hug a woman. I want her warmth and curves and softness.' Not that he'd done much hugging for a long time. He used to love hugs. There was something relaxed and friendly and caring between two people who were close when they hugged. Like saying the world was good.

'Each to their own.' Hope tripped through her gaze.

'Well, you're my partner so I get to say what I like.' When they called it all off he would still think Kelli had a body to die for. He should ask his mother to start sending her care packages. As if that'd go down well with this prickly woman. 'Feel like ice cream tonight?' he teased, aware she'd hate him asking, but wanting to show her there was no harm in indulging occasionally. As long as she was healthy and stayed that way, eating was all about balance.

'I hate you,' she muttered as she stared longingly at the menu listing a multitude of ice-cream flavours.

'I know.' Did she realise he was still holding her hand? He should withdraw but this was cool. Cosy. Nice. Something he hadn't done since… Cherie. Mac sat back, taking his hand away. From another chance at happiness.

Happiness was good; everyone deserved it. Even he did. Maybe. But when happiness went belly up then… Then the pain was unbearable. Terrifying. Inexplicable. It tore a man apart, left him unable to put the pieces back together, definitely not the way they'd been before.

Cherie's death had changed him. The loss of their child

before he or she had seen the light of day had crippled him. But losing Cherie had been indescribable. All he really knew was he couldn't face that again. The guilt at not realising what was happening still ate at him, demanded a price be paid. Staying single and focused on helping as many folk as possible through his career was that price, and one he was comfortable with.

So Kelli. He was more than okay with helping her out as long as he kept his mind-set in front. Mac swallowed the bile at the back of his throat. Irony was a bitter pill. He'd offered to be Kelli's fiancé for the weekend. For longer if that was what it took to sort out Jason. But he couldn't take on the role for real. As tempting as it might become. He would not. That meant opening his heart wide, letting Kelli in to everything that made him tick, risking hurt.

Kelli was pushing away from the table. 'Time I headed home. See you tomorrow.'

'Not so fast.' Mac was upright, the tab in his hand. 'I'll get this then give you a ride home.'

Ride. That damned word again. When Kelli had used it earlier his brain had not been picturing her sitting in his four-wheel drive, that was for sure.

Nor had hers if that cute shade of pink pouring into her cheeks was an indicator.

'I don't need you running around after me.'

'So you said last night, and I'm giving back the same reply. I am giving you a—lift.' Better, not perfect, but one degree up from ride. 'I heard you tell your mother your car is in the workshop until tomorrow.' Sensible talk might abate the growing need to touch this tantalising woman, to hold her close and feel her skin against his, and kiss her until his world spun. Might. Didn't. His world was already spinning. He wanted a hug and kiss. He wanted the whole nine yards. With Kelli. The sex nine yards, not the commitment nine yards. Which made him a heel. Not who he was or wanted to be.

'Tomorrow I'll pick you up for lunch as repayment,' Miss Independence muttered.

Tomorrow was another day. Tomorrow his head and body would be back under control and he'd be able to talk sense. Tonight he was all out of any kind of sense. 'Let's go.'

The sooner they hit the road, the sooner he'd be on his own and able to loosen off the tension gripping him in unexpected places. This *was* only a fleeting problem.

CHAPTER FIVE

'HI, MUM,' KELLI answered her phone. 'How's your day going?'

'From bad to worse. I can't make lunch, my girl. Those imbeciles at the catering company say they can't get crayfish for the entrée. Something about an order not going through. I can forgive them that, everyone makes mistakes.'

Huh? Can I have whatever it is you're on, Mum? 'But?'

'They've done nothing about coming up with a suitable replacement dish. The wedding's only three days away. What's wrong with these people?' Her distress poured through the ether.

'Take a breath, Mum. A big one.' *Think, Kelli, think. Find a solution. Mum needs a solution.* 'Do you know where the caterers were getting the crayfish from?'

'The caterers said the Kaikoura region but supplies are intermittent from there since the earthquake so you'd think they'd have outsourced further afield.'

'You could have a chicken entrée. A vegetarian one.'

'Wash your mouth out, my girl. This is me you're suggesting that to. The queen of organising events does not take a soft option when something goes wrong.'

How true. Mum hated to be wrong-footed.

So think of something. Someone. Ah.

'Jack Harris. You know, Andy's mate from university. He runs a fishing company in Milford Sound. Lots of crayfish down there. Get Andy to call him asap.'

'Kelli, darling, you're a gem. Why didn't I think of that? Jack's coming up for the wedding, too.'

Kelli let out a relieved sigh. 'He can bring cartons of live lobsters under his arm.'

'Have you got an answer for my next problem?' Mum asked. 'I've learned this morning that one of the brides-maids gets seasick *and* airsick.'

'The helicopter will be a lot faster than the ferry. Fill her up with travel pills but don't overdose her as she'll need to be fully compos once she's on Waiheke.'

'My thoughts exactly. Guess there's really no other way round this one. I'll go talk to my friendly pharmacist.'

'You've got a busy morning, Mum.'

'I'm sorry to cancel lunch. I've got too much to sort out. And your father's busy with his Sydney counterpart.' Not a lot of conviction in Mum's voice about Dad being unable to do lunch. That was definitely an add-on. 'Friday will have to be it.'

'Sure, not a problem.' The relief at her reprieve just wasn't coming. Instead disappointment was the dominating emotion. She wanted her parents to meet Mac? Today instead of Friday? *Not making sense here, Kelli.*

Mac was a temporary fix, not a lifelong commitment. Commitment? Didn't she mean decision? Commitment? No way. He was a sexy hunk, an intelligent man with a sense of humour that he occasionally let out of the bag, but commitment material? When she wasn't ready to commit to anyone? Hadn't completely laid the past to bed? Mac never hesitated saying she looked good, which gave her hope and relief and some happiness. But... But she wasn't one hundred per cent certain she could trust herself in believing him. She'd once believed Steve loved her and look how that ended.

'You still there, Kelli?'

'Friday night it is.' When there would be a crowd of family to dilute the impact on Mac and hopefully not scare him away until after the wedding.

Next she called Mac. 'Lunch's cancelled. Mum's got problems to sort for Saturday.'

'Let's go anyway. I'll still pick you up a little after twelve.' Click.

Thought I was picking you up.

This was a bit like a date. No, it was a date. Possibly a backhanded one, but she and Mac going out. She needed to get a wriggle on and collect her car, then go get her dress from the dry-cleaner's. Then make sure she looked perfect for her 'date'. With Mac. A smile lifted her mouth and warmth crept in under her skin. That skirt and the blouse with three-quarter-length sleeves she'd created for autumn were about to get their first outing.

Stop it. You're getting too keen on the man, and there are no guarantees he won't hurt you.

If only she could drop the mantra. Learn to accept who she was and demand everyone else do the same.

Mac held open the four-wheel drive's door, his gaze fixed on her thighs. 'You look stunning. Is that skirt new?'

Kelli automatically ran her hand down the soft leather of her short black skirt, one she hadn't had any opportunities to wear, what with being away in Fiji since the weather had begun to cool into autumn. It fitted perfectly and the red top made to hide her large breasts wasn't too shabby either. But stunning? 'You say the nicest things.'

'Kelli,' Mac growled. 'I mean it. I am not trying to

suck up to you by uttering niceties for the sake of it. If I hadn't liked the effect I'd have kept quiet.'

That took her breath away, along with the ability to reply. Mac believed she looked stunning. Those butterflies started up behind her ribs, flappity flap. He was way more than a quick fix to her weekend problem. With an abrupt nod she concentrated on pulling her seat belt into place. Her fingers weren't as steady as they should be, and those butterflies had relatives beating in her tummy. Stunning. Might be an exaggeration, but she could live with that. Enjoy it, grab it and pretend it was true—until proven otherwise. *How's that for standing strong?*

Mac pulled out onto the street. 'Will the booking at Cardo's still be available?'

'Yes.' Cardo's always had a table available for her family or any Barnett family business meals. 'Are you sure you want to go there? I don't mind if you change the plan.'

'And miss out on the best seafood ravioli in the city? I don't think so.'

'You frequent Cardo's?' The man had taste. What was there not to like about him? Like? Try adore. Something stronger? L-lo… No. No. Please no. Her mouth clamped shut.

'I wouldn't say frequent, but I go there occasionally when I can't be bothered to make my own pasta, or I need to get out of the apartment for a few hours because I'm sick of my own company.'

The clamp slipped. 'You make your own pasta?' This man just kept on getting better and better. He wasn't only a very good doctor and a good-looking hunk at the gym. He made pasta. Please, not the L word. That would wreck everything.

'Beats the packet stuff any day.' Mac smiled. Or was that a smirk?

'Who'd have thought it? Where did you learn to do that?'

'Mum's parents came out from Italy to Wellington sixty years ago.'

'So you grew up on Italian food. I'm so jealous.'

'Don't be. We only had it as a treat. My father thought eating pasta was like eating flour and water.' The smile had gone, his mouth now grim. 'He refused any kind of Italian food.'

'You aren't close?' Definitely some problem there. His hands were gripping the steering wheel and his arms were tight. As were his thighs, she noted as she cruised down his body.

'Not at all. He passed away ten years ago.' The four-wheel drive jerked as Mac roared away on the green light. 'We didn't see eye to eye on anything.'

Thoughtlessly she placed her hand on his forearm, felt the tension in the muscles under her palm. Went to withdraw, decided against it. 'I'm sorry.'

Mac didn't shrug her away. 'Don't worry about it. It's old hat.'

Yes, and still hurts. 'I got lucky. My family might be bossy and like to run my life for me at times, but we are close. Even the two, soon to be three, sisters-in-law fit right in.'

'Is that another reason for them foisting Jason on you? He already fits in.'

'You might have a point. He's someone we all know well, no hidden agendas.'

'Interesting.'

Maybe. 'Did you grow up in Wellington?' She needed to know stuff too, right?

'Yep, Lyall Bay, where many Italians settled years back. Dad desperately wanted to move away but as my *nonno* bought the house I grew up in as a wedding gift to my parents Dad was tied. Something he resented all his married life.'

'*Nonno?* Grandfather?'

'Yeah. A fabulous old guy. Loved him to bits.' The tension backed off.

Loved, as in the past. Someone else Mac had lost. 'Your mother?'

'Still lives in the same house, only now it's party central for seniors. My word, not hers. She is getting older and wiser, but she's not a senior, if you please.' Mac was smiling softly. 'Croquet, Bridge games, Tai Chi. You name it, it happens at Maria's place.'

Kelli had never seen him so relaxed. His mother was special to him. 'Do you get to see her often?'

'I try to get down every couple of months, but I don't always make it. I'm going the weekend after the wedding.'

'You didn't cancel this weekend for me, did you?' She'd feel terrible when Mac obviously adored his mother.

'No. It's her birthday in ten days and I'm taking a crowd of her cronies to dinner at one of the top restaurants in town. Can you imagine what that's going to be like? A dozen seniors who think they're teenagers in wrinkly skin.'

The laughter wouldn't hold back. Kelli bent forward as it roared out of her. 'Bedlam, I reckon,' she finally managed to gasp. 'You are going to be toast, mister. They will give you endless teasing and stress.' What she wouldn't give to see that.

'You're sounding too gleeful. Might have to extend the engagement to cover the following weekend. Wouldn't my fiancée attend her future mother-in-law's birthday?'

Careful what you wish for, Kelli. Not laughing now.

'You'd tell her the same stuff we're going to tell my family? For what reason?'

'To make you eat your words.' He grinned back. 'But no, I won't do that. She'd get too excited and smother you with love and questions.'

'Your mother wants you settled down?' It did make sense. Mac had to be in his mid-thirties. 'How old are you?'

'Yes, she does. Thirty-six. And before you ask, I am a widower.'

Her lungs deflated like popped balloons. The fun evaporated. The black hole he'd fallen into. The reason he kept aloof—except not always with her. No idea what that meant. 'That's sad. Awful. Hell, I don't know what to say.'

'You're doing fine.' Mac flicked her a dark look. 'It's all been said a hundred times. Don't get me wrong, I'm grateful that people care enough to say something. It's just that it doesn't make a handful of difference.' He drew a breath. 'Thank you for caring.'

For a man who didn't put much out there that was some speech. 'So time's not the greatest healer?' Did this explain why he'd left her that night? Not because he'd changed his mind about her, but because he'd remembered how much he loved his wife?

He grunted. 'I guess it has helped. It's been four years. Sometimes I feel as though she went only yesterday, but more often lately I am aware it's been a long while.' He scrubbed a hand down his face. 'But not long enough.'

'This was what you were referring to when I asked why you were helping me.'

'Yeah.' His fingers were tight on the steering wheel. 'After Cherie died I was in a bad place. Not sleeping, barely eating, struggling to get through a day's work without making mistakes. Basically I hated being alive.' His chest rose, fell back. 'My mentor at the hospital turned up one morning and hauled me out of ED, drove me to his cabin two hours away in the hills where there was nothing, no one, but the trees, the weather and the birds.'

'That'd be confronting.'

'It got more so. Tom stayed the first night with me, told me how I'd nearly screwed up with a patient—I hadn't even noticed—and that I had to get my act together. He understood what I was going through because he'd lost his wife two years earlier. Then he just sat and waited and, sure enough, the words spilled, my pain, my grief, not understanding why it had to happen to me and Cherie, everything.' His voice was barely a whisper.

Kelli laid her hand on his thigh.

'He left the next morning, telling me he'd be back at the end of the week. Thought I'd go mad at first. The bush was quiet, even the birdsong didn't register with me. With nothing to occupy my mind I couldn't hold back all the images of Cherie and our future I'd been denying.' Mac cleared his throat. 'Anyway, I survived the week and went back to work totally focused on why I was there. Tom saved me that day, and I'll never forget it.'

Out of words without sounding crass or condescending, Kelli kept quiet for the rest of the ride to the restaurant. But her mind whirled. No wonder he was so serious. Or had appeared to be until she'd begun getting to know him better. How did anyone get over losing the love of their life? Because that was who Mac's wife would've been. He didn't do things by halves, would've loved her with all his being. Kelli had been devastated when her ninety-two-year-old grandmother died quietly in her sleep one night after a good innings. Nothing like what Mac must've dealt with.

'Must be my lucky day,' Mac said with forced lightness as he swung into a park directly over the road from Cardo's.

Kelli placed her hand in his forearm. Touching him a lot lately. 'If you want to cancel I won't beat you up.'

'Miss out on tortellini? I don't think so. Come on. Hustle your butt, woman. I'm starving.' This time there was warmth in his voice and a soft smile that went straight to her belly to spread heat in all directions. Which was not a good idea when she'd just learned that Mac wasn't in the running for a new partner. He was still grieving for his wife.

Definitely the wake-up call she needed to get back on track with keeping their bizarre relationship story working and not spreading into something neither of them wanted. Because, despite feeling closer to Mac than ever before, she wasn't ready for a relationship. Strange how she had to keep reminding herself when being with Mac felt so right. 'Pizza for me.'

'Eat some real food, woman. You'll work it off at the gym tonight, I bet.'

She shook her head. 'Pizza.' Mac might like her shape but there was that tight dress to wear to the wedding.

'Hello, Kelli. The family table?' The head waiter gave her a friendly smile.

'If it's available, James. I don't want to put you out.'

'No problem. After you.' He picked up two menus, the wine list, and waved a hand in the direction of their table tucked into a private corner of the spacious restaurant.

After hearing about her parents not being able to come, James removed two of the settings as Kelli and Mac settled into their places.

Mac waved away the wine menu. 'It'll have to be water or something equally innocuous. Kelli?'

'Water for me. And I'll have a margherita pizza.'

Mac placed his order, then sat back to look around at the lunchtime crowd filling the room. 'It's always busy in here.'

'And noisy. The food's fun, the atmosphere's fun.' The company was fun. Though after that revelation about his wife Kelli no longer felt she was on a date with Mac. She didn't know what she felt, but that excitement had evaporated.

'Relax and enjoy, Kelli. I didn't mean to spoil our time together.'

'How do you know what I was thinking?'

'You have a very expressive face. Especially when you're not with patients you're trying to keep details from.'

'I hate the bad stuff. I couldn't be the doctor giving people awful news. It's hard enough helping them after they've learned it, but I like being there to help them through it.'

'That's why you make a great nurse. And I doubt it stops there.'

Maybe this was still a date of sorts. It sure was starting to feel like one again. Keep the compliments flowing and for the next hour she'd sideline her determination to enjoy Mac from a distance.

'Hello, Kelli,' boomed her father from above her.

'Dad! You're joining us for lunch? I thought Mum cancelled.' Disappointment at not having Mac to herself warred with happiness and trepidation.

'Your mother wasn't cancelling my lunch with my girl and her new man.' Dad turned to Mac with his hand out. 'I'm Dale Barnett, Kelli's father as you've probably gathered.'

Mac stood and took the outstretched hand to shake. 'Pleased to meet you. I'm Mac Taylor.'

'Sit down, sit down.' Her father pulled out a chair beside her, and directly opposite Mac, no doubt to observe him. 'You two work together, then?'

'Yes, we do,' Mac agreed. 'The dreaded night shift.'

'Lots of quiet time to hide away in storerooms together?'

'Dad,' Kelli protested. 'It's not like that.'

Both men stared at her, one amused and one, Mac... wistful?

'The emergency department's always busy,' she muttered. Nearly always.

'There are times...' Mac stopped when she ramped up her glare to I-will-kill-you-if-you-keep-going. He shrugged. 'Just—you know.'

Playing his role to its full potential? Regret floored her. She wanted to hide away in a tiny room at work with Mac and kiss him till she couldn't breathe. Wanted, wanted, *wanted* it. But it wasn't happening outside her imagination, an imagination that was only operating to keep the hoax up to speed. 'Mac's head of ED. He has to be super careful.'

Her dad did a mean eye-roll, one she'd known all her life and it always made her laugh. Today was no exception. 'You are my *father*. Not my girlfriend. I'm shutting up about now.' She gave an exaggerated shudder.

Mac was watching them both with amusement all over his face. He really did relax more when he was away from work. Or could be it was when he was with her? She wasn't sure which, but was more than happy to see him like this.

Their meals arrived, including her father's usual carbonara. 'Wine?' he asked.

'Not when I'm working in a couple of hours' time, thanks, Dad.'

'Likewise, Dale.'

'Then I'll just order a glass for me.' He nodded at the waiter before turning back to them. 'How long have you two been going out?'

First question and they hadn't prepared for it. As Kelli floundered for an answer Mac spoke up. 'Since Tamara and Conor's wedding.'

She locked her gaze on him and nodded. Smart. True in a warped way. 'Guess the romance of the occasion got to us.'

Mac leaned back in his chair, his eyes flaring. Hadn't thought of that, had he? 'Yeah,' he drawled.

Kelli couldn't take her eyes off him. When flustered, he was adorable. Gone was that haughty I-am-always-in-control thing, replaced with apprehension and possibly excitement. He was getting to her in more ways than she'd have imagined. And didn't need.

Dad cleared his throat. 'Hate to interrupt, but your food's getting cold.' Meaning he wanted to talk.

Heat swamped her cheeks, and there was a reciprocal colour going on in Mac's too. 'Sorry,' she muttered.

'Don't,' warned Mac softly.

'Don't what?' Oh, sorry. 'Got it.' She'd been working at keeping that word off her tongue but embarrassment had got in the way.

'You okay with the lift-off time arranged for you on Friday?'

Thank you, Dad. Keep it simple and we'll get through lunch unscathed. 'No problem.'

She should've known better than to think unscathed. This was the man who'd known her from the moment she arrived in the world. 'You're booked into one of the front suites overlooking the beach. Secluded for when you want to get away from the crowd.'

Dad. 'Err, thanks.'

Mac was pressing his lips together, as if he was smothering a smile. 'We're very appreciative, Dale. Aren't we, Kelli?'

Mac. 'Err, yes.'

Mac pushed back his chair and stood up. 'Excuse me.'

Kelli watched him head to the men's room, thinking she wanted to strangle him for leaving her to deal with her father's amusement. 'I suppose it's time to leave. I've got heaps to do before I go to work.'

'I like him,' Dad said. 'A lot.'

Trouble was stirring. 'You hardly know him.'

'I make instant decisions every day of my working life. I am good at reading people. Your Mac is an excellent man.' Dad rose and tugged her up onto her feet and into a familiar hug. 'I'm pleased for you.'

Tears threatened and she had to blink hard to prevent the spill-over. 'I'm pleased too.' She meant that. When she shouldn't.

'How serious are you?'

'We're engaged.' Agh! Where did that come from? Being with someone she was never on edge around had its downside.

Dad leaned back to stare at her. 'You are? When were you going to tell us?'

'After the wedding.' Liar. 'Or maybe on Friday at the family dinner. We didn't want to steal the show from Billy.'

'This isn't a bit sudden?' The hug was over, the mood serious. Not that hugs weren't serious in her family, but they interfered with straight questions and answers in Dad's book. 'You might've got together at Tamara's wedding but since then you've spent most of your time in Fiji.' Nothing but love and concern stared out at her from those faded blue eyes. Eyes that rarely missed a trick. 'You're not doing this to spite Jason?'

Absolutely. 'No. Please start believing me.'

'How sure of your feelings for Mac are you?'

She got brave. 'The first time you met Mum how did you feel?'

'Baffled, bemused, and… I'm not telling my daughter what I was feeling.'

'Touché.'

'That's how you feel about Mac?'

'I'm not telling my father.' She wasn't even admitting it to herself. Not much.

Dad chuckled. 'Then I'm happy for you. Your mum's going to be ecstatic.'

'Don't rush us. I want to enjoy this one day at a time.' Her heart slowed. Now she seemed to be believing her own lies. Even a faux engagement to Mac was proving to be intriguing and exciting, and she was beginning to wonder how she'd walk away from it. No walking away from Mac though. He'd be in her life every day, every shift, every visit to the gym—though she could change that. Male and pine scent would be in the air she breathed. Mac induced heat under her skin. No, not that close. Yes, that close. Grr. Now she'd have to fight harder to keep her distance.

'Love you, baby girl.' Those comforting arms returned, winding around her shaking body and holding her against that familiar, to-go-to-in-moments-of-pain chest that had been a part of her whole life.

Tears leaked down her face. What a mess. Breathing in, she dug deep for composure. It was all a lie and she'd told it to this man who'd always had her back. 'It's okay.'

Then Dad was letting her go and turning around. 'Mac, I hear congratulations are in order.' He slapped Mac on the shoulder in that way guys did these things and nodded. 'I'm thrilled at the news.'

Mac shot her a startled glance, then quickly recovered. 'Thank you, Dale. I'm only sorry we've kept quiet about this, but Kelli was concerned about spoiling her brother's big day.'

'I'm going to tell your mother the moment I get back to the office. Teach her for letting all those little wedding details keep her running around like a headless chook.' He was grinning like the toddler with ice cream. 'I'm so going to love this. Payback for when I had to miss Billy and Leanne telling her last week they're pregnant.'

'They're pregnant?' Wow. 'That's wonderful, brilliant. I'm going to be an auntie? When?'

'Some time in September.' His chest was expanding with pride. 'The next generation begins.'

Mac dropped an arm over Kelli's shoulders. 'Is this to be kept secret until after the wedding?'

Could divert interest off them.

'I shouldn't have mentioned it but the excitement of your news got to me. Keep it between yourselves, will you?' Her father didn't look at all contrite.

'Of course.' If only she could say the same about their engagement. But a baby? The first in their generation. Awesome. *Go, Billy.* Then her heart flip-flopped as if it were in thick mud. A baby. Would she ever get the chance to have one, to be a mum?

Her eyes slid sideways, drank in the man talking to Dad while watching her too closely. She'd found a great man for the dad role.

Flip, flop.

Her heart ached through its sluggish moves.

She'd made a colossal mistake involving Mac in the

weekend. She just couldn't do it. She would have to back out, tell her parents it was all wrong and that she'd lied.

Running away from Mac wasn't going to change what was going on in her head. Forget her head. If she'd relied on that there'd be no problem. No, her heart was to blame for making such a botch-up of a simple plan. It—all right, *she* was falling for the tall, enigmatic man who'd stood by her all week and seemed more than ready to go as far as it took to make her weekend enjoyable.

Six weeks working in Fiji hadn't calmed the simmering in her veins. Perhaps she should apply for twelve months on base in Antarctica. Except personnel were usually sent south in late spring, not mid-autumn. She'd have to come up with another plan to save her heart. If she wasn't already too late.

CHAPTER SIX

Kelli clicked the safety harness into place, silently cursing herself for not finding a way out of the weekend, and gazed out over the harbour. An offshore breeze had the water skipping as it pushed towards the downtown wharves. 'We do live in a beautiful city,' she murmured in Mac's direction.

'I agree.' Sitting next to her, he appeared relaxed despite two of her brothers and their wives also on board the flying machine. The family had heard the news, and Andy and Phil had been giving Mac the eye from the moment they showed up at the helipad. Mac had been holding her hand until they'd boarded, no doubt to add authenticity to their relationship.

Validation or not, she'd been more than happy to go along with it since it meant having those long, strong fingers entwined with hers. Meant feeling his palm pressed against hers, heat radiating up her arm and tightening her belly. And bringing pictures of a large bed to mind. Was she sex-starved, or what?

Sitting so close her thigh was touching Mac's, she fought the urge to grab his hand again. *Pretend you hate flying.* As if. One big fib was one too many. She wasn't about to start telling more to anyone, and especially not to Mac. He'd stepped up to the mark for her when he didn't have to and somehow not being totally honest would undermine her feelings for him. There was an idea. Put the kibosh on her ever-increasing awareness of him.

Then Mac reached over and took her hand in his again, slid those fingers she adored back into place. More authenticity? Or was he by any chance feeling the same need as her? No answer to that—because she wasn't going to ask. That would be laying too much on the line, and at the moment there was still time to pull back, withdraw entirely, be remote over the weekend. Remote when they were sharing a suite, *with* a double bed? Remote negated the whole purpose of Mac partnering her.

Remember the rules. That shouldn't be hard, knowing Mac was still grieving. Except sometimes she felt he forgot that and enjoyed himself.

The helicopter shook as the rotors wound up to speed, and everything vibrated as they left the ground behind and rose into the blue sky. Tiny puffs of white cloud lightened the blue, made it pretty. Kelli loved flying, had even contemplated getting a private licence but put it in the 'too hard' basket because of the hours required to train and all the exams that had to be sat.

'You're enjoying this, aren't you?' Mac had leaned close so as she could hear him.

Breathing deep to take in that smell of pine and something else she couldn't put her finger on except that it was uniquely Mac, she nodded. 'It's a great way to start what's going to be a fantastic weekend.' Fingers crossed.

Below and to the right the volcanic Rangitoto Island stood proud against the backdrop of sea. Not extinct but in a slumberous state, the iconic double-coned shape looked inviting. Not frightening. Bit like the approaching weekend. Approaching? It had already started. There was no going back now.

When they walked into their suite, Kelli was sure that there was no way she would ever get her fingers to straighten again. She had to force her hand away from Mac's as she scoped the classy room. Fantastic was only the beginning. The room's full-length glass doors opened onto a small deck overlooking the beach and the expansive Waitemata Harbour beyond with the outlying islands and innumerable pleasure craft criss-crossing the sparkling waters.

That was only the view. There was the man who'd walked beside her from the helipad to the resort's reception and on to their room, laughing at her brothers' cheeky taunts and not letting a thing frazzle him.

Then there was that super-king-sized bed dominating the centre of the room they'd be sharing for two days—and two nights. 'Mac, this is all a mistake,' she whispered.

Not so quiet he didn't hear. 'Want me to hitch a ride back when the helicopter returns to the city for more guests?' A wistful note had entered his voice, softened his mouth. 'I can if you want me to.'

'It would've been easier if we'd been given a shoebox-sized room with grotty furnishings and a view of the other side of the resort building's back wall.'

'No romance factor?'

Kelli's head dipped in acknowledgement. 'It all seemed so easy back in the city.' Spreading her fingers wide, she waved her hand at the scene before them. 'This is real. This has nothing to do with the story I've made up to keep my family off my back.'

Mac caught her shoulders, pulled her closer to him. 'Stay focused, Kelli. Keep reminding yourself why we're sharing this amazing suite. And I'll…' He faltered. Tipped his head back and swallowed hard. 'I'll only do what you ask of me. No more, no less.'

He'd put it back on her. Thanks, Mac. She should be grateful. Only she wasn't. She wanted what they had never planned on, what hovered between them in memories of one hot night after another wedding in another city. If they spent the coming nights in bed making love would she finally get the fizz out of her blood? At last be able to look at Mac and know she didn't want him for ever?

No answers blindsided her. Just the heat from those hands on her shoulders to remind her.

You don't always get what you want in this world.

Or did you?

Get real.

Even when her body was crying out for release, and her head was saying go for it, make the most of the situation, tomorrow was just another day.

But then there was want and there was *want*. She wanted a night with Mac. Wanted to trust him enough to fall completely in love with him. Wanted a future with him that involved the picket fence and two-point-seven kids, or whatever the national average was these days. She did? Yes, a brood of knee-huggers was on her bucket list—once she'd found the right man to have them with.

Tick. Done that.

Shut up, brain.

'Kelli? You're spooking me with that worried look.'

Sorry. Didn't count if she didn't say it out loud. 'I'm fine. Just a few nerves. You haven't seen me like this before. I like to do everything perfectly. I get that from my mum. For a moment there I felt there was a deep chasm I had to cross before everything would work out for me.'

'For us.'

'Us, yes.' Mac was totally here for her. Amazing, and scary. No other man, certainly not her real fiancé, had done that no questions asked. 'Thank you.' Apparently of their own accord her feet lifted her up so her lips could reach Mac's. When her mouth grazed his gently she shuddered with need, and felt a returning movement from Mac. Pressing closer, she opened her mouth, expanded the kiss, and tasted him.

Mac's hands landed on her waist, held her like a fragile package, and kept her from moving closer—or away. His mouth took over the kiss, deepening it, allowing their tongues to tangle. If not for those hands Kelli would've sagged against him, length to length, thighs touching, her breasts pushed against his chest, his growing reaction pressing into her stomach. If not for those blasted hands holding her in place. As though Mac was as uncertain as she was how far to take this.

Kelli froze. 'We have rules in place for this very reason.'

Instantly Mac dropped his hands and stepped back. 'Two minutes in the room and I can't control myself.'

'I think I have to take responsibility. I did start the kiss.' Her body was screaming: more, more. What there was of a brain in her head, and that was up for debate, was shouting, *Get away from him. He's not yours, not your future. Only your date for the weekend.*

'Let's go for a walk on the beach before we join the others at the bar,' Mac suggested.

'Separately. You go left, I'll go right.'

'No can do. We're a couple, remember? Newly engaged at that. I'm thinking those brothers would notice faster than a jet on take-off if we don't do this properly.'

'You're right.' Did properly mean more kisses? *If so, bring it on.*

I am toast. Burnt toast.

Falling for Mac is a huge mistake. He's been married, is still grieving the first one. And those are only his points *against a relationship.* She hadn't the energy to drag up all hers. They'd spoil the weekend—if she hadn't already done that by kissing Mac within moments of walking in here. 'I'll change out of my heels. That sand isn't going to be as forgiving as the promenade at Darling Harbour.'

Mac became busy, unzipping his suit bag and withdrawing two suits to hang in the wardrobe. Shirts followed, jeans and chinos. He hadn't skimped when it came to packing. 'Better hang that dress up,' he commented.

'Good thinking.' She hadn't gone to the trouble of getting it pressed to just leave it lying over the back of a chair in a full-length carry bag. Like Mac, she'd unpack everything now. Anything to keep her distracted from Mr Diversion who was quickly becoming Mr Attraction. Ah ha, could be why he was so intent on emptying his bag too. 'Did you leave anything behind?' she asked when he began to fill a drawer with tee shirts and a jersey and everything a man could need when isolated on an island for a month.

Mac shrugged. 'There was room in my bag so I kept putting clothes in until I couldn't any more.'

'You weren't a Boy Scout, then?'

'No. I don't like being caught short and having to make do.' He looked over at her bag, nearly as large as his, and shook his head at her. 'You weren't one either?'

'As if. Did you leave any hangers for me?' Hotels never provided enough.

'One or two.' Mac grinned. 'Want a water before we hit the beach?' Obviously over that awkward moment.

'I'd better.' Once they reached the bar it wouldn't be water she'd be drinking. Her brothers would make a bee-line for the drinks department and line them up as soon as they'd dumped their bags in their rooms. No fussing about hanging clothes for them, though these days their

wives didn't let them get away with such behaviour quite
so easily.

Mac was opening two small bottles from the fridge,
looking relaxed. Looking as if he were on holiday, not in
the middle of a family occasion where he knew no one.
She'd be uptight and fearful of making mistakes if it were
her. Taking a closer look at him, Kelli couldn't find any
hint of stress or worry. No, that heart-stopping face was
open and happy, so unlike the doctor she worked with.
Yes, her heart was doing the stop-start thing as she gazed
at him.

Snatching up a light jersey to sling around her shoulders in case the breeze turned chilly, Kelli slugged back
some water and aimed for the door. 'Let's go.' The room
had become airless and small. At least the beach was wide
and long and there'd be lots of fresh air coming in on the
light sou'wester.

Mac strolled along the beach, his hands jammed into his
pockets, his stance relaxed, his mind anything but quiet.
Kelli did this to him. Stirred him up something shocking,
tossing possibilities of happiness at him, then knocking
reality back in place with her honesty.

Beside him she was chirping away non-stop about inci-
dentals: one of her brothers' passion for rugby, the colour
of her outfit for tonight's dinner, her mother's penchant
for arriving exactly on time for everything. Kelli was nervous, and it was becoming contagious. Trying to lighten
the atmosphere, he said, 'I am house-trained: don't pee
on the carpet or hoick my food back up under the table.'

She flipped around so she was walking backwards, annoyance fighting with laughter in her expression. 'I am
acting over the top, aren't I?'

'Totally. Why the nerves? You were okay up until we got here.'

And you kissed me in our suite.

Was that the cause of her jumpiness? That kiss had been unexpected, and the perfect antidote to his nervousness. It had loosened the tension that had begun gripping him since they'd gathered with her brothers at the helipad. Not that he had any difficulty with meeting new people and sharing a weekend at a special occasion with them, but the lie he and Kelli were living had hit home when he saw Andy wrap his sister up in a bear hug and get swiped for crushing her new blouse. Family stuff that spoke volumes about love and understanding and didn't need a lie sitting bang in the middle.

As a kid he'd never minded being the only child because it had meant he'd got all his mother's attention. Not that there was a lot going spare after she'd seen to his father's demands. Watching Kelli with her lot, he felt a pang of envy. If he'd had siblings he might've coped a little better with losing Cherie. Not gone off into solitude in an attempt to shut down his feelings. Something he'd achieved all too well. Now it was difficult letting go of the restraints he'd placed on those emotions.

Not when you're around Kelli.

And that was the problem with being here.

Impervious to where his thoughts had gone, Kelli was answering his question in some depth. He focused and tried to catch up.

She was saying, 'You're already fitting in. It's like they've always known you, but don't be fooled. The boys will test you, make sure you're good enough for me. Hardly fair, considering.'

'You want my take on that?' When she nodded, her teeth nibbling her bottom lip, he ignored the cuteness and continued. 'It's good they do that, shows how much they care. And for the record, I can handle whatever they throw at me.'

'You're as cocky as them.'

He winced. Bad word. While his body might appear relaxed there was a lot of tension in certain areas that needed relief—and that wasn't going to happen any time soon, if at all. He hadn't come here with the intention of becoming intimate with Kelli. But if it was on offer how would he be able to turn her down? 'You reckon?'

'Yes, I do.'

'Watch out!'

Too late. Still walking backwards, she hadn't seen the piece of driftwood in the sand. Mac grabbed her before she could trip and fall to the ground. Holding her again. Twice since they'd arrived. His hands burned from the feel of her skin under his palms. Other parts of his anatomy tightened. 'I'm going to sleep on the deck tonight.'

'What?' Cobalt eyes locked on him.

Showed how thrown he was, saying that out loud. Now that he had, he might as well put it all out there. 'If you think I can share that huge bed with you and not touch you, then, lady, you ain't got a clue.'

Kelli stared and stared. The air cracked with heat between them. And still she stared. Then she did that lifting-up-on-her-toes thing and he knew what was coming, and was incapable of stopping her. Didn't even want to.

Those full lips he pretended not to fantasise about brushed his mouth softly, left to right, and her tongue did a slow lap of his lips. A groan ripped out of him. He had to hold her close, to kiss her senseless, to feel her body pulsing against his.

His hands found the edge of her blouse and tugged to

make room to slide up underneath, to caress that hot, silky skin. Her breasts pressed against his chest, her nipples pebbles against his pecs. Driving him insane with need. Tipping him further into the mire he did not want to be in. Yet *had* to be in. It was unavoidable. Kelli did that to him.

Her arms were around his neck, keeping him close as that sweet, tormenting mouth worked magic on him. Kisses weren't meant to knock your knees out from under you.

'Oi, you two, this is a public beach,' Phil called out from a balcony nearby.

Kelli spun out of his hold, her hands caressing as they slid from his neck. 'Great. Now there'll be no end to the teasing.' Her forefinger ran slowly over her lips, touching where his lips had been, as though sealing in the kiss.

Mac fought the urge to take her hand and draw that finger into his mouth, to brush his tongue up and down the length. He won, but only just. His hands remained at his sides in tight fists as he strived for nonchalance. To be seen in a horny state in front of Kelli's brothers would only give her more grief and lead to a weekend of hell. In the nicest possible way.

He ground his teeth and banged on a smile. False, fake, whatever; it was a smile that hopefully said, 'I'm here for your sister and don't dare interfere,' in case Phil could read him across the fifty metres of sand that separated them. Mac nudged Kelli. 'Game face, remember. We've got to act the part or everyone will know.'

Kelli flipped her head back to glare at him, a big, fat question in her eyes. 'That kiss wasn't genuine? You were role playing?' Hurt darkened her words.

Say yes, and he wouldn't even get the deck to sleep on. Say no, and there was a possibility he'd be raising hope in Kelli for something he wasn't prepared to contemplate. Rock or hard place? Try honesty. Then buy a shovel to get out of the mess that'd get him into. 'I only do genuine kisses.'

The glare softened, but didn't completely vanish.

Mac leapt further into the mire. 'When we kiss I forget everything sane and sensible.'

Her mouth dropped open. 'Oh.' That familiar red shade coloured her cheeks and she looked away, out to sea.

Bet she wasn't noticing the water or the boats buzzing past.

Why had he told her she distracted him so much? Because he'd been distracted. Why else? Thing was, what would she do with that gem of information? Toss him off the deck, or send him home when the helicopter returned shortly?

'Mac, I shouldn't have kissed you. Both times. It's my fault we're going to get stick from the family.'

He was off the hook. If he let her take the blame. 'It took both of us to make that kiss so hot. If I hadn't been totally immersed in kissing you I'd have remembered what we agreed to.' It was impossible not to lose himself in her kisses. This was like coming out of a drought and soaking up all available water to the point of saturation. Doubt there was any such thing as too many of Kelli's kisses, but he had to try. 'Let's aim to keep ourselves under control. A little bit anyway.'

'Got any suggestions on how to go about that? Apart from one of us moving to a different resort for the weekend?' The words were sharp but there was confusion in Kelli's beautiful eyes. 'I don't understand. It's as though when we're away from work there's nothing keeping us apart. Like when we were in Sydney.'

Don't mention Sydney.

That night was etched into his brain, right at the front where there was no avoiding it. 'Unfinished business?'

Ouch. 'We didn't want that night to finish.' Until he'd wised up outside her door and left to go to his room alone.

Relief pushed aside whatever else Kelli had been thinking. 'You're right. We've had one amazing time together so naturally we want to do it again. But we can't. We work together now. Imagine how we'd deal with spending eight hours a day in the same department if we repeated ourselves? It would be next to impossible. I'll stop kissing you.'

At least one of them was being rational. Shame it wasn't him. 'You're right.'

He wanted to risk messing with his job? To take Kelli to bed and put up some more memories, then have to see her day in, day out, so close he would know her scent, her voice, her everything? 'Come on. Let's head to the bar and join the rest of your family.'

No amount of challenges or teasing from those guys could be as difficult as this conversation. There were no answers to half the things they were talking or thinking about. He was not in the market for romance. Could not bear the thought of losing someone else even if he had love to spare. Somehow over the coming hours and days he'd have to dig deep and find that remote place he favoured so much. The place that kept his heart safe and his head on the job, not on a lovely, sexy, fun woman.

'The helicopter's back. That means everyone from my family's here. And Jason.'

'Can't wait to meet him,' Mac muttered. Couldn't wait to show him that Kelli was unavailable. For the next few days at any rate.

And then what? When the wedding was done and they'd all returned to Auckland City what would happen between him and Kelli? Would Monday night be the big announcement night?

Hey, guys, Kelli and I are calling our engagement off. See you around some time.

Mac shuddered.

Kelli nudged him with an elbow. Even that was a hot move. 'You realise this is when we break the news of our engagement to everybody outside my immediate family? Mum will be expecting it, and Dad will have got the champagne ready.'

'How did your mother take the news?' Kelli had sent him a text to say her father had done as he'd said and spilled the beans. She hadn't said anything else and he didn't know how to read that.

'She's all over the place with it. Excited to have another wedding to plan for. Believe me, she gets her thrills from organising events and people. But then she rang me and demanded to know why you and not Jason, and gave me the low-down on all his good points. I can recite them off by heart. Then her next call was to ask when we want to get married. How many people we would be inviting.'

'It's going to break her heart when we pull out.'

'No, it won't. She'll carry on, changing one groom for the other. Win, win. Or should that be lose, lose?'

'You're nibbling your bottom lip again.' Cute and spoke volumes of her distress. 'Is it okay to hold hands while we walk in to join everyone?' He wanted to give her security, show he was on her side, at her side, had no regrets about volunteering to be here for her. 'Or is that a bit like kissing? Too much contact?'

'We're going to drink to our engagement. We're meant to hold hands.' Nibble, nibble.

He wanted to kiss those lips, gently possess them so she'd stop gnawing. He couldn't, not if he wanted to keep the fire roaring through him under control—at least a little bit.

CHAPTER SEVEN

'BILLY, LEANNE—THIS is Mac Taylor. I'm sure you've heard about him by now.' Kelli bit back on the excitement. If this moment had been for real she wouldn't have been able to contain herself.

Mac and Billy were shaking hands, her brother giving her *fiancé* a thorough going-over.

'Give him a break.' Kelli elbowed Billy.

Leanne gave her infectious laugh. 'Mac, you and I have to talk about the Barnett crowd and how they like to flex their muscles around outsiders. I have a few tips that'll help you contain them.'

Mac gave Leanne a peck on her cheek. 'What are you doing now?'

'About to sip a drop of champagne to celebrate your engagement.' Leanne didn't sound the least put out that this was supposed to be exclusively her night.

But Kelli had to make doubly sure she knew she hadn't deliberately tried to spoil her fun. 'I'm really sorry this got out, Leanne.' Sort of true, though no point going through the whole deal if no one knew. 'We don't want to take anything from your special weekend.'

'Believe me, I'm glad some of the heat's being transferred off us. I'm already feeling overwhelmed, and it's only going to get worse. What if I botch the ceremony? Trip up, or get my words all wrong?'

Kelli slipped her arm through Leanne's. 'Who cares? This is all about you and Billy. He loves you and if you say something not in the script he isn't going to mind. Perfect's highly overrated and boring. Just relax and enjoy the weekend. It's your wedding, not a movie set with a tyrant for a director.'

Leanne sniffed and squeezed her arm tight against Kelli's. 'Thanks, sister-in-law-to-be. You're right, but it's hard to be calm when everyone's rushing around asking have you got this, done that, ready for it all.'

'Go hug Billy,' *and get him away from interrogating Mac*. She nudged Leanne gently. 'He's your rock, and understands what you're going through.'

'You know the right thing to say when people are in a state, don't you?' Mac was back at her side, none the worse for having Billy check him out.

'I try.' Something she'd learned as a youngster dealing with the bullies, and had never stopped doing.

Loud voices and laughter came from the reception area that ran the length of the bar room. Mac stared across the heads. 'I take it that's your mother?'

Kelli didn't need to look. 'That's Mum in full organisational mode. She'll be counting heads, checking who's still in their suite and not here for the first glass of champagne.' Pride filled her. Mum was good at this sort of thing.

'You're a little like that, though a lot quieter,' Mac commented. 'There's no doubting you're related. She's a very good-looking woman.'

The air hissed out of her lungs. How was she supposed to walk away from this man next week? 'You could charm a rattlesnake if you tried,' she gasped.

'Never had the opportunity.' That was all Mac had time for before his hand was grabbed by her mother.

'You must be Mac. Welcome to our weekend.' Mum was doing a fast but thorough perusal of Kelli's fiancé.

'Thank you, Mrs Barnett. I'm happy to meet you all.'

'Then you're a brave man,' her mother said. 'Warning, drop the Mrs Barnett fast. I'm Trish.' Her eyes were still watching him too closely.

Feeling sorry for Mac, Kelli interceded. 'Did you get the crayfish sorted?'

Of course she would have, but for once Kelli was all out of things to say. Having Mac here as her fiancé was making her belly wind tight, and tighter. This was not how she'd ever thought she'd be announcing to the world she'd be getting married. The fact it was a lie only made it worse, and she wanted to call a halt, to tell everyone she'd made a mistake and wipe the untruth away. But once it had been put out there it would never go away. Even when she announced the engagement was off there would be comments and commiserations.

'Hey, Kelli, how are you? I hear you've got some news to share.'

Jason. The moment had arrived. Would he accept it? Or put up a fight? He was smiling that open, friendly way he always did with her. Genuine and caring. Confident and totally misguided.

She was engulfed in a friendly hug. 'Jason, hi.' Then she felt a hand at her back. Mac had stepped up. *Here we go.* This was what the whole deal with Mac was about. Pulling free, she said, 'Jason, I'd like you to meet Mac Taylor.' She couldn't add, 'my fiancé'. She just couldn't.

'Mac.' Like everyone else in her family Jason put his hand out, shook politely. There was the same challenge in Jason's eyes as her brothers had put out there. But not like a jealous man who'd been thwarted in love. *Not making sense here, Jason.*

'Pleased to meet you.' Mac sounded relaxed and unconcerned, but the hand on her back had tensed. 'I hear you're almost one of the family.' Not as much as Mac would be if he actually were to marry Kelli.

Jason nodded, studying Mac thoroughly. 'Dale and Trish have been good to me, probably saved me from going off the rails.' His scrutiny moved to her, but he said nothing more.

Clink, clink. A spoon tapping against a glass quietened the room. 'Listen up, everyone.' Dad to the rescue without knowing he was needed.

Then Kelli realised he was looking around for her and Mac, and her stomach sank. 'Here we go.' Not the right diversion at this moment.

Mac leaned close. 'You're doing great.'

Never had she felt so supported by anyone whose surname was not Barnett. She snuggled a little bit nearer to her rock. 'Are you ready for this?'

'As ready as I'm ever going to be.' His hand found hers, held her firmly.

When Kelli looked at him she fully expected to see a grim expression on his beautiful face. Surprise rattled her. Mac looked happy. Happy? Because they were announcing a fake engagement? Or because he was doing this to help her out of a bind? As she stretched up on her toes he suddenly looked startled. No, she wasn't about to kiss him. 'You're wonderful.'

Delight returned. 'Of course.' He grinned.

'Glasses of champagne are being passed around. When you've all got one I'd like to propose a toast.' Dad was suddenly in front of her and Mac, Mum's arm through his.

A tray appeared before her and Kelli picked up a glass,

not surprised to find her hand was shaking. It still wasn't too late to back out, to admit what she'd done and then go into hiding. Mac squeezed her hand, giving her the confidence to continue.

Looking around at the smiling faces she wanted to believe this was for real. Then she saw Jason. His mouth had flat-lined. No cajoling smile now. She should feel sorry for him, but that emotion wasn't coming to the fore. Instead anger that he'd helped her to take this unusual step began expanding throughout her. Until Mac squeezed her hand again.

Thank goodness for Mac. She'd been about to ruin the evening, especially for her family. Plastering on a smile, she waited for the next instalment of this crazy ride.

Back to Dad. 'This weekend is about Billy and Leanne, and Trish and I are thrilled we're all here to share it with them.' He raised his glass. 'To Billy and Leanne.'

'To Billy and Leanne.' The champagne was delicious. Kelli dipped her head in acknowledgement to her father. He'd done the right thing. She wasn't off the hook, but he'd put her brother first.

Then, 'I've also got some more wonderful news to share.' Dad and Mum moved closer to her and Mac. 'For those of you who haven't met him yet, this imposing man is Mac Taylor, and, as of this week, Kelli's fiancé.'

It was Billy who raised his glass and said, 'To Kelli and Mac.'

Billy, who didn't mind his sister nudging in on his weekend, was grinning at her as he used to when he'd put something horrible and wet and cold in her bed.

Tears spurted out and down her cheeks. Her beloved family might give her a hard time but they were always there for her. As was the man holding her hand and tugging gently. When she looked up into Mac's eyes, her heart broke. It was too much. If only this were for real. She was falling in love with him. Not a doubt lifted, not a question waved at her. But he wouldn't love her back.

'To Kelli and Mac.' The toasts bounced off her, echoing throughout the room, and the tears flowed.

'Hey, come here.' Mac wrapped her in his arms and held her gently.

Laughter broke out and the usual cheeky comments from her brothers added to the good cheer. Kelli shivered. Everyone thought her tears were about her joy. Only Mac knew they weren't and he was sticking to her like glue until her meltdown dried up. She really had given him a lot to deal with. 'Sorry,' she whispered.

'I'm not, okay? It was never going to be easy. Let's take our drinks and go sit at an outside table.'

'We won't be left alone.'

'You don't want to be. That'd look odd.'

'Where did you learn all this stuff?' She gazed at Mac. 'It can't have been in any medical training manual.' And he didn't have siblings.

He laughed. Really laughed, as though there was nothing wrong here. 'You want sensible? I've got loads of it. Too much.' He removed her glass from her fingers. 'Let's get refills and head out into the twilight.'

That would be romantic if only they hadn't just put out a big fat lie to everyone. Kelli sucked in her stomach, straightened her back and went with Mac, acknowledging the good wishes as they moved through her family. They were barely seated when her brothers and their wives joined them. Disappointment warred with common sense. Being alone with Mac would add to her confusion and longing; having the guys here meant putting up with relentless teasing.

Teasing was likely the safer option. She couldn't get into any trouble that way.

* * *

Mac stood up from the table where he'd been seated with Kelli and her brother, Andy, and his wife for dinner. 'Seems we're the last ones left,' he said unnecessarily. There was no further putting off heading to that suite with Kelli. The barman was wiping down the counter and tipping semi-defrosted ice into the sink with a loud clatter.

'Thought you two would've been the first to head to your room.' Andy winked as he too stood.

Kelli slowly unwound her body and came up beside Mac, holding herself rigid.

Mac nudged her softly. Be careful or Andy would notice something wasn't kosher. She nodded and slipped her arm through his. 'Goodnight, you two. See you bright and early for breakfast, Rach. It's going to be full on with hair, nails, and make-up to be done.'

'Let's hope that rain doesn't eventuate. Leanne must be having kittens worrying about that.' Rach was looking through the windows at what was now a gloomy scene.

The ceremony would take place in the gardens, and from what Mac had seen of Trish Barnett the weather had better clear up or she'd create havoc. The woman was a mini-storm all of her own. Something he needed to remember in the coming days. She was not going to let him break up with Kelli easily, if at all. Though she did have a contingency plan—Jason.

The man had sat through drinks and then dinner looking a little stunned, as though he was slowly absorbing the truth about his relationship with Kelli. He didn't appear too upset, more surprised. Probably felt stupid for continuing to try and win Kelli over when it had never been on the cards. Mac couldn't find it in himself to feel too sorry. If Kelli had any feelings for Jason at all then it'd be different, but he'd watched her over the night and she treated the guy no differently from anyone else.

Mac swallowed an inappropriate smile. His earlier guess about Jason being like family had strengthened, which made *him* feel better. About *his* role in this. About his own feelings for Kelli. For every hour he spent with her there was an increasing sense that he might be getting another chance at happiness. Of course, in the hours he wasn't with her the reasons why he was an idiot were easier to hear. Not that he seemed to be taking a blind bit of notice.

From the moment they'd lifted off the ground in the city he'd felt like a different man: free from the past and those locks he'd put on his heart and now stepping into the unknown. Even excited about being amongst this family and their special weekend, certainly eager to be with Kelli for days, not just hours.

'Goodnight,' Kelli muttered and headed in the direction of their suite, striding out with determination. As if she had something to face and get out of the way.

Mac followed, quickly catching up. 'I mightn't be sleeping on the deck if those showers arrive.'

'You reckon?' The face she tipped up to him was strained and her smile tired.

'I could try the floor.'

'We've got this far—we can manage the rest.' Her mouth stretched into a yawn. 'What have you guys got planned for tomorrow while the females get glammed up?'

'A round of golf.'

'Can you play?'

'I can swing a club, and someone uttered the word "challenge".'

'And you can't turn one of those down.' She paused, giving him the once-over. 'You fit in so well it's scary.'

Pride puffed out his chest, then reality flattened it

again. 'I'm not meant to fit in. These are the men who are going to come after me when you tell them I've dumped you.'

'I'm not going to say that.'

Really? He was in with a chance? But did he want one? He wouldn't have put up his hand to help Kelli out if going their separate ways afterwards hadn't been the conclusion to their engagement. Would he? This was starting to feel more about helping himself, not Kelli. Not only Kelli.

She flashed her entry key at the door pad and shouldered the door open, stepped inside and came to a halt, staring at that enormous bed.

Mac walked past her, trying not to let any X-rated thoughts push aside what little reason lurked in his skull. Continuing to the doors opening onto the deck, he slid one open, peered out and swallowed the need clawing up his throat, tightening *all* of his body. 'Please don't kick me out tonight.'

When Kelli didn't answer he turned to face her. A breath stuck halfway between his lungs and his nose. She was gazing at him with sadness in those cobalt eyes. 'Kelli?' he whispered. 'What's up?'

She blinked, shook away that look. 'Wishful thinking, that's all.' Dropping her clutch purse on a bedside table, she stared around the room, before her gaze came back to him. 'You okay?'

If he didn't want what he couldn't have, then yes, he'd say he was in top form. The air was getting tight, the walls closing in on him. Three steps and he'd be close enough to raise his arms and hug this distracting woman, or kiss her, or pick her up and carry her to that bed to lie together and make love. But that sadness in her eyes had wrought havoc with his emotions. He needed to lighten the mood, to wipe away that despondency. Sex might do the trick, but if Kelli wasn't in the mood then he'd be adding to her problems. 'I'm good. Let's try to get some sleep. I imagine tomorrow's going to be full on for you. Lying back while someone paints your nails. Drinking coffee—or will that be wine?—as your hair's styled and your warpaint applied. Definitely a massive day ahead. Then there's the wedding. With tears.'

She'd cried at Tamara and Conor's wedding.

'The reception dinner with speeches and lots of laughter, the dancing with your brothers and fiancé.' He slapped his forehead. 'Why are you standing there and not rushing to get into your pyjamas?' Another slap. 'I forgot to bring my racing car PJs.'

Kelli's mouth was a startled O. 'Thank goodness for something.' Then she started to laugh. 'You're mad. You know that? At least I don't have to try and hit a tiny ball into a tinier hole a hundred metres down the lawn, and then have to shout a round of top-shelf drinks because I missed hitting the ball in the first place.'

It was good to hear that laughter. It warmed him right to his toes. Tomorrow, fingers crossed, he'd ramp it up when he beat the pants off her brothers. Unless they were top-class golfers, and from the few comments made at dinner he doubted it. 'You want the bathroom while I turn down the covers?'

The bed had already been turned down, but Mac intended being in his side well before she returned from doing whatever took females a lifetime in the bathroom.

'Don't touch my chocolate while I'm in there,' Kelli warned as she pointed at the confections on the bedside tables.

'You won't eat yours.' She was particular about what she put in that delectable mouth. Didn't seem to eat bad food ever.

'I might, after tomorrow.' Kelli rummaged in her case and pulled out some red satin creation. 'But then again, I know what's on the menu for the dinner and I probably won't eat again for a week after that.'

'Kelli, why are you so fixated with what you eat? You're not overweight, not even a tiny bit, so there must be another reason.' His hands had fitted perfectly over her curves when he'd held her earlier, curves that filled his palms with heat, turning him on fast.

Her eyes popped wide, like bugs caught in headlights. 'I'm not exactly svelte.'

'Svelte? Isn't that another word for skinny?'

'Mac, don't. Please.'

Crossing to where she stood, looking as if she was ready to run if he said the wrong thing, Mac lifted a stray strand of hair from her cheek and slipped it behind her ear. The only thing he could say was the truth. 'In my book, you're perfect. Ten out of ten. Beautiful, inside and out.'

A lone tear slowly slid down her cheek. 'That's the nicest thing any man has ever said to me.'

Nice? Blah word that it was, he got her sentiment. And the atmosphere was getting heavy again. So, deep breath, and a quick slap on her bottom. 'Go clean off the warpaint and get into whatever that red outfit is.' It had better be a sack with drawstrings at each end to prevent any access for his hands. The night was going to be one of the longest of his life, and there'd been some doozies in the past.

Only her bedside light was on when Kelli slipped out of the bathroom, her light robe wound tight around her. She should've gone shopping for a winceyette nightgown that reached her ankles, not packed this little number. She hadn't been thinking about the nightwear, only what to bring for the days and evenings right down to the last G-string.

Mac was lying on the edge of the far side, his hands behind his head, and a wobbly smile aimed at her.

Thump-thump. Her heart was cranking up the tempo at the sight of the man she had to share the bed with. Share, but not touch. Rule number one. How did she manage that? There wouldn't be much sleeping going on for sure, and tomorrow she was going to look awful. 'Don't roll over or you'll fall out of bed,' she warned and gave him a quick smile.

'I did mention sleeping on the floor.'

Talk about hopeless. Here she was about to climb into bed with Mac, the guy who had a short while ago told her she was not fat, and who she had started falling for: and nothing was meant to happen.

Nothing's going to happen.

A strangled laugh broke free of her tense body. 'We're crazy,' she spluttered.

Mac grinned at her. 'Absolutely crazy.'

Still laughing, she slid under the cover and switched the light off, plunging the room into complete darkness. 'I'm glad you agreed to do this.'

The mattress moved as he rolled onto his side to face her. 'You had a problem, I had a solution.'

'No regrets?' She held her breath and tried to see his expression in the dim light beginning to push into the room from behind the curtains.

But his face was in shadow. 'Not for a moment.'

She wanted to believe him—she really did. 'A weekend with strangers who are happy to give you a hard time and no regrets? Think I've said it before—you're crazy.'

'That's me.' He laughed softly. 'It's odd but I'm starting to feel alive again. As though I belong somewhere. Not that I'm saying I'm becoming a part of your family. I know that's not on the cards, but they're so friendly and easy to be around that I forget our relationship isn't for real.'

It could be, if he meant what he was saying. 'I suppose that's why you're so convincing.' To the others, not her, though there had been moments when she'd wondered if he did want to be with her. As in properly, completely, every day, with her. 'I'm glad for you. Could be this weekend helps you as much as me.'

'Kelli, can I make love to you? I know it wasn't meant to be, but I want you so much. You make me feel again, to want things I thought I'd never want again.' He wasn't reaching for her, no touch to soften her, tempt her, if she wanted to say no.

Rules one, two and three. No touching or kissing in bed. No sex anywhere.

Rules are made to be broken, repeated that annoying voice in her head.

If they made love then they'd do it again tomorrow night, and it would be harder to walk away from the relationship next week. On the other hand, she was halfway to being in love with Mac and resisting him was nigh on impossible. When her blood was fizzing, muscles tightening in anticipation, and desire winding up fast. She could make and store up exquisite memories for the long, lonely nights to come. Besides, she wanted to give back something to him, and if making him feel alive again was it then she was more than happy. 'Yes,' she sighed around a lump in the back of her throat. 'Please.'

'Don't move.' Mac tossed the covers aside and came over to her. His fingers traced a line from beneath her earlobe to her breast, followed by his lips, soft and tantalising.

When Kelli placed her arms around his neck Mac gently pushed them away. 'Lie back and enjoy.'

'But I want to touch you, to rub you, make you come.'

'Trust me, you're doing that in spades.' His mouth returned to her nipple and with one hot flick her back was arching as need sparked through her.

How? She hadn't done anything. Mac's hands touched her as though with wonder. *Her.* Amazing…

'You're beautiful,' he whispered against her breasts.

She tensed. He couldn't see her properly in the semi-dark.

'I mean it,' he growled against her skin, sending shivers of heat through her.

To hell with not touching him. It was agony, and ecstasy. It was wonderful and frustrating and oh… 'Do that again.'

Her body was shattering as a conflagration of desire and love rolled through her, took her out of this world and shut her mind down, leaving her free to absorb the wonder of Mac's lovemaking.

And then he was above her, entering her, taking her to a whole new level of wonder, going with her, until they both peaked and the heat exploded around, through, between them.

Breaking the rules wasn't so bad.

CHAPTER EIGHT

KELLI HADN'T STOPPED smiling since Mac made love to her last night, and everyone was noticing.

'You two are hot together.' Leanne grinned as they walked into the salon where they were to be made beautiful. 'I've never seen you so happy.'

Mac had told her she was beautiful and she'd begun to go with it. To trust him on this. He hadn't turned away from her that morning when they'd woken in full daylight, he hadn't studied her like a specimen to be catalogued, or the night before's mistake. No scalpels in sight. Instead Mac had reached for her and caressed her before making love with her again. He'd made them late for breakfast and earned a whole load of witty comments from her obnoxious brothers. Mac was in for a long morning on the golf course unless he managed to shut them down.

'I hope those men don't wear themselves out playing golf. Especially Billy. He's going to need his stamina for the wedding and the wedding night.' Kelli poked Leanne on the arm. *Back at you.*

The bride-to-be only laughed. 'No worries on that score.' Then she stopped and hugged Kelli. 'As long as you're happy, that's all anyone wants.'

Her heart stuttered. This wasn't how it was meant to go. The crash was going to hurt a lot more than she'd expected. But then she'd never meant to make love with Mac, or to find herself falling for him. 'I am,' she managed around her doubts. If it were all true then she'd be crazy happy, not just warily perched on cloud nine. Next time Tamara had any insane suggestions like asking Mac to accompany her to something, she'd hang up and stay hung up. Not that it had been her friend's idea to fake an engagement; that brainwave lay entirely with Mac.

But if she'd ignored Tamara she'd have missed out on getting close to Mac, last night being the icing on the cake so far. Tonight might lead to an even sweeter topping. Then tomorrow would come and they'd continue the charade but on Monday reality would strike and the show would be over. Her stomach cramped. Her mouth dried. No. She didn't want that. But perhaps Mac did. He'd signed up for a weekend, not a lifetime. By his own admission this was his first foray back into the dating world. Apparently she had a lot to do with his willingness to participate, but he'd be wanting to test the waters, try out other offerings.

What if she made him fall in love with her? Was that even possible? Where to start?

'Kelli, my girl, don't stand there looking lost.' Mum was at her side. 'You're up for nails first.'

Was this a sign? An answer to her question? Get made to look more than her best, starting with her nails? Be so alluring Mac couldn't resist her. It was a start, and the only one she could come up with. Though it did reek with falseness. Shallow. Not how she wanted any relationship she was involved in to go. She knew first-hand the downside to that. But striving to look fabulous so as to deflect Mac seeing the real her was being honest to herself in a way. Though she was meant to be toughening up about that, it was hard to stop hiding behind amazing clothes and hairstyles and sometimes even witty conversation. Incredible how many people bought it, saw only what she wanted them to.

Mac's not like that.

Could explain her feelings for him. But it'd be a big step to trust him never to see her faults.

'Kelli, you're daydreaming.'

'Yes, Mum.' Sinking onto the chair being held out for her by the nail technician, she smothered a wry smile. If only she were truly engaged and could enjoy the moments of excitement like Leanne, but since she couldn't she'd make the most of the day and have some fun, maybe even figure out how to make Mac think twice about walking away next week.

She could try just being herself. There was a novel idea, and it fitted with being strong.

The hour of the wedding ceremony sped towards Kelli so fast she thought she'd never be ready in time. With chaos surrounding her Leanne had become cool and calm, organising her best friend into the bridesmaid dress and not panicking when some buttons popped off. Kelli took over there, reattaching them with needle and thread after realigning others to allow a bit more room so the dress wasn't quite as tight.

When Kelli went to get dressed in her specially made teal silk shift Mac was nowhere to be seen. His suit was gone so she presumed he'd already showered and dressed and was with the guys somewhere. She swallowed her disappointment at not preparing alongside him. That was what couples did; not them. To be fair, she'd left him with the brothers for most of the day so couldn't expect him to be hanging around waiting for her when she chose to make an appearance. They'd managed lunch together, along with most of the family: a rushed meal with people coming and going, grabbing sandwiches and coffee to have on the run.

Andy had come over when Mac was with her to say, 'Don't believe this one whenever he says he's not good at something. He aced the golf.'

Mac had looked the picture of innocence as he'd said, 'I don't recall saying I wasn't any good at golf.'

Not those exact words, no. 'You did kind of imply it,' she'd laughed before devouring a small salad. This getting glammed up was hard work.

Kelli had just slipped into her dress when the door to the suite opened and Mac strolled in, looking divine in his dark grey evening suit and white shirt. 'Oh, my.'

'Have I got grease on my chin?' The hunk grinned.

She fixed him a look that said 'don't fool with me', and growled, 'Can you do up my zip?' How like a couple that sounded. 'Would you mind?'

'No, I'd hate it.' He was still grinning, which took the edge off what he'd said.

'Then I'll pop down the hallway and knock on the next door to find someone else to help me.'

'Oh, no, you won't,' he growled back. 'While we're a couple, that's my job.' He stepped behind her and sucked in a breath.

While we're a couple. A thrill shivered through her. Mac wasn't touching her zipper. 'Problem?'

A gentle tug where the zip started, then zilch. Only the sensation of kisses whispering over the skin between her shoulder blades. 'Mac.' She had no idea if she said his name out loud, no idea of anything except those kisses caressing her, of whispers of breath as his mouth caressed her skin. 'Mac. Please.'

'Please what?' he asked quietly beside her ear.

Tipping her head back, she felt his lips moving slowly

up her neck, tasting her, awakening her, tightening her belly and creating a tsunami of need centred at her core. 'Take me.'

His laugh was low and sexy and intensified everything she was feeling. 'And have your mother banging down the door asking why we're not already waiting in the ceremony garden? No, Kelli, this is something to be going on with until tonight.'

Mac said that? Nothing like his usual measured speech and words, more like a hot man in need of getting close and personal—with her. Twisting around in his arms her hip swept across his need, rock hard and pushing the front of his trousers out of shape. What was going on? Apart from lust? Did Mac want more too? More likely now he'd got back in the saddle he'd be unable to stop. There was a drought of four years to make up for. Kelli shuddered as if a bucket of icy water had been dumped on her.

Knock, knock. 'Kelli, Mac, are you in there?' Dad called from the hallway.

'What did I tell you?' Mac grinned. 'Trish has sent the cavalry. I'm in the bathroom until Dale's gone.'

'Good idea,' Kelli muttered, glancing at the evidence of his need. 'But first, my zip?'

Nothing sensual about the way Mac dealt with it this time; up and closed, done deal, and her skin was bereft.

Opening the door, she gasped. 'Hey, Dad, what's up?'

'Your mother needs you. Something to do with her jacket not sitting right.' Dad glanced around. 'Where's Mac? He's not gone down already?'

'He's in the bathroom.' She slipped her arm through her father's. 'Come on. Let's go sort Mum out.'

'We can wait for Mac. It's nothing urgent, just Trish flapping in panic with nothing to do. She's so organised, every box ticked twice, nothing going wrong, I swear she's made this crisis up because she can't deal with quiet time.'

Wait for Mac? Kelli could feel laughter beginning to unleash inside. She'd be waiting for ever. 'Mac,' she called and swallowed. 'You going to be long? We're waiting for you.' If only she could see his face. It'd be a picture for sure.

The bathroom door cracked open. 'Nearly ready,' Mac said in such a normal I-am-in-control voice that she had to wonder if there weren't two Macs hanging out in the bathroom.

'That was quick.' The devil had got her tongue. When his eyes widened, she laughed. And then turned away to distract her father. Just in case all was not quite 'ready'.

Of course Kelli cried when Leanne walked down the petal-strewn path towards Billy and the marriage celebrant. She cried as her brother said his vows, and when he slid the ring onto Leanne's finger. It would've been rude not to when there were tears tracking down Billy's cheeks too. Mac kept handing her tissues from what seemed like a never-ending supply in his pockets. With his other hand he held one of hers, fingers laced, and his thumb rubbing circles on her skin.

'I'll need to find the make-up artist for a repair job soon,' she murmured as she mopped up yet more tears. These ones were for what might have been if only she and Mac were for real.

Mac's fingers squeezed hers. 'You don't need make-up.'

'What is it about weddings that makes me cry? It's not something I go around doing much.'

'You're happy for Billy and Leanne. And…' he leaned

closer '…you're not the only one. There's hardly a dry-eyed female around here.'

'And Dad.' An emotional man, her father, not afraid to show his feelings. 'Third and last son married off.'

'The focus on you is going to be turned up something awful.' Mac stared at her for a long moment.

'What?'

He shook his head. 'Nothing.'

Kelli stood up. 'I'm going to kiss my new sister-in-law then get us some champagne.' She wasn't going to waste time and a wonderful day worrying what was behind that look. Plenty of time once she was back in Auckland to try unravelling what went on in that craggy head focused on her.

For the dinner Mac sat with Kelli at the family table in front of the wedding party. The food was divine, the speeches heart-wrenching at times and hilarious at others. He couldn't remember the last time he'd been so relaxed amongst people who twenty-four hours ago had been strangers. When he and Cherie got married there'd only been a handful of friends and relatives, and while it had been wonderful there hadn't been this amazing family atmosphere.

Dale and Trish had accepted him as Kelli's fiancé and all her brothers had gone out of their way to make him welcome. Which meant trying to catch him out with questions about his past, and challenging him to a game of darts—blindfolded. As for that golf, thank the lucky stars his game had been on. The guys would never have let him live it down if he'd lost to them.

It was all fun and friendly, not a hint of unacceptance. It threatened to drag him in; to tempt him to make this a permanent arrangement; to let go the past and aim for a future. With the gorgeous and loving woman sitting beside him, her hand on his thigh. Possessively? Or lovingly? Or what?

Leaning back in his chair, he covered Kelli's hand with his, felt her jerk as though she hadn't realised what she'd been doing. Pressing down gently, he kept her from withdrawing. He liked her touch, liked that she was happy to be seen touching him. This wasn't a game, wasn't for show to underline their engagement. Kelli had acted impulsively and that stirred him deeply, suggested he might be able to move on some day. Was already easing out of the gloom.

Pulling the brakes back on his emotions was impossible right now. He wanted to let loose a bit, and plain old enjoy a weekend with a woman without having to worry about what tomorrow might bring. As though someone had lifted the shutters on his grief and light had spilled in to banish the darkness. Monday would be the end of this so he might as well grab today and tomorrow with both hands and have a blast. Which included giving Kelli a good time. She deserved it, and he was happy to oblige.

'Up to dancing?' Kelli leaned in to ask, teasing his senses with the smell of roses.

'Now there's a loaded question.' The band had started up a few minutes ago and already the dance floor was heaving. He stood up, tugging Kelli with him, still holding her hand. He never wanted to let her go again.

But he would. He had to. She needed someone she could trust to watch her back. Someone like Jason. That man was perfect for her. Her parents hadn't done her a disservice trying to convince her to date him. Not once since they'd all arrived on Waiheke had he been rude or nasty to him, or Kelli. He'd taken their engagement on the chin like a real bloke.

Kelli was moving to the music as though she'd invented

dancing. Her long body swaying and her hips gyrating, her head tipped back so those dark blonde waves of hair fell down her back.

Mac went with her, his moves matching hers. His mouth was dry and his gut tight. Keep this up and he'd need to take her to the beach before the music stopped. Kiss her senseless, make love to her behind the trees like a crazed teen, hear her groan with pleasure. Come to think of it, he felt like a teen who'd just discovered sex. No slow reawakening for him. Instead wham, bam, can we do it again? He'd gone from low, low, low to a searing high.

There was only one way to go after that.

The band had packed up, the bride and groom had left for their suite, and some of the guests were sitting around the tables leisurely drinking more champagne while they talked and laughed the night away.

Mac and Kelli went for a stroll along the beach, hand in hand, Kelli's shoes swinging from the fingers of her free hand. 'It's good to see Billy so happy,' she said. 'There've been times when none of us believed he'd ever be again.'

Mac felt a hitch in his chest. 'What do you mean?'

'Like you he is, was, a widower.'

The hitch became an ache. 'No one's said a word all weekend.'

'Why would we? Everyone knows about it, no one wanted to blight his and Leanne's special day. Billy has moved on, found happiness again, but I know he hasn't forgotten Carla. Why would he? Why should he? They were a couple in love when life took a tragic turn. Carla would've been the first person to kick his butt and tell him to get on with being happy.'

'What happened?' There was a blockage in Mac's throat impeding his words, flattening them.

'They'd been at Billy's rugby club Christmas party and he'd had too much to drink so Carla drove them home. It was a wet night and she took a corner too fast, spun out and slammed into a power pole.'

Game over. Mac could feel Billy's pain. 'Bet he felt guilty about not being able to drive.'

Kelli nodded as understanding filled her eyes. 'You'd know about that. The guilt, I mean.'

'Yeah.' The word sighed out of him. 'Totally.'

'Want to talk about it?'

Strangely, he did. Which was a first, apart from Tom. Not even his mother had been able to get a word about Cherie's death. 'Cherie had an aneurism.'

Kelli squeezed his fingers and kept walking. 'That made you feel guilty how?'

Not he shouldn't be guilty, but why. 'I'm a doctor.'

'She'd had symptoms? There usually aren't any for an aneurism.'

'I should've known something was wrong. I didn't. Not a whisper, not a hint. I had come home late and Cherie was already in bed asleep.' Tipping his head back, he stared up at the stars, swallowing the pain. 'I remember feeling relieved I could slide in beside her, tuck my arm around her waist, and give into the exhaustion overwhelming me.' He'd been working horrendous hours as he studied for his final exam in emergency medicine and did the days and nights in ED. 'The alarm woke me. Not Cherie. She was gone. According to the autopsy report she'd died about three hours before I woke up. How could I not have known?' The despair, guilt, the anguish all poured out of him in that last question. 'How?' They'd been so connected, so in touch with each other, loved and understood one another so well. 'How?' he cried at the stars.

Kelli's arms wound around him, held him tight. Her

head was tucked against his shoulder, her mouth quiet, her body supple and giving.

Mac breathed deep, drawing in Kelli's scent. Kelli's. The rose fragrance stirred him, reminded him of other things that used to be a part of his life. His family history, the home he grew up in, the laughter whenever Dad was away, the love, the anger. The good and bad. There'd been difficult times, days when he'd nearly run away out of fear of his father, yet he'd stayed because of his mum. Stayed and survived to go on to become a successful doctor, to marry a wonderful woman—and lose her. His heart banged against his ribs. He should've known Cherie was unwell. He'd survived that. If being wary and holding onto his heart and not wanting to get involved with anyone for fear of not being able to protect them, save them, was survival.

Slowly, slowly Kelli's warmth moved into him, heating the cold that had settled around his heart all those years ago. Making room for new emotions. Making way for life. Really? Could he let go of the anguish that had kept him in limbo for so long and find happiness again?

Was he prepared to take the risk?

Was he prepared not to?

The answers weren't bombarding him, but he could go with the flow for now.

Standing in Kelli's arms, waiting, enjoying a new-found peace within himself as he soaked up the moments drifting by, allowing it to fill him with a relaxing quietness. Across the beach the tide rolled in, reaching up the sand, an occasional gull squawked, and behind them laughter and voices stabbed the air intermittently.

Kelli's lips were moving on his neck, soft yet fiery, gentle yet demanding. Warmth was turning to heat, hot strobes searing him inside and out, building a desire he had to do something about.

His mouth caught hers, his lips demanded possession and his tongue made a foray into her heat. He wanted to lose himself in Kelli, to give as much as he needed to take. His hands cupped her butt, pressed her hard against his need.

'Mac,' she whispered.

His name hung on the night air, vibrating with Kelli's longing. For him. An endorsement of his emotions, of the need to satisfy her too. He scooped her up into his arms and strode fast towards the trees at the end of the bay, which were closer than their room, and way more romantic.

Kelli suddenly started laughing, causing Mac to pause and ask, 'You okay?'

'What is it about us and weddings?'

Phew. 'I have no idea but I'm liking it. We'll have to attend more.'

Her laughter faded. 'Think I've done my dash with those.'

Hey, they might be temporarily engaged but there'd never been any suggestion of a wedding. Mac lowered her to the ground. It was one thing to be rushing to the trees with Kelli in his arms, quite another to stand here holding her discussing unlikely events. Events that came with a dose of reality. This was a temporary situation. 'Let's finish this one before thinking about any more.'

Running her hands down the front of her dress, Kelli had no idea how she affected him. He had to turn away, stare out to sea. Or…

Mac turned back to Kelli, placed his hands on her shoulders and leaned in to kiss her. 'You okay?'

She stared at him for a long moment. 'Yes. Yes, I am.'

Did she just add 'for now' under her breath?

Mac wasn't sure if he wanted to know. If Kelli was hurting then he had to stop all thoughts of sex and kisses. At least until she was comfortable with him again. 'Let's walk a bit more.'

'No, let's kiss, and follow through on that.' She was up on her toes again.

Mac was over talking and trying to analyse everything. Kissing Kelli was way more exciting and rewarding and fun. And kissing was going to lead to those trees.

CHAPTER NINE

'RISE AND SHINE,' Kelli squeaked as the sun inched up over the horizon. 'Let's go kayaking.'

'Didn't you get enough exercise during the night?' Mac groaned as he pulled the pillow over his head.

She tugged it away. 'Nope. I've got energy to burn.'

'Then I know how to fix that.'

Suddenly she was trapped in Mac's arms and sprawled across that big chest. His knee was pushing between her legs, and already she was reacting with need. 'I like your idea.' She grinned before beginning a trail of kisses over his chest, not thinking too much about how she looked this morning.

Or that this was probably her last day as Mac's fiancé. The engagement wouldn't count once back at work.

Nope, she was grabbing everything with both hands and going to have the day of her life with the man she loved. Tomorrow was going to hurt anyway, might as well get as much out of today as possible. And give as much back so as Mac could never say he'd been used, and possibly, just possibly, he might see what he was walking away from and decide not to go. Instead stay and learn to love her.

Kayaking offshore in the morning sun added to the afterglow of their lovemaking and as Kelli powered ahead she couldn't believe the sense of amazement filling her. This was how she'd always imagined being in love would be. But Steve had put paid to that, dampening down any joy she'd felt with him.

Mac paddled up beside her, not slowing, calling as he passed, 'Race you to that boat anchored beyond the bay.' He was off, not waiting to see if she was on for it. He knew she liked a challenge.

He wasn't getting off lightly with this one. She was no stranger to kayaks, having spent many hours in them every summer at the family beach house. She dug deep with the paddle and began a slow, steady overhaul of the kayak in front. Those broad, muscular shoulders could be a distraction—if she let them.

Keeping her eyes fixed on the boat she was aiming for, she managed to keep her hormones in lockdown and begin to draw closer. And closer. Then, 'Hey, slowcoach, stop mucking about and put some elbow into paddling.' Her kayak nosed past, got in front and that was the last she saw of Mac until she reached their target and spun her craft around in the water to gloat. 'And you thought you could beat me.' She grinned moments later as his kayak nudged hers none too softly.

'I didn't want to hurt your feelings,' he gave back.

'Sure, buddy.'

'Not a valid reason for losing? Fair enough. Brunch's on me.'

Everything they ate at the resort was covered by her parents. 'Does that mean we're going into the town? Just the two of us?'

'I'd like to see the town centre.'

'We should check out some of the art shops and galleries. I need a small frame for a photo I got in Fiji.'

'We have a plan. Is it okay we're not joining your family this morning?' Mac looked concerned.

'I bet half them will be in town, doing other things. Today is wind-down time.'

She was right. Seemed every time they turned a corner they'd bump into someone from the wedding party. 'There's no getting away from them,' she muttered.

'Sounding disgruntled, sweetheart,' Mac laughed. 'Did you want time alone with me?'

Sweetheart, eh? Oh, boy. 'Yes, I did.'

His eyes widened before he took her hand and dragged her along to the end of the street and a café overlooking the water. 'In here, quick, before we're spotted.'

As long as no one else had beaten them to the place. 'This is like running from the media,' she quipped.

'You know about that?' Surprise blinked out at her from those stunning green eyes.

She elbowed him. 'I might've been famous in another life.'

'Thought I recognised you from somewhere.' He nodded at a waitress. 'A table for two, please.'

As Kelli slipped onto the chair he held out, she grimaced. 'Too often I saw Tamara trying to avoid the press. It was harrowing when all she wanted was to be left alone to get over what that awful man did by stealing her family's fortune.'

Mac sat beside her. 'She's moved on. There was no looking back at their wedding.'

'You're right. She's so happy in love.' If Tamara had got another crack at the love game surely *she* was entitled to a chance? With Mac? He was her pick. And she was entitled. Just not trusting herself yet.

'What are you having for breakfast? Salad? Or something decadent?' Mac teased.

'After all the exercise I've had? Eggs Benedict at least. Or should that be pancakes with berries and maple syrup?' She licked her lips and tried to ignore the way Mac's gaze fixed on them. 'What are you having?' she asked mischievously.

'What?' His gaze lifted to meet hers, and his eyes filled with lust. Or was that something stronger?

'Eggs for you?' She'd love to give him what he wanted. Again. Making love had never been so incredible, so exquisite, so—everything.

'Stop looking at me with those eyes,' her lover growled.

'They're the only ones I've got.'

Then the waitress interrupted the fun, and they had to make up their minds what they were going to eat. Kelli figured a plate of chaff could be put in front of her and she'd hardly notice, the distraction sitting opposite her large.

Afterwards, out in the sunshine, heading towards an art shop, Kelli felt as if she were walking on air. She was living in a magic bubble, and refused to acknowledge it was about to pop. Not this morning, hopefully not any time today, and that was enough to be getting on with for now.

Mac strode along beside Kelli, his hands firmly jammed in his pockets. The morning was turning into one of the best he'd had in a long time. *The* best. Which was why he had to hold back and not grab Kelli's hand in his and swing their arms between them while feeling her heat zing through his palm and into his veins.

Tipping into the well of excitement and happiness was all too easy to go along with, and would have consequences he wasn't prepared to face. It wasn't as though the pain of losing Cherie would suddenly disappear in a flash of lust. No, the pain was a familiar jacket he'd worn day and night since Cherie left him. Strange how comfortable that jacket was. Safety. Safety from the fear of trying again, moving forward. He'd had the love of his life. No one got two shots at that.

Billy has.

Mac stumbled. Where was he going with this? His eyes sought out Kelli, drank her in. His heart curled in on itself, tightened that comfort jacket around him. Kelli needed someone to love her with no restraint, and he couldn't guarantee that.

'Hey, Billy, Leanne, didn't expect to see you two out of your rooms before midday.' Kelli rushed to her brother to wrap him in a hug before giving Leanne one.

Had his thoughts conjured up Billy? The man looked relaxed and utterly happy. So it was possible to start again. Mac gave Leanne a light hug and Billy a back slap. 'Great wedding, guys.'

Billy, the man who'd faced tragedy and moved on to find new happiness, grinned. 'We thought so.'

Did he ever worry about losing Leanne? About history repeating itself? He had to. He was human. 'I was glad to be a part of the proceedings.'

'The family will be gearing up for another wedding now ours is done and dusted.' Billy smiled. 'Any idea when you might tie the knot, sis?'

Kelli's face paled. 'Um…no, not yet. There's plenty of time, no need to rush.'

Mac moved closer to her, said, 'We'll make some decisions later.'

'Watching you two together, I'd have said next week would be a good time.' Leanne fanned her face with her hand. 'I mean, you two are hot together.'

Draping an arm over Kelli's shoulders, Mac struggled to come up with something to deflect these two who only meant the best for Kelli. 'We'll keep you posted. Now we need to get to the art shop, and I presume you've got lots you want to do before heading to the airport for your flight to Australia.'

'Have a great honeymoon, you two.' Kelli put her arm around his waist and began to walk away. 'Spare me all the details when you get back.' Laughter followed them down the road. 'Phew,' she muttered.

'It's getting harder, isn't it?'

Her shoulders rose and fell under his arm. 'It sure is.'

One day to get through and then Kelli would release him from their engagement, mission accomplished. 'Jason's been great about the whole thing.'

Kelli slipped out from under his arm. 'He's been brilliant.'

'I wonder if he'd felt obligated to your parents for everything they've done for him?'

Kelli's eyes all but popped out of her head. 'He'd go so far as to marry me because of that?'

'You work it out. You know him and your family better than I do.' The more Mac thought about it, the more he felt he'd hit the button bang on. 'It's not too late to set the record straight.'

The nibbling stopped. 'Because when everyone learns you and I are not engaged the pressure's going back on? Got you. I'll talk to Jason later.'

'Good. Now let's enjoy what's left of our time together.' He pointed to a shop. 'Is that where we're headed?'

With a nod Kelli changed direction, aiming for the wide store with big windows letting in lots of sunlight. Inside paintings dotted the walls, placed artfully so as not to encroach on the next and spoil the viewer's enjoyment of what was on the canvas.

Kelli wandered around the room, stopping to gaze at

two paintings in particular. 'If only I had a big house to put works of art like these in.' She sighed wistfully as she studied a watercolour of Rangitoto Island with a storm brewing around the peak. 'That is particularly beautiful. Brings back memories of a day when Dad took me and Phil across to walk to the top. We got soaked, but I didn't care. It was wonderful being on the island with only a couple of other people also walking the track to the summit.'

'You wouldn't want it where you live now?' Mac asked.

'It would have to go in my bedroom and that's small and dark. No, that painting needs light and space to itself.' She moved on.

What if he bought it for her? As a gift for a wonderful weekend? No. Not wise. She might misinterpret the gesture, think he wanted more from her, or think he was trying to buy his way into her bed again. Moving along, he studied the next two paintings, liked them but wasn't overly moved. But the next one brought him up short. An abstract that spoke to him of tension and danger and risks and a softening in one corner that said maybe good things could happen if he was prepared to open up to them.

Mac stared and stared, taking in the brush strokes almost one by one. Dazzling red shades, subtle greens, angry blues, and a hint of summer blue. The more he looked, the more he found. He didn't do art, wasn't into paintings and pictures at all.

Kelli nudged him. 'Buy it.'

'No.' Apart from a calendar and a photo of Mum with him and Cherie his apartment walls were bare. Sterile. Safe. Undemanding.

'Dare you.' The challenge was loud and clear.

He wasn't having a bar of it. Not this one. He shook his head abruptly. 'You finished in here?'

'Sure.' She followed quietly, but he could feel her eyes boring into the back of his skull.

Out on the footpath he looked around, saw a pottery shop and headed that way. 'Let's look in there.'

'Okay,' was all she said, but her disappointment was obvious. She expected more of him. An explanation for starters.

'You're not keen on pottery?' he asked.

'Not my thing. Whereas paintings are. Especially when it grabs me and won't let me walk away. Then I know it's special. Like that one did for you.' She changed direction, heading for the beach.

Why did Kelli think one painting mattered? It wasn't as though he'd shouted with glee or said he had to have it. No, he'd studied it in depth, that was all. Then he'd walked away, leaving it behind where it couldn't bug him every time he saw it.

'Where do you live?' Kelli asked out of left field. Or maybe it wasn't given he'd been looking at a painting and decided not to buy it.

'In a Ponsonby apartment.' It was modern, comfortable and boring. That painting would liven the place up no end.

'Yours? Or do you rent?'

'It's mine.'

'Any flatmates?'

'No.'

'Pets?' she persisted.

What was this? Fifty questions? Might be lucky if she stopped at fifty. 'I occasionally toss the neighbour's spaniel a bone. Does that count?'

Kelli was shaking her head over something he didn't get. 'Sounds lonely. I bet your walls are bare and the furniture is minimal.'

'It's perfect.'

'Speaks of lack of involvement.'

He'd done that deliberately. 'Okay, I'll play ball with pooch next time I see him.'

'Stop being a prat, Mac.' Anger glittered out of those serious eyes, directed solely at him. 'Why did you come here with me if you don't want to mix with people?'

Go for the solar plexus, why don't you?

'I told you. You needed help and I offered.'

Her hands were on her hips, her feet slightly splayed. 'So you said, but I don't buy it. You've fitted right in. You are a people person, Mac. Don't say you don't like most of them back.'

'I used to be a people person.' But Kelli had a valid point. 'You're right. I've enjoyed myself immensely these past couple of days. I've remembered what it's like to be involved with friends, and to have someone special at my side.' Ouch. Shouldn't have said that. 'That special person is you, Kelli. I have no idea where we're going with what started out as a solution to your problem, but I do like you a lot.' Like? Pathetic. But as far as he was prepared to go for now. The most he'd admit even to himself.

'Thank you, I think.' She wasn't smiling at him, or bursting with happiness.

Did Kelli expect more of him? Slam. What if she didn't like him half as much as he did her? He'd set himself up for a crash. He'd better toughen up and get over himself. This was what getting involved meant. Suddenly he thought he might want more with Kelli, that he mightn't be happy to rock off into the sunset come Monday. Was this love? He did not know. It didn't feel like last time. Could be it was taking the long way round to his heart. If it wasn't then it could be the beginning of a strong friendship. Mac shuddered. Being friends with Kelli was imperative, but nowhere near enough.

Kelli leaned close and placed the softest of kisses on his mouth, then she took his hand. 'We're going back to the art shop and you are going to buy yourself a painting. It's past time you got out in the real world again.'

'And you think a painting is the answer?'

She stopped at that, turned so her fierce cobalt gaze locked on him. 'You felt that painting—the moods it invoked were there in your eyes, on your face. It pulled you right in and touched something deep. I don't know what that was but I do know that painting has your name on it.'

'What if I don't want to look at it every day and feel those emotions it brought back?'

She hesitated, and he thought he'd won. But no, this was Kelli. 'Maybe it's time you did feel all those emotions you've obviously kept clamped down deep inside. Maybe you're ready to face living fully again, moving on and finding happiness. Everyone deserves it, Mac. Even you.'

Blimey, she didn't hold back. Gave it like a metal truck dumping its load at the quarry. It was too much to take in right now. He did best when he let thoughts and emotions infiltrate slowly, one fact at a time. 'What about you? Don't you deserve it too?'

'I wasn't aware I was avoiding it,' was her acerbic retort.

'Oh, really?'

'I am not shutting out happiness. I'm just afraid I won't find anyone to love me enough to overlook my imperfections so that I can trust that happiness.'

Her ex had done a right number on her. What he wouldn't like to do to him. How to put his feelings out there without getting too involved and giving Kelli hope he was afraid to follow up on? 'I truly don't understand. You are so beautiful, inside and out. No one's perfect but in my book you're damned close.'

Her mouth fell open, quickly followed by tears tracking down her cheeks. He wrapped her into a tight hug, his shirt getting a soaking and his heart a pounding.

When Kelli finally pulled back in his arms to look at him, she asked, 'What are we doing to each other?'

Setting ourselves up for a big fall. 'Telling it how we see it. Being honest, in other words.' Except he wasn't totally. Opening his heart wasn't— A scream shattered the fragile air around them. 'What's going on?' Mac stared around the shops and the street, saw two women running out of a café, and headed their way.

'The chef's been electrocuted!' one of them shouted. 'We need help. I think his heart's stopped.'

Help. Mac's key word. 'I'm a doctor. Kelli here's a nurse.' He looked around at the shocked faces of pedestrians. 'Is anyone a local? We need to find a defibrillator.'

'There's one in the superette. I'll grab it,' a man called, already racing away.

Kelli ran into the café, pushing through the throng of people gaping into the interior, not waiting for anything.

Mac took after her. Arriving in the kitchen, he heard Kelli ask as she knelt beside the stricken young chef, 'How long has she been down?'

'A minute, a bit longer.' The guy swallowed. 'Lauren— she was using the hand-beater, whipping the gravy. It must've short-circuited.' Another swallow. 'I'm the manager, haven't had anything like this happen before.'

'Stay clear everyone,' Mac warned. 'Don't touch that beater,' he snapped at Kelli as she reached for the girl's hand gripping the utensil.

'I've turned off the power to the switches,' the manager informed them.

Kelli was onto it, immediately kicking the beater out

of Lauren's hand, then starting CPR. The girl was pale as sand while blue around her lips.

'Where's that defib?' Mac asked as he dropped to his knees on the other side of their patient. 'Have you called the ambulance?' He flicked a quick look to the manager.

'They're on their way.' The man was calming down now that he had medical help for his chef. 'So's the air ambulance.'

'Here's the defib,' someone yelled.

'Get it charging,' Mac instructed as he tore Lauren's chef jacket down the middle. 'Wish we had some oxygen.'

Kelli kept up the compressions, a sweat breaking out on her forehead. 'Your wish is about to be granted. I hear a siren.'

'Clear the area around your patient,' intoned the defibrillator.

'Everyone stand back,' Mac repeated the message as he placed the paddles on Lauren's chest. With a quick glance around to make sure those in the room had heeded his request, he shocked the chef.

Her body jerked upward, fell back.

Feeling for a pulse, Kelli shook her head.

'Stand back,' Mac commanded though no one had moved.

Another shock, another jerk off the floor, and then a flicker of an eyelid, a slight rise of Lauren's chest.

'Yay, we have a result.' Kelli huffed air over her lips. 'A good result.' Her fingers were on the pulse, nodding as she silently counted the beats.

'The best.' Mac sat back on his haunches as paramedics rushed purposefully into the room, carrying oxygen and all the other necessary paraphernalia to keep Lauren alive and well. Quickly explaining what he knew, he moved out of the way and left the experts to the job.

'That calls for a very strong coffee,' he told Kelli as they walked through the humming café.

The talking stopped and clapping broke out.

The manager pointed to a table out on the pavement. 'Take a seat and I'll bring you those coffees. On the house. I can't thank you enough for your rapid response. Lauren was very lucky you were in town.'

'Glad to be of help,' Mac agreed.

'How do you take your coffees?'

With their orders in place Mac settled on a seat and stretched his legs along the side of the table. 'Things like what just happened remind me why I became a doctor. The unexpected can happen to anyone anywhere and it's an awesome feeling being able to step in and do something constructive.' He was feeling good.

'Then you should shout yourself a reward. That painting's got your name on it.' Kelli grinned at him. Then her breath seemed to hitch in her throat and her teeth did that nibbly thing on her bottom lip as the grin faded. She looked away as her cheeks began turning a strawberry shade.

Mac understood that breathing problem. It was going on in his lungs too. He didn't think his cheeks had taken on the red hue but he definitely wanted to nibble something. His brain was not in sync with the rest of his body. 'We don't have to wait for the coffee.'

'Here you go, folks.' Two large cups appeared on the periphery of Mac's vision, along with a plate of chocolate and strawberry muffins. Strawberry? Yes, the same shade as Kelli's cheeks. 'Thanks,' he muttered.

'Thank you,' Kelli told the hovering manager and picked up the huge coffee cup and wrapped her shaking hands around it. 'Those muffins look delicious.'

Don't spill the coffee, Mac warned silently. *We'll be*

*here all day while another round is made and more food
brought out.*

She must've got the message because her grip tightened.

'You're welcome.' Finally the guy moved off.

'Isn't that too hot to hold onto?' Mac queried lamely,
all out of what to say to her without double entendre. Her
fingers had to be burning.

The colour in Kelli's cheeks intensified. She sipped
at the frothy milk on top of her coffee. Still not looking
at him.

Now what? Hot? Too hot to hold onto? She had it bad.
So did he. His gut had tightened in anticipation. 'I suppose it would be rude to leave right now,' he half asked,
half stated.

Kelli nodded emphatically, making a moue with her
mouth. 'I reckon.'

'And this *is* too hot.' He blew on his long black. 'Boiling, can't drink it just yet.'

Suddenly Kelli laughed, a free and happy sound that
went straight to his heart. 'I hope the resort staff haven't
cleaned our room and sent our bags to the luggage room
yet.'

Mac wanted to wrap her hand in his, kiss her knuckles, knew that'd only turn him on even more. 'We don't
have to be out until two. Should be just enough time for
what's on your mind.'

Those alluring eyes widened, and colour crept into
her cheeks again. 'My mind hasn't a lot to say at the moment. Except we are going back to that art shop on the
way to the resort.'

'Persistent, aren't you?'

'Yes.'

And he'd better not forget that. Nor could he deny any

longer that he wanted to take another look at the painting. It would look perfect on the west wall of his sitting room, the first thing someone would see when they entered the room. It would demand attention, more than the view of the harbour bridge and the sea beyond. But still he said, 'I don't need a blasted painting any more than I need a pet dog.'

'Don't tempt me.'

CHAPTER TEN

MONDAY, AND KELLI hit the gym before starting work. Her body was exhausted, every muscle had its own tune of cramps and tiredness, but there'd been a lot of serious eating and drinking over the weekend that needed dealing with.

She'd done some weights and was clocking onto the treadmill when that sexy deep voice that lifted bumps on her skin and kept her awake the night before interrupted her concentration.

'Hey, Kelli. Didn't expect to see you in here this early.' Mac strolled into sight.

'I was at a loose end.' Restless and wound up tighter than a ball of string and unable to focus on anything. 'You're early too.'

'I'd done my laundry, cleaned the bathroom and got in groceries for the week, and still had time to kill before going into work.' How Mac managed to step onto the treadmill beside her without doing a face plant was beyond her. He hadn't taken his eyes off her legs from the moment he'd turned up.

Heat and need spread through her, blanketing her hang-ups about her body with something far more exciting and game changing because now she understood what that look meant, had experienced how Mac followed up with his hands and mouth. They were in the middle of the gym, surrounded by people working out. Get real. This was not the place to be craving Mac's touch. Struggling for normality—her old normality—Kelli dredged up an inane comment. 'I did pretty much the same things this morning.'

Mac nodded, still focused on her legs. 'Way too wired to be hanging out doing nothing.'

So he felt the same as she did. There was no holding in the smile now spreading across her face. 'I didn't know you could be so domestic.'

'Needs must,' he grunted as he hit the buttons, finally dragging his eyes forward. 'Now for a hard workout.'

Kelli was already jogging slowly, warming up before hitting the hills button. 'That painting look good on your wall?'

'Yeah.'

'What's wrong? You regretting your purchase?'

'Too late for that. I'm enamoured with it, which is un-nerving. I live a very clean-cut style; no mementos other than one photo, no pictures cluttering the walls, or un-necessary lampshades and furniture to dust.'

Sterile. Uninvolved. 'Keeping the world at arm's length.' He'd have fifty fits if he saw her bedroom.

'It's who I am, Kelli.' Oh-oh, the serious tone had switched on. 'You'd best remember that.'

Her stomach knotted. 'Hard to gel that version of you with the man I spent the weekend with. Sure you like liv-ing so remotely?'

'It's safer that way.'

'Safe can be restrictive,' Kelli argued, knowing she was guilty of doing the same until Mac came into her life.

'Less confronting.'

'To what?' Her heart had already taken a tumble and

there was quite likely a load of pain waiting in the background for the day Mac didn't want to stare at her legs.

A pager sounded and it wasn't until she saw Mac tug something from his waistband that she realised where the peeps had come from.

'There goes my workout.' Mac hit the slow button. 'I'm wanted in ED. Seems Michael's got a problem.'

Kelli nodded, swallowed the flare of annoyance that she'd been relegated to second. As head of department he had to go. It was bad timing, was all. They were actually talking about something serious and probably important to their future. If there was going to be a future, and she had no idea where they stood on that. No point trying to keep Mac here when he was wanted in the department. That was a no go. 'See you later.'

'Back to reality.' A brief twisted smile accompanied his words.

'Saved by the pager,' she acknowledged.

Mac didn't hear her. Or chose not to, striding out of the gym without finishing that uncomfortable conversation.

Suddenly the leftover fizz from the weekend dropped away, leaving her lethargic and barely able to put one foot in front of the other. The bubble had burst. Mac hadn't changed anything. His offer to stand by her had been for the duration of the wedding. No need to discuss breaking up. Confronting her family to explain had always been part of the deal.

The problem was that she'd gone and given away her heart to Mac. Of course she shouldn't have, but that suggested she'd had control over it. Fat chance. Spending so much time with Mac, having fun and getting to know him better, seeing a different side to the serious specialist—what was there not to fall in love with? The sparks had flown, back and forth. Leanne had commented about how hot she and Mac were together and that took involvement from both parties.

Involvement, Mac. When you get close to someone. When you share things—conversations, meals, friends and family. Involvement.

Sweat trickled down her back, soaked the waistband of her knee-length sports pants. *Yuck.* Her legs protested every step and her lungs moved in and out as if they were under water. Was she drowning? Under a blanket of unrequited love? Whatever Mac thought was a mystery. She'd seen desire light up his eyes uncountable times over the past three days. Had been loved with skill and abandonment, with wonder and joy. *What do you think of me, Mac? Huh? Do you care enough to carry on seeing me?*

Her legs won. No point in hauling them through the kilometres when they moved like lead weights.

Hitting the 'stop' button, she lurched against the hand bar and kept her balance. Just. Time for a shower and a coffee then she'd sign on for the shift.

Hopefully Mac would be friendly and not doing his serious thing as if she was a problem that had to be put in its box.

The department was full to bursting when Kelli slouched in. Mac was nowhere to be seen for handover, and those in the day shift were subdued. Too quiet.

'What's going on?' Kelli asked Stephanie, who'd been standing behind the counter flicking through patient notes.

'Everyone will hear soon enough.' Then Stephanie sniffed. 'Michael lost a patient, and he's not coping very well. A wee boy with a massive allergic reaction to some food product.'

A wee boy. That was hard to take and, for the doctor

in charge, distressing beyond imagination. 'That's why Mac got that message.' And she'd been thinking he'd been in a hurry to leave her. Selfish didn't begin to cover her thoughts. *Sorry, Mac. Sorry, Michael.*

'They're shut in his office going over what happened. Hopefully Mac can reassure Michael that he did everything right.' Stephanie looked worried.

'That explains the full cubicles. Down a doctor. What was Michael doing on day shift anyway?'

'He started early to cover another registrar who went off sick. One of those kind of days.' Stephanie handed her a file. 'Cubicle three, male, fifty-five, arrhythmia, SOBOE, no known history. Monitor him and I'll send a doctor as soon as I have one available. We need to get things moving around here, even if we only clear some of the minor cases until Mac's able to join us.'

'No problem.' Heading across to the cubicle opposite the department centre where more serious patients were kept under watch, Kelli glanced down the page of notes she'd been handed, took in the relevant details, and tried not to think about Michael and how he must be feeling. The guy was good, didn't make mistakes, but all doctors met their challenges, and today was his turn. 'Hi, Will. I'm Kelli, the nurse who's going to be keeping an eye on you for the next hour or two.'

'A lot of fuss about nothing, if you ask me. You've got far more serious patients needing your attention,' Will blustered.

The woman beside him introduced herself as his wife and said, 'Will, no one's asking you. The nurses are telling you there's something wrong with your heart and if you think I want you at home before we know what's going on, then think again.'

Kelli raised a thumb in the woman's direction. 'Will,

your wife's right. We can't be discharging you only to have you brought back in a far worse condition later, now can we?'

Will blanched. 'I guess not.'

'You've had a shock, physically and mentally.' She was reading the heart monitor's printout. 'See how those peaks are not nice and even? That's an abnormal rhythm and the doctors will want to find out the cause.'

'Am I going to have heart surgery?' All the bluster had gone out of her patient's voice. 'I've never been under the knife before.'

His wife gripped his hand. 'It won't be as serious as that.' The look that she threw Kelli was imploring her to reassure her husband.

'Let's not get ahead of ourselves. Your BP is high, but your lungs are clear of fluid, which is good. I'm here to keep monitoring you. A doctor will be along soon—' cross her fingers '—to explain what's happened and what your treatment might be. He'll discuss your symptoms and results with a cardiologist who will decide the next move.'

Stephanie joined them. 'Because of what's happening elsewhere, I've talked to Penny and she asked that we take blood for a troponin.' Penny being a cardiologist. 'Can you do that, Kelli?'

'Sure can.'

'What's a troponin?' Will asked.

'It's a test to see if you've had a heart attack in the last twenty-four hours. I'd say the cardiologist asked for it because of your problems breathing yesterday when you were trying to walk that hill.' The notes said he'd been on a walking challenge in Cornwall Park and had been stopping every hundred metres or so to get his breath back.

'Told you we should've come in straight away.' His wife looked ready to burst into tears.

Kelli nodded. 'It's okay, you're here now. But—' she aimed for stern '—any time this happens, or any chest pain, you must call an ambulance.'

'I don't like being a bother. It's not like it was urgent.'

'It could've been. We'd prefer to send you home healthy and with no heart problems, than have to deal with the consequences of a heart attack.' Or worse, but the embarrassed look on his face said he'd got the message and didn't need more horrific details. 'Right, I'll get the phlebotomy kit and take that blood sample. The sooner I do that, the sooner we'll know what's going on.'

The blood was taken and sent up to the lab. Kelli regularly checked the monitor printout and reassured her patient nothing had changed for the worse.

She worked with a young woman suffering acute abdo pain in the next cubicle as well. Another registrar had joined the shift and between them they arranged bloods for a CBC and CRP. Appendicitis was on the cards, soon confirmed with an increased white cell count and a raised CRP. The girl disappeared with an orderly, heading to Theatre.

Nearly an hour after she'd come into the department Mac strode into Will's cubicle, his serious face on and his eyes sad. 'Hello, I'm Mac Turner, an emergency doctor,' he said. 'I've read all your results and talked to the cardiologist. The good news is that you haven't had a heart attack.'

'And the bad?' Will asked.

'There's still your irregular heartbeat to sort out. I'm going to put you on blood thinners, starting today, to negate the chances of having a stroke until you see the cardiologist in approximately six weeks when the thinners have had time to stabilise.'

Mac was in efficiency mode, checking off points as

though he held a bulletin board. Kelli watched closely. Saw the distress in the back of his eyes and knew he was worried for Michael. 'You're discharging Will now?'

'Yes. There's nothing untoward going on.' He nodded at their patient. 'You'll have regular INR blood tests to monitor how the thinners are working. I'm emailing a copy of everything to your GP and you should visit her tomorrow to establish what's happening over the next few weeks. Any questions?'

The couple was quiet. Most likely shocked, as was Kelli at Mac's abrupt comments. Unlike him even at his most serious. She could forgive him, knowing he had problems to deal with, but his patient would've expected more.

'Okay, Will, let's take this slowly,' Kelli said as Mac disappeared out of the cubicle. 'No leaping out of bed and dancing around the ward.'

'Am I going to have to sit in a chair all day until I see the specialist?'

'Not at all.' She laughed. 'I was exaggerating just a little. Carry on as normal. But I'm sure you're going to have a hundred questions by nightfall so write them down so you can ask your GP tomorrow.'

Soon he was up and dressed. 'I'll be fine,' he muttered.

'Yes, you will,' Kelli agreed. 'I don't want to see you in here again. In the nicest possible way.'

Mac stood up from the desk when she crossed to pick up a file. 'Thanks. You were great with Will and his wife.'

Only doing what she was trained for. 'What about you? And Michael?'

'Want a quick break? I could do with a coffee.'

And someone to talk to. It hung between them, warming her to her toes. Mac Taylor had turned to her when in need. She glanced around, looking for Stephanie, who was only a couple of metres away at the chute for sending samples to the lab.

Stephanie nodded. 'I've got you covered.'

With a full department she was being extra kind, but then that was Stephanie to a T. 'Won't be long,' Kelli promised as she walked past the senior nurse, hoping she could keep that assurance.

They made instant coffee and took it to Mac's office. 'How's Michael?' Kelli asked the moment the door was shut.

'Badly shaken, and in need of a few hours away from here.'

'Shaken's not too bad, is it?'

Mac's lips twitched. 'No, Kelli, it's not.' Then he got serious again. 'Losing any patient is dreadful, but a child dying is every doctor's worst nightmare.'

She nodded. 'Especially when it's your first in charge of the case.'

'Yeah.' Sadness filled the air. 'My first one was a girl, seven and the cutest little minx you'd ever come across. Meningitis. The family had been hiking in the Rimataka Ranges and by the time they realised Juliette was seriously ill and tried to get her out they were already too late.'

He'd not forgotten her name. 'Yet you still blame yourself.' It was a no brainer. She'd seen it often enough throughout her career.

Mac's mouth turned down and his focus appeared to be miles away. 'It's what we train for, saving people in every eventuality even when we understand that's impossible.'

'Will Michael be all right?'

'He has to be, or take a change in direction as far as his career is concerned. If that sounds harsh, I'm only stating the facts as dealt to me over Juliette. Blunt but true. Unfortunately.' Mac dragged his hands down his face. 'But

I'm thinking Michael will come through this just fine. He's talked about it with me and is going to call me any time it gets on top of him.'

'Talking's good.' Often not a guy thing. Nor hers. Telling all and sundry about the bullies who'd shaped her had never been possible, because that'd be exposing her weaknesses and showing others how to get to her. Of course she'd told Steve. They were in love. But he'd used it against her, saying the bullies had a point and shouldn't she take the opportunity to have surgery. Drinking her bland and now cool coffee, Kelli shuddered. 'Yuk.'

Mac's smile was small but it was coming out, slowly, lightening the atmosphere. 'Not up to Waiheke café standards.'

That coffee at the café where they'd helped the chef had been hot and intense and full of flavour. Not that she'd been thinking of the coffee they'd tried to drink super quick, and the muffins she couldn't taste for all the need in her mouth. Nothing but returning to their suite at the resort had mattered. 'Not a patch,' she replied around the longing building in her again.

Inappropriate, Kells. Mac's worrying for Michael, and recalling his own unhappy medical stories and you're thinking of sex.

Mac did that to her. Stole all sense, replaced it with sex-crazed thoughts—no, make that sensations. Because there was no thinking straight whenever Mac was close, unless they were beside a patient, but that didn't count. He'd tossed her world sideways, leaving her not knowing whether she was up or down, left or right. She was lost. And in love.

'We'd better be getting back to work.' Mac stood up slowly, reluctantly. Even sad he was good enough to want to eat.

Or hug. To give warmth to, to show she understood and cared. Easy. Wrapping her arms around him, she held him tight. 'It's what you do. Help everyone who needs you.'

'I do. It's ingrained in me, and probably Michael feels the same, so when the outcome goes wrong it's hard to accept we're not gods.' The pain in his voice smudged out any arrogance there might've been in that statement.

He was a hero in her book. 'Want to share bacon and eggs at the All-Nighter after work? We can talk some more if you need to vent.'

Or we can hurry through our meals and head to your apartment.

She'd love to see where he'd hung that painting. *Ha.* Right. Sure. On the way to his bedroom maybe. Or on the way out after an intense night. Like going to his place would happen.

Mac's mouth covered hers, not softly but hungrily, taking from her, devouring in his intensity. A kiss like no other. A kiss that said he needed her in a way he hadn't admitted before. A personal way.

Her knees were jelly, tipping her into Mac's long, hard body. Exquisite sensations pummelled her from curled-up toes to skin-tightening forehead. 'Mac,' she groaned between their mouths before immediately pressing her lips back on his. How had she survived before Mac? How could she have believed she knew all about sex, or love-making, or whatever it was called. There was no one word to describe what was ripping through her right this moment.

Those lips she hankered after when they weren't available were torn away from hers. 'Work.' Mac's chest was rising and falling rapidly.

Kelli spread her hand flat on his pecs, absorbed his heat and harsh breathing. 'Yeah.'

'Rain check?'

'End of shift.'

Mac smiled a long, slow, knowing smile that went no-where towards toughening up her knees. 'Bacon and eggs at my place.'

Truly? She was being invited into his sanctum? A place no one seemed to be invited to. Sex, food and a glimpse at how Mac lived. This was right up there with being awe-some. 'You're on.'

The light in his eyes dimmed. Just realised what he'd got himself into?

Not about to give him a chance to change his mind she spun out of his arms and aimed for the door, unsteady on those knees. 'Let's get cracking. The busier we are, the sooner the hours will be gone.'

'We haven't just been busy?' His smile was back, wider, cheekier and, yes, a whole load sexier—if that was possible.

Getting through the shift without climbing the walls with need seemed a remote possibility. Flapping her hands in front of her fiery cheeks, she straightened her back and blew Mac a kiss to be going on with. 'That was merely a warm up.'

Mac followed Kelli out into the department, his gaze locked on those endless legs in baggy scrubs. Whoever designed the shapeless, boring outfits hadn't had a woman like Kelli in mind. She filled the loose folds out in all the right places and turned the ugly scrubs into a fashion state-ment. Her butt rounded out the back and was moving in a tantalising way that made his mouth water and his heart do cartwheels. Not thinking about the tightness in his groin.

End of shift was for ever away. Might have to find an empty storeroom next break. So much for moving on from the weekend and calling it a day. He wanted Kelli more than ever. Hadn't got enough of her yet. Would he ever?

He had to. There was an engagement to call off. Once that happened those protective brothers wouldn't allow him near her. Nor would her mother.

A breath hissed over Mac's lips as Kelli reached the counter and leaned over the top for a file. Those scrubs took on a whole other rounded shape as her butt stretched them tight.

She's mine.

'Looks like we've got an urgent case on the way in.' Kelli waved the file at him. 'Sixteen-year-old male, knocked off his skateboard outside school. Suspected fractured tib and fib.'

'How far away?' Mac dragged his concentration back to where it should be.

The buzzer sounded.

'About now, I'm thinking.' Kelli grinned as she thrust the file at him and immediately headed for the ambulance bay.

How was a bloke supposed to focus on a patient when that involved working with a siren?

Drawing air in right down to his stomach, Mac counted to ten and stared at the file in his hand. The words flickered, came into focus, and the details nudged Kelli aside in his mind. The teen had a history of broken bones from skateboarding. Slow learner or a lad who didn't believe in holding back when it came to putting his body on the line?

The only good point was that time would whizz past and the shift would be over sooner than later. And then the fun could really start.

At five past nine Kelli leaned back in the chair where she'd been entering data on her last patient. 'I'm for a coffee. Anyone else?'

The waiting room was suspiciously quiet. It'd probably fill up at ten forty-five and there'd be no getting away for hours.

Can't happen.

Her body hadn't stopped thrumming with need since that sizzling kiss in Mac's office. If they didn't get down and busy together soon she was going to explode.

'I'll be along in five,' Mac called from the resus directly opposite.

'Want me to order your usual?'

'Please.'

Settled in a corner of the cafeteria, two coffees and a donut that looked as if it'd been made a week ago in front of her, Kelli read her emails. Nothing earth-shattering. Tamara was still pregnant and getting antsier by the hour. Dad wanted to do lunch one day this week.

'You've got a donut,' Mac drawled as he dropped into the chair opposite her.

'I more than made up for it over the weekend with all that exercise,' she retorted around a grin as she put the phone down on the table.

'Kelli.' He drew her name out like warm liquid honey. 'Tonight. You want to stay with me?'

Oh, boy. Did she what? 'As in a sleepover in your apartment?'

He spluttered with laughter. 'Something like that.'

The phone rang. 'I could ignore it, but it's Mum.'

'We know she won't go away. Better see what she wants.' Mac leaned back and sipped his long black.

'Hi, Mum. Getting back to normal now the wedding's over?' The moment the words were out Kelli wanted them back. She just knew what was coming and had no way of stopping any of it.

Mac reached for her donut and took a big bite.

'Hey.' She snatched at it and got cream squeezed over her hand for her trouble. Mac's eyes locked on her as she began licking her fingers clean.

'I thought we could start planning yours.'

See? 'Mum? What did you say?' The donut tasted like glue.

'That you and Mac should come to dinner one night next weekend, then we can set a date and start the ball rolling for your wedding. What do you think?'

That I'm in deep doo-doo.

'There's no rush, Mum.' She couldn't look at Mac. Didn't want to see the truth blaze out from those sexy eyes she dreamed about every night. The fun would be over as soon as she explained to her family she was no longer engaged. It was going to finish when he heard her tell Mum they wouldn't be coming to dinner this weekend. Or any weekend.

'Maybe not in your eyes, Kelli, but I like to be prepared.'

When Kelli remained mute her mother sighed heavily before continuing.

'At least come for a meal. Your father and I would love to spend more time getting to know Mac better.'

Getting harder.

'I'll talk to Mac and get back to you. Love you, Mum.' *Click.*

Now what? All the fun and the greatest sex ever and falling in love with the man responsible had not gone any way to prevent the fact that she needed to tell her parents the truth.

'The game's up?' Mac leaned forward, his hand reaching for hers. 'It doesn't…' He hesitated, stared at her for so long a wart must've begun growing on her chin, and then he leaned back against his chair again.

Raw pain sliced through her. 'It doesn't what?' she asked in a high-pitched squeak.

He shrugged. 'Nothing.'

The pain opened wider. Nothing? This was nothing? The weekend, the way they fitted together so well, how they were opening up to each other was nothing? He knew what her mother had asked. The knowledge was there, darkening those eyes, crowding out the previous look of fun and laughter. 'Nothing. As in we're done now that it's Monday? When you've just invited me to stay at your apartment tonight?'

'The deal was I was your fiancé for the weekend, Kelli. This was how it was always going to end.'

'In the beginning there'd been the suggestion we'd take a couple of weeks before calling it off so it didn't look so obvious it had been a hoax.' *Except I went and fell in love with you.* 'Wait a minute. That kiss earlier on? That was a break-up kiss? A false kiss for a false break up? You weren't really going to take me to your apartment?'

Now he reached for her hands. She was shaking. And so was Mac. Maybe there was hope after all. She'd got it wrong, hadn't given him a chance to say anything before leaping in the deep end to rabbit on and on at him.

'I kissed you because I couldn't not. You're beautiful, amazing, and I have had a wonderful few days. Could go on having some more, but in the end we have to tell your family the truth no matter what we get up to.'

She gaped at him, trying hard to keep up, and failing.

He hadn't finished. 'Your mother's invitation to dinner is the wake-up call we need. Continuing what we've started would only make it all the harder to pull the plug further down the track.'

Pull the plug? Nice turn of phrase for her heart to hear. 'Why do we have to finish at all?' The words were out before she'd thought about them. Thank goodness she hadn't cried out that she loved him. How humiliating would that be?

Her hands were suddenly bereft of warmth, or anything, as they were dumped. Mac's face was white, his lips flat. 'I am so sorry. I never meant for this to happen.'

And she'd thought she couldn't hurt any deeper. The genuineness of those words cut her to the core. 'Of course. Helping people is what you do. Staying around and getting involved is not.' Vitriol was not pretty, but again her tongue had raced away on her.

'I can't do anything about that. I've been involved, married, about to become a father, and lost it all. I am never going there again. You have to understand.' He was pleading with her.

Damn it, her heart softened a little. Of course he'd been hurt dreadfully when he'd lost his wife. And apparently an unborn baby. But did he have to lock his heart up for ever? She was asking that? She who'd never wanted to risk being hurt again? That she'd fallen in love with Mac had been completely by accident, but she was prepared to allow him in. 'Why not give us a chance?'

He looked her up and down, and shook his head. 'I don't think so.'

That look made her feel stupid, told her she still wasn't any good at reading men. Her chair legs screeched across the floor as she leapt up. She wanted to beg, to lick her hand again to create that need in his eyes, place her heart in front of him. But that was how she used to deal with people, always trying to appease them. Not any more. Mac either wanted her or he didn't, and, anyway, it was there in his sad but steady gaze—she'd be wasting her time and making a goat of herself into the bargain.

'Time I went back to work.' Heading for the lift to

take her down to the department, she concentrated on holding back the hot tears gathering in the corners of her eyes. Crying never got her anywhere, and tonight would be no exception.

CHAPTER ELEVEN

MAC SAT ON his deck, a thick jersey keeping the cold out, and looked out at the bridge and harbour and saw nothing. Nothing except the agony in Kelli's eyes.

But hell, was he feeling. A deep pain he'd hoped to never know again. The loss of something so important it paralysed him. Something he hadn't yet had the guts to acknowledge. Love. For. Kelli.

Not ready. Too fast. Can't get involved.

Tipping his head back, he stared up at the cloudy sky. Not visible in the dark, it would be grey, he knew, like his heart, heavy with rain as he was with unshed tears. Despite not wanting to he'd gone and got himself in love with the most wonderful woman walking the city.

Slow learner. Hadn't he spent the years between Cherie's death and now denying the need to love, to cherish and adore a woman? To have someone to bare his soul with, and have hers back? Hadn't he accepted he'd had his chance and needn't expect a second shot at happiness? He'd believed it was impossible to know love twice.

Afraid to take it, more like.

Not that he was happy right now. Far from it. Falling in love was a foolish mistake. Letting it cut him off at the knees worse. If only he'd walked away last night after they'd returned to the city, told Kelli thanks and to have a great life. There'd been no reason to postpone the ending to their pretend engagement. The sooner the better for everyone really.

The fact he couldn't not kiss Kelli again and follow up with wanting to make love had nothing to do with this sense of slip sliding, into an abyss.

When the helicopter had touched down yesterday he and Kelli had had to go in separate directions. Kelli's mother had invited them back to the family home for a barbecue. He'd declined, knowing how close to the wire that would take him. One lie too many. But Kelli had gone. She'd been torn, but he'd nudged her. She adored her family and he'd thought they might have tonight together, stalling on ending their relationship because he was selfish, wanted it all without giving his heart.

Ha. Showed what he knew about anything. He'd done his bit and now they were back to being colleagues in the department. But he was greedy, had wanted one more day, and he'd got it. In spades.

Leaping up, he charged inside and came to an abrupt halt in front of the blasted painting that also messed with his mind. His hands gripped his hips as he stared at it, felt it. From the sharp strokes of colour he knew that his future hung in the balance. He either leapt without looking any further, or he crawled into a hole and hid away until his head and heart returned to normal. Uninvolved normal. Cold. Lonely. Sad. Gutless.

Who'd brought his smile back after dealing with Michael's grief and his own memories of a similar experience? The first person he'd ever let that close since Cherie, and now he'd gone and shunted her out of his life. There'd be no coming back from that horrid conversation in the cafeteria. He'd hurt Kelli. All because he refused to acknowledge his feelings. Yet now that he had nothing would change. The past still held him captive.

His phone chirped. He'd ignore it, didn't want to talk to anyone tonight. But it was nearly two a.m. so unless it was Kelli—unlikely—then it could be an emergency. Or Michael struggling to cope with his day.

The display showed Conor. The thumping in his heart slowed as he pressed talk. 'Hey, man. How's things?'

'I'm a dad. To the cutest little girl you'll ever meet. She's awesome, dude, seriously awesome. Tamara is a legend...twelve hours' labour and yet she's smiling like there's no end to Christmas.'

When Conor paused to take a breath he cut in. 'Congratulations to you both. That's wonderful news. I'm glad it went well.' He felt a heel, as if he was raining on his friend's parade with his stilted comments. But it was all he could manage. His mate had to recognise the distress in his polite words.

Stop thinking of yourself for once.

Thankfully Conor was on a different planet, and the Irish accent thick with excitement. 'She's tiny, and looks like Tam. Wait, I'll send you a photo. You've got to see this.'

An email arrived. 'Hold on, I'm going to check this out.' Without cutting Conor off? 'Keep yabbering on while I crank up the laptop.'

'Wish you were here, man. We could have a beer or three.' Conor laughed as if that were the funniest thing he'd ever said. 'And afterwards Tam would kill me.'

Clicking on Conor's email and bringing up the photo of Tamara holding the most beautiful baby against her breast, Mac felt his heart splinter. 'Oh, man.' Sniff. 'You weren't exaggerating. She's lovely.'

'Gabriella. That's her name.'

'How soon before you're saying Gaby?' Mac struggled to find a chuckle in the thick of tears clogging his throat. If jealous was the word to describe what was suffocating him right now, then he was jealous. He and Cherie had nearly had this. He and Kelli *could* have this.

'Already have,' replied Conor. 'Got the wicked-witch eyes from you know who.' Not that he sounded as if that was a punishment.

Mac bit down on the jealousy. Wrong time and place, if there ever was a right one. It was his choice to be where he was at in his life, no one else's. 'I'm thrilled for you. I know how determined you were not to have a family and now listen to you. Happier than a toddler on chocolate.'

'I don't intend having the low that usually follows that. The cardiologist thinks Gaby's heart is fine, and as that's all I ask for I'm going to run with it. Relax and enjoy my family. Got to go. Mum's calling from Dublin.'

'Catch you tomorrow. Hugs to Tamara.'

Had Conor heard any of that? In his excitement he'd been quick to cut the call.

Mac wanted to call Kelli, share the good news, go over the details. Hear her sweet voice. She'd have been the first person Tamara would've called; they were that tight.

He pushed his phone aside. Time he went to bed and got some shut-eye.

Still running away.

His mate's fabulous luck added to his own uncertainty. Underscored what was missing from his life. As Mac made his way through the darkened apartment as confident as if he had possum vision, he couldn't shake the sense that everything he wanted was right there, beckoning, waiting for him to take that last step, take the risk, chance his heart with Kelli.

* * *

'She's gorgeous,' Kelli whispered through the tears drenching her face, dripping onto her nightwear tee shirt.

'I know,' giggled Tamara. They were on their second phone conversation in less than an hour. 'Who'd have believed I'd produce a child so beautiful?'

'You'll choke on that pride,' Kelli giggled back. It was good to hear Tam so besotted. If ever there was someone who deserved happiness that was Tamara. Her past had been diabolical and then along came Conor and the stars hadn't stopped shining for her friend since. If only there were more stars to go round, she might get a bite of the pie too.

With Mac? Only with Mac. And since that wasn't about to happen any time this century, then she was plumb out of luck.

'You've got to come over to Sydney and meet Gabriella,' Tam was yabbering on. 'Asap. She'll grow so fast you'll miss so much.'

'I'll flip across for a weekend as soon as I can arrange it.' That'd give her something to focus on rather than an unobtainable man and the heartache he'd started up for her. 'With a bit of luck I'll get flights that fit in with my shifts. I can't ask for another Friday off just yet.'

'Let me know when you've booked.' The giggles had stopped, but the wonder was still in Tam's voice. 'Seriously, Kelli, this motherhood stuff's amazing. I know there are going to be days and nights when I'll be pulling my hair out, but today I fell instantly in love with this little human. She's stolen my heart and I'm never going to let go.'

'Stop it.' Kelli sniffed back another flood. Until now babies had always been on the back burner, something to get serious about later. Couldn't have one without having a partner and she wasn't getting tied to any man to be trashed again. Then along came Mac, cool as, sexy as, kind and fun as. And bang. All the theories in the world sloped out of the back door leaving her slam dunked in love.

'Was Mac as hot as you'd hoped?'

Where did that come from? 'Sure, he's hot.' That was all she was admitting. The first time she'd ever kept something from her bestie, and it didn't sit easy, but Tam wouldn't let it go if she had any clue.

'Hot to look at? Or hot up close and touching?' drilled her *bestie*.

'Does it matter?'

'Conor, you hold Gabriella for a minute. I've got some serious talking to do here.'

Great, she was in for a speech. 'I've got to go, Tam. It's two-thirty in the morning and I should be sleeping. I'll call tomorrow morning.'

'Don't hang up on me, Kells. You answered my call before the first ring finished so you weren't even trying to sleep.'

Kells. Said it all, really. Even though she knew she wasn't going to like whatever was coming her heart swelled for her friend. 'Go on.' Might as well get it over. Sleep would be impossible anyway.

'I saw you and Mac together at my wedding. Sparks were flying between you.'

'You've told me this.' Could be she was getting off with only a warning.

'So? The weekend? Spill.'

'Just as hot.' More so. 'But there's a catch.'

'Isn't there always? You have to make allowances.'

'Mac went as my fiancé. Not true, of course,' Kelli was quick to point out, just in case Tam got some strange ideas in that sharp head of hers. 'It was meant to put Jason firmly out of the picture and on that score we succeeded.'

Laughter was peeling through cyber into her ear. 'You and Mac pretended to be engaged. Wow, that's way more than I suggested, or believed you'd have the guts to undertake.'

'It's not funny.'

'It's hilarious. Hey, Conor, wait till I tell you this.'

'Hanging up now.' But she didn't. Her fingers tightened around the phone, pressing it painfully hard against her ear. 'Tam, I'm in a fix.'

'You've got to explain to your family. Hope Mac's got medical insurance.' Tam was still laughing.

Anger flared. This was not funny.

Suddenly Tamara sobered up. 'Kells, the family will understand, might even be embarrassed that you had to take such drastic measures. Ah, no, cancel that. They'll tear your hide off, wrap you in big Barnett hugs, and shake Mac's hand for helping you out.'

'I'll keep you posted. Tomorrow has to be the big reveal. I can't go on living under this any longer.' Not when Mac had made it plain they weren't going anywhere.

'What's the real issue here? You gone and got too close to Dr Hunk?'

There shouldn't be any tears left in the tank. Seemed she knew Jack nothing. 'Something like that.'

'What are you going to do about it?' Only sympathy now.

'Tie bricks to my feet and jump off the wharf.'

'Yep, I can see that working. Then again, you could try going with this something, spend more time with Mac, get to know him even better, not only in the sack. Find out if he's the guy you want to spend the rest of your life with.'

She already knew the answer to that.

'Kells? I get it. You do, don't you?'

Again she couldn't find the words to explain herself.

'You're afraid. I get that too. Been there, got the man and baby to show for it. And guess what, I'm over the moon with happiness. I want you to have this. I really do.'

'Easy for you to say,' she croaked.

'Nothing about getting to where I am now was easy. But it was worth all the crap that went down.'

'Mac's not interested in me.' Other than between the sheets, and in the shower, behind the trees. Certainly not as a lifelong partner who might get to know what made him tick. 'Please don't share this with Conor. I know he's your nearest and dearest but I did hold that position platonically for years before he turned up.'

'All between you and me.'

'Thanks. I'd better let you go. You've got a daughter to feed or change or hug. Yes, hug her from me, will you? Love you, Tam.' Kelli cut the call and tossed the phone onto the bedside table.

Telling Tam that much about her feelings for Mac was too much. Not that her friend would ever say a word to anyone else but now she'd enunciated it she could no longer pretend she was in control, no longer pretend that she'd be able to shove her love in a dark corner and forget about it, bring it out only on dull days and Billy's wedding anniversaries. Now she had to face up to the fact she loved Mac with a capital L and that it wasn't going anywhere.

Sleep would never happen tonight. Kelli tossed the bedcovers aside, found her thick dressing gown, the soft, warm, comfort blanket one that did nothing to enhance her figure but a lot to soothe her jangled nerves, and went to boot up the laptop. If she couldn't rest then she might as well make use of the time and check out flights to Sydney.

* * *

'Look at these gorgeous pictures of Gabriella, Stephanie.' Kelli handed her phone over to the head nurse. 'Tam had her at midnight Australia time last night. Isn't she a little cutey?'

'Mac showed me a couple of photos earlier. She's gorgeous.' Stephanie sighed. 'Lucky girl.'

'You want babies?' Kelli asked. So Mac hadn't been backward in sharing the news. His usual reticence about friendships must be missing. Where was he anyway? She'd been vigilant when she'd entered the department, not wanting to be caught unawares in case she gave herself away to those all-seeing eyes.

'Sure. Don't you some time?'

'Haven't given it too much thought. Got other things to sort before worrying about getting pregnant, if you know what I mean.'

'Figured you were halfway to getting that done.' Stephanie handed the phone back, a big, cheeky grin on her dial.

'Nope. Haven't even started,' Kelli told her. 'Who have you got for me?' She held out a hand for a patient report form.

'We'll have handover first,' came the steady, uninvolved voice of the man who'd kept her awake all night.

Plastering on a smile as false as her engagement, Kelli slowly turned to face Mac. *'No problemo.'* Not like everything else.

'I called around to your place after lunch but you weren't answering the door,' Mac told her.

'I was out.' His face paled. Tough. 'Shopping.' Nothing like a bit of retail therapy.

'Not having lunch with your parents, then?'

'I look whole, don't I?'

His eyes scanned the length of her, hesitating at her breasts. 'We need to talk about that.'

'There's nothing to talk about. I've got it sorted.'

'You've told them?'

'Not yet. But I will. On my own.'

His nod was abrupt. 'Right.' He glanced around, found they had an audience, and shivered. 'Listen up, everyone. I'm sure you've all heard the news about Conor and Tamara's baby arriving last night. Gabriella. What say we all put in and send flowers to the happy family?'

Amongst murmurings of agreement Kelli watched Mac. Shadows darkened his upper cheeks, filled his eyes. As if he hadn't slept either. It was going to be a long week. If only she'd been able to get a flight across the Tasman for Saturday but there was a rugby league match on between New Zealand and Australia in Sydney and not a seat to spare. She'd even checked business class thinking the money would be worth it if it got her out of town. But that'd been a waste of time. She'd just have to go hiking on Rangitoto Island all weekend, up and down, up and down, ten times till the ferry returned late Sunday to pick her up.

The ambulance bay buzzer buzzed. Loud, demanding, and the perfect solution to wanting to get away from standing in the same air as Mac.

Michael nodded at her. 'You and me. Let's go see what we've got.' So he hadn't been listening to handover either. Hopefully that wasn't an ongoing problem from yesterday and the patient he'd lost.

'Sure.'

They got a hit and run patient. Broken legs, fractured ribs, and a smashed spleen, which kept them busy for a long time, only to be followed by a stroke victim arriving towards the end of his golden hour. The man survived but was a long way from walking and talking as he used to. As an orderly wheeled him away Kelli stretched up onto her toes and rubbed the small of her back. Exhaustion oozed out of every pore. A big weekend, no sleep last night and being constantly on guard around Mac had taken its toll. And there were more than five hours to go.

Looking around, she spied Mac busy in resus one with a patient whose heart had stopped, and must be where the emergency buzzer had come from. 'I'm going for my break,' she told Michael and Stephanie. Without Mac, and any discussion about telling her family what they'd done.

Sinking onto a hard chair in the cafeteria, Kelli stared into the depths of murky coffee and fiddled with the dried arrangement that was supposed to be a sandwich. No appetite for anything—she couldn't even find the energy to lift either hand to her mouth for liquid or food. The room was rolling around her, as if she were sitting in the centre of a merry-go-round watching the horses rising and falling on their poles. Her eyelids were heavier than pot lids and eventually she gave up fighting to keep them open. Her chin tapped her sternum, and still those blasted horses kept bobbing up and down.

Mac strode into the cafeteria, scanning the mostly empty tables until his gaze alighted on the object of his search. No wonder Kelli hadn't returned from her break. She was sound asleep.

After ordering a long black and a cappuccino from the annoyingly perky girl behind the counter, he crossed and sat opposite Kelli. In sleep she looked vulnerable. And beautiful, but then she looked that all the time. Back to the vulnerable. There were definitely some issues from her past that had kept her hands up in the off-limits zone— until last weekend.

But then he'd appreciated that, wanting nothing more

involved than a fling with her, and he hadn't even re-alised that until he'd spent three days—and two incred-ible nights—with her.

Or had the slippery slide into getting close to Kelli begun in Sydney? Yes, buster, it probably had.

Whichever, letting go was proving impossible. So he had to find out what those issues were. The bullies? The guy she'd been engaged to before had done a number on her. Had someone else been as cruel? There weren't any problems regarding her family. They all got on brilliantly.

But by knowing what could hurt her he could shore up his resolve to walk away while he still could. Cruel to be kind. His guilt at not coping when he lost someone was stronger now that Kelli had become special. Special? Come on. Admit that this stabbing in his chest had nothing to do with special and all to do with… With… He could not say the word. There was a roadblock in the way. A roadblock in the form of heartache and lost love and feel-ing more secure when he only had himself to look out for.

Their coffees were on the way. Mac put a finger to his lips as the girl got closer and smiled his thanks as she placed the mugs ever so carefully on the table.

Kelli hadn't moved once since he'd joined her, and the aroma of fresh coffee didn't awaken her. A thick strand of that glorious hair had fallen across her face and he ached to lift it away, but daredn't. If she awoke while he was doing that she'd have fifty fits and go ballistic.

Which was what he should do. Return to the depart-ment and pretend he hadn't been here. But Kelli would look for an explanation for the coffee and the girl be-hind the counter would be happy to oblige for sure. Any-way Kelli had to return to work soon or the others would start asking where she was. He could cover for her. Why wouldn't he? If he cared about her why not do something so small but hopefully kind?

Mac stood up too quickly, causing the chair to scrape on the floor.

Kelli moved. Her eyes blinked before her chin sagged back on her chest.

He'd got away with it. Leaving the chair where it was, he turned away.

'Mac?' When his name was sleep-filled on Kelli's tongue it sounded warm and tender and loving.

He had to look over his shoulder. Had to. His heart did loop the loop at the sight of Kelli leaning back, still blinking away the sleep and staring at him as though she wasn't sure where she was. He told her, 'There's a cappuccino. Get it into you before coming back.'

Her gaze dropped to the table, returned to him. 'You not drinking your coffee now that I'm awake?'

Not so asleep any more. Acerbic and annoyed instead. 'I wasn't running away.' Those lush lips didn't lift anywhere near a glimmer of a smile. 'I just didn't want to wake you.'

'Then have your coffee.' When he didn't move she snapped, 'Get over yourself, Mac. We can be civil enough to share our break.'

'You're right.' Reaching for the chair, he spun it around to straddle the seat. Like a wall between them. There was no getting any of this right. 'You didn't sleep much last night with Tamara phoning and everything?'

'No.' Kelli tested the heat of her coffee with a slow sip, sending his gut into turmoil. When she replaced the mug on the table there was a smudge of frothy milk on her upper lip. He even began to lift his hand to wipe it away, froze. Not wise. Worse, Kelli's tongue lapped her mouth, removing the froth.

Mac's mouth dried. That tongue had done wondrous things on his skin. South of his belt there was a load of tightening going on. 'I'll see you back in the department.' Whether she could understand him when his tongue was stuck to the roof of his mouth was anyone's guess, but he was out of there before he did something they'd both regret. Like rekindle everything that had been between them all weekend, the heat and need that had driven them into that super-king-sized bed again and again.

Silence followed him out of the cafeteria, but cobalt eyes were drilling holes between his shoulder blades. Not a good look for getting through the rest of the shift. And this was only Tuesday. Three more nights before he got a break and could tuck his heart out of sight, away from danger. Though there'd be no hiding out in Wellington for the weekend with his mother and her cronies. She'd cancelled, having booked to go to Melbourne shopping with a friend instead.

Too late on the danger factor. What he was supposed to be doing now was raising barriers to save himself any further anguish, to keep Kelli safe.

Because after the coming weekend there'd be another five shifts to get through, again and again and again. Might have to ask Conor to look out for a job for him in Sydney.

CHAPTER TWELVE

THE WEEK WAS HIDEOUS. Every day Mac struggled with going into work, so he'd gone earlier than normal, hiding away in his office doing paperwork until handover. But once shift started there was no avoiding Kelli and that continuous snub she'd managed to hold onto since Monday night.

He'd hurt her. No getting away from that. He was hurting too. Denying his love for her was a fail. It didn't go away, instead held his heart in a vice, shaking his carefully put-together world like that seven-point-eight earthquake last year in Kaikoura. The damage felt as monumental. Hopefully the repair work wouldn't be as long as some of the roads and railway lines were going to take down south.

He wouldn't survive like this.

I want you, Kelli. In my home, my bed, my life. Everywhere I breathe.

Now it was Friday night. No more mucking around. He had to talk to Kelli, lay his heart on the line and hope like stink she didn't jump all over it.

Over the week Mac had picked up the phone twice to call Billy and ask how he'd allowed himself to be happy again and both times he'd put it away. The guy was on his honeymoon and didn't need some nutter asking difficult questions. He had to work this out for himself or the happiness would be shallow.

But it was the moving-forward bit he was stuck on.

'Goodnight, everyone. Have a great weekend.' Kelli waved a hand over her shoulder as she headed for the stairway leading to the basement, not a glance in his direction.

Right. 'See you all on Monday.' He headed the same way.

She didn't look back when she pushed her way through the heavy doors, just charged down the stairs as if she was late for something.

Mac raced down behind her. 'Hey, Kelli, you heading home or to the gym?'

Kelli kept moving.

'Kelli, wait.' *Please. Okay,* 'Please?'

Her pace slowed but she didn't stop.

As Mac caught up he forced himself not to let those sad eyes put him off his stride. 'Going to the gym?'

'No. Home to a mug of soup and some tea.'

'A woman could get an ulcer on that diet.' Mac put a hand out to stop her mad dash and looked directly into those beautiful eyes. 'Want to hit the All-Nighter for bacon and eggs? Or lash out and try something different?'

'No, thanks.' She pushed past his hand.

He was right beside her, his steps matching hers. The only thing they had in sync at the moment. 'Any chance of a rethink on that?'

She snapped, 'What's the point, Mac? It's over, whatever it was going on between us. You put your hand up for the weekend, and today is Friday, tomorrow heralds a new weekend, one that doesn't involve us doing things together. You're free to do whatever you like as long as it doesn't involve me.' *Ouch.* Go for the throat, why didn't she? Then, 'What happened to going to Wellington for your mother's birthday?'

They'd reached the landing between floor one and the basement. She carried on down. He followed. 'My mother's flown to Aussie with a friend. But before you even think it, that is not why I asked you to join me for a meal. I want to talk with you.'

'I can't imagine there's anything I want to hear.' She glared at him. 'That's still a no from me.'

'Have you told your family yet?'

She understood what he was talking about. 'Tomorrow at dinner.'

Less than twenty-four hours to change her mind. 'Give me a chance. Come and hear me out.'

'I already listened once, didn't like what I heard.' Kelli stopped one stair below and stared up at him as though wondering how she was going to get it across to him. 'You aren't ready for what I want, Mac. Might never be. Best you spend your energy sorting yourself out.' That steady gaze seemed stuck on him. As though she couldn't look away.

He winced. 'You didn't used to be so hard hitting.'

'I've finally learned to protect myself.' Now she turned away. Slowly but oh-so deliberately. 'See you Monday, Mac.' There wasn't a shred of sarcasm in her voice. Just deep sadness.

'Don't do it, Kelli,' he called after her. 'We're right together.'

Her foot missed the next step and she pitched forward.

Mac reached her as she grabbed at the rail to stop from falling. His heart was going crazy as fear of her hurting herself hit him. He grasped her upper arm, held her tight, close to his body, but not so close as to crowd her. 'Kelli. You crazy girl, not looking where you're going.'

'Don't call me crazy.' She was trembling. Which didn't stop her tugging free and stepping away. 'Though it is a new one for me.'

Mac sat down, held her eye. 'Join me.'

If only he knew how to banish that load of caution darkening the cobalt in his favourite eyes.

'So you can go on and on about why we should remain engaged after telling me there was no future for us? No, Mac. I heard your message, loud and clear. I am not setting myself up to be dropped when the use-by date rocks around.'

She hadn't moved away. Good sign? Or wishful thinking on his part? 'I know you've been hurt in the past.'

'Yep. We both have.' Her eyes slowly lowered to stare down the stairwell. 'Goodnight, Mac.' That sounded, felt, like goodbye. He watched her take a step down, and another, another. On the next landing she looked up, her eyes bleak. 'Enjoy your weekend. Get out and do something rash, like go fishing, or play a round of golf. Get involved with people.'

In other words, get a life.

'What do you want, Kelli? A fling? A wedding? The whole nine yards with kids and a home? Or are you serious about calling this quits?' When she said nothing he continued. 'When we started out I got the feeling you weren't willing to take a chance on any of the happy-ever-after stuff. That you believed everyone was out to hurt you one way or another. So come on. Tell me.'

'It doesn't matter any more.'

'Yes, it does, sweetheart. I know this now. I have been an ass, afraid to step outside my comfort zone, scared to give you my heart. I have been hiding behind Cherie's death for so long it was easier to stay there. Do you feel like that?'

Kelli lifted her gaze back onto him. A bleak gaze that had him fighting not to leap up and hold her tight. Do that and they'd be no further ahead. 'Don't turn everything back on me, Mac. You have issues from here to Africa and I don't hear you talking about them.'

Don't give this woman a laser gun. Her aim was phenomenal. 'Cherie's gone. It wasn't her fault she died, any more than I could've saved her had I known what was happening. It's taken you to wake me up from the guilt. Because I want to be with you. I want *us*. She'll always be a part of me, but my future is mine. Yours and mine, Kelli.'

The mixture of sorrow and disbelief that stared out at him angered him. He didn't need sympathy or understanding. No, he just wanted to love and be loved. Simple as. Complex as. Hard to do.

'If only it was that easy.' She sank down to sit on the stairs. 'The weekend was unbelievable. For the first time in a long time I have found someone I can trust not to deliberately hurt me. But you're not really ready for involvement, and I get that. It took me long enough to come around. But we only signed up for the weekend, not for ever.' Sadness rolled off her in waves.

Then suddenly she was on her feet again, heading down to her car.

'Kelli, I want to be there when you tell your family our engagement's off.'

'What? You want to be whipped?'

'I want them to know the truth.'

Kelli felt her mouth dry up as she stared at Mac. Did she even know him? *Really* know him?

I trust him. I love him. What more do I want?

'And what would that be?' she squeaked. 'What's your

truth, Mac?' Why was there a knitting needle attacking her stomach? Stab, stab.

'Kelli.' Sweet heaven. Two large, firm hands, familiar hands, on her shoulders, holding her ever so gently. 'Kelli, sweetheart.' Sex in two words. Say her name like that and the man could have anything.

Dragging her eyes upward, she finally locked onto his steady gaze. 'Mac?'

'I don't want to call our engagement off. I want to make it real.'

'I don't understand.' But she might be beginning to. Her stomach was quivering and her head spun, but her heart was strangely steady as a rock.

'I've been a fool, a slow learner. I tried to hold you away when all the time I wanted to drag you so close you could never leave me. Every day I stare at that painting and see what I'm missing out on. I love you, Kelli Barnett. Simple and as complicated as that.' No doubt in his eyes. Not a drop.

She sank a bit under his hands, her knees not as strong as they were meant to be. 'Y-you love me?' Mac loved her. 'You love me,' she shouted, and then heard her words echo up the stairwell.

'Tell the world, why don't you?' A glimmer of a smile appeared, wound through her. 'Is this your way of saying you might reciprocate my feelings?'

'I do. I love you so much it hurts.' Her fist banged between her breasts. 'In here. This week has been hell watching you, hearing you, remembering how well we fit together.' She took a step up, and another to stand beside him. Reached up on her tiptoes. 'Yes, Mac Taylor, I love you.' Her lips sought his, touched lightly.

Mac's arms wound round her, brought her up against that hard, soft, warm body.

She deepened the kiss, lips pressed to lips, her tongue plunging into his mouth, tasting. Her knees weakened some more, so she was forced to lean further into him.

This was what kissing the man she loved felt like. What being kissed by the man who loved her back was all about.

She couldn't get enough.

Eight days later Mac lifted Kelli's case off the luggage carousel at Sydney's Kingsford Smith Airport and groaned. 'What didn't you leave behind?'

'Last week's laundry and a bag of stale crisps.' Her case was stuffed full with toys and cute little dresses for Gabriella that would take at least a year for her to grow into. Kelli pinched those straining arm muscles and grinned. 'Not going all soft on me?'

'Soft?' he chortled. 'Complaining about the goods already?'

Maybe it was their happiness but they were shooed through Immigration so fast they were outside and climbing into a taxi before they'd caught their breaths.

'Darling Harbour, please,' Mac directed the driver, adding the name of the hotel they'd stayed at for Tamara and Conor's wedding.

Kelli felt a knot of excitement unfurling in her tummy. They were going to unload their bags before heading across the city to see Tamara, Conor, and wee Gabriella. Then tonight—anything could happen. So much to be excited about. Her hand sought Mac's.

His fingers wound around hers, giving her a gentle squeeze. 'Welcome back to our special place.'

Her lips found his, and this kiss was no sweet, soft one but a hungry, love-filled one. Bringing everything together for them. When Kelli thought about it she felt her whole life had been heading for this day, this man. Then

Mac's tongue slid into her mouth and danced across her tongue. And she couldn't think any more.

'Excuse me, but here's your hotel,' the driver interrupted them.

They broke apart with an unspoken promise this kiss and its consequences were not over, merely on hold until they were upstairs in their room.

Upstairs on the top floor, Kelli discovered, when the lift doors slid open to reveal two apartments, one apparently theirs for the weekend. 'Oh, Mac, you've gone overboard, but I won't let you change your mind.' She did a twirl of the massive lounge room before going to check out the bedroom and en-suite. 'Come in here. This bed is ridiculous.' It was the size of a football field. 'I'll never find you in the night.'

Mac stood in the doorway, laughing. 'I'll wear reflective pyjamas.'

'The day you wear any pyjamas I'll know you've gone off me.'

His laughter stopped. 'That's never going to happen.'

'Good answer.' Her smile was filled with love for this man who'd seen behind her barriers to the fears that had dogged her most of her life and still loved her. With her forefinger she beckoned him into the room. That bed was made for using, not staring at. 'Come here.'

'Hate to disappoint but we've got a booking down on Darling Harbour.' He didn't look at all repentant, more like cocky. Or was that pleased with himself?

'We have?' What was going on? He hadn't mentioned anything until now. 'We're not going to meet Gabriella?'

'A man's allowed to surprise his woman occasionally.'

Her tummy sucked in on itself. Stepping up to him, she peered into his eyes, trusting him with everything she had. 'Mac?'

'We will be using that bed, just not yet.' He hooked an arm over her shoulders and turned them to the door leading out to the lift.

Once again the excitement was bubbling. 'Where are we going specifically?'

'Which part of "surprise" don't you understand?' he mock growled before dropping a kiss on a particular hot spot below her ear.

Snuggling closer, she refrained from uttering another word for the next ten minutes as they made their way out of the hotel and down to the pier and along to... 'The restaurant Tamara and Conor were married in. Where our gazes got all fogged up staring at each other,' she gasped.

'We're having brunch. Along with champagne. Thought we should celebrate where it all began.' Mac wasn't smiling now; instead he looked purposeful and serious as he gave his name to the waiter.

There was a lot of activity amongst the waiters and the sound of a cork popping, champagne being poured, chairs pulled out, serviettes shaken open, then the staff disappeared.

As Kelli sank onto the chair Mac held for her she caught his hand over her shoulder. 'You're such a romantic, you know that?'

He came around to face her and picked up both glasses and handed her one. Then he dropped to one knee.

Kelli's heart went into overdrive and she had to pinch herself to see if she was alive and this was real. The glass wobbled in her fingers; cool liquid splashed over the rim.

'Kelli.' Mac reached for her other hand. 'I can't imagine my life without you in it. Will you please marry me and make me the happiest man on the planet?'

'You're proposing.'

'Yes, sweetheart, I am. No way were you getting away without a proper proposal.'

'Like I said, a romantic. And yes, Mac Taylor, I will marry you.'

'And make me happy as I will you.'

'All of that.' Leaning forward, she kissed those accomplished lips. 'I love you.'

Pulling back, Mac removed her glass from its precarious hold and placed both on the table before wrapping her into the biggest, warmest, lovingest hug of her life with a kiss to match.

Sometimes life did deliver on your wishes, Kelli acknowledged silently as she melted further into the man who'd brought her all the happiness she could want. More importantly, she was able to pour her heart into giving Mac all his heart's desires.

Then Mac stood up and put his hand in his pocket, retrieved a tiny jeweller's box and opened it, held it out to her. 'I know I should've got you to choose a ring but when I saw this sapphire I had to have it. It's the same cobalt shade as your eyes when you're laughing.'

Slowly she held a now very shaky hand out to him. Her gaze was fixed on the sapphire set in gold. 'It's beautiful,' she choked. 'You got it so right.' Not that she'd have been able to describe something like this if asked.

As the gold band slid onto her finger she sighed. What a ride, but worth every bump and glitch along the way to be here with Mac.

Sure, there was champagne, and a ring, and Mac had got down on his knees, but this time she heard the love, the genuine need to be with her and love and cherish her and accept her as she was. Love. This proposal was all about love, the right kind of love. Sharing, caring, happy.

Picking up the glasses again, she handed one to Mac

and raised hers. 'To us, and whatever the future brings.'
They had another wedding to look forward to.

Mac clinked his glass against hers. 'To us, my love.'

And then they drank the nectar of love, the bubbles
fizzing along Kelli's veins to her toes, along her fingers
where that ring gleamed, and slap bang into her heart
where her love for Mac sat ready for anything.

* * * * *

*If you enjoyed this story, check out
these other great reads
from Sue MacKay:*

*PREGNANT WITH THE BOSS'S BABY
RESISTING HER ARMY DOC RIVAL
THE ARMY DOC'S BABY BOMBSHELL
DR WHITE'S BABY WISH*

All available now!

THE FAMILY
SHE'S LONGED FOR

BY
LUCY CLARK

Published in Great Britain 2017
By Mills & Boon, an imprint of HarperCollins*Publishers*
1 London Bridge Street, London, SE1 9GF

© 2017 Anne Clark

ISBN: 978-0-263-92673-6

Dear Reader,

At times it feels as though the world spins at a faster pace than normal, and at other times it drags on. One thing I've been learning is to live in the moment, to enjoy the road trip of life and appreciate those who have chosen to share it with you.

As for Clara, she's endured a wild ride—with heartbreak and physical injuries to overcome. At times I'm sure she feels as though life has dealt her a cruel hand. Thankfully, with the help of her family, she has been able to rebuild her life, and is happy to settle for a mediocre existence.

Virgil has also endured his fair share of heartbreak, but through the unconditional love of his daughter, Rosie, he's able not only to conquer his own fears about moving forward into happiness, but also to help Clara. Together they risk it all, to take a second chance at the love they lost all those years ago. For Clara, Virgil and little Rosie, a mediocre existence is not an option. Instead they choose vibrancy and a passion for life.

I hope you enjoy *The Family She's Longed For*.

Warmest regards,

Lucy

For my babies—
once you were small and now you're grown.
Where did the time go? Thank you for loving me
back and choosing to spend your time with me.

Ecc 7:9

Books by Lucy Clark

Mills & Boon Medical Romance

The Lewis Doctors

Reunited with His Runaway Doc

Outback Surgeons

English Rose in the Outback
A Family for Chloe

The Secret Between Them
Her Mistletoe Wish
His Diamond Like No Other
Dr Perfect on Her Doorstep
A Child to Bind Them
Still Married to Her Ex!

Visit the Author Profile page
at millsandboon.co.uk for more titles.

PROLOGUE

CLARA LEWIS KEPT her head down as she walked to her car. It was close to three o'clock in the morning and her shift in the Emergency Department at Melbourne General Hospital had run very late, but that was the way life was when you were an overworked doctor. She sniffed, telling herself she wouldn't cry—not again, and definitely not within the hospital grounds. Even at this time of the morning she felt as though there were prying eyes, watching her through the darkness.

It wasn't the long hours she spent at the hospital which was upsetting her, it wasn't because the registrar on call had snapped at her, and it wasn't because a patient had decided to share the contents of his stomach all over her shoes. That wasn't the reason she was trying so hard not to burst into tears. No, her reason was the age-old one of a breaking heart. Was it possible to actually *feel* your heart break in two? She hadn't thought so before, but now she most definitely believed it.

Thankfully, Clara made it to the sanctuary of her car and quickly shut the driver's door. After putting the key into the ignition and clipping her seatbelt into place, she gripped the steering wheel and allowed her tears their release. If she bottled up her emotions any more than she already was, she ran the risk of exploding at an unsuspecting person for the most minor infraction.

She wanted to throw back her head and wail, to scream and shout, to share her heartbreak with anyone who cared enough to listen. But at the same time she didn't want anyone to know just how distraught she really was. Clara was well aware of the way the gossips whispered about her as she walked down the corridor. As soon as she came into earshot they would quickly stop and turn their attention to something else, but as soon as she passed them by, off they'd go again.

'How terrible for her.'

'I heard he dumped her at the fundraising dinner.'

'He is so *incredibly* good-looking. Perhaps too good looking for her.'

'I'm not sure what he saw in her anyway.'

'I thought they were just friends. At least they were all through medical school. Some women are meant to stay firmly in the friend-zone rather than trying to chase after a man too good for them.'

That last one she'd heard as she'd been sitting in the cafeteria. The woman who had been gossiping about her had spoken rather too loudly—loud enough for Clara to hear—and even though Clara had tried to rationalise that the gossip might not actually be about *her*, as soon as the gossiper in question had turned and seen Clara sitting there she'd gasped.

'I'm so sorry for what's happened, Clara,' she had mumbled, before scuttling away.

And if it wasn't the whispers in the corridors and back rooms, it was the pitying looks which were shared openly by those staff who knew her. It was getting beyond a joke, and it didn't make working her shifts any easier as it provided a constant reminder of just how Virgil had broken her heart.

At least she only had another fortnight at the Melbourne General until her contract was up. She'd agreed to do a twelve-month specialisation in emergency medicine before taking up a position as junior GP with a busy practice in her home town of Loggeen, forty minutes outside of Melbourne city.

She was looking forward to getting to know her patients, to making sure they weren't just some numbers in a file. She wanted to help people, but apparently Virgil hadn't been able to see that. Now he thought the world of general practice far too mundane for him, and their previous plans to settle down after their internship, and open up a practice together, had evaporated into thin air.

Virgil had fallen in love with general surgery, and the instant he'd changed his preference for the specialisation he'd stopped being the Virgil Arterton she'd come to know and love.

They'd been best friends throughout medical school, and for the past eighteen months they'd been a lot more than friends. Virgil had been accepted onto the service registrar programme before he'd even finished his internship. He was hungry to climb the hierarchical ladder—to become the best general surgeon he could. He was also planning to write his PhD thesis during his registrar training, which Clara had suggested might be a bit foolish.

'You'll be burning the candle at both ends. That won't be good for your health.'

Nor for their relationship, she'd added silently. She hadn't spoken the words out loud because she hadn't wanted to hear him say that their relationship was over. She realised now that all the signs had been there: all the signs that she'd been losing his attention, losing his love, losing his desire to be with her. But she'd ignored them, not wanting to believe that *her* Virgil was like so many of the other egocentric surgeons who walked the hospital corridors.

'I'll be fine.' He'd brushed her concerns away as though her words were nothing more than an annoying fly. 'You could do your PhD with me,' he'd suggested. 'We could both be studying and working together.'

'I'm not interested in doing that.'

And that had been the problem. Virgil had a clear idea of what *he* thought Clara should do with her life, and he wasn't interested in listening to what she had to say.

'I want to be a GP.'

And so the debate had continued between them, until the night when they'd been at a hospital fundraising dinner.

'I was positive you would change your mind during this past twelve months—that you'd agree to do more emergency medicine,' Virgil had told her.

The other thing he'd told her was that he'd been accepted on to the full surgical registrar training programme and would be heading overseas.

'You're not going straight away, are you?'

Clara had felt the nagging pain at the back of her mind, which had been increasing over the past six months, begin to pulse with dread at what he might say next.

'Of course I'm going. It's such an honour—and it's in Montreal. At one of the most ground-breaking hospitals in general surgical medicine.'

'But what about *us*?'

'Clara…' He'd sat back in his chair, his air matter-of-fact. 'We don't want the same things any more. You've made that abundantly clear. Besides, I won't have time for any sort of private life. I'll be constantly at the hospital or studying and brushing up on my French.'

'But what about the other things we've discussed—marriage? Children?'

He'd sighed, as though explaining his plans to an imbecile. 'I'll have no time for any of that. I know that sort of thing is important to you, but it's not my priority—not my focus any more.'

As she'd sat there, watching his mouth move, his words penetrating her heart, she had realised that her Virgil—the man she'd been such close friends with, the man who had once shared all her hopes and dreams for the future—was gone. He was gone, and in his place was an arrogant workaholic.

Yes, she wanted to get married and have children one day, and she'd always thought she'd end up doing that with him. But that wasn't the end of her plans for the future. Clara had hoped that one day she would have her own GP practice—that she'd be a respected member of the community and be known for helping others in their time of need. Wasn't that more important than being the best of the best of the best, with honours?

Shaking her head, Clara sniffed and reached into her bag, hunting for a tissue but finding none. She looked around her car, searching the glove box and other areas for a tissue, or a serviette, or even a piece of paper. Eventually she found an old sticky note, which had a phone number on it written in Virgil's handwriting. She used it to blow her nose.

He'd ended their relationship and the next day he'd flown out to work for a year in Montreal. Clara knew she should be happy he'd shown his true colours—that she hadn't wasted even more years of her life changing her plans to suit his ideals. She'd had a lucky escape.

That had been three weeks ago, and she'd been left to endure the gossips and the pitying looks.

Starting the car's engine, she hiccupped a few times before pulling out onto the road. Thankfully, at this time of the morning, there was little traffic which meant the drive back to her apartment shouldn't take too long.

Determined not to think any more about Virgil while she was driving, she switched on the radio and was trying to find a decent song when out of the blue there were bright lights in front of her...heading straight for her...

Clara braked and tried to swerve, but the last thing she could remember was the sickening sound of crunching metal as two cars collided.

CHAPTER ONE

'CHECK THE LEG PULSE,' Clara Lewis instructed her co-worker, while she continued with chest compressions on their patient.

She'd been working with her retrieval team for almost two years since she'd returned to Australia in time for her brother's wedding. Prior to Arthur tying the knot with her long-time friend Maybelle, Clara had been working in the UK for two and a half years, desperate to forget all about Virgil Arterton. She'd filled those years with meeting new people and getting her life back on track.

'Pulse is present on the left leg, but not on the right.'

'Check for fractures,' she said, before checking her patient's pulse. 'No pulse.'

It was necessary to report all the details to her team to ensure everyone knew the status. That way, they could perform their duties effectively. She continued with chest compressions.

'Possible fracture to the right femur,' Tony stated.

'Pulse!' she called a moment later as the man drew in a staggered breath. 'It's weak, but it's there. Suspected internal bleeding. Geoff—oxygen, stat. Then set up an IV. Push fluids. Tony, deal with the fracture.'

She looked to her patient, a twenty-three-year-old male who was still unconscious but at least breathing again. She tried calling to him while she checked his pulse once more.

'Hello? Can you hear me?'

No response.

'Pulse is stronger.'

She picked up a stethoscope and checked the man's heart rhythm, pleased with the result.

'Administer an injection of Methoxyflurane to provide pain relief.'

Her team worked together as Tony continued to stabilise the femoral fracture.

'Tony, have we got a pulse in that right leg yet?' Clara performed neurological observations. 'Pupils equal and reacting to light.'

'Right leg pulse is faint, but present,' Tony reported half a minute later.

Once Geoff had the IV set up, Clara dug into her emergency medical backpack for the medication, which was already drawn up and clearly labelled. 'Check medication,' she said to Geoff, who duly confirmed the medication before administering it via the intravenous drip.

Once that was done, Geoff addressed the fracture to the right upper arm, while Clara placed a bandage on a laceration to the left thigh.

Within another five minutes their patient's breathing and blood pressure had stabilised, which meant they were ready to transfer him, with the use of a PAT slide, onto a stretcher and into the waiting ambulance.

Ensuring the man's head was secured in a head and neck brace, and that he was strapped firmly onto the stretcher, they levered him into the ambulance, handing his care over to the paramedics.

Clara shut the doors to the ambulance, then received a round of applause from the crowd. The onlookers, who had been kept away by the barriers, clapped and some even whistled.

'Well done, Dr Lewis. You and your team have successfully stabilised the patient and completed the aims in under the projected time frame.'

Dr Fielding, one of the adjudicators of the retrieval team examination, shook her hand. The entire exercise had been designed not only to test the retrieval teams from different hospitals but also to raise public awareness of the importance of first aid courses.

'If you wouldn't mind delivering the verbal report, we can conclude your proceedings.'

'Thank you, Dr Fielding.'

Clara took a deep breath and looked out at the crowd. She held up her hands for silence and the applause died down.

'I'm Dr Clara Lewis. General Practitioner at the Victory Hospital Specialist Centre, located near Loggeen. This—' she indicated her team '—is RN Tony Simpkin and RN Geoff Thompson, both of whom have trained long and hard in emergency trauma management retrieval procedures.'

There was another round of clapping.

Clara applauded her team as well, then waited for silence. 'Let me state here and now that our patient today was a volunteer from the Melbourne Institute for Dramatic Arts and did a superb acting job. As a team, we were given a medical scenario to follow and we addressed each point in turn. The medications were not really injected into our volunteer and he is perfectly fit and healthy. We thank him for his part in the exercise.'

More clapping.

'Today we were faced with an accident victim who had

sustained a fractured right humerus, which is the bone above the elbow—'

She pointed to the areas on her own body as she listed them.

'Also severe laceration to the left thigh, which involved damaged muscle tissue and a damaged femoral artery, and a minor concussion. But, more importantly, our patient had stopped breathing. After restoring the patient's breathing, through chest compression and oxygen, we were able to stabilise the fractured femoral artery which, if left unattended, can cause a patient to bleed out. The right arm had minor bruises and abrasions, and upon examination it was surmised that the bone was probably broken in at least two places. When the patient was handed over to the paramedics, his breathing, blood pressure and pulse were all stable. His injuries were also stable.'

She paused for a breath, then delivered the point of why these emergency and trauma retrieval scenarios were being played out in the public arena.

'Learning first aid is a valuable asset for each and every person to have. Please,' she implored, 'sign up for a course. The St John's Ambulance and the Red Cross run courses on a regular basis throughout the year. And remember, if *you* were the person lying on the road in need of help, wouldn't you like a passer-by to be trained in first aid so they could help you? *Be* that person. Be that passer-by who could potentially save someone else's life. Sign up today. Thank you.'

She paused as another round of applause broke out.

'Well done again, Dr Lewis,' Dr Fielding reiterated. 'Your team is well trained and your speech was delivered in layman's terms. From checking the preliminary scores of the other adjudicators, I'd say you're in the lead—and with only one more retrieval team to perform, you're in with a good chance.'

'Thank you, Dr Fielding.'

Clara shook the other woman's hand and smiled. As she walked over to her team she glimpsed, out of the corner of her eye, a tall man with jet-black hair walking towards them.

Turning her head sharply in his direction, she recognised him immediately, and felt her heart skip a beat.

'Virgil…'

His name was a disbelieving whisper on her lips. It had been almost six years since she'd last set eyes on him, and she had to admit that, from afar, he looked every bit as handsome as always.

He was wearing navy trousers, a white shirt with rolled up cuffs, a colourful tie and dark sunglasses. Clara didn't need to be told what colour his eyes were. She'd looked into them too many times in the past and lost herself in their depths. Blue. The most compelling and hypnotic blue she'd ever seen.

Shaking the memory away, Clara clenched her jaw, trying to calm her increased heart-rate, needing to get her thoughts onto a more even keel. But her mouth was suddenly dry and a wave of repressed longing washed over her.

Yes, Virgil had broken her heart—but that was in the past. She'd moved on. She'd changed. She wasn't the easygoing Clara of yesteryear. She was a strong, independent woman who had conquered the issues of her past—both emotionally and physically. Still, that didn't mean she had to stick around and talk to people she didn't want to.

'Clara? Are you all right? You've gone pale.'

It was Tony who had spoken, and she looked at her colleague, staring at him blankly for a moment before her mind kicked back into gear.

She forced a smile. 'I'm fine.' She tucked a stray strand of hair back into the tight bun at the nape of her neck. 'You know, I'm a little thirsty. Do you guys want to get a drink?'

'Uh… I was going to hang around here for a bit,' Tony replied, as he gazed across at some of the nurses who had been part of other teams.

'Yeah, me too,' Geoff added, following Tony's gaze.

'You're both wolves in sheep's clothing,' she retorted good-naturedly.

'And if we win this competition we'll have a lot of those lovely nurses wanting us—not only for our sexy bodies,' Tony continued, 'but also for our brains.'

'Exactly,' Geoff replied. 'We're not just pretty faces.'

Clara shook her head at their antics. 'Fair enough.'

It was good that she was working with men who could make her smile, and yet not feel physically attracted to them.

However, the man who had held her interest for far too many years was most definitely heading her way. When she risked a peek over her shoulder it was to find him bearing down on their location, his strides purposeful and direct.

'Uh…well… I might go. Now. I might go now and get that drink. See you both later.'

'You're not going to wait around for the results?' Geoff called, but she'd already started to walk away and didn't want to stop to answer.

She needed to put as much distance between herself and Virgil Arterton as possible.

He had no idea where she'd disappeared to. One minute Clara had been chatting with the nurses in her retrieval team and the next she'd vanished. Virgil stopped in his tracks and looked around before going to speak to her team.

As one of the adjudicators, he'd known she was going to be here today, and had been hoping for an opportunity to talk to her. He hadn't wanted to disturb her concentration before she and her team had performed their retrieval exercise, but as soon as it was over, Virgil had made a beeline for her.

He couldn't believe how incredible she'd looked—performing her retrieval, giving her speech. He'd always been attracted to her—even when they'd just been friends throughout medical school—and then, after medical school, when they'd taken their relationship to the next level, he'd gone and ruined everything with his stupidity.

Years ago he'd tried to make contact, to ask her to forgive him, but he'd received no reply. Clearly Clara had been done with him. Now, though—now that he was back in Victoria—he wanted the chance to make things right between them. He wanted to beg her forgiveness, to ask her if it was too late for them to try again.

Although his life had taken several unexpected twists and turns throughout these past years, Virgil had finally figured out what it was he wanted out of life. He wanted Clara back, and he was determined to do everything he could to let her know he'd changed.

'G'day. Dr Virgil Arterton.' He removed his sunglasses and proffered his hand to the two nurses who had been working alongside Clara. 'Well done on your retrieval procedures.'

'Thanks, mate,' Tony replied, noting the badge Virgil was wearing, which declared him to be one of the adjudicators for the retrieval team examinations.

'Uh… I was looking for Clara…er… I mean Dr Lewis.' Seeing the way Tony gave him a concerned look, Virgil added, 'We went to medical school together. I just wanted to catch up and find out how she's doing.'

He shifted his stance, hoping to seem casual as he made the enquiry.

Geoff glanced over his shoulder. 'She was heading to the pub, I think. Said she was thirsty. And the closest place to get a drink is the pub on the corner.'

Virgil followed the direction Geoff was looking. 'Thanks. I'll see if I can catch her up.'

He slipped his sunglasses back into place and walked towards the pub. Had she rushed off because she'd seen him? If that was the case, it clearly meant she didn't want to talk to him. He'd been a jerk all those years ago, full of his own arrogance, his own career, rather than focusing on what was really important in life. And of late, there hadn't been a day that went by when he didn't think about Clara in one way or another.

Sometimes he'd hear an old song on the radio, and it would take him back to when they'd been studying together for their final medical exams, music playing in the background as they'd tried to cram as much information into their brains as possible. Or he'd smell the scent of a greasy diner and remember when they were interns, finishing an excessively long shift at the hospital, and would go for a burger and chips.

Now that he'd returned to the hospital where they'd both once worked—Melbourne General Hospital—the memories came hard and fast. Even the street he was on right now was one he'd traversed with Clara in the past. The pub he was heading to was one where they would often have a drink with all their friends whenever they'd had time off.

When he entered the pub he removed his sunglasses, astonished to find the place as crowded as it had been all those years ago. Several of the people there were medics, either those who were competing in the retrieval examinations or those who had just finished their shift and needed a cold one. At any rate, the front bar of the old Australian pub was crowded.

Was Clara here? If she was, would she be happy to see him? He hoped so. Yes, their lives had gone along different paths for the last almost six years, but surely that was enough time for her to forgive and forget.

Virgil continued his way towards the bar, rationalising that if Clara wanted a drink that would be the place she'd go. As he politely nudged his way through the throng he saw her. She was standing at the bar, waiting impatiently to be served. He could tell she was impatient by the way she drummed her fingers on the counter—a habit it appeared she hadn't conquered.

A smile touched his face at just how well he'd known this woman in the past. Would she let him get to know her again in the future?

Another woman was beside her, chatting away. Clara was feigning polite interest in between doing her best to attract the bartender's attention. Virgil's smile brightened and his heart filled with anticipation as he neared her location.

He made it to the bar and, as he was tall, drew the immediate attention of the bartender—the same bartender Clara had been trying to get to serve her.

'G'day, mate, what can I get you?' the bartender asked.

'I'll have a beer and…' Virgil paused and glanced down into Clara's upturned face.

At first, she looked annoyed that the bartender was serving someone else before her, but upon seeing just who he was serving she openly gaped in astonishment.

'A lemon squash with a slice of lime?'

It had been her favourite refreshing drink on a hot day. Was he still right? He quirked an eyebrow, waiting for her to respond.

'Actually, I'd like a cranberry juice with sparkling mineral water, please,' she said, after giving Virgil a solid glare, then turned to smile at the bartender. She reached into her pocket for some money.

'It's on me,' Virgil said. 'It's the least I can do.'

He was having a difficult time keeping his mind focused on trying to talk, as even just being this near to her again was causing a tightening in his gut. Nervousness? More than likely. He had a lot riding on this meeting and it wasn't going at all the way he'd planned—probably because her fresh, floral scent was teasing at his senses, reviving even more memories of those intimate times they'd spent together.

Clara shrugged one shoulder, then returned her attention to the woman beside her. 'Sorry, Helen. You were saying…?'

All her attention was on this Helen, which meant none of her attention was on him—or at least that was what she wanted him to think. But he could tell by the way she shifted her body, so there was half a centimetre more distance between them, that she was well aware of his presence.

Helen, however, had a different idea. She looked from Clara to Virgil, then down to Virgil's adjudicator's badge.

'Virgil Arterton? As in *the* Virgil Arterton? The general surgeon who invented a new surgical method which has revolutionised invasive incision procedures?'

Virgil held Clara's gaze for a split second longer before turning to look at Helen. 'You've read my papers?'

'Well, who wouldn't?' Helen asked rhetorically as she held her hand out towards him. 'I'm Helen Simperton. I find your work to be incredibly insightful, as well as revolutionary.'

The bartender had finished making their drinks and, much to Virgil's chagrin, Clara used the excuse of him being trapped by Helen's raptures, to take her drink and leave the bar area.

'What was it that first made you consider changing the usual way for incising a patient?' Helen asked as Virgil watched Clara almost rush to the other side of the room.

A moment later she disappeared from sight as more people came in through the front doors.

Trying to appear outwardly calm, he sipped his drink and gave Helen brief answers to her questions. He needed to find Clara, to talk to her for more than half a second. It was clear from his reception that she wasn't interested in talking to him, so if he didn't go after her now he might not get another chance until it was too late.

If he were to walk into her consulting rooms at the Specialist Centre and announce that he was the newly appointed general surgeon, she might well resign on the spot—and he didn't want that.

'Will you excuse me, Helen? I need to catch up to Clara.'

Without waiting for Helen to ask another question, he picked up his drink and followed in the direction Clara had gone. He looked in one of the back rooms of the pub, but she wasn't there. He checked another room off to the side. She wasn't there either. Was she in the bathroom? He hovered momentarily outside of the door to the ladies' room, but knew he couldn't barge in there calling her name.

Virgil turned and headed back towards the main bar, and it was then that he spotted half a glass of what looked to be cranberry juice and mineral water sitting on a table near the door. Was it her drink?

He asked some of the people nearby about the drink's owner, and their description matched Clara.

She'd left.

Putting his own drink on the table, Virgil stepped outside into the Melbourne heat. Slipping his sunglasses back into place, he glanced first one way and then the other, and finally spotted her. She was walking briskly down the street, back towards the retrieval teams. When she glanced over her shoulder and saw him standing there, she hastened her pace.

Clearly she was trying to avoid him as much as possible.

Virgil shook his head as he set off after her again, not surprised at her stubbornness. It had been one of those traits which had either endeared her to him, or frustrated him. Today it was the latter. No other woman had ever affected him the way Clara did. She could drive him crazy, make him laugh, and make his heart melt like butter, all within the space of a few minutes. The woman was an enigma, and he'd been captivated by her from the beginning.

With his long strides, he managed to catch up to her just as she was about to cross the road.

'Clara. I need to speak to you. Please?'

She stopped. Sighing heavily, as though admitting defeat, she turned and stared up at him, lifting her arms wide before dropping them back to her sides.

'What do you want, Virgil?'

Now that he was face to face with her—now that he wasn't playing this game of cat and mouse—his mind went momentarily blank, as he stared into her upturned face. Good heavens, didn't the woman have *any* idea just what she did to his insides? That defiant lift of her chin... the way her back and shoulders were rigid, as though preparing for a fight. The way small wisps of her hair escaped their bonds and floated around her face in the warm breeze. *Gorgeous.*

And her eyes, although glaring at him with distrust, were as hypnotic as ever. Why had he been so incredibly stupid in the past? How different their lives might have been if only he hadn't been such a jerk.

'Uh…' He finally managed to stammer the sound, as he shifted his feet and tried to get his brain to work.

'*Uh…?* You've just chased me around the streets of Melbourne to utter "uh"?' She crossed her arms and angled her head to the side. 'Are you sure it's me you want to speak to, or rather a speech therapist?'

He couldn't help but laugh at her sassiness. She'd always had a sharp wit. 'Oh, Clara. Sweetheart, you haven't changed.'

'Don't call me that.'

'Sorry.' It was then he realised he was wearing his sunglasses and quickly lifted them onto his head. 'OK…' He cleared his throat once again and met her gaze. 'I've been chasing you because I need to tell you something.'

He paused for a second, and again her impatience got the better of her.

'That you're sorry for the way you treated me all those years ago?'

'Well…there's that—and I am deeply sorry—' His words received an eye-roll from her. 'But, more importantly, I wanted to let you know that I've returned to Melbourne.'

'I can see that. You're standing right in front of me,' she retorted.

'To live,' he added.

There was a moment of silence between them as she processed his words. 'You'll be working at Melbourne General?'

'Uh…no… Well…when I say I've returned to Melbourne, I mean I'm going to be living in Loggeen.'

'What?'

'And…working at Victory Hospital… and at the Specialist Centre.'

At his words, her expression changed from one of impatient annoyance to one of horrified disbelief. Then she closed her eyes and shook her head.

'No, you're not.'

'Yes. I am. I start there in two weeks' time.'

'Then you can *un*-start. Get out of your contract. Take a different job. Anywhere. Anywhere but at *my* hospital and *my* specialist centre. *No!*'

Her words were firm, direct, and yet he detected a hint of desperation—as though she *really* did not want him anywhere near her. Did she hate him that much?

'I've already bought a house in the district.' He cleared his throat. 'We start moving in tomorrow.' His words were rolling from his mouth quite fast. 'I wanted you to hear this from me, not from any gossip or the rumour mill.'

'We?'

She clenched her jaw, and a moment later he could have sworn he saw her eyes brim with tears. Were they tears of anger or tears of joy? He hoped it was the latter, but was pretty sure it was the former.

Clara immediately looked down at the ground, as though she were wishing it would open up and swallow her. When she spoke her voice was polite. Too polite. And when she lifted her head, she didn't quite meet his gaze.

'Thank you for letting me know, Dr Arterton.'

With that, she turned and continued on her way back to her retrieval team.

Virgil wanted to call out to her—to let her know where he'd be living, to invite her to dinner so she could meet his daughter. He wanted to gather her into his arms and never let her go. He wanted to rectify the mistakes from his past, to ask for forgiveness and beg her to give him another chance. Even the small amount of time he'd spent in her company had reignited the desire he'd had for her in the past. Of course he did none of that, because her reception of him had shown him exactly where he stood—far, far away from her.

The hopes he'd had, the plans he'd made, the way he'd wanted to find a way to get her back into his life, had all come crashing down.

Clara hated him.

CHAPTER TWO

'TODAY I THINK I'll have…' Clara surveyed the mouthwatering row of different fudges, trying to decide. 'Peppermint chocolate.'

'Coming right up.' Marni cut the fudge and placed it into the mixer.

This was Clara's favourite time of the day. She watched as Marni operated the machine that would mix the ice-cream with the fudge, producing the most scrumptious taste Clara had ever experienced.

'There you go.'

Marni handed over the small bowl filled with the dessert and Clara paid.

'Thanks.'

Clara eyed the dish she now held so protectively in her hand. As always, she would have at least one spoonful before leaving the shop. She swirled the spoon around the edge of the bowl and scooped some up. Her lips parted in anticipation and the spoon slipped between them.

Clara closed her eyes. 'Mmm…' She could feel her body begin to relax from the pressures of her rigorous medical practice. 'Heaven!'

The small pieces of the fudge mixed with the smooth, creamy ice-cream as she swirled them around in her mouth before swallowing.

'It really is the small things in life that can bring you so much joy.'

Marni laughed. 'Enjoy. I'll see you later.' She moved off to serve other customers.

As Clara stepped out of the shop, she heard one of the new customers saying, 'What was she eating? It looked delicious.'

Taking slow steps, she placed another spoonful into her mouth, then stopped at the kerb to enjoy the flavours. There were at least thirty different varieties of fudge at Marni's shop, and Clara had sampled each and every one of the them at least fifty times over.

She was so busy focusing on her delicious dessert that she almost walked into a man pushing a pram with a toddler in it, and the pregnant woman beside him. The woman looked to be in her second trimester, and the pang of envy which always ripped through Clara when she saw a pregnant woman came swift and fast.

She skirted around the young family, neatly avoiding the collision, and scooped another spoonful into her mouth, willing the sensation to calm the feeling of emptiness she'd carried with her for almost six years.

She would never be able to give birth to a child.

She pressed the button for the pedestrian crossing, eating more ice-cream while she waited for the lights to change. And then she saw him. Virgil Arterton. So he had come. He was here. He was back in Loggeen and he would be working at the Specialist Centre and Victory Hospital.

She'd held out a vain hope that after their brief conversation in Melbourne he would change his mind, that somehow a strange twist of fate would cause his plans to be altered.

When she'd returned to Loggeen after the retrieval exercise, she'd checked with her colleagues and discovered that Virgil had spoken the truth. The two of them would be working in the same building as well as the same hospital.

Thankfully, their paths shouldn't cross when she was doing her twice-monthly stints in the Emergency Department at Victory Hospital, given that Virgil was a qualified general surgeon and would be using the hospital to hold public clinics and operate on his patients. In fact, she was hopeful that their paths would rarely cross, and that when they did they would be able to nod politely to each other and go about their business.

Gone were the days when she had pined over him. Clara was in control of her own future, and right now she was more than happy with the way her life was turning out. Good general practice, helping people at the Specialist Centre and in the ED, as well as going out with the retrieval teams when necessary. Her family lived close— her brother and his family even lived in the same building as her—and although her parents were presently overseas, enjoying another long cruise, the Lewis family was a close-knit one.

Yes, she was more than happy with her life—and, as such, there was absolutely no room for Virgil Arterton in it.

A car horn beeped, bringing her out of her reverie. It was then she realised that the light had turned green, indicating it was safe for her to cross the road, but like a ninny she'd simply stood there, speculating about Virgil, while a bowl of ice-cream and fudge melted in her hand.

Crossing the street, she walked up the paved pathway to the doors of the Specialist Centre. After they'd whooshed open, Clara continued walking through the lobby to her consulting rooms. Pushing open the glass door, she was met by her ever-smiling receptionist, Jane.

'You'll never guess who was just in here!' she gushed as Clara placed her bowl on the desktop.

'The King of Persia?' she growled, preoccupied with her anger.

Now she had one more thing to add to her dislike of *'him'*. One glimpse of Virgil Arterton and she'd lost all enjoyment of the confection she loved so much. She spooned some more into her mouth, hoping to recapture the sensations again. *Nothing.*

'Oh, what flavour did you get today?' Jane asked, eyeing the greenish tinge to the ice-cream. 'Peppermint chocolate,' she guessed, before Clara could say a word. 'I thought you had that last week?'

'Does it matter?' Clara snapped, then immediately apologised. 'I'm sorry, Jane. When's my next patient due?'

'You've got another ten minutes before Mrs Holden comes in.'

Clara walked through to her office and put the bowl on her desk. 'Coffee?' she asked Jane.

'Sure—if you're getting some.'

'Hey, I've got ten whole minutes to spare and I've got the best dessert in the world sitting on my desk. I may as well go the entire way and have a hot cup of coffee instead of sculling a lukewarm one.'

'Talk about spoilt.' Jane grinned. 'Oh, I forgot to tell you who was here. The most dashingly handsome and gorgeous man I've ever seen in my life. He was really tall—about six feet four inches, I'd say—with the most wonderful thick black hair that I could just run my fingers through for ever, and—'

'Hypnotic blue eyes?' Clara finished, trying desperately to ignore the way the description was permanently burned into her memory. She shook her head, annoyed with herself for describing his eyes as 'hypnotic'. Why hadn't she just said 'blue'? 'Virgil Arterton.'

'You *know* him?' Jane's eyebrows rose to meet her fringe.

'You could say that.' Clara shook her head dejectedly and sighed. 'Milk, no sugar—right?'

'Yeah. But, Clara…'

Clara didn't wait to be questioned. She stalked to the communal kitchen, which was shared by the staff at the medical centre, and started to make coffee for herself and Jane.

Cedric Fowler, the local obstetrician, was sitting at the table with a smile on his face.

'You look happy, Cedric,' Clara stated.

'Our new general surgeon was just in here. Actually, he asked after you.'

'He did?' Dread instantly washed over her. 'Why? What did you say? You didn't tell him anything, did you? Did you tell him I wasn't here?'

The words tumbled out of Clara's mouth, her eyes wide with a mixture of fear and annoyance.

It wasn't that she was afraid to see Virgil. Rather, she was sceptical about working in such close proximity with him. She needed Virgil to be professional about their relationship—not blab about their past to all and sundry. She'd done everything she could to move forward with her life, to put her past behind her, and the last thing she needed was Virgil digging it up again, telling people they'd been a couple, reigniting the old gossip.

'Uh…' Cedric eyed her in confusion. 'You *weren't* here, Clara. Besides, didn't the two of you used to know each other? I thought you were at med school together?'

Darn Cedric and his perfect memory. 'Yes. Yes, we were close friends. And then we weren't—aren't.'

Cedric's frown increased. 'I hope whatever it is that exists between the two of you won't interfere with—'

'We're both professionals, Cedric,' Clara interrupted, reassuring him.

'Good, because we need Virgil here consulting as our resident general surgeon. We're lucky to have a man as widely published as him agree to come to Victory Hospital.'

Clara smiled politely at Cedric and nodded once more. She'd grasped his meaning. GPs like her were found everywhere—yet established and successful surgeons like Virgil usually worked at larger hospitals in capital cities, not in smaller cities or outer suburbs.

'There'll be no drama between Virgil and myself,' she promised as she returned her attention to making coffee.

'That's good to know,' a deep voice said from the doorway.

Clara immediately closed her eyes as an unbidden wave of desire swept through her at the sound of Virgil's modulated tones. Darn the man! She hadn't even looked at him and already her body was betraying her. Well that was OK, she quickly rationalised. It was OK to be attracted to him—after all, he *was* a good-looking man. However, she knew the real Virgil—the man behind the façade—and she knew there was no way she'd ever be able to trust him again. Therefore the attraction, and the way he could cause goosebumps to tickle their way across her skin with the sound of his voice, meant nothing. *Nothing!*

'Ah, Virgil, you've returned,' Cedric said. 'You didn't forget anything, did you?'

'No.'

Clara could hear the two men shaking hands.

'Just needed a quick word with Clara.'

'Right. I'll leave you to it,' Cedric said, before exiting the small room and closing the door behind him.

Clara felt completely trapped. She was standing at the bench where the coffee things were and Virgil was near the door. There was a table and chairs between them. She didn't want to be here. She didn't want to see him. She most certainly didn't want to talk to him. But what she wanted didn't matter.

Cedric was right. The Specialist Centre needed Virgil to consult here. It would allow a lot of patients to have their surgeries at Victory Hospital rather than having to travel to Melbourne for treatment. She needed to be professional. She needed to be cool, calm and collected. She could do it. She could work alongside the man who had broken her heart and shattered her world to pieces. She was strong. She was different now. *She could do this.*

Turning slowly, she consciously unclenched her jaw and wrapped a mental shield around herself. The Arterton charm had been known to break through all the barriers she could erect, and she had vowed never to leave herself that vulnerable again.

Their eyes met and held for a second. Jane's description of him had been accurate. He was devastatingly handsome. He was dressed in denim jeans and a white polo shirt. His hair was as dark as midnight, with a hint of grey at the temples, but it was his lovely blue eyes that had always been able to make her knees go weak and her heart skip a beat.

'Clara.' Virgil smiled. 'Good to see you again.'

She nodded in his direction, but didn't return his smile. 'Virgil.'

Considering his presence had once again shaken her foundations, she was pleased that at least her voice sounded calm and controlled.

'Can I talk to you a moment, please?'

Clara closed her eyes and shook her head. 'What do you want, Virgil?' The question was soft, but she knew he'd heard her.

'I wanted to make sure you were OK with me working here.'

'It's a bit late to consider my feelings now.'

'True,' he acquiesced as he sat at the table. 'But had I given you a choice—if I'd run my plans by you—chances are you would have said no, you *didn't* want me working here.'

'Well, you're here now,' she stated as she crossed to the fridge and removed the milk.

She was positive she could feel his eyes watching her every move. The subtle sway of her hips beneath the navy cotton skirt. The rigidity of her spine under the light blue shirt.

With her back still to him, she asked, 'Just out of curiosity, what *are* your reasons for moving here?'

She collected two cups and spooned in some instant coffee and sugar. The actions were automatic, but after putting three sugars into her own cup, when she usually only had one, she knew she wasn't concentrating on anything but awaiting Virgil's response.

'Well…besides wanting to be nearer to you and to spend time with you—'

'Whoa!' She turned to face him, teaspoon upheld in her hand. 'Wait a second. *Nearer* to me? Spend *time* with me? What planet are you living on?' She scowled. '*You* may be quite comfortable cheating on your wife, but I am most definitely *not* happy to be "the other woman"—so you can forget about it.' She shook the teaspoon at him as though that would help to prove her point.

'How did you know I was married?'

'I bumped into Misty Fox from med school about three years ago. She told me that you'd got married—which surprised me, because I was pretty sure one of the reasons we broke up was because you didn't want to get married and have a family. You wanted to focus on your career. You didn't want me cramping your style.'

'I never said that last bit.'

'It was implied. So clearly your career's going well, *and* you found someone you wanted to marry, so why on earth would you want to spend more time with *me*?'

'Clara, can we sit down and just talk?'

'No. I have a clinic and I need to make coffee for myself and Jane.' She busied herself with adding hot water to the cups and starting to stir them.

'I'm not married.'

He seemed to blurt out the words and she glared at him over her shoulder.

'You just told me you were!'

'No. I asked how you knew I was married.' He shook his head and stood. 'I'm a widower.'

'Oh.' She slowly exhaled, the anger she'd been holding so close starting to wane a little. 'I'm sorry, Virgil. That must be difficult for you.'

'She died in a car accident—with her lover.'

'Oh!'

Car accidents... They really had a way of changing things.

'Clara, it's true my career is going great—so great that I can choose where I want to go. And I've chosen to come back to my old stomping ground of Loggeen.'

'But why? Seriously, it can't be because of me—so why?'

'It's a great place to raise a family.'

'You have *children*!'

She couldn't believe the pain that pierced her heart at this news. Not only had he broken her heart all those years ago, declaring he didn't want to be with her because he needed to focus on his career, but the reasons he'd given—that he didn't want to get married and have a family—meant the truth of the matter was that he hadn't wanted to have those things with *her*.

Clenching her jaw, she tried to keep her voice neutral. She'd promised Cedric that she would be professional, and by golly she was going to be as professional as possible.

'I'm very happy you've chosen to raise your family here. It is a great part of the country, with a lot of good schools.'

'I have one child, Clara. Her name is Rosie and she's three years old, so not quite ready for school.'

'And you've moved her here because…?' She tried hard to keep the pain from her voice.

'Because she's young enough to make a fresh start.'

'I see. Well, I hope you'll be very happy working here at the Specialist Centre.' She picked up the coffee cups, holding them in front of her like a barrier. 'As far as we're concerned, I think it's best if we just forget the past and continue on like the professionals we are.' She took a step forward. 'Would you mind opening the door for me, please?'

'Don't be like this.'

She forced a smile. 'Like what?'

'Like…like an automaton.'

Clara sighed with exasperation. She was standing near the door and so was he. It had been a mistake to move closer to him, because now all her senses were attuned to every little thing about him. The scent surrounding him was the same spicy aura she'd always equated with him.

'So you're really going to be working here?' Her words were barely a whisper.

He edged a little closer to her. 'Afraid so.'

His breath fanned her neck. She could feel her body respond to his closeness, even though he wasn't touching her. Clara tried to control not only her breathing but her wayward emotions as well. How was it that whenever he got within coo-ee of her, every sense went on alert, every fibre of her being became attuned to his every move.

'You've cut your hair,' he stated, his voice still soft. 'The last time I saw you it was almost down to your waist.'

'It needed cutting.'

'It looks good shoulder-length. Professional.'

Clara fought against his deep, sensual tone. It washed over her like silk, making her feel vulnerable.

'I've always loved the colour. Rich, dark brown—to match your eyes.'

Clara sucked in her breath at his words. Her whole body seemed to be tingling with awareness at his close proximity. Although he wasn't touching her, she could feel the warmth his body exuded and it enveloped her like a glove. How was it that after all this time—after all the therapy she'd undergone both physically and emotionally—he could still affect her in such a way? Did she *really* have no self-control where he was concerned?

'Clara!'

A female voice called from the distance, breaking the small bubble surrounding herself and Virgil. Clara almost spilt the coffees at hearing Jane's voice.

'Quick, open the door,' she stated.

He rested his hand on the doorknob, but paused. 'Do you have patients now?'

'Yes—and you've just completely ruined the only ten minutes I've had to myself all day.'

'Are you free for dinner tonight?'

'No.'

'Tomorrow night?'

'No.'

'But we need to talk, Clara. We need to sort things out.'

'Will you please just open the door?'

'The next night?'

'*Yes*. Just open the door!'

With a goofy grin at her acceptance, he opened the door just in time for Clara to see Jane walking towards the kitchenette.

'I knew you'd get sidetracked,' her receptionist said. 'Mrs Holden's here.'

Without seeing Virgil on the other side of the kitchenette door, Jane took the coffee Clara had made and immediately took a sip.

'If you don't hustle, you'll be running late,' Jane remarked as she turned and headed back the way she'd come.

Clara looked up at Virgil in disdain. 'That was a dirty trick and there's no way you can hold me to that acceptance.'

'Yes, I can.'

'No, you can't. Agreeing to have dinner with you was the only way I could get you to open the door. Desperate times sometimes call for desperate measures.'

'I completely agree—which is why I had to trap you into dining with me.'

'Aha! So you admit it was a trap.'

Virgil smiled widely at her words. 'I've missed this, Clara. This crazy banter we used to share.'

And so had she, but she wasn't going to admit it.

'Please—have dinner with me some time before I officially start next Monday. Sunday night would be good for me, if it's good for you.'

Sighing, she knew she wasn't going to get her Friday afternoon clinic done unless she agreed. 'Fine. Sunday night.'

'I'll email you the details.'

'OK. My email address is—'

'I have a list of everyone's email here at the Specialist Centre,' he told her, then took her free hand in his and brought it to his lips, pressing a soft and sweet kiss to her knuckles. 'Until Sunday.'

'Ugh!' She jerked her hand free and rolled her eyes at his corny action, then headed towards her consulting room.

She made sure she walked in a calm and controlled manner down the corridor, once again feeling his gaze watching her movements. The effects from that gentle kiss on her hand had sent a wave of wildfire spreading throughout her body. It *had* to be wrong that she was still this attracted to him, right?

Placing the now lukewarm coffee on her desk, she looked at the melted bowl of ice-cream and fudge. That was exactly how she felt. Once upon a time she'd been the most important person in Virgil's life. Then visions of being the best in his profession, of working all the time and spending little or no time with the people who mattered most, had become his main focus. And she'd been discarded—shoved aside as though she were nothing but a distant memory.

'Why did he have to come back?'

The question was spoken to her empty consulting room, the words filled with pain from the past and desperation for the future. If he'd affected her this strongly just by being in the small kitchenette with her, how on earth was she supposed to cope dining with him on Sunday evening?

What she needed to do was to prescribe herself a healthy dose of living in the present and ignoring the past—and a double dose of self-preservation.

CHAPTER THREE

VIRGIL SAT ON his bed on Sunday evening, amazed at how nervous he was about actually sitting down to talk to Clara face to face. They'd been friends for such a long time during medical school—studying together and buoying each other up, especially around exam time. Several times they'd discussed whether or not they should change the nature of their relationship.

'If we do that,' Clara had rationalised once, 'if we become *more* than friends, what happens if we have a fight? I need you to help me through these next few years, Virgil. You're my study partner, my lab partner, my cheer team—just as I'm yours.'

'You're right,' he'd agreed. 'That's far more important at the moment.'

'And, besides, who knows what might happen if we change the dynamic? What if we don't like kissing each other?'

'We're only going to find out if we try,' he'd encouraged, too embarrassed to tell her how he hadn't been able to stop thinking about it. They were friends, and he hadn't wanted to ruin that friendship by taking their relationship to the next level.

They'd been sitting in one of the back corners of the Loggeen City Library, studying for a coming practical exam. Several medical texts had been scattered between the two of them, and Virgil had been leaning on the table, his elbow almost knocking one of the books off as he propped up his head.

Clara had stared at him for a moment, looking severely tempted. And after a long moment of contemplation, of staring longingly at each other's mouths, wondering and wishing, it had been Clara who had broken the tension surrounding them, shaking her head and tapping the text in front of him.

'Let's just focus on learning the anatomy of the abdomen, so when we dissect the cadaver we actually know what we're doing.'

And that had been the end of the discussion—until the next time the subject had arisen. The following time it had been *his* turn to be the strong one and again insist that they remain friends.

'At least until medical school is over and done with.'

When they had finally been done with studying, he wasn't sure who had been more surprised—himself or Clara—at the way they'd congratulated each other, wrapping their arms around each other, their lips melding in perfect synchronicity.

'Oh, it's *there*,' he'd breathed triumphantly against her lips. 'I knew it would be.'

'Shut up and kiss me,' she'd ordered, and he'd willingly complied.

Now, raking a hand through his hair, Virgil exhaled and stood, walking over to the tallboy in his bedroom, which was adorned with framed photographs of his daughter. He reached into the top drawer and pulled out a bundle of other photographs from the back—photographs of himself and Clara. Her hair was pulled back into a long braid in most of them, although there were one or two where her hair was loose. He'd always loved to run his fingers through those gorgeous locks.

He flicked through the photos, and stopped at what had been the last photo of them taken together. They'd been attending a fundraising dinner for the Melbourne General Hospital's cancer centre. A professional photographer had taken their picture at the table. Even though they'd pasted on their smiles, looking at Clara now, he could see just how unhappy he'd made her.

'This has been going on for months,' she'd told him earlier that night. 'You're always at the hospital—even when you don't need to be. If you don't slow down you're going to end up sick from exhaustion.'

'Just because *you* don't have any desire to specialise, and are more than happy to be a GP for the rest of your life, it doesn't mean you should criticise *me* for chasing my dreams. I want to be a general surgeon. Do you know how difficult it is to get onto the training programme, Clara? I've managed that after only doing one year as a service registrar. *One year.*'

He'd spread his arms wide.

'And now I've been accepted to go and train overseas for the next twelve months—again, for a first-year registrar that is almost unheard of, and yet they've chosen *me*.'

'I'm very happy for you, but—'

'*Are* you? Or are you completely jealous of my success?'

He'd fixed her with a stare that had indicated he wouldn't believe a word that came out of her mouth, because as far as he had been concerned, she was the biggest liability in his career plan.

'Perhaps it's best if we take a break from each other while I'm overseas. I think you were right all those years ago when we were in medical school—we should never have changed the nature of our friendship. At least now that you're done with your training, you don't need me to hold your hand any longer.'

Virgil closed his eyes at recalling the words his past self had sprouted to Clara. How *could* he have treated her in such a fashion? He'd been so full of his own self-importance, so determined to succeed, that he'd pushed away the one person who had always been there for him, who had always shared in his successes.

It had been almost eight months into his overseas placement in Montreal, after he'd presented a paper and received an award, that he'd realised he had no one special to share it with. What had been worse was that when he'd tried to contact Clara to apologise, he'd received no response.

'She's giving you a second chance tonight,' he told his reflection sternly. 'Don't blow it.'

The knock at his bedroom door made him turn to see Gwenda standing in the doorway, looking at him with a small smirk on her face.

Gwenda had been an old friend of his mother's, and after she'd nursed her husband through terminal cancer she'd been at a loose end, her children all grown with lives of their own. When Virgil had found himself a widower, with a six-month-old daughter to care for, as well as a full workload, Gwenda had offered to help out as his live-in housekeeper and nanny.

'I'm nervous,' he told her.

'You'll be fine.'

'What if she doesn't show up?'

'What if she *does*?'

'What if she refuses to listen to what I have to say?'

'What if she *doesn't*?'

Virgil closed his eyes. 'I hope she listens. I hope so much that Clara and I can patch things up.'

'Rosie's ready for bed. Go and say goodnight, then off you go to get some answers to these questions.'

Virgil opened his eyes and smiled at the mention of his daughter. 'Good plan.'

He'd thought about asking Clara to come to his house for dinner and meet Rosie, but they really did have a lot to discuss. They needed to try and put the past in the past and hopefully forge a future together. At least that was what *he* wanted. Was he being foolish putting all his cards on the table?

As he went through the nightly routine with his gorgeous girl, checking her teeth and reading her stories, Virgil embraced the love he felt for his daughter. Rosie didn't judge him—she simply loved him because he was her daddy. That innocent, unconditional love had been the starting point for his present plan. Being upfront and honest with Clara was the only way he knew how to try and win her back.

Clara arrived way too early at the restaurant, but she wanted to be there when Virgil arrived. She wanted to show him that she was a different person from the one he'd known all those years ago—the woman who had run late for dates, late for classes and late for everything in between. Now she was a successful GP, with her own thriving practice. She was well respected by her peers and within her community. She was happy, content, and she didn't need a boyfriend from her past to insinuate himself back into her life.

The problem was that Virgil wasn't *just* an old boyfriend. He'd been the true love of her life, and long before their relationship had changed from one of friendship to one that was much, much more, Clara had been in love with him. However, as she constantly reminded herself, the past was the past—and regardless of what Virgil had planned for his move back to his old stomping ground, it definitely wouldn't be including her. Not in a romantic light anyway. Professional colleagues she could cope with. Nothing more.

Finally he arrived, ten minutes before their appointed time. She saw his eyebrows rise when the maître d' indicated that Clara was already there. She watched as he walked towards the table, his stride sure and steadfast. She liked the way he walked. She'd liked watching him walk in the past, and now was no exception.

It wasn't until he stood before her that she realised she'd been staring.

'Shall I add a little pivot for you?' He quirked his eyebrow, his gaze filled with memories of the past, his lips pulled into an intriguing smile.

It wasn't the first time he'd asked her that question, but she was determined tonight would be the last. Ignoring the way his smile had caused a flood of tingles to invade her body, and the way his spicy scent teased her senses, she indicated a chair.

As he sat, he continued to smile. 'You're early!'

'I've changed, and I want you to know that I'm not interested in picking up the threads of our old relationship.'

'Straight to the point. Good.' He opened the menu and glanced at it for a whole three seconds before declaring, 'Well, I know what I'm having. How about you?'

'Yes.'

'Excellent.'

He summoned a waiter and they gave their orders.

Once they were alone, he shifted in his chair before leaning forward. 'Thank you for agreeing to dine with me.'

'As far as I'm concerned, Virgil, it's merely a strategy to ensure we can keep the past where it belongs and work alongside each other like professionals.'

'I couldn't agree more.'

Upon hearing those words, Clara sighed. 'Good.'

He was going to see sense. Thank goodness for that. No more talk of moving back to Loggeen just so he could see her again. Clara picked up her glass of water and took a sip. Perhaps this dinner wouldn't be so bad after all.

'But that doesn't mean we can't investigate whether or not there are any residual feelings remaining from our past relationship,' he continued.

She accidentally sprayed some of her mouthful of water on him, before choking on the rest as she swallowed the wrong way. Coughing and spluttering, she was powerless to stop him from patting her on the back in an effort to ease the obstruction.

'Steady on.' He picked up a napkin and dabbed at where the water had landed.

'I didn't mean to spit on you,' she remarked between coughs.

Virgil chuckled. 'Just like old times. The two of us having fun together.'

Clara gave one last cough, then shook her head. 'No, Virgil. It's not. It can never be like old times again.'

She tried to make her words sound firm, definite, but her throat was still recovering from the coughing spasm and therefore sounded a little croaky.

'As we're speaking frankly, I've got to ask why you won't even consider it.' He went to reach for her hand but she shifted back in her chair. Virgil looked at both his own hands for a moment before saying softly, 'I've changed too, Clara. I really have. I'm not the idiotic moron I was back then. I apologise for what I said and for the way I treated you.'

Clara pondered his words for a long moment. 'Thank you for apologising.' She tilted her head to the side and aimed her next question at him. 'So what are you planning? To waltz back into my life, woo me once more and then—what?'

He held her gaze, his tone filled with conviction. 'Then we fall in love again. Marriage. Children. Careers. Happy families until death do us part.'

Clara openly gaped at him in astonishment. 'And you told me you'd changed.' She shook her head. 'What absolute rubbish!'

'I *have* changed, Clara.'

'Really? Hmm…let's review. In the past you wanted to break up with me, head overseas and focus on your career. Check.' She mimed the act of making an imaginary tick in the air. 'Then you decided to get married and have children.' She mimed another tick. 'Check. Then things didn't turn out exactly as you planned so you thought, *Hmm... Clara wanted to marry me in the past, so I think I'll return to Loggeen and pick up where we left off. I'll wine and dine her, I'll woo her, and she'll remember what we once had. I'll tell her I've changed. I'll apologise for the pain I caused and then everything will be fine.*'

Clara twisted her napkin beneath the table, the piece of material receiving a good portion of her pent-up frustration.

'It's always what *you* want, Virgil. *Your* career. *Your* plan. You haven't changed one bit and I'm not falling for you again.'

'But I *have* changed,' he said imploringly, his words urgent. Even his facial expression showed he thought he spoke the truth. 'I'm not as selfish as I was before.

I've learned, Clara. I really have learned how to put others first.'

She laughed with disbelief. 'Really?'

'Yes.'

'So why didn't you *ask* me? Why didn't you take my feelings into consideration before barrelling your way back into my life?'

'You would have said no.'

'And I'm still saying no.' Clara twisted the napkin tighter as she tried to hold on to her frustrations. 'You never listened in the past and you're not listening now, Virgil. I don't *want* to renew our past relationship. I'll work alongside you. I'll be professional and friendly. But nothing more.'

She paused and swallowed, focusing on her breathing in an effort to get her emotions under control. He didn't venture any comment and she was pleased about that. She needed to say what she'd come here to say and then she could leave—could return to her apartment, hug her dog and cry over what might have been for the very last time.

'I can't do this, Virgil. I can't do "you and me" again. It almost killed me last time—literally—and it's taken me years to get to where I am now. I just can't do it.'

Clara was certain the napkin in her hands was about to break, she was twisting it so much. Now that she'd told him how she felt—now that he could be sure there was no future for the two of them—she wasn't sure whether she should stay and wait for her meal or simply leave. However, she didn't want to leave him to pay for her meal. One of the other ways she'd changed was in taking care of herself. She was an emancipated woman and she liked it.

Deciding it was best to leave and pay for her uneaten meal on the way out, Clara shifted her chair back slightly to make her exit easier. It had been a whole fifteen seconds since she'd finished talking, and he hadn't made any comment.

'I'm sorry to skip out on dinner,' she stated as she started to rise from her chair, the napkin still in her hands. 'But I think it's best if I go.'

'What do you mean our break-up almost killed you *literally*? What—what happened?'

Clara's eyes widened in surprise. For some reason she'd thought he'd know about her accident, but how could he? It wasn't as though they moved in the same circles, except for bumping into the occasional friend from medical school, like Misty Fox.

'Oh. I guess you wouldn't know, would you?'

'Wouldn't know what?'

Clara sat back in her chair and met his gaze across the table. 'It was three weeks after you left for Montreal. I was involved in a horrific car accident.'

Virgil stared at her, his mouth dropping open slightly. 'Clara…' He shook his head. 'I didn't know.'

'How could you? You'd left.'

'That's unfair.'

'Granted,' she acquiesced. 'I was heading home from the hospital and a drunk driver side-swiped my car. I was in a bad way—pelvic fracture, lots of operations, lots of intensive therapy which lasted the better part of a year—and once I was back on my feet again I headed overseas myself for a few years.'

'Why did you go overseas?'

She closed her eyes and rubbed her forehead. 'Because of my parents…because of Arthur.'

She opened her eyes and looked at him, locking the memories away before they could take hold. Whenever she'd thought about the accident in the past, she'd usually ended up with a terrible migraine and a sleepless night.

'They all gave up so much for me. I moved back home. Mum looked after me. Arthur drove me to rehabilitation. Dad paid my hospital bills when my savings ran out. They all gave and gave and gave.'

'Probably because they love you.'

'And that's why I needed to go away—not only to try and find myself, to heal myself emotionally and mentally, but to give them all a break. I came back in time for Arthur's wedding.' She smiled when she thought of her brother and his lovely wife Maybelle. 'He's so happy.'

'I'm glad for Arthur—but what about you? Are *you* happy?'

Virgil's words were soft and caring, creating the beginnings of an intimate bubble between them.

Clara met and held his gaze. 'Yes.'

'*Really* happy? Not just happy enough?'

'Virgil…'

She sighed, trying not to lose herself in the depths of his wonderful eyes. She could see his concern for her— could see that he was genuinely interested in her answer. *Was* she happy?

'I'm content with my life. I like things the way they are. I have a good job, people who love and care about me, and a gorgeous dog who cuddles me and loves me unconditionally.'

They sat there, looking at each other for a long moment, lost in so many of the unspoken conversations they should have had over the years but never had.

Virgil was the first to look away, straightening the cutlery on the table and making way for their waiter to place their meals in front of them. The wine was poured and they began to eat, both clearly happy to have something else to focus on.

'I tried to call you,' he stated after a few minutes.

Clara swallowed her mouthful. 'What? When?'

She went to pull her smartphone from her pocket but he stopped her.

'Not tonight. I meant I tried to call you several months after I'd been in Montreal. You were right. That's what I was ringing to tell you. I wanted to tell you that you'd been right—that I'd ended up burning the candle at both ends, that I was overworked, exhausted and running myself ragged. I had no balance in my life any more and I realised, belatedly, that you were the person who had always provided me with that balance. Throughout medical school, during our internships… You were the one, Clara.'

He put down his fork and picked up his wine glass, taking a sip.

'I called you because I wanted to apologise, to tell you how incredibly sorry I was for the way I'd treated you and to ask if there was any possibility of us starting over.'

'Virgil.' She shook her head slowly. 'I didn't receive any calls from you.'

'When I called the phone service said the number was no longer valid. I tried emailing you. Still no response. I wrote to you but never received any reply.'

'Wait. You emailed me? Which email address? Where did you send the letter? I never received anything.'

Virgil stared at her for a long moment, his mind processing her words before he leaned his head back and slowly exhaled, unable to believe the weight which had just been lifted off his heart. She hadn't been ignoring him. She hadn't received his emails, hadn't received his letters—all of them begging her for another chance. A ray of hope sprang to life as he realised she hadn't rejected him at all.

'You didn't receive anything?' He slowly repeated her words.

'I was in hospital for months, and when I was discharged from the rehabilitation centre I moved in with my parents. Those first few months, Arthur took care of all my day-to-day issues, like paying bills, cancelling rental agreements, sorting things out with the hospital.'

'And you didn't receive anything from me?'

When she shook her head in confirmation he couldn't help but smile. It was short-lived.

'Wait.' He held up one hand. 'That means you never knew how sorry I was for the horrible way I'd treated you.' He shook his head sadly. 'My behaviour was arrogant, thoughtless and downright rude, and I'm *so* sorry, Clara. You deserved better.'

This news also made him realise why she wasn't willing to give him a chance now.

'I always thought you didn't reply as a way of telling me it was over. You were giving me the brush-off, letting me know that I'd blown it once and for all, and that there was no chance of a reconciliation.'

Hope continued to increase within him.

'Oh? So you thought that as you'd rejected me it was my turn to reject you?' Clearly he didn't know her at all. 'You thought I was that petty and wouldn't give you another chance?'

'I didn't say that.' He picked up his fork and started to eat his dinner again. 'But now that you know the truth—that I did try and apologise—does it make you want to change your mind about giving me another chance now?'

Her fork clattered to her plate as she stared at him in astonishment. 'Weren't you listening before?'

'I was listening,' he returned after finishing his mouthful. 'I heard everything you said. But it doesn't mean I'm going to stop hoping.'

'Hoping that there might be something other than professional friendship between us?' Clara shook her head. 'Stop hoping, Virgil, and just accept that this is the way it's going to be from now on.'

'But *why*?'

He needed to know. He felt certain there was something she wasn't telling him. But if he pressed her too much right now, she might stand up and walk out of the restaurant. He wanted to get things sorted out between them—to know exactly where he stood. He knew her of old, and he couldn't shake the sense that she wasn't telling him everything.

Clara put her knife and fork together on her plate, indicating she was done with her meal even though there was still half of it left.

'I think I should leave.'

'No. Wait. Clara, please stay.'

'Why?'

'Because…' He racked his brain, trying to think of a good reason. 'Because I want to tell you about my daughter. I have a phone full of pictures.'

She shook her head. 'I don't want to see them. Professional friends, Virgil.'

'Does Cedric have children?'

Clara frowned at the mention of the obstetrician at the Specialist Centre. 'Yes.'

'Have you seen pictures of them? Met them?'

'They've come to the Specialist Centre on occasion, yes.'

'So you've met them.'

'Yes.'

'What about Jane? Your receptionist? Does *she* have children?'

Sighing with impatience, she held up her hand. 'Yes, Jane has children. Yes, I've met them.'

'Then why, purely from a professional friendship point of view, can't you stay to let me be the proud, boasting daddy and show you some pictures of my Rosie?'

There was a hint of hurt in his tone and she knew she'd capitulate—but only because he'd made a valid point.

'OK. Fine.' She held out her hand. 'Give me your smartphone.'

Looking at pictures of an old boyfriend's child with another woman wasn't her idea of a fun evening, but with Virgil working at the Specialist Centre and hospital, there was every chance that Clara would eventually meet his daughter. Best to get the initial pain of accepting he'd had a child with someone else over and done with now.

Grinning, he was quick to find the pictures of his little girl and pass his phone to her.

'That first one was taken today. She's a cheeky thing.'

Clara stared at the photograph of the little girl with blonde hair, her eyes as perfectly blue as her father's. 'She's gorgeous, Virgil. How old did you say she was?'

'Three. My cheeky three-year-old. It doesn't end with the terrible twos!' He chuckled at his own joke and she nodded.

'Arthur has twin girls, only eighteen months old, and they get into so much mischief.' She continued to scroll through the photos on his phone. 'So I take it your wife was blonde?' The words were out before she could stop them and she quickly handed Virgil back his phone. 'Sorry. It's none of my business.'

'But it is, Clara—or at least I want it to be.'

'Virgil, we're just professional—'

'Diana. That was her name. She was French-Canadian and she reminded me a lot of you.'

'Really? Except that I'm very much Australian and have dark hair,' she felt compelled to point out.

She wanted to hear what Virgil had to say about the woman he'd married, but by the same token she didn't want to know anything. Knowing more about Virgil's life during the past six years would only make her more intrigued by him, and that was the last thing she wanted. Her life was great the way it was—wasn't it?

'Personality-wise, I mean. She liked old movies, like you. She liked the same authors you did. She loved to sing off-key in the shower and was always late for appointments.' He smiled sadly.

'Were you happy with her?' Again the question seemed to spring from her lips without thought.

'In the beginning, yes.' Virgil took a sip of his wine. 'After I didn't hear back from you I was—depressed. Lonely. Diana was a nurse, and we became friends. She helped me to heal a broken heart.' Another sip of his wine. 'Our wedding was a pure impulse at the end of a clinical convention in Las Vegas. Tacky, I know, but it happens.'

'Chapel of Love?' she asked, trying to keep her emotional distance from what he was saying by injecting some humour.

'Something like that. Anyway, we decided to try and make a go of it.' He put his glass down and leaned forward. 'I thought there was no hope of reconciling with you, Clara. I had to move on with my life, try and find some new form of "normal".'

'Just like I had to move on with *my* life—to heal from my accident and travel overseas in order to find my new life.' She nodded, her words soft. 'I *do* understand, Virgil.'

When he reached for her hand she let him take it, linking their fingers together. When he gazed into her eyes she didn't look away, but instead saw the sincerity of his convictions. Perhaps she'd judged him too harshly. Perhaps he *had* changed. But if he truly had, did that mean she should give him another chance?

Her heart was screaming *yes*, but her mind… Her mind was definitely not saying no, and that was a scary prospect to consider. *Was* there a future for herself and Virgil just waiting to be explored? *Should* she take the chance? She honestly didn't know.

CHAPTER FOUR

WHEN CLARA ARRIVED home from her dinner with Virgil she sent her brother a text message to check if he was free to talk. A moment later her phone rang.

'Hey, sis.'

'You busy?'

'Nope. Just waiting up for my wife to get home from her long shift at the hospital. The wine is chilling and I'm about to draw her a long and relaxing bubble bath.'

'And the girls?'

'Sound asleep—at the moment.' Arthur chuckled. 'But tonight Daddy's on duty and Mummy gets to relax.'

Clara sighed. 'See? Why can't I find a guy like you?'

She sat down on the lounge and a moment later, her dog, Fuzzy-Juzzy, jumped up beside her, expecting to be patted. Clara didn't disappoint the dog.

'You're all about the caring and the listening and the supportive attitude.'

Arthur chuckled. 'I know. I'm quite a catch—as I remind Maybelle on a semi-regular basis. Anyway, little sis, what's up?'

'Why would anything be up?'

'Because you don't usually call me this late at night, sounding so serious.'

'Uh—well—I had dinner with Virgil tonight.'

There was a momentary silence on the other end of the line, and for a second she thought her brother had hung up.

'Arthur?'

'I'm here. I just didn't think you were going to have anything to do with him—apart from being professional, I mean. At least that's what you told me before he arrived back in town.'

The protective note in Arthur's tone was unmistakable.

'It wasn't a romantic dinner.'

She tried to block out the mental vision of them sitting at that table for two, fingers linked, staring into each other's eyes. What had she been *thinking*? That was the problem. She hadn't been thinking. All she'd been feeling at that moment when she'd let him link his hand with hers, was that she'd missed him. Even though she'd been through therapy, even though she'd tried new things, met new people, done everything and anything she could in order to pull her life back together, at the end of the day the simple and honest fact was that she'd missed him.

Of course there was no way she could say that to Arthur, or else he'd don his protective big brother superhero cape and stand guard over her as he'd done in the past. She didn't need him to do that any more. She was more than capable of donning her own superhero cape.

Clara cleared her throat. 'We—ah—we simply needed to set out some ground rules so we know where each other stands.'

'And where *does* the almighty Virgil Arterton stand? Still on his pedestal? With a pole stuck up his—?'

'Actually, he was very apologetic.'

Arthur snorted. 'I'll bet he was.'

'Arthur…' She hesitated for a moment, unsure how to ask what she needed to ask. 'Virgil mentioned that several months after he'd been in Montreal, he tried to contact me again. Do you know anything about that?'

'No!' The surprise in Arthur's tone was clear.

'He said he tried to call but the number was disconnected.'

'He would have tried your old number at your old apartment.'

'He also said that he tried to email me and even wrote me a letter.'

'He did?'

'You seriously don't know anything about this?

'I don't. I really don't. Back when you were in hospital I cancelled your phone, your internet connection and your lease. I had your mail redirected to Mum and Dad's house for six months. I figured six months was enough time to change over any details. With regard to your emails, I think the only email address you had at the time was the one at Melbourne General, and that was shut down when you stopped working there.'

She continued to stroke Juzzy as she mulled over what her brother was saying. 'So you and Mum and Dad weren't protecting me from Virgil?'

'Honestly, Clara, if an email or a letter from Virgil had found its way to me, I would have given it to you. I would have discussed the possible emotional outcome with Mum and Dad, and probably your doctors, before giving it to you, but I would never have kept it from you. Neither would Mum or Dad. We love you, yes. We want to protect you, yes, but we wouldn't have hidden something like that from you.'

'That's what I thought. I just needed to check—just needed to be sure.'

Her phone had been disconnected, her email address had been wiped from the hospital server and her mail redirection had probably expired by the time Virgil had tried to get in touch.

'OK.' She heaved a heavy sigh. 'Thanks.'

'Are you OK? You don't want to talk about things some more? You could come down and join us for a drink. Maybelle won't mind. She loves seeing you and—'

Clara smiled. 'I'm OK, Arthur. Humpty Dumpty *has* been put back together again, remember?'

'I know, but I'm always going to worry about you—and especially where Virgil Arterton is concerned.'

Clara felt the warmth of his brotherly love. 'I'm fine,' she reiterated, before signing off with their usual farewell. 'Love you, bro.'

'Love you, too, sis.'

Clara disconnected the call and looked down at Fuzzy-Juzzy.

'Virgil tried to contact me, to apologise and ask for a second chance. What do you make of that, Juzzy?'

The dog's answer was to snuggle in closer.

'All these years and now he's back. I guess it's time for me to start walking through the next chapter of my life. The chapter where Virgil and I are nothing more than professional friends, consulting about patients together and being polite.'

So why couldn't she stop thinking about the way he'd held her hand, the way he'd looked into her eyes? She'd seen his hope that they'd be able to patch up the past and move forward into a happier future. He was wearing his heart on his sleeve and that was yet another indication that he'd changed.

'I just need to walk very carefully,' she told her dog. 'Very carefully indeed.'

* * *

During the week following their dinner—Virgil's first week working at the Specialist Centre as well as at Victory Hospital—Clara was surprised at how little she actually saw him. Twice she'd seen him walking through the corridors of the Specialist Centre, but both times he'd been deep in conversation with Cedric. The two men had nodded politely, acknowledging her, before continuing to discuss a patient they shared.

Perhaps this could work after all. Virgil had listened, and was clearly being the professional friend she'd asked him to be.

So why did the knowledge make her feel forlorn, as though she was missing out on something really special?

She shook the thought away and went back to work.

On the weekend she was rostered for an evening shift in the ED, and as Virgil didn't hold any clinics at the weekend, there was no real chance of her running into him.

'And even if he *is* at the hospital he'll probably be up on the surgical wards, doing a quick check on his patients before going home to spend time with his daughter,' she told Juzzy. 'Nothing to worry about.'

Clara finished pinning her hair into a bun at the nape of her neck.

'He has his professional life, I have mine, and that's that. No reason to feel forlorn. No reason to think I'm missing out on something great. I'm happy with my life the way it is.'

She nuzzled closer to the fluffy Pomeranian, receiving a lick on her cheek in return.

'I love you, too, Juzzy,' she told the dog.

After putting Juzzy to bed, Clara headed out of the apartment and drove to the hospital.

Her shift turned out to be an average one for a Saturday night. Kids with coughs, teenagers who had been drinking too much and a few patients with broken bones.

An hour before her shift was due to end, early Sunday morning, Larissa, one of the ED nurses, beckoned her over to the nurses' station.

'Just received a call from the paramedics. They're on their way in with Michelle DeCosta, who's been complaining of—'

'Abdominal pains,' Clara finished for her, and nodded. 'Michelle's one of my patients. I saw her in the clinic last week and made an appointment for her to see Dr Arterton as soon as possible. Virgil was able to squeeze her in yesterday, but apparently she didn't show. I was going to follow-up her no-show on Monday.'

'Clearly the pains have become more intense. Do you want me to call Dr Arterton in for the consult?'

'Let's order some tests first—see what we're dealing with.'

Clara didn't want to bother Virgil.

She turned and headed towards a treatment room, wanting to ensure it was ready for Michelle's impending arrival, but after a few steps she stopped and sighed.

Michelle suffered from acute anxiety. Even when Clara had told her patient she was referring her to Virgil, Michelle had had a minor panic attack. Clara had managed to calm the woman down, telling her that Virgil was an exceptional surgeon, that he would take good care of her and that Victory Hospital was fortunate he'd come to operate there. She didn't want Michelle having another anxiety attack now.

Clara turned back to Larissa. 'On second thoughts,

call Virgil in now. When Michelle gets here I'll order an abdominal ultrasound and see if my suspicions are confirmed.'

'What do you think it is?'

'Gallstones.'

'I'll call him in right away.' Larissa picked up the phone.

When the ambulance arrived Clara was waiting for Michelle, ready to care for her patient. As the paramedics wheeled Michelle's stretcher into the hospital, Clara realised Michelle was slap-bang in the middle of a panic attack.

'She's refused all medication,' Adrian, Michelle's husband, told her. 'She doesn't want to take anything—either for the pain or to help calm her nerves.'

He was clearly worried about his wife, trying to hold her hand as the stretcher was taken through to the treatment room.

'I know she doesn't have any allergies so I'll draw up some Methoxyflurane—which should help calm her down long enough to get some tests done.'

Clara headed over to Michelle, eager to calm the woman down.

'Clara. Clara! I'm so happy you're here. Why *are* you here? This is the hospital. I'm sorry I didn't see Dr Arterton.' Michelle spoke fast, her words tumbling out in a rush. 'I was too scared. I was—I was shaking and unable to move. Adrian tried to get me to go but I was scared, Clara. I was *so* scared.'

Even now Michelle was shaking. She was white, her breathing was rapid, and even if Clara had wanted to check the other woman's blood pressure there was no way she'd be able to get a cuff onto her arm.

'It's OK, Michelle.' Clara hooked up the oxygen and

held the mask out to Michelle. 'Nice deep breaths. You can do it.'

'You're not angry?' Michelle checked, accepting the mask from Clara.

'Of course not. What I *am* concerned about is the pain you're in.' Clara spoke in soothing tones, placing her hand on the woman's shoulder in a show of support. 'I'm here, and I'm not going to leave you until we know exactly what's causing the pain and how it's going to be treated. OK? Now, I want you to try and focus on your breathing. Slow it down. In and out.'

Her words were calming, yet firm. She needed Michelle to focus and thankfully, as Michelle held her gaze, the two of them practised breathing in slowly and then exhaling slowly.

Once her breathing was more steady, the nursing staff were able to take Michelle's vitals and Clara was able to give the injection of Methoxyflurane, which would not only help to keep Michelle calm, but also assist with the abdominal pain.

By the time Virgil arrived she had the results of Michelle's abdominal ultrasound, which confirmed her diagnosis of gallstones.

'Clara! What are you doing here?' he asked when he saw her standing at the nurses' station.

His tone had resonated with a hint of delight at seeing her so unexpectedly and he'd smiled. Darn it—*why* had he smiled? She hated it when he smiled, because when he did it caused the butterflies in her stomach to churn with excitement. She didn't want to be aware of his nearness, his scent, of the way he held his body so perfectly that his polo shirt pulled across his broad shoulders. She didn't want to be this attracted to him.

'It's my bi-monthly shift in Emergency at the hospital.'

She didn't want to dwell on anything but the main reason why *he* was here. She didn't want chit-chat—she just wanted to focus on getting Michelle sorted out. She handed him Michelle's file and began discussing the case.

Virgil read the results of the scans and tests Clara had ordered. 'She has anxiety?'

'I've been treating her for the past two years. She's actually much better than previously, but coming to hospital and being out of her comfort zone has triggered her anxiety.'

'Of course.' He held Michelle's notes in his hand. 'As you're Michelle's GP, I think it might be best if you come with me when I go and talk to her. That way she'll have your reassuring presence to fall back on when she learns she'll need to have surgery.'

Clara nodded, pleased he was thinking about the emotional welfare of their patient rather than playing the part of brisk, arrogant surgeon.

As they headed to Michelle's room, he asked, 'Have you told her the diagnosis?'

'I've told her she has gallstones and that she may need surgery.'

'How did she react to that news?'

'She started to hyperventilate. But it didn't last too long and she was able to control her breathing. Last time I checked, she was sleeping.'

He sighed. 'Unfortunately, we're going to need to wake her.'

Together they woke Michelle, who was far more relaxed now than when she'd arrived. Her husband Adrian sat in the corner.

'Hello, Michelle. I'm Virgil Arterton, the new general surgeon here at Victory Hospital. It appears, as I'm sure you've been told, that you have gallstones.'

Michelle nodded, tears springing to her eyes. 'I'm sorry I didn't have the scan sooner. I'm sorry to be causing all this trouble. And I'm sorr—'

'It's perfectly all right,' Virgil interrupted, putting his hand on hers and instantly soothing his patient. 'One of the gallstones is quite large, measuring in at almost one centimetre. The other isn't quite as big, but both will need to be removed.'

'H-how?' The worry in Michelle's voice was prominent.

'It'll be a short procedure in which I'll remove your gallbladder. It's all done in the day surgery unit, so you'll be able to go home the same day.'

'What?' Michelle's eyes widened at this information. 'The same day? But what if I have problems—what if the pain comes back and—?'

Her breathing started to accelerate again and she reached blindly for her husband's hand. Adrian was instantly on his feet, taking her hand in his and trying to soothe her.

'Would you prefer to say in overnight?' Clara asked. 'That way we can keep you under observation for twenty-four hours after the operation. And once you're home we can put you on the district nursing roster. I can also come and do a house-call to check on you,' she offered.

She glanced at Virgil and the unspoken communication they'd used to share, seemed to kick in. With one look she was able to convey to him that whilst Michelle indeed only required a small operation, it was her anxiety which was the bigger threat.

'That sounds like an excellent solution, Dr Lewis.' He nodded in Clara's direction before addressing his comments to Michelle. 'I'll admit you to the ward now, and then I can organise a theatre for later this afternoon. All being well, you can go home tomorrow.' He smiled at his patient, his tone reassuring.

Michelle looked from Clara to Virgil and then to Adrian, who nodded encouragingly. 'Uh… OK…'

'You're not alone, Michelle. We're here to look after you,' Clara reassured her, before she and Virgil headed back to the nurses' station.

Throughout the consult Clara had been aware of Virgil's every move, and she had to admit that his bedside manner was exemplary. Was he trying to show her how much he had changed? If so, it was working—because she *was* noticing. It seemed the chauvinistic, arrogant man he'd been all those years ago had been replaced by someone who was calm, caring and absolutely charming. He clearly didn't see his patients as just a number on a file, but rather as the individuals they were.

They left Michelle in the care of the nurses who were organising her transfer to the ward, while Clara helped Virgil with the necessary paperwork to book an operating theatre for later that day and contact the anaesthetist.

'Where would I be without you?' he crooned as he leaned back in the chair and flexed his arms above his head.

The action caused the polo shirt he was wearing to pull tightly across his upper arms and chest, and Clara found it difficult to look away. Clearly, he'd kept in shape. When she finally raised her gaze to meet his, it was to find him regarding her with an interested smile.

'Like what you see?' he teased.

Clara felt an instant heat come to her cheeks as he flexed his muscles in the familiar pose body builders used. Although it was early Sunday morning in the ED, there were still quite a few of the night staff around to witness him teasing her.

'Behave,' she warned him, looking away and straightening some papers on the desk.

She needed to be doing something other than looking at the way that shirt fitted him to perfection. She had so many memories of him teasing her this way, of joking together, of laughing and enjoying themselves, and until that moment she hadn't realised how much she'd missed that easy camaraderie they'd shared. She'd missed him. Missed his friendship, missed his calming manner, missed the way he would stare into her eyes and make her feel as though she were the most important person in the world to him.

Clara glanced at him over her shoulder, only to discover he was watching her intently, the smile still in place.

'Do I really need to behave?'

'Yes.'

'Why?' He glanced around. 'No one's looking—and, besides, it used to be *me* who was always telling *you* to behave.'

'Untrue,' she declared instantly.

'*You* were the one who had the idea to put sticky tape over all the taps in our lab at medical school. *You* were the one with the party trick of drinking a whole glass of water whilst doing a handstand. And I distinctly remember several of us turning up to ward round wearing cartoon masks.'

'OK. OK.' She couldn't help but smile at the memories he was recounting.

Virgil pointed at her. 'Another one of your brilliant ideas.'

He chuckled, the warm sound washing over her.

'And *I* was the one who took the blame for them all—well, for the sticking tape over the taps, at least.'

'The cartoon masks were when we were doing a rotation in Paediatrics. The kids loved them,' she felt compelled to point out.

Virgil stood and looked down into her upturned face. 'We used to have so much fun together, Clara.'

'We did, but we're not medical students any more.'

He rolled his eyes. 'Tell me about it. I found another grey hair yesterday—on my chest!'

Clara couldn't help but laugh at the disgusted look on his face. 'Oh, Virgil. We have so many wonderful shared memories.'

'We do.' He placed one hand on her shoulder. 'Which is why I really want to be more than just nodding-in-the-corridor professional friends with you.'

'But you're wanting something I can't give.'

'All I want is a second chance—and you can give me that. A chance to be your friend again. A *real* friend, not just an acquaintance.'

'Friends?' She mulled it over. A large part of her wanted so desperately to say yes, but she needed to protect her heart. 'It's not as easy as that.'

'Yes, it is.'

She closed her eyes for a moment before meeting his gaze. 'You broke my heart. You really broke it, Virgil. So much pain…' Tears welled in her eyes.

He shook his head. 'It wasn't me…it wasn't the *real* me. My mind was overtaken by my own stupidity, my own arrogance, my own self-importance and I hurt you. But I've worked on those negative qualities, Clara. I'm a wiser, more well-rounded person nowadays. Please?'

His words had been soft and intimate, yet imploring. She could see the sincerity in his eyes and she knew she was about to capitulate—against her better judgement.

'OK.'

'OK? OK, you'll give me a second chance?'

'To be my *friend*.'

'Yeah. *Yeah*. That's good. That's excellent.'

And before she knew what he was about he'd drawn her close and hugged her.

'Thank you. You won't regret it.'

'I'd better not,' she mumbled against his chest, doing her best not become hypnotised by his alluring scent.

Although he'd surprised her with the hug, the warmth from his body meshed with hers and she closed her eyes, savouring every second to think about later.

'Now, let me go, you big oaf, before someone sees us.'

'And what if they do?' He released his hold on her and shrugged one shoulder. 'We're just two old friends enjoying a quick hug. Nothing wrong with that.'

'Hmm…' She frowned at him and couldn't help but laugh. She hoped it was true—that her old friend was back—because she had missed him. She'd missed the good times, the sad times and the quiet times.

'And my first act of friendship is to ask you over to my house for dinner next weekend.'

'Virgil, take it easy.'

He held up his hands to ward off her words. 'I know. You think I'm rushing things.'

'A bit, yeah.'

'But I really want you to meet Rosie. She's my world, Clara, and I want to share that with you. Oh, and you can meet my housekeeper, Gwenda. She's nice, too.'

'Will you be cooking?'

'No.'

'Good. You were always really bad.'

'Then you'll be pleased to know I've improved.'

He seemed to be filled with energy, his eyes alive with excitement at the thought of her coming to dinner at his house and meeting his daughter.

'But Gwenda will be cooking. I have a clinic at the Specialist Centre on Saturday morning and I promised Rosie we'd go to the park in the afternoon.' He angled his head to the side and raised an eyebrow. 'You could come to the park if you'd like? Then we could go back to my house for dinner.'

'Let's just take it one small step at a time. Besides, I have house calls.'

'Right.' He nodded. 'And Michelle will probably be on that list, won't she?' he stated.

'More than likely.'

'Good.' He paused, his stance changing from her cheeky friend, to the serious surgeon. 'It's *good* that anxiety disorders are now more widely accepted by practitioners as well as the community at large.'

'Hear, hear.'

'Actually, would you like to be there for her surgery? I'm sure if she saw you in the ante-chamber of the surgical suite she'd be more comfortable. She has a lot of confidence in you, Clara.'

'You sound surprised.'

'No. I'm not at all surprised that you're a great GP— that you not only care about your patients but they care about you in return and value your opinions. You made the right decision about your career and I'm glad it's worked out for you.'

'Really?'

'Yes. When I'm wrong, I say I'm wrong—and I was wrong.'

Clara clutched her hands to her chest as she looked up at him. 'Thank you, Virgil. That means a lot.'

'So… Michelle's surgery? Think you'll be able to make it?'

As she pondered coming back to the hospital this af-

ternoon to see Michelle, after doing a full night in the
ED, she began to realise how tired she was. Still, it wasn't
every day she received an invitation to watch a surgical
procedure—even if it was just the removal of a gallbladder.

'Yes. I'll be there. You're right. It will help Michelle.'

'You really are a kind and caring doctor, Clara. I'm
proud of you.'

As he headed off to do whatever it was he needed to
do, and as Clara finished her shift and headed home to get
some sleep, she couldn't believe how wonderful it felt—
not only to have her friend Virgil back in her life—but to
hear that he was proud of her. That meant a lot.

CHAPTER FIVE

WHY AM I happy that I have his approval? That he's proud of me? It's not like I need his approval to be content with my life. I'm already content...so why does it matter?

Did she still care what Virgil thought of her? *Did* she still care that much about his opinions? She had in the past—until he'd changed from Dr Jekyll to Mr Hyde.

She opened the door to her apartment, greeted instantly by Fuzzy-Juzzy.

'Oh, hello, darling. Hello!' She picked up the dog and cuddled her close before letting the fuzzy Pomeranian go. 'Yes. It's breakfast time. Were you a good girl, sleeping all night in your bed or did you sleep on my bed?'

Clara put her bag and keys down, then checked her bedroom. Sure enough, there was a little round spot in the middle of her bed where her dog had slept. At the end of the bed was a step stool, so that Juzzy could get up and down from Clara's bed. When Clara really didn't want the dog to disturb her sleep, she would move the stool away, but on nights when she was at the hospital she left it there, pleased that the dog missed her enough to curl up on her bed. It made her feel loved.

There was a knock at her door and she quickly went to answer it. Juzzy was equally excited.

Clara was pleased to find her sister-in-law on the other side.

'Morning!' Maybelle said, and gave Clara a hug. 'We're just about to take the girls and the dogs for a walk. Shall we take Juzzy for you so you can get some sleep?'

'Oh…that would be wonderful.' Clara sighed and went to get Juzzy's leash. 'I *love* having family living in the same building.'

'How was your shift?' Maybelle asked as Clara tried to clip the leash to a very excited Juzzy.

'Good.'

As she said the word Clara couldn't help but smile as memories of Virgil teasing her, Virgil laughing with her, Virgil being absolutely delighted she was giving him a second chance, flashed through her mind.

'Wait. What was *that*?' Maybelle queried.

'What? What was what?'

'You were doing that little half-smile—that smile you do when you're secretly excited about something.'

'No, I wasn't.'

'Yeah, you were.' Maybelle nodded, then gasped as realisation dawned. 'Was *Virgil* at the hospital?' she asked.

'Yes. I had a patient with gallstones. He was called in for a consult.' Clara waved her words away as though it had all been nothing but completely professional.

'But—*Virgil*. I've seen him around the hospital, Clara. He's gorgeous.' At Clara's raised eyebrows, Maybelle continued. 'But definitely not my type. My type is my husband.'

Clara smiled at her friend. 'Yes, Virgil was there. Yes, we chatted. Yes, it was…nice.'

'Exciting! Are you going to give him another chance?' Maybelle asked.

'Another chance to break my heart?' Clara stared sceptically at her friend. 'No. A chance to be my friend again, yes. I mean, we're working together, and we have so much history, and we know each other so well—'

'And he's totally your type,' Maybelle added softly.

Clara sighed. 'He *was* my type of man, once upon a time.'

'Maybe he has really changed. People do. *I* did.'

'But you're you and you were forced to change—forced into a life you never really asked for until you were able to find your way back to total happiness.'

'Perhaps Virgil thought he *had* to change—that he had to impress all the other arrogant surgeons and be just like them in order to get ahead in the surgical world?'

Clara frowned. 'Hmm… I never thought of it like that before.'

'Granted, the way he treated you was horrible and heartbreaking, but what if he really has changed, Clara?'

She sighed again. 'If he has, then taking it very, *very* slowly is the only way to go. I might like laughing with him, being friends with him, but I don't know if I can ever trust him again.'

The door to the downstairs apartment closed and the noise level immediately rose as Arthur pushed the double pram, complete with chattering little girls, into the entryway. Their dogs barked with excitement and Juzzy joined in.

'It's a good decision to take things slow,' Maybelle said with a determined look as she took Juzzy's leash and allowed herself to be pulled away. 'I'm glad you've agreed to be friends. Now, eat breakfast and sleep. Doctor's orders.'

Clara closed the door and couldn't help but do a little dance. It was exciting to know Virgil was back to being her friend. 'And *just* your friend,' she warned herself aloud as she went to the kitchen.

As she ate some food, she reflected on how he'd smiled at her, and how she'd been moved by the sincerity of his expressions and impressed with his treatment of Michelle. He wasn't the same man she'd known during medical school, but he seemed to be a new and improved version, one with wisdom—and another grey hair on his chest.

She smiled at the thought as she brushed her teeth and fell into bed, pulling the covers around her and feeling just as happy and secure as she'd felt when being hugged in Virgil's arms.

'Virgil...' She sighed with contentment before drifting off to sleep.

Clara managed to return to the hospital in time for Michelle's gallbladder surgery, and saw her patient relaxing when she realised Clara would be present.

'Thank you. *Both* of you,' Michelle said, looking at Clara and then Virgil before closing her eyes and allowing the anaesthetist to do his job.

The surgery was completed without complications, and as Michelle was taken through to recovery, Virgil wrote up the notes.

'How was that?' he asked as he added his signature and closed the notes.

'Watching keyhole surgery?' Clara gave him two thumbs up. 'A perfectly fun way to spend an afternoon.'

Virgil laughed at her antics and Clara grinned. It was so nice to feel as though she had her friend back. 'Thanks again for letting me be here. I know it made a difference to Michelle.'

'You may be surprised by this, Clara, but there are quite a lot of surgeons who aren't just scalpel-happy jerks. Sure, there are the arrogant holier-than-thou types, and

for a while I felt I had to be one of them in order to impress them, but at the end of the day I do what I do in
order to help people. There are plenty of us who actually
care about our patients.'

'Huh. I *am* surprised. But I'm glad you're one of them.'

As they exited the theatre, heading to the change
rooms, she was highly aware of her *friend* walking beside
her. Highly aware that he was incredibly tall and somehow
looked incredibly sexy in theatre scrubs. Highly aware of
the way his hand almost brushed hers. Highly aware of
that subtle spicy scent he wore. She didn't want to be—
she wanted to view him as she had in medical school, as
her very good-looking friend who was there to support
her, to have fun and to laugh with her.

Upon reaching the changing room doors, he paused.
'Listen, are you free to grab a cup of coffee in the cafeteria before heading home?'

She smiled up at him as she put in the code for the female changing rooms. Opening the door, she shook her
head. 'I've got so many household chores to do before tomorrow morning, the most important of which is washing my clothes so I have something to wear to work in
the morning.' She tilted her head to the side. 'Not *all* of
us employ housekeepers, you know.'

'It's only because I have a child who can't be left alone,'
he defended quickly, but grinned at her as he put in the
code for the male changing rooms. 'OK. I guess I'll see
you around the Specialist Centre and—' he proffered as
he opened the door '—hopefully wearing clean clothes.'

He winked at her, his teasing tone rushing over her
with delight.

Entering the changing rooms, she walked to the bench
and sat down because her knees were starting to wobble.

Friends. They were friends. Friends *only* and at her insistence. It was great to know that Virgil wanted more—that he wanted to give their relationship another go and that he had visions of spending the rest of his life with her—but that was far too much for her to compute and accept right now.

He was back in her life. She'd accepted that. They were giving their friendship another go. She'd accepted that too. And although she was attracted to him—although she was being driven insane by his scent and her heart rate increased whenever he winked or smiled or laughed with her—that didn't mean she had to rush headlong into a full reunion with him.

'He hurt you. He hurt you badly,' she whispered to herself, needing to find logic and common sense in her crazy new world. 'You've been friends before and you can be friends again. Nothing more.'

With that, she drew in a deep, cleansing breath and stood up, heading to her locker so she could get changed and head home. She sniffed the clothes she'd worn to the hospital and screwed up her nose. Yep. Definitely time to do the laundry.

For some reason the thought of not looking her best, the thought of not smelling like a sweet-scented rose, especially when she was around Virgil, made her feel highly self-conscious.

It's not for Virgil, she told herself as she drove home. *It's for yourself. Dress for yourself. Wear your hair the way you want to.*

And if Virgil found her irresistibly attractive, then so be it.

Monday and Tuesday were both hectic days, and Clara was glad when she arrived home that she could eat dinner then fall into bed, resting and relaxing with Juzzy by her side.

On Wednesday, she had a patient cancel just before lunch.

'You can take a whole forty minutes,' Jane told her.

'It's sad that that's the most exciting thing to happen to me all week,' Clara said as she grabbed her wallet and headed out through the door.

Around the Specialist Centre and the hospital were several cafés and novelty shops, as well as two florists. She'd just stepped outside the centre when someone called her name. She turned to see Virgil heading her way.

'Where are you off to?' he asked.

'A patient cancelled and I have forty minutes for lunch.'

'Whoa! Pure luxury,' he exaggerated as he fell into step beside her. 'Mind some company?'

'Sure. Who did you have in mind?'

He groaned at her lame joke. 'You're *funny*. Hey, how's Michelle doing?'

'Really great. Once she arrived home her anxiety settled down and she's letting her husband pamper her. I *have* sent you a professional progress report with words to that effect.'

'Good to hear. So, what do you feel like for lunch? Salad? Burger and fries? Chicken roll?'

'Ice-cream and fudge,' she stated, and pointed to Marni's café, which was next to one of the florists.

'Ice-cream for lunch? I should have guessed. After all, I do remember you eating a whole litre of fudge ripple when studying for exams.'

'I like ice-cream. It's not a crime.'

'No, it is not.' He held the door to Marni's café open and together they went in. 'I've never had anything mixed in with my ice-cream before.'

'You do *not* know what you're missing out on, buddy. You're going to love it.'

'I don't know… I don't mind having things on the side, but mixed in?' Virgil frowned and shook his head.

'Go on. Live life on the edge.' She chuckled before perusing the selection of ice-creams.

'Yeah. I need to do more crazy things in my life. OK. You've talked me into it.'

It was nice. Nice to be around Clara, nice to hear her laugh, nice to tease her, and incredible to see her smiling—not only smiling but smiling at *him*.

When he'd seen her in Melbourne at the retrieval examinations, he'd really had second thoughts about moving back to Loggeen, but now, being with her, sitting opposite her whilst eating ice-cream and enjoying an easy camaraderie, warmed his heart.

Perhaps there was a chance that he could win her back. Although he'd blurted out his true intentions when they'd had dinner, and had thought such a declaration would send her running for the hills, here he was, sitting with her, eating ice-cream with bits of fudge mixed through it.

After Diana's death, when he'd been left alone to raise their daughter, he'd gone to therapy, needing to find some semblance of meaning to his life. Yes, his work made him happy. Yes, he loved spending time with his little girl. But even with Diana, there had always been one aspect of true happiness which had been missing, and he'd realised, belatedly, that Clara was that one aspect.

He was content with his life—just as she'd told him she was content with hers—however, there was more to life than simply being content. What about being incredibly happy? What about finding that one person who was your other half? Spending time with them, sharing the ups and downs with them, growing old together with them?

Through his therapy sessions he'd come to realise that the only time in his life he'd been truly happy was when he'd been with Clara. It wasn't that he'd relied on her for his own happiness, but rather that being with her had enhanced his joy.

Although Diana had helped him through a difficult time in his life, they hadn't had the solid foundation of friendship he'd needed in which to succeed at marriage. If Diana hadn't passed away, he knew their marriage would have required a lot of work. Even then, there would have been no guarantee that it wouldn't have ended in divorce. That hadn't been an easy realisation for him to deal with, but slowly he'd come to terms with it.

'Happiness isn't a myth,' his therapist had told him. 'But happiness *is* made up of a lot of small things—and being content with who you are as a person, is a big part of that. Finding someone who is content within themselves, someone you're compatible with, someone you just can't wait to share good or bad news with, knowing they'll be there for you no matter what, is the difficult part.'

And that was when Virgil had had his epiphany. He'd already found that one person, and he'd let her go. Diana's death had taught him something else as well—that life was too short not to go after what you really wanted, and *he* really wanted to spend the rest of his life with Clara.

'You're frowning at your ice-cream,' she pointed out as she finished her delicious confectionery.

'Huh?' He jerked his head up and looked at her. 'Sorry. Deep in thought.'

'Ooh. Deep thoughts are dangerous—which is why I don't mind the occasional brain-freeze. It helps me not to think too deeply.'

He chuckled at her words.

'You don't like the fudge mixed in, do you?' she asked.

Virgil slowly shook his head. 'I don't, but I know Rosie would. I'll have to bring her here to try it out.'

'At least you're not letting your own dislikes influence her. Let me know when you're bringing her here and I'll join you.'

'You will?' He was surprised at her words.

'Sure. I never pass up the opportunity to eat fudge and ice-cream.'

'All right, then.' He held out his hand and Clara shook it. 'It's a date.' He paused, still holding her hand, still needing that contact, still delighting in the softness of her skin. 'You *are* still coming to dinner this Saturday?'

'Yeah.'

She nodded and he released her hand, then watched as Clara eyed his half-finished ice-cream as it melted in the bowl.

'Are you going to finish that?'

Chuckling, he passed the bowl to her. 'Here you go, you ice-cream-a-holic.'

Wanting to finish his leftovers? This was good. This was *very* good.

Clara shifted her present for Virgil's daughter to her other hand and smoothed down her top. Ridiculous, she chided herself. Being so preoccupied with her appearance simply for Virgil. She'd told herself over and over that they were simply friends and nothing more, yet this was the fourth outfit she'd changed into before leaving home.

She'd stopped by the toy store yesterday, and after long minutes of deliberation had ended up buying an animated clock, which was guaranteed to lull any child to sleep at night and bring a giggle to their lips during the day. She hoped Rosie liked it.

Resisting the impulse to press the doorbell again, Clara

fluffed her ankle-length skirt and smoothed her white top again. Where on earth *was* he? Didn't he realise she was nervous about meeting his daughter? If Rosie didn't like her then— Clara stopped. Then what? Why did it matter whether or not Virgil's daughter liked her? Sure, they'd managed to make it through a whole week being a bit more than professional acquaintances, and Clara had enjoyed every moment she'd spent with Virgil, but if his three-year-old daughter didn't take a shine to her, it wouldn't be the end of the world.

After a few more impatient moments, she heard footsteps heading towards the door. Exhaling a deep, calming breath, she pasted a smile in place.

'Clara Lewis?' The door was opened by a plump, elderly woman with short grey hair and green eyes.

'Yes.' Clara quickly responded.

'Come on in. Virgil won't be a moment. He's just putting away his toys.'

There was a slight smirk on the other woman's lips and Clara instantly warmed to her.

'*His* toys?' she queried as she came inside.

The woman closed the door behind them. 'He needs to set a good example for his daughter by removing his computer and paperwork from the dining room table.' She chuckled.

'OK…' Clara remarked, feeling a little unsure of the correct response.

The woman held out her hand. 'I'm Gwenda, by the way.' Gwenda glanced at the beautifully wrapped present and smiled. 'Rosie is going to love that wrapping paper.'

Clara nodded. 'I specifically chose shiny paper for that very reason. My nieces always love this kind of wrapping.'

'How old are they?' Gwenda asked as she led them

through the house, Clara's flat shoes making a faint tapping sound on the polished wooden floor.

'Eighteen months old—they're twins.'

'Double the trouble, double the love!' Gwenda stated.

'And double the nappies, as my sister-in-law says.'

Clara followed Gwenda.

'Come through to the dining room. We'll be eating straight away, so Rosie can have her bath and go to bed.'

'Sounds good,' Clara agreed.

The large dining table was set at one end with four place settings—the fourth having a Mickey Mouse theme. Placemat, fork, spoon and cup were all adorned with Disney characters. A booster seat was on the chair and Virgil, with his back to Clara, was seating his daughter comfortably.

When he stepped back, Clara was captivated by the little girl, with her blonde hair and the same perfect blue eyes as her father. She'd looked adorable in the pictures Virgil had shown her, but in person there was definitely a hint of mischief about her. At the moment, though, she was gazing lovingly up at her father, as though he'd hung the moon just for her.

'Thanks for coming, Clara,' Virgil stated, and it was only then that Clara glanced his way.

He was dressed casually in jeans and a cotton shirt. She looked back at his daughter, who had spied the present in Clara's hands.

'It's a present? A present for Rosie?'

Her blue eyes twinkled with delight, her little hands coming forward with anticipation. Best of all, her little voice held the hint of a French accent, and Clara realised the girl was most likely bilingual. Having been born in Montreal, it was little wonder.

'Uh—' Clara seemed to snap out of the fog which had

surrounded her at seeing Virgil with his daughter. 'Yes. This is for you.'

'You shouldn't have. She's spoiled enough.' He watched as his daughter took the present, prompting, 'Manners, Rosie?'

'Merci,' Rosie replied dutifully, her little hands trying to find the join in the paper where the sticky tape was located.

As the little girl unwrapped the gift, Virgil edged a little closer to Clara.

'You look lovely,' he said quietly.

Clara turned her head. 'Thank you.' She allowed her gaze to flit fleetingly over his lithe frame. 'You don't look so bad yourself.'

'Why, thank you, Dr Lewis.'

'You're welcome, Dr Arterton.'

They stared into each other's eyes for a long moment, and then the smiles started to slip, their easy, joking manner being replaced by one of tantalising awareness. He looked good. He smelled good. He was looking at her lips—and she was looking at his.

As though both realising the danger they might find themselves in, they looked away, focusing on the little girl, who had managed to get the ribbon off and was scrunching the shiny gold paper.

'Would you like some help, blossom?' Virgil carefully removed the sticky tape and helped her to open the box. 'Hey. What's in here?'

As Virgil helped Rosie to remove the clock, Clara took the opportunity to put her attraction to Virgil out of her mind. She was here to meet his daughter, not to ogle him in front of the child.

'Wow!' Rosie exclaimed. 'Cow. Dog. Cat. Spoon.'

'It's "Hey Diddle Diddle",' Virgil told her. Rosie

reached for the clock and her father quickly said, 'Gently, blossom. Touch lightly.'

The clock, shaped like a moon, had three-dimensional characters from the nursery rhyme around it.

'It plays two different tunes,' Clara volunteered. 'One for bedtime and one for daytime.' She'd put a battery in and set the clock to the correct time before wrapping it.

Virgil sat it on the table, out of reach of little fingers, and flicked the button that controlled the music.

The strains of 'Hey Diddle Diddle' filled the room as the cat fiddled, the cow jumped over the moon, the dog laughed and a small dish and spoon moved across the base.

Rosie's eyes grew wide and she clapped her hands when it had finished. 'Again, Daddy. Play it again.'

Virgil flicked the switch over to the night-time song and soon the strains of Brahms' 'Lullaby' filled the room. Rosie clapped her hands again. Although the characters continued to move in the same way, the music was softer and more peaceful.

Virgil yawned and stretched and Clara laughed.

'It definitely works for Daddy,' he told Rosie with a grin, then tickled his daughter.

The girl giggled, the sound making Clara fall in love with the child.

'Thanks, Clara.'

She flicked her attention from Rosie to Virgil, who was smiling at her in the way that had often made her knees weaken. Now was no exception.

'It's a wonderful gift.'

'My pleasure.' Their gazes held for a moment. Both seemed to be remembering happier times—times they'd shared together.

When the music began for the third time, Virgil groaned and switched it off.

'More, please. More, Daddy.'

'Later. It's time for dinner now. Say thank you to Clara.'

'Thank you, Clara,' Rosie repeated.

'You're welcome,' Clara replied.

'I presume both tunes are on continuous play?' Virgil asked. When Clara nodded he groaned.

'And I made sure I put long-life batteries in.' Her smile was wide.

'How considerate,' he teased, and winked at her.

The action caused her heart to skip a beat, and she knew that as she was already instantly enthralled with his daughter, she'd do well to keep guarding her heart against becoming enthralled with Rosie's father.

CHAPTER SIX

'SORRY FOR THE slight delay,' Gwenda announced as she came through the swinging door from the kitchen. She carried a large tray with steaming plates. Placing them on the table she said, 'Sit down, before it gets cold. Virgil, can you pour the wine, please?'

Virgil instantly reached for the bottle of white wine that stood chilling in a silver bucket. He wiped the base and offered it to Clara. 'Wine?'

'Yes, please.'

He poured one for himself and one for Gwenda, before passing Rosie a sippy cup of water. Clara watched as the three-year-old fed herself quite well, sometimes using the fork and spoon as well as her fingers. If the food was too hot she would blow on it, or ask her daddy to blow on it for her. The child was incredibly adorable.

The conversation over dinner was kept rolling by Gwenda, who explained that she'd known Virgil all his life and that she'd been more than happy to come and help him out after his wife had passed away.

Rosie also offered several topics of conversation such as not wanting to eat her carrots, demanding sauce on everything, and wanting Clara to help her finish the final three mouthfuls.

'You don't have to. I can do it,' Virgil told her.

'It's fine. I'm more than happy to help. I often help Arthur and Maybelle with their twins.'

'Aunty Clara to the rescue, eh?'

Her answer was a tinkling laugh and Virgil had to stop himself from staring at her. When she laughed, it illuminated her entire face and made her look radiant. He liked making her laugh. He liked being near her, watching her graceful movements, and he was pleased at the way both Rosie and Gwenda seemed to like this very special woman.

Rosie dropped her spoon on the floor and he quickly bent to retrieve it. 'There you are, funny face.'

Rosie giggled and blew a kiss to her beloved daddy.

As he continued to watch the way Clara interacted with Rosie, he couldn't help but wonder what might have happened if he hadn't taken that position in Montreal. Would they have stayed together as they'd planned? Would both of them have found fulfilment in their careers? Would they now be married with a gaggle of children? Would Clara still have had her accident and had to endure so much pain?

It was stupid to play the 'what if' game because there was no way he could go back and change the past, but he could most definitely change the future.

Once Rosie had finished eating it was time for her bath. Clara thanked Gwenda for the delicious meal, and when Gwenda headed to the kitchen with the first load of dishes Clara instantly stood and began helping to clear.

'You don't have to do that,' Virgil stated. 'You're a guest.'

'Oh, piffle. With our history, I'm hardly a *real* guest,' Clara stated as she took the next load of dishes through to the kitchen.

Virgil conceded she had a point. The fact that they'd

known each other for almost two decades meant that she didn't expect to be treated like a true first-time guest. He was glad, in a way, because it meant she felt comfortable—not only around Gwenda and Rosie, but around him.

While Clara and Gwenda cleared he helped Rosie from her booster seat and went to start her bath. He could hear Gwenda and Clara chatting in the kitchen before Gwenda gave Clara directions to Rosie's bedroom. Then he heard his daughter showing Clara around her bedroom, introducing her soft toys.

With the bath running, Virgil walked to Rosie's room, leaning on the doorframe and watching the two of them together.

'This is my tea set. I play with my toys and have tea parties, but Gwenda says that I have to have 'maginary food and drink only—no real food and drink.'

'That's a good idea,' Clara agreed as another teddy bear and a doll were shoved into her hands for inspection. 'Imaginary food and drink means you don't get any ants in your bedroom.'

''Sactly! And Daddy sits down on the blanket and he drinks his tea with his little finger in the air.' Rosie burst into a fit of giggles at this, and held the cup in her hand and tried desperately to hold it with her little finger in the air. 'And he makes slurpy noises.'

Rosie slurped, clearly to ensure Clara understood what she meant. Clara laughed and lifted a small cup to her lips, putting her little finger in the air and making slurping noises, causing Rosie to laugh even more.

It warmed his heart to see them interact like his. She was so natural with Rosie—so open and accepting. His hope began to increase once more that Clara might one day change the nature of their relationship and allow him to court her properly. That was a mistake he'd made the first time. They'd gone from being friends to being a couple without all the lovely in-between moments of really finding the romance within their relationship.

When he'd decided upon this course of action—to see whether he could find a future with Clara—he'd been surprised to discover she hadn't married. Of course, back then, he hadn't known about her accident and months of rehab, but even still, she might have met someone when she'd been overseas.

Now, getting to know this new Clara, he had to admit that she was far more content and confident within her own life than she'd ever been in the past. She'd always had that inner strength, but now she had the confidence to use it. It was great to see and very alluring.

As Rosie started to show Clara her favourite story books Virgil cleared his throat. 'Bathtime, Rosie.'

'Non, non, non!'

Rosie quickly tried to climb onto the bed behind Clara, but Virgil was too fast for her and came into the room, scooping her up in his arms. Then he started to blow raspberries onto her tummy, making Rosie squeal loudly with delight. The child's infectious laughter filled the room with vibrancy and colour, making Virgil and Clara laugh as well.

'Arrêtes, Papa!' she ordered between giggles, not meaning a word she said.

Virgil repeated the action, the sound of his lips on her stomach echoing around the room as Rosie's laughter bubbled over.

'Ready to get drenched?' Virgil asked Clara as he led the procession to the bathroom.

The tub had been half filled with water and was covered with foaming masses of white bubbles. Virgil tested the water and, after ensuring it wouldn't burn Rosie's delicate skin, shut the taps off and went to undress his daughter. Surprisingly, he found Clara helping Rosie to get her T-shirt over her head.

'Thanks.'

Clara grinned at him. 'I'm an experienced aunty, remember?'

'I can see that.' He grinned as he helped the little girl into the bath.

Rosie searched for her toys amongst the bubbles, enjoying a game that was obviously a nightly ritual. She pulled out cups and boats and animals, delighting in each find. The two adults stood side by side, watching the child play.

'She's gorgeous, Virgil. I didn't expect her to be bilingual.'

'That's because most three-year-olds aren't. But I want her to continue to be raised speaking both languages.'

'You talk to her in both French and English?'

'Yes, but since we returned to Australia last year, she's really started to pick up the Aussie twang.'

Clara was surprised. 'You left Montreal last year?'

He nodded and beckoned her out into the hallway. That way they could talk without disturbing Rosie.

'Rosie was only six months old when Diana passed away, and for a while I wasn't sure what to do. Diana had no family in Canada, and as a qualified surgeon, I knew I could get work anywhere. Gwenda came over and lived with us, taking care of Rosie so I could work, but Gwenda doesn't speak much French so it was difficult for her. I took a locum position at Sydney General for six months, so we could acclimatise ourselves to the Australian climate, and after that Victoria seemed like the logical choice. My parents are here, when they're not travelling, so after giving it much thought, I decided to move back to the last place I could remember being really happy.'

He looked into her upturned face and couldn't resist brushing a strand of hair from her face, tucking it behind her ear.

They stood like that for a long moment, staring into each other's eyes, unsure what to say or do next. What he wanted to do was to gather her into his arms, hold her as close as possible and press his lips to hers—but he'd promised her they would remain friends. *Friends*. He knew that if all Clara could ever give him was friendship, then he would take it. Of course he wanted more—he was a red-blooded male in love with this incredible woman—but it was because he loved her and respected her that he knew he would accept whatever verdict she gave on the status of their relationship.

'Sounds as though you've had a few difficult years.' Clara was the first to speak, the first to break eye contact and glance over at Rosie, playing happily in the bath.

'I think we both have,' he added. 'The question is, where do we go from here?'

He couldn't help but look at her lips as he spoke, remembering all too vividly just how incredible it had been to kiss that mouth. In the past, their lips had meshed with perfect synchronicity. Would it be the same now?

When she looked at him again, he was positive he saw repressed desire in her eyes. Was that possible? Did Clara *want* him to kiss her? When she stared at his lips before meeting his gaze once more, he was certain those were the signals she was sending.

'I—I don't know.'

The words were barely a whisper, but he heard them. Virgil cleared his throat, needing to break this moment, needing to take things slowly even though he wanted nothing more than to follow through on that urge. Clara followed suit, both of them turning their attention to the little girl still enjoying playing with her toys in the bath.

'Rosie means the world to me, Clara. I've cut my workload in half so we can have more time together. It was one of the major reasons for moving back to Loggeen. I loved growing up here, and I know it's the best thing for Rosie. She'll make close friends, have people watching out for her, caring about her. It will make a vast difference to her life,' Virgil continued.

Rosie looked across at both of them, standing outside the bathroom, and held out her hands to them. 'Look! Look!'

Both adults went into the bathroom and over to the tub. Clara crouched down and looked at the toy Rosie was holding out to her.

'Oooh! A turtle. What's his name?'

'Mr Turtle,' Rosie said, as though that was completely obvious.

While Clara was inspecting Mr Turtle, Rosie took great delight in bringing one hand firmly down onto the surface of the water.

Splash!

With one single motion they were thoroughly wet. They both laughed, which made Rosie think she should do it again.

'Funny!' She giggled before splashing once more.

'I think that's enough, scallywag.' Virgil smiled but spoke firmly, so the child understood he wasn't playing games.

'She'd get along so well with my nieces. Mischief. All three of them are pure mischief.'

'It would be great to meet them,' Virgil said as he reached into the bath for a washcloth and began quickly washing his daughter. 'Gwenda's enrolled Rosie in a play-group, but that's only one day a week. Meeting other children would be really good.'

'I'll call Maybelle and get her to set up a play date.'

'Sounds fun—I think?'

'What? Three little girls aged three and under? Sounds like madness to me!'

She laughed, and the sound washed over him like the breeze on a fresh summer's day. He marvelled at how natural Clara was with his daughter. He watched the way she scooped his daughter carefully out of the bath and wrapped her in the waiting towel before drawing Rosie closer.

'Cuddle this little girl dry!'

She wriggled Rosie from side to side, making the child laugh. The sound was music to his heart.

'Come on—let's get you to your room and dressed for bed.'

Gwenda was ready and waiting to take over. Rosie's arms went out to her and she smiled gleefully. Clara watched as Gwenda quickly dried and dressed the wriggling toddler, amazed at the other woman's speed at performing the task.

'Give Daddy a kiss goodnight,' Gwenda instructed, and Rosie instantly puckered her little lips for her father. 'And a cuddle and kiss for Clara.' That was Gwenda's next order.

Rosie eyed Clara briefly, before holding out her arms for a cuddle. A lump caught in Clara's throat as she held the child tenderly, closing her eyes to savour the moment.

A kiss was placed on her cheek, then Rosie marched back into the bathroom proclaiming, 'Teef time,' and waited patiently for Gwenda to hand her the toothbrush.

'Goodnight, darling.' Virgil kissed her again and motioned for Clara to leave.

'Don't you put her to bed?' Clara asked as they walked downstairs.

'Usually—but tonight, considering you're here, Gwenda will do it.'

'Please,' Clara implored, 'I don't want to disrupt the routine. You go back up and I'll let myself out.'

'Just like that—you're leaving?' He quirked an eyebrow at her.

Clara shrugged and looked down at her hands. 'I think I should.'

There had already been several moments tonight when she'd fallen in thrall to Virgil Arterton once again. Hadn't she given herself a stern lecture before she'd arrived? Hadn't she told herself to keep her distance and not let his natural boyish charm infect her? Yet when they'd been standing in the hallway outside the bathroom, all she'd wanted was to feel the touch of his lips on hers, to taste the delight only he had been able to give her, to breathe in his scent and allow herself to drown in it.

Virgil really was as dangerous to her sense of self-preservation as she'd expected. The fact that after all this time, she'd only tonight realised she still wasn't over him, was perhaps the revelation she'd needed in order to find the strength to leave his presence.

'But why? Why do you need to rush off?' He reached out and took her hand gently in his own.

Clara bit her lip. If she told him the truth he would know she wasn't over him. He would know that the instant she'd seen him again, her heart had leapt with joy and delight but she'd quashed it. It was true things hadn't turned out the way either of them had wanted, but the past was the past and the present was the present—and hopefully the present might lead to a future she'd often dreamed about.

Was it possible? Was it really possible that she and Virgil could have a fresh start?

Everything he'd done and said since returning to Loggeen—the way he treated the staff he worked with, the way he was thoughtful and considerate of his patients, not to mention his doting daddy routine with Rosie—all of it, every aspect of his personality, was showing her that he *had* changed.

Even the way he was now holding her hand, stroking her skin while gazing into her eyes as though he really couldn't get enough of her, rather than just taking charge of the situation, was different. He was letting her choose whether this was the road she wanted to take. He was proving that he'd listened to her when she'd said she just wanted to be friends.

She *did* want to be friends, but was it wrong for her to want more? If they changed the nature of their friendship wouldn't history simply repeat itself?

Clara swallowed, looking at those blue eyes she'd always loved to stare into. Her mind was in turmoil, her body betraying every rational thought she had, in its need for the man before her.

'Virgil…' His name was a whispered caress and her heart began to pound even more wildly against her chest as he closed the distance between them.

They were standing at the bottom of the stairs, the lounge room in one direction, the front door in the other. She should leave. She knew she should leave. But that was her head talking, not her heart. Her heart was hammering out a rhythm which wanted to urge him closer, urge him to lower his head, urge him to kiss her just as he had so many times in the past.

'Clara?'

Her name was a question upon his lips, and she knew Virgil was offering her a way out of this bubble filled with desire and need, which seemed to have captured both of them.

She couldn't move. She didn't want to. She wanted this. She wanted to kiss him. And, if she was honest with herself, she was curious to see whether the magic which had flared between them so many years ago, was still present.

'Clara…' He murmured her name again. 'If you keep standing here I'm not going to be able to resist you.'

His words only fuelled the fire within her.

'There are too many…' She paused, her words breathless, her tone filled with repressed desire as she gazed longingly at his mouth once more.

He was *her* Virgil. He'd burst back into her life and turned her contented world upside down. How was she supposed to resist him when he looked so perfect? When he smelled so good? When he was being the perfect gentleman and allowing her to choose what happened next? What would happen if she did kiss him now? What would it change?

The answer came hard and fast after the question. It would change *everything*—and Clara wasn't sure she was ready for that.

'Virgil…' She breathed his name again, then closed her eyes and found the superhuman strength from somewhere to edge backwards. Swallowing, she looked into his handsome face, shaking her head. 'I need—' She licked her dry lips. 'I need more time.'

His gaze dropped to encompass her lips one last time before he nodded and brought her hand to his lips, pressing a long, tender kiss to her knuckles.

'Take all the time you need. I'm not going anywhere.'

CHAPTER SEVEN

'WHY AREN'T YOU in your bed? You're supposed to be sleeping by now.' Clara spoke lovingly to her dog as she entered her apartment.

Darling Juzzy always insisted on greeting her whenever she came home, and tonight Clara really needed it.

'I'm so confused, Juzzy,' she told the dog as she checked Juzzy's automatic food, and bubbling water dispensers. Yes, Juzzy had enough food and fresh water. As Clara continued to talk, the dog followed her around the apartment. 'One minute I think everything is going great between myself and Virgil, and the next I just don't know.'

As Clara prepared for bed she thought back to those intense moments she'd shared with Virgil at the bottom of the staircase. How was it possible that the man could still get her all hot and bothered with only one look?

It was a look that said, *I want you, Clara. I need you, Clara. I adore you, Clara.* How could one glance say so much and cause her to forget her resolve to remain as friends? She couldn't believe how tempted she'd been to close the distance between them and press her lips to his. He had been waiting for her to do just that, but when she'd moved back, deciding not to follow through on the impulse, he hadn't made any effort to talk her round as he would have in the past. He'd let her take control of the situation and it had only made her appreciate him more.

Getting involved in a romantic relationship with him would make her life way more complicated than it needed to be. Wasn't she in a good place with her life? Wasn't she happy? She'd told Virgil only a few weeks ago that she was more than content with her life, but now here she was questioning that decision. Yes, she was pleased with how she'd managed to pull her life back together, but what if there was *more* happiness just waiting for her to claim it? What if being with Virgil was her destiny?

Then there was Rosie. Virgil's gorgeous daughter had stolen her heart, so what would happen if things progressed between them and Rosie became attached? That would be all well and good if everything worked out between herself and Virgil, but given their history there was no guarantee.

The last thing Clara wanted to do was to hurt the child, but the real question was, could she completely trust Virgil again? Would he turn on her as he had in the past? If she made a decision he didn't agree with, would he try persuading her to change her mind? She'd stood her ground last time, and she'd do it again, but would she be able to cope with yet another heartbreak? She wasn't so sure.

'Am I overreacting?' she asked the dog as she finished brushing her teeth and climbed beneath the covers.

Juzzy looked up at her expectantly, and when Clara gave in and patted the bedcovers beside her, the dog climbed up the little step stool and jumped up onto the bed, snuggling next to Clara.

She stroked the dog, the rhythmic movements helping her to relax. 'I like him, Juzzy. I like this new and improved version of Virgil. And if this is our second chance—well, I don't want to blow it.'

There was still a long way to go—a lot of things which needed to be discussed. She needed to tell him about the outcome of her devastating accident and just how it had changed the course of her life. Yes, it had taken a lot of rehabilitation to put herself back together, but with the help of her family and close friends she'd managed it. Yes, there were lasting devastating repercussions, and, yes, those issues might be detrimental to the rekindling of the frighteningly natural chemistry which seemed to exist between herself and Virgil.

If things were going to get permanently serious between them, she needed to know how he felt about having more children. She wanted children. She really did, but due to the accident her badly crushed pelvis and subsequent surgeries had put paid to any possibility of her ever carrying a child. Clara had endured several years of both physical and psychological therapy in order to recover from the effects of the accident—the main one being that to start with, she'd felt less of a woman simply because she'd never have children.

'You don't need to carry a child inside you and give birth just to prove you're a woman,' her psychologist had told her. 'Many women don't go through the trauma you've endured—women who, medically, have nothing wrong with them—and yet they still can't conceive naturally. You're not alone in the way you feel, Clara. In fact, given the extent of your injuries, it's a miracle you're walking. Perhaps you need to cut yourself some slack… be a bit kinder to yourself. Not all women need children to complete their lives.'

The problem was she *did*, and spending time with her nieces and Rosie only intensified that sensation. Being with Virgil's little girl, hearing her giggle, seeing the way she wrapped her arms around her father's neck and pressed wet and sloppy kisses to his cheek, had only made her yearn to have a little mischief-maker of her own—hers and Virgil's.

That had always been the plan. The two of them together. The two of them getting married and raising a family. That had been all she'd wanted for so long, and now—now that there was the slightest possibility it might happen—she was scared that should Virgil learn the truth, learn that she could never have children, he might reject her for a second time.

'You're borrowing trouble,' she told herself aloud as she switched on the radio, allowing the soothing classical music being played to calm her mind.

She needed to sleep, and in order to do that she needed to shut her mind down—and that meant she needed to stop worrying about what might or might not happen with Virgil.

'Easier said than done,' she whispered to Juzzy.

For the next week Clara made sure she was polite and professional every time she came into contact with Virgil. It wasn't that she was trying to avoid him, but rather she was trying to come to terms with the numerous events which had happened since he'd re-entered her life. She'd tried not to overthink the time they'd already spent together, which was difficult for her as her family had used to joke that she should hold a degree in overthinking things.

If things were going to move smoothly between herself and the gorgeous man working alongside her, then Clara knew she needed to relax more.

It wasn't until she was doing her second Saturday night shift at the hospital that he caught up with her. It was just after eleven p.m., and he'd been in Theatre for the past five hours with a motor vehicle accident patient. He was still in scrubs as he walked over to the nurses' station, where she was busy typing information into the computer, and slumped down into the chair beside her.

'So, have you been avoiding me or have we both just been insanely busy this past week?'

'Definitely busy—although I *have* enjoyed our game of voicemail tag.'

He chuckled at her words, then looked around the ED. 'Slow night?'

'Shh.' She frowned. 'Don't ever say that. Saying that is like begging for a horde of patients to come bursting through the doors.'

'Well, they wouldn't exactly *burst*,' he pointed out. 'They'd have to go through triage first, and then sit in the waiting room for—'

'Stop being so pedantic,' she interrupted. 'How's Rosie?'

Changing the subject to his daughter was a good distraction. Clara was able to finish entering the information into the computer before saving the files. Once that was done she began clearing up the desk in front of her, needing to do something to distract her from Virgil's close proximity. How could the man still smell so sexy after such a long stint in Theatre?

'She's settling in well. Your sister-in-law got in touch with Gwenda, and I think they've arranged a play date for tomorrow. Thanks for mentioning it to Maybelle. The more little friends Rosie can make, the better—and, besides, I'm looking forward to meeting them.'

He passed Clara a few paperclips which were on the long desk, close to where he was sitting. She accepted them with a nod and put them into the paperclip container, ensuring their hands didn't touch so she wouldn't have to endure that overpowering zing of awareness which occurred every time Virgil's fingers came into contact with hers.

'Is Rosie excited to meet the twins?'

'She is—and it'll do her good to learn to share her toys.'

'Is she enjoying the clock?'

'Oh, she loves it. You chose a winner there. Although both those songs have become permanently lodged in my psyche and I've found myself humming Brahms' "Lullaby" several times of a morning.' He tapped the side of head with the heel of his hand, as though trying to dislodge the ear worm.

'Glad to be of service!' She laughed.

The desk was now shipshape and everything was tidied away. What could she do next to distract her? His nearness was already creating havoc with her senses, and it was all she could do not to stop herself from leaning close to him and doing the one thing she'd been dreaming about for the past week—pressing a kiss to his lips. Didn't the man realise just how addictive he could be?

'Do you give your nieces piles of noisy toys?'

'Of course. It's an aunty's responsibility.'

Virgil chuckled again. 'I'm sure Arthur is looking forward to getting his own back when you start having children.'

The smile instantly slid from Clara's face and she quickly stood. 'I should go and check on the patients in the treatment bays. That way, when a horde of emergencies come flooding in—thanks to your earlier comment—' she tried to keep a light and teasing tone to her voice, but even to her own ears she knew she hadn't succeeded '—the rounds will have been done.'

'Hey.' Virgil stood and put a hand gently on her arm. She tried not to gasp as the zing of desire spread up her arm and burst throughout her body. 'Clara, what's wrong?'

'Nothing. Just doing my job.' She forced a smile and took a step away.

Virgil instantly dropped his hand and let her go. What had he said? Did Clara not want children of her own? If that was the case, how did he feel about that? With the re-emergence of Clara into his life, his hopes of having more children had increased. It wasn't just that he wanted to spend the rest of his life with Clara, he wanted to build a family with her. Was that wanting too much?

After the successful dinner at his house last weekend, when that moment at the bottom of the stairs had shown him that she was as captivated with him as he was with her, his hopes had continued to increase. Still, he needed to be aware of Clara's own feelings, to *listen* to her and take his cues from her.

He'd been wanting all week to ask her for another date—one on which Rosie would be able to join them so she could get to know his daughter better. Rosie was such an integral part of his life that he wanted his little love to be as comfortable around Clara as he was—but would Clara be happy to go on a date with himself and a three-year-old? She and Rosie had connected beautifully last weekend, but had that been just a one-off? If Clara saw Rosie having a temper tantrum, would that put her off wanting to get involved with him? Especially if she *didn't* want to have children in the future?

The phone on the desk rang, and as he was the closest he picked it up. 'Emergency Department,' he said, then reached for a pen in order to note the details from the paramedics.

An elderly woman had injured both ankles after a fall from a stepladder. Both she and her elderly husband, who was in a wheelchair, were being brought in via ambulance. Estimated time of arrival was ten minutes. After hanging up the phone, he went in search of Clara, finding her just finishing off checking on the three patients who were presently being monitored for a variety of injuries.

'Ambulance arriving in just under ten minutes,' he said, and gave her the details. 'Do you need help?'

She shook her head. 'Should be fine. Besides, we have enough staff here to deal with a non-life-threatening emergency—which this is.' She headed back to the nurses' station. 'I'll call the orthopaedic registrar for a consult on her ankles, but until we've been through the X-ray process there's no urgency.'

'See? My earlier gaffe didn't result in a horde of emergencies,' he pointed out, and was rewarded with quizzical smile.

'Not yet.'

Virgil knew he should go home, but he'd just finished a five-hour emergency surgery, missing the opportunity to say goodnight on the phone to Rosie, so there was no reason for him to dash home. If he was honest with himself, what he really wanted to do was stay here with Clara.

When the ambulance arrived he stayed out of the way, watching as the patient's husband, still in his wheelchair, was lowered to the ground via the hydraulic lift before an orderly pushed him inside. The paramedics soon followed, with the stretcher holding the man's wife.

'Henry hates to leave me and I hate to leave him,' Clara's patient, Mrs Linda Santorino, told her as the paramedics took her into a treatment room. 'We've been through so much during our lives, and now, as we're coming to the end of our race, we really do like doing things together.'

'That's lovely to hear,' Clara responded as she got into position, ready to transfer Mrs Santorino from the paramedic stretcher to the hospital barouche.

When Virgil came to stand next to her, ready to help, she found it momentarily difficult to concentrate on what she needed to do. Why wouldn't he go home? He wasn't supposed to be here, driving her to distraction.

'One, two, *three*,' the paramedic counted.

They shifted Mrs Santorino—or Linda, as she'd invited them all to call her—onto the hospital bed. The paramedics finished giving their handover, letting Clara know what pain relief had already been administered, and Clara started her own assessment of the patient. After a brief clinical assessment of Linda's ankles, Clara requested X-rays and a few pathology tests.

'Both ankles are most definitely sprained, but as they're so swollen I'm unable to assess whether they're broken. The X-rays will tell us more.'

'Once she's had the X-rays, can we go home?' Henry asked, coughing a little as he spoke.

Clara eyed him carefully. His skin was pale and his lips seemed a little dry.

'I'm afraid Linda will need to stay in for at least a day or two.'

'What?' Linda seemed surprised at this. 'But—but even if I have to stay off my feet, I can still go home, can't I? We're set up with wheelchair ramps and everything for Henry, so surely I can just hire myself a wheelchair and head back home?'

There was a hint of desperation in Linda's tone and Clara really felt for them. It must be so difficult to get to a stage in your life, when your mind was as sharp as ever but your body was starting to fail you.

'Henry can't be at home on his own. I'm his full-time carer.'

'Oh. Uh—do you have any family close by who could perhaps come and help out?' Virgil asked, but both of them shook their head.

'Well, why don't we see what the X-rays reveal and we can plan from there?' Clara stated, not wanting to upset either of them. 'In the meantime—Henry, can I get you a cup of tea?'

The elderly man's eyes softened at her words. 'That would be great, love. Thanks.'

'I can do that,' Virgil offered. 'I'll even see if I can find a few biscuits for you, Henry.'

'Thanks, lad.' Henry nodded.

'Do *I* get a cuppa?' Linda asked hopefully.

'I'd rather you don't have anything at this present time,' Clara told her patient. 'At least until I get the results of your scans.'

She didn't want to tell them that if Linda's ankles were broken, there was a high possibility that surgery would be required.

'What are you *doing*?' Clara asked Virgil in a stage whisper as they headed back to the nurses' station. 'You're not the tea lady.'

'And neither are you. The brilliant volunteers who do our tea runs are well and truly off duty and the nurses have other things to do right now. Besides, I don't mind.'

Clara sighed heavily. 'Just go home, Virgil.'

'Why? Rosie's asleep. Gwenda's probably asleep. I have a lot of energy at the moment. I don't mind help-ing out.'

She rolled her eyes. 'Ugh! I give up. Right. Go make

the tea for Henry. I need to get these X-rays and tests sorted out.'

She turned her back on him, deciding that he could do whatever he wanted. She wasn't in charge of the ED, her brother was, and at present Arthur wasn't there—so far be it from her to dictate what Victory Hospital's leading general surgeon should and shouldn't do!

The orderlies came and wheeled Linda's barouche to the radiology department. Clara had thought Henry would want to go with her, but when she went to check on him he was sitting in his wheelchair, sipping his cup of tea. Virgil was seated nearby, chatting amicably.

'Comfy?' she asked.

'Absolutely. Henry was just telling me that he used to be in the Air Force.'

'Over thirty years,' Henry added. 'Plane went down twice and I survived both times.' He took a bite of biscuit and when he started to chew, he coughed at the same time, breathing in and getting some biscuit lodged in his throat.

'Henry?' Clara watched him closely.

The man coughed again.

'You OK?'

She came closer and Virgil stood up from his chair, both of them on alert to see if Henry needed help. He tried to suck in some air but it was clearly difficult for him. The elderly man's eyes widened in terror as he tried to breathe once more. He gasped several times, each one a valiant attempt, but it was no good.

Although time seemed to have stood still, it was only a matter of seconds before Clara and Virgil were by Henry's side. Clara hit Henry firmly on the back, hoping to dislodge the obstruction. It didn't work.

'Help me get him out of the wheelchair.' Clara ensured the wheels were locked in place as Virgil put both his arms beneath Henry's armpits and performed the Heimlich manoeuvre.

Nothing!

Clara pressed the emergency button, alerting staff that they required help.

'There's no way to dislodge it,' she told Virgil. 'Get me a barouche,' she told the first nurse who appeared in the treatment room. 'His glands are starting to swell,' she announced.

'I'll need to do a tracheotomy,' Virgil stated as Henry tried desperately to breathe.

Only the smallest amount of air was getting through. The elderly man looked even more frail than before, and Clara was exceedingly worried for him.

'Set up for emergency tracheotomy,' she told Kate, the sister in charge this evening. 'Let's get Henry onto the bed,' she added when a barouche was wheeled in from another room.

Staff were helping out everywhere. A tray was set up for Virgil to use while he pulled on a pair of gloves. Clara placed her hands on either side of Henry's head to keep him as still as possible, seeing the look in the man's eyes conveying his distress at finding himself in such a situation.

'It's OK, Henry. You'll be fine in no time. Virgil's one of our finest surgeons and he's going to take excellent care of you.'

'Yes, I am,' he stated firmly as he carefully palpated the tracheal rings, ensuring he made the incision into the correct space. 'Scalpel,' he stated, and Kate put the instrument into his hand.

A moment later Virgil had a piece of tubing in place and with a gurgling, rasping sound Henry was able successfully to get air into his lungs. Clara breathed a sigh of relief, very happy now that Virgil had indeed stuck around. It wasn't that she wouldn't have been able to perform the emergency procedure, but it was much better to have a surgeon do it.

Now that Henry was breathing, Virgil turned and thanked the staff. 'I think we'll transfer Henry to one of the emergency bays,' he said. 'So that when Linda comes back there's room for her here. Besides, the emergency bays have the equipment needed to completely remove this obstruction. Kate, can you get me the anaesthetics registrar, please? Given Henry's age, we'll need to sedate him in order to successfully remove the obstruction.'

'Let's get you something for the pain,' Clara said.

Thankfully, Henry was wearing a medical alert bracelet on his wrist, and after checking the information contained there, she was able to draw up some analgesics for Henry to assist him with his immediate pain.

When Henry was in the emergency bay, which was bigger and had more equipment, the anaesthetics registrar came and consulted alongside Virgil. It was decided, due to Henry's age, not to give him a full sedative. A local would be enough to keep Henry relaxed enough for Virgil to use the equipment to dislodge the obstruction.

Once they began, the procedure didn't take long, and when Linda came back from the radiology department Clara explained the situation to her.

'So where is Henry now?' a shocked Linda asked.

'He's being admitted to a ward for observation,' Clara told her as she checked the scans of Linda's ankles. 'I'm very happy to tell you that neither of your ankles are broken, just very badly sprained. You're going to need a lot of bed-rest as well as physiotherapy for the next few months.'

'*Months?*' Linda laid her head back against the pillows and promptly burst into tears. It was all too much for her.

'We'll be admitting you tonight, and I'll do my best to ensure you and Henry are side by side in the ward.' Clara gave Linda a tissue and wrote up a prescription for more pain relief. 'I'll be around to see you in the morning.'

'And you'll look after my treatment?'

Clara shook her head. 'You're being admitted under one of our physicians—Dr Presley. He'll also be around in the morning to introduce himself to you. You'll love him. He was an Air Force doctor for many years.'

'Oh, well. If he was Air Force…' Linda let her words trail off as she wiped her eyes and blew her nose. 'It's going to be a bit of an upheaval, but Henry and I can get through it.'

Now that she'd had her cry, it was as though Linda was ready to cope with the latest challenge in her life.

'What an amazing woman,' Clara said to Virgil when they both ended up back at the nurses' station.

'What an amazing *couple*,' Virgil agreed. 'So devoted to each other.'

'Linda must have been through a lot of hard times during her life—especially as Henry said he'd gone down with his plane twice!'

'It would have been difficult for her.' Virgil sat back in his chair, resting his head and closing his eyes. 'He'd head off to work on a top secret Air Force mission and she'd probably have no idea whether he was dead or alive until he walked in the front door.'

'I don't know if I could live like that—not knowing what was happening to the people I loved.'

'That's how I used to feel whenever I thought about you.'

Virgil's words were soft and Clara couldn't help but stare at him.

'What?'

'I used to think about you a lot, Clara.'

'Even when you were married?'

He smiled sadly. 'Thinking about an old girlfriend isn't a crime—even for a married man.'

'What happened?' she asked softly, pleased that the ED was indeed quiet and there weren't a lot of staff around. 'You said your wife died in a car accident with her lover. That must have brought you a lot of mixed emotions.'

'It did. When a person gets married, no one ever thinks their happiness is going to change—but it can and it does. I think Diana was fed up with me spending so much time at the hospital, devoting more time to my patients than to her. She was right, though. I *did* spend too much time at the hospital because I wasn't happy in my marriage.'

'Why weren't you happy?'

He met and held her gaze. 'Because I married the wrong woman.' He shook his head sadly. 'I tried to make it work. You'd rejected me—or so I thought—and I needed to get on with my life. Diana and I went to marriage counselling and things actually turned around for a while. It was good. It was happy. And she became pregnant with Rosie.'

Virgil exhaled slowly and shook his head.

'But Diana had a bad pregnancy. She was sick. Gestational diabetes, pre-eclampsia—the works. She was bedridden from five months onwards, and when Rosie was born via emergency C-section…' He shook his head again. 'Diana didn't bond with her. She didn't want to hold her, feed her, look at her.'

'Oh, Virgil. How sad…'

'When they returned home from the hospital, Diana still couldn't attach herself to Rosie. I took several months off work so I could care for the baby—feeding, changing, bathing… I was Daddy, and caring for Rosie was the most important job I'd ever had. Diana…' He trailed off. 'I didn't know she was seeing someone else. He was one of the district nurses who had been coming around to check on her during her third trimester. Both of them were killed outright when the car hit a tree.'

Clara gasped and covered her mouth with her hand.

'She was leaving me. That's where the two of them had been going. Off to start a new life together.' He held his palms up and shrugged. 'She'd left me a note saying it was over. She didn't want custody of Rosie, and she didn't want to be married to me. She wanted to be happy, and I wasn't the man to make her happy.'

'Oh, Virgil.' Clara shook her head and within the next instant she'd thrown her arms around him, hugging him close. 'I wish I'd been there to help you through those times.'

He eased back a little and looked into her face. 'I wish I'd been there to help you through *your* bad times.'

When Clara continued to stare into his eyes, wanting to convey her desire to support him, there was only one way she could think of to do that—she pressed her mouth to his.

CHAPTER EIGHT

VIRGIL COULDN'T BELIEVE the way it felt to have her lips pressed to his once again, but no sooner had she kissed him than he put his hands on her shoulders and eased her away. 'Not here,' he whispered. 'I don't want to give the gossipers any ammunition.'

Clara's eyes went from being glazed over with a mixture of sadness, regret and desire to widening in shock, as she realised exactly what she'd done and where they were presently situated.

'Oh, my gosh!' She sprang back from him and stood. 'I'm— I'm—' She shook her head.

Virgil stood, but kept his distance. 'It's OK.' He glanced around them. 'No one saw.'

He could feel fatigue starting to set in, and unsuccessfully smothered a yawn.

'Perhaps you should head home and get some rest. If Rosie's anything like my nieces, she wakes up early.'

'That she does—and she loves coming into Daddy's bed to cuddle him for a few minutes and then jump on him for half an hour in an effort to ensure he's really awake.'

Clara laughed. He liked seeing her smile.

'Listen, are you free tomorrow afternoon? I know you'll be here until the morning shift arrives, and then you'll need to sleep, but after that—'

Clara shook her head. 'I'm looking after the girls tomorrow afternoon and evening. Maybelle has a shift, and Arthur's away this weekend in Sydney at a conference.'

'How about next weekend?'

She hesitated. 'What did you have in mind?'

'Perhaps a picnic in the park. You, me and Rosie.'

'Can I bring my dog? Fuzzy-Juzzy loves the park.'

Virgil grinned, realising she couldn't have given him a better response to his invitation. 'I'd love to meet your dog—as, I'm sure, would Rosie.'

'OK, well—emergencies permitting—it's a date.'

Virgil reached for her hand, giving it a little squeeze. 'It's a date,' he reiterated, more than delighted that she was accepting this new level of their relationship.

As he headed home he felt a weight lift from his shoulders. He'd told Clara about his marriage, not hiding from her his own faults in the scenario, and she'd accepted him. He could still feel the burning heat on his lips where hers had brushed his—oh, so gently and filled with compassion.

Yes, they'd both been through a lot, and he knew that whilst Clara had told him she'd been in an accident, she hadn't talked about it further. The fact that she'd been in hospital and rehabilitation for so long could only mean the accident had been quite horrific. The patient he'd operated on earlier tonight would require future surgery, and it made him wonder exactly what Clara's injuries had been.

She might be willing to spend time with him, to get to know his daughter, introduce him to her dog, but that didn't mean she was willing to trust him. He had so much at stake here, and he wanted to do whatever he could to ensure they had the opportunity of a future. But with one wrong move Clara might reject him for ever.

Sure, he'd go on with his life—working, parenting, existing—but without Clara by his side, sharing, laughing, loving, his world would feel like an empty shell. He'd lived that sort of life with Diana, appearing happy on the outside but feeling hollow and broken on the inside. Clara was the only one who could fix him, make him whole again.

He had to continue to hope. Hope that everything would turn out all right in the end and that he and Clara would get their happily-ever-after. Because if they didn't, he knew he'd end up in the pit of despair—and he really didn't want to go back there again.

To say Fuzzy-Juzzy was excited to be going out with her mistress was an understatement.

'I need to take you out more,' she told the dog.

Yes, they went for their daily walks, and if Clara wasn't able to take Juzzy then Maybelle and Arthur would take the Pomeranian whenever they took their own dogs for a walk. Still, having time to take Juzzy to the park was a luxury they were both going to enjoy.

When she arrived at the park, late Saturday afternoon, her clinic and house-calls completed for another week, she saw Virgil pushing Rosie on the swings and couldn't help the instant smile which beamed on her face. She parked her car and came around to the passenger side to get the excited Fuzzy-Juzzy from the back seat. She clipped the leash to Juzzy's collar and headed towards Rosie and Virgil.

'Higher, Daddy!' Rosie was calling.

'Well, well, well. Don't you look lovely?' Virgil stated as Clara walked up to him, reining Juzzy in a little closer to her side. 'Hey, Rosie, look who's here!' Virgil reached out and carefully grabbed the swing, gently slowing it down. 'It's Clara, and she's brought someone new for you to meet.'

When Rosie saw the dog she clapped her hands with delight, and found it difficult to sit still long enough for Virgil to unclip the restraints which had held the little girl firmly in the swing.

'There you go, wriggle-pot,' he said, and helped her to the ground.

Rosie instantly raced over to Clara and Juzzy, running both her small chubby hands through the dog's fur. Juzzy yapped excitedly at this new undivided attention from a little girl. Then the dog was tugging on her leash, as though eager to go for a walk.

'Why don't we take Juzzy for a walk? We have quite a few hours before the sun starts to set.'

'True—and Gwenda made Rosie have a sleep earlier, so my daughter is well rested and can stay up past her bedtime.'

'Yay!' Rosie had clearly overheard the last bit.

'Just for tonight, sweetheart,' he warned as they started walking along the waterfront.

Rosie wanted to have a go at holding Juzzy's leash, and after giving her a lesson in how to hold it, so it didn't hurt her hand, Rosie and Juzzy ran off. Juzzy stopped every now and then to sniff out all sorts of nooks and crannies. It was funny to watch as the dog took the toddler for a walk!

Virgil held out his hand to her. 'May I hold your hand whilst we stroll, ma'am?' he asked, and Clara couldn't help but giggle at his proper, gentlemanly behaviour.

She nodded eagerly and a moment later his soft fingers were laced with her own, the warmth from his touch spreading up her arm to burst throughout her body with delight. They strolled along hand in hand for a while, with Rosie very content to be in charge of the dog but often having a disagreement with Juzzy as to which way they should head next.

Clara knew that if Juzzy started leading Rosie off towards a dangerous path—perhaps towards the lake they were walking around—then all Clara needed to do was give a little whistle and the dog would turn and come straight to her. Years of puppy school were finally paying off.

When it looked as though Rosie was starting to get tired they decided to head back towards the car, where Virgil had left the picnic basket and a rug.

'It is so nice to get away from the hospital and the clinic,' Clara remarked as they started tucking into the picnic Gwenda had packed.

Clara had brought some food for Juzzy and the dog was more than happy to sit near them and eat up.

'And this cold chicken and salad is yummy.'

'Yummy,' Rosie repeated, before Virgil once again told his daughter not to give the dog her lettuce.

Virgil picked up the bottle of wine and gestured to Clara's glass. 'More?'

'Just half a glass, please.' Clara lazed back on the rug and joined him in watching the child eat as though she'd never been fed before. 'Rosie certainly likes her food. It's not always easy to get children to eat.'

'She has her days. A few months ago she would only eat breakfast, so Gwenda made sure it was a breakfast packed with as many of the five food groups as she could. Besides, as long as they drink enough fluids, they won't waste away.'

Clara sighed. 'She really is adorable, Virgil. You are a lucky man.'

'She's not always such an angel.' He chuckled. 'Sometimes there are smiles all round—the next it's tantrum after tantrum.'

'Rosie?' Clara joked. 'Have a tantrum?'

Virgil grinned. 'Generally she's a happy little princess, and one thing I know for sure: she's my little girl and I wouldn't be without her. I know I finally have my priorities right.'

They sat in a companionable silence as the pressures of life seemed to ebb away. 'It's so peaceful here,' Clara murmured as Juzzy snuggled up next to her.

A moment later, Rosie decided she wanted to be a dog, like Juzzy, and settled herself down on Clara's lap. Rosie pretended to bark and stick her tongue out, breathing fast like she'd seen Juzzy do.

'Good doggie,' Clara praised, and patted Rosie on the head.

Snuggling in closer, Rosie leaned against Clara, yawning and sighing, clearly displaying her contentment. Clara absorbed the gorgeousness of the child, knowing she would love nothing more than to become a mother to the precious little moppet. The child *and* her daddy were proving far too hard to resist.

'I think she likes you,' Virgil remarked softly as he sipped his wine.

'You think so? Or is she just tired and I was the closest lap for a nap?'

He chuckled. 'Children are honest.'

'And usually have no filter whatsoever,' she added, smiling at him.

It was nice to sit here so content, so relaxed with Virgil and his daughter. If she'd told herself two months ago that she'd be sitting in the park enjoying an evening picnic with Virgil Arterton she never would have believed it. Two months ago she'd been busy going over various scenarios to ensure she and her team were ready for the up and coming retrieval examinations. So much had changed since Virgil had re-entered her life, and she had to admit that she liked spending time with him.

'You look quite content there, with Rosie snuggled against you.'

Clara glanced across at him, his long legs sprawled out in front of him as he propped himself up on his elbow. He was relaxed, charming and sexy.

'Is she falling asleep?'

'Her eyes are closed. She'll become a bit of a dead weight soon.'

'Oh. Do you *want* her to go to sleep?'

He shrugged. 'It'll make putting her in the car a whole lot easier.' He shook his head. 'The other day she went as stiff as a board. It was like she didn't bend any more. Took me almost five minutes to get her arms into the straps and buckle her in safely.'

Clara chuckled. 'They're so funny, these toddlers.' She ran her fingers gently through Rosie's hair.

'Do you want to have any?'

'Toddlers?' she queried, unsure that was what he'd meant.

'Yeah. Babies of your own.'

At his words she looked away, dipping her head down to drop a kiss to the top of Rosie's head, allowing her hair to slide forward and shield her face from his view.

'I mean, I know we talked about getting married and having a family all those years ago, but is that what you still want?'

Clara's mind was starting to slip into panic mode, telling her that she should get out of there as soon as possible, because Virgil was entering dangerous territory. *Just tell him. Just tell him,* her logical side was pushing. *Tell him about your injuries. Tell him about your heartbreak. Tell him—*

'Clara?' There was a hint of confusion in his tone. 'Do you *not* want to have children any more?'

She lifted her head, opened her eyes and tucked her hair behind her ear, knowing she needed to address this with him—but she couldn't do it now.

When they'd first gone out to dinner he'd declared his intentions, which were to woo her back, to spend the rest of his life with her. At the time she'd dismissed it, because she'd thought she'd be able to resist him. She'd been wrong. She'd forgotten how charming he could be. And that was the problem. He'd made her *want* again. He'd made her want to spend the rest of her life with him—with him and Rosie.

And no other children. Because she couldn't give that to him. Yes, they could adopt, but would he want to? Would he be able to love a child that wasn't biologically his? She didn't know, and right now, after the most perfect afternoon, when they'd been happy and relaxed with each other, when they'd laughed and held hands and connected in a way they never had before, she didn't want to ruin it.

'Ugh—you were right about the dead weight part.' She tried to shift. 'I think my legs are lacking blood.'

Clara chuckled, trying to cover up her nervousness. Virgil obliged by kneeling up and lifting Rosie off Clara and into his arms, so the child rested her head on her father's shoulder. Juzzy was also disturbed, and as Clara quickly stood, patting both her legs which were now developing pins and needles, she made sure she had hold of Juzzy's leash.

'I'd better get her home,' said Virgil.

'OK. You carry her to the car. I'll pack up here.'

Thankfully Virgil did as she suggested, but Clara couldn't help but feel as though she'd firmly shut the door on any hope of rekindling a deep and abiding relationship with him for ever. It was clear he knew she'd just brushed him off. That because she hadn't answered his question— hadn't told him that, whether or not she *wanted* to have children, she was physically incapable of doing so—he'd gathered his daughter up and was leaving her. Again.

This time, though, it really was her fault.

Biting her lips, to stop the tears from springing to her eyes as she quickly packed everything into the picnic basket and gathered up the rug whilst trying to ensure Juzzy didn't run away, Clara managed to get things neat and tidy before she dragged in a soothing breath and walked on shaky legs towards Virgil's car.

This would be over soon. He'd bid her a polite farewell, get in his car, take his daughter home, put her to bed and then figure out a way to extract himself from Clara's life. It would happen gradually. He'd see her now and then, but whenever she would suggest getting together he'd tell her how much work he had to do, or say that Rosie needed to spend time with him and—

She stopped the negative hamster wheel from spinning in her mind. She was overthinking things again. She was borrowing trouble. She was selling Virgil short—or at least she hoped she was.

When she reached his car, she placed the basket and rug on the ground as he closed the door, Rosie safely secured inside.

'Did she wake up?' Clara bent to pick up Juzzy, who was starting to weave in and out of her legs, winding the leash into a knot.

'No.'

His one-word answer pierced her heart. Short and to the point.

He collected the picnic basket and rug and stowed them in the boot of his car before jangling the keys from his finger, a sure sign that he was ready to leave her. Well, if this was it—if this was the end of any new beginning for herself and Virgil—she was going to behave with as much dignity as she could muster.

'Thank you for suggesting this.' She gestured to the park, the sky behind them now a lovely mix of pinks, purples and yellows. 'Both Juzzy and I had a lovely time.'

Clara stroked Juzzy's head as she spoke, then jerked her thumb towards her car.

'I'm parked over there, so I'll let you go and see you around the Specialist Centre some time.'

She turned, promising herself she could cry as much as she wanted when she arrived home.

'Clara—wait.' He put his hand on her arm, stopping her from leaving.

She wasn't sure she wanted him to say the words that would bring these wonderful past weeks to an end.

'Could you put Juzzy down on the ground for a moment?'

'Why?'

Virgil quirked an eyebrow at her. 'Because I don't want the dog to get squashed when I kiss you goodnight.'

His perfect lips curved into a half-smile as he took the dog from her arms and placed the Pomeranian on the ground, putting the leash under his shoe to ensure Juzzy remained safely nearby.

A short laugh of disbelief erupted from her before she could stop it. 'Kiss me?'

'Yes.' He chuckled. 'What did you *think* I was going to do?' As he spoke, he reached for her, drawing her close, sliding his arms around her waist. 'A perfect afternoon deserves the perfect ending, and I can think of no better ending than kissing you.'

'But—' Clara frowned, completely thrown by his behaviour. 'But before, when you—'

It didn't matter what she'd been about to say because it appeared Virgil could wait no longer, and he was pressing his lips to hers.

Memories flooded back at his touch—familiarity, acceptance, delight. Virgil was kissing her! Her heart sang with utter excitement. The kiss was soft and questioning, as though he was testing the waters. Slowly—ever so slowly—he moved his lips over hers, tenderly caressing and filling the emptiness she'd tried to lock away for almost six years.

For a brief moment she was certain she could feel raw passion surge through him, but in the next instant his mouth was gently exploring, gently coaxing, to ensure she was right there with him, side by side on this journey into the familiar.

This was Virgil—*her* Virgil—and the love she'd banished all those years ago flooded her like a raging torrent of emotions.

With ardent desire Clara leaned closer to Virgil, thinking how great it felt to feel this way again. She'd thought he would end their budding relationship tonight, but she'd been completely wrong, and it once again proved to her just how much he'd changed. He wasn't her friend from medical school, and he wasn't the focused surgeon eager to make a name for himself. No, the man who was presently making her feel as though she could fly, was someone with wisdom, experience and a clear direction of what he wanted out of life.

She lifted her hands to his head, lacing her fingers in his hair, ensuring his head remained in place so he would continue this sweet, sweet delight upon her senses. Her body was zinging to life, reigniting the spark from so long ago, and their pheromones were combining together to make a heady combination.

Never had she been kissed so tenderly—as though he really did cherish her. It was as though he was trying to show her that she didn't need to be afraid of the electrifying attraction which seemed to hum every time they were near each other. He gently nipped at her lips, causing her eyelids to flutter closed with longing. She wanted to savour every aspect of his kisses, wanted to show him without saying the words just how much she loved being with him.

Eventually it was the need for air which made her tip her head back, unwillingly breaking their connection. As they both dragged air into their lungs, he pressed a smattering of light, feathery kisses to her cheeks, stopping momentarily in the middle to cover her lips with his once more.

'You're addictive,' he murmured against her mouth. 'From the first moment I kissed you until now, you've been like fire in my veins.'

'Mmm…' She kissed him once more before opening her eyes, looking at him through heavy eyelids. 'You make me swoon.' She drew in a slow breath. 'I'm not sure I can stand without help at the moment.'

Virgil smiled and pressed a kiss to the tip of her nose. 'You and me both.' He eased back to look at her. 'Sweetheart, I know there's something bothering you.' His words were as soft and as tender as his kisses. 'I know you too well not to pick up on the signals.'

'Virgil, I—'

'Shh. I won't pry. I'll just continue to show you that you can trust me. I'm here, Clara. For the long haul.'

His tenderness was dangerous, unravelling her tightly wound emotions. Hoping her legs were ready to support her weight, Clara gently eased herself from Virgil's wonderfully strong and protective arms, looking into his hypnotic blue eyes.

'We both need to go our separate ways,' she whispered, unable to believe he'd said he wouldn't pry, that he wanted her to trust him, that he was here for the long haul. A second chance at happiness was at her disposal, and if she tried to explain her swirling emotions now she might make a mess of things. 'You need to get Rosie home.'

'And you need to get Juzzy home.' He kissed her briefly once more, before releasing her from his arms and bending to hand her the dog. 'Just remember one thing for me,' he stated as she took a step backwards. 'This really *is* a new beginning for us, Clara.'

'New beginning…' she repeated, her heart singing with delight. And she ignored that little voice inside which told her it would never last.

CHAPTER NINE

CLARA COULDN'T BELIEVE how well she'd slept last night. 'Kisses from Virgil will do that to you,' she laughingly told her reflection the next day.

As it was Sunday, and neither of them were on call, Virgil phoned her just after midday to see if she was free to spend some more time with him and Rosie.

'We'll just be here—hanging out, playing with toys and avoiding paperwork.'

'Oh? Does Rosie have a lot of paperwork?' she asked, grinning widely as she spoke.

'Stacks. What do you say? Bring Juzzy if you like.'

'I'd really love to, Virgil—'

'But…?' he interrupted, drawing the word out.

'I'm spending time with Arthur and the girls while Maybelle's at work.'

'They can come, too,' Virgil stated. 'I know Rosie would love to play with your nieces.'

'It does sound interesting, but…uh…' She hesitated and Virgil waited expectantly. 'I haven't told Arthur that we're seeing each other again.'

'Ah.' There was silence on the other end of the line for a long moment. 'I take it he isn't my biggest fan?'

'Not really, no.'

'That's understandable. I did break his sister's heart.'

'I was going to tell him this afternoon. Let him know how much you've changed…that things are different this time.'

'At least he allowed his daughters to come and enjoy a play date with Rosie.'

'He's fine with you living and working here. And he's fine with his daughters playing with your daughter.'

'But he's not fine when it comes to you and me together?'

'Something like that. I *will* talk to him, Virgil. Today.'

'It's all right, Clara. Take your time.'

Although his impatience was beginning to surge, he reminded himself that he had the rest of his life to show Clara—and the rest of her family—that he was a changed man, that he adored her and that his intentions were extremely honourable.

He spoke to Clara for a few more minutes, then rang off and leaned back in his chair. He shouldn't have been surprised that Clara's brother wasn't his biggest fan, and it was good that Arthur was still looking out for his sister.

Before arriving back in Loggeen, the last time he'd seen Arthur Lewis had been the night before his early flight to Montreal. Arthur had turned up at Virgil's apartment, giving him an earful.

'She loves you!' Arthur had stated. 'And this is how you treat her?'

'It's my *career*, Arthur. I thought at least *you'd* understand. You're chasing your own career dreams.'

'Not overseas. I'm not running away when the going gets tough.'

'What? I'm not running away.'

'Clara told me that you had plans to get married and start a family. She wants that with you.'

'I never asked her to marry me.'

That revelation had brought Arthur up short. 'But Clara said—'

'We've discussed it on occasions, but there have been no firm plans made. I can't make firm plans until I've sorted out my career. This opportunity in Montreal is a once-in-a-lifetime sort of deal and I'm not going to turn it down. Not for you. Not for Clara. Not for anyone.'

'Your career isn't your *life*, Virgil.'

'Yes, it is.'

'No. Your career is just your job. It's not where you live.' Arthur had pointed to his heart. 'Jobs will come and go, but do you know how difficult it is to find the love of a woman who adores you the way Clara does? When you have your big successes in your career, who are you going to share them with? When you've have a bad day at work, who's going to support you?'

Arthur's words had made him stop, had made him ponder those questions for a moment or two, but then he'd shaken his head. 'It's too late to think like that. I've made my decision. My flight leaves in ten hours' time and I still have packing to do.'

He'd indicated the front door to his apartment.

'You'd better go.'

'So that's it? You're just going to *leave* her?'

'She'll be fine. She's a smart, intelligent woman.'

'Yeah. She is.' Arthur had walked to the door, wrenching it open. 'And *you're* the fool who let her go.'

And what a fool he'd been. He didn't blame Arthur for being over-protective of Clara. He was glad she had a family who loved and supported her, and he knew that if he was to stand any chance with Clara in the future, he needed to make amends with Arthur, too. Family was important. Rosie had taught him that. For now he would follow Clara's lead where Arthur was concerned, trusting her to guide him.

Later that evening Virgil received a phone call from the ED, calling him in.

'There's been a bad accident. Retrieval teams are preparing,' the nurse told him.

Thankfully, Rosie was already in bed, and after quickly telling Gwenda he was heading to the hospital Virgil walked briskly to his car. If the retrieval teams were getting ready to go out, there was a high probability that Clara was leading the team.

When he arrived at the hospital it was to find it a hive of activity. He stood still for one long moment, scanning the room until he found her. She was standing at the nurses' desk, talking to Arthur and Larissa, one of the ED nurses.

He headed towards them and upon greeting them, received a normal 'Hello', from Larissa; a growl accompanied by a frown from Arthur, and a subdued but happy, 'Hello, thank goodness you could make it,' from Clara. It wasn't so much what she said, but the softening of her gaze as it came to rest on him. It was a nice sensation to have.

'What's the situation?'

'Briefing in five minutes,' she told him. 'Why don't you get changed into retrieval overalls?' She indicated her bright orange jumpsuit, covered with pockets and reflective tape here and there. 'Meet us in the briefing room?'

'Good.' He nodded and left to do as instructed.

How was it possible she could make those clothes look as though they were the latest fashion? The woman was amazing.

She ran a successful and very busy general practice, and he knew she was up to date with her paperwork as he'd received reports on Michelle and also Linda and Henry Santorino, who had been discharged and were doing well. She worked two shifts per month at the hospital's Emergency Department and led the retrieval teams, helped out with her nieces and was well liked by everyone she met. Was it any wonder he was completely and utterly smitten with her?

He knew there was something deep that was troubling her, but he had to trust her to tell him when she was ready. He wouldn't push. He wouldn't pry—no matter how badly he wanted to know why she would sometimes sit and stare at nothing, tears springing to her eyes. Or why she would abruptly change the subject or distract him from discussing things further.

When he entered the briefing room, it was to find it almost full to bursting. Clara was standing at the front of the room, and as soon as she saw him enter she started to speak. Had she been waiting for him? Just as well he hadn't dilly-dallied.

'Right, listen up.'

She spoke to all the people who were in the small briefing room, some of them already in their bright orange retrieval overalls and others who were just arriving. Virgil stood near the back. As a general surgeon, the best place for him to be would be here at the hospital, waiting for the casualties to be brought to Theatre, but after reading the particulars of this accident, Clara knew she needed him at the crash site.

'There are two people trapped in a car, and the car has gone over an embankment on the road heading to the coast.' Clara spoke clearly. 'One male, one female in the car. The Country Fire Service and police are in attendance. The car has rolled several times, so we can expect head injuries, seatbelt injuries and a plethora of internal injuries.'

She glanced towards Virgil as she spoke.

'You all know your strengths—work to them. Let's work as a team and attend to our patients. Go and grab your gear. Meet out at the ambulances in five minutes.'

With that, she dismissed everyone and people scattered to do their jobs.

Virgil was the only one left. 'You sounded like a coach. What's your strategy?'

'Pumping everyone up. Adrenaline. We have no idea what we're going to find and, quite frankly, Virgil, sometimes even the less gory scenes can still turn my stomach. Getting pumped up and preparing our minds mentally for what we'll find is a big issue. It helps us cope.' She crossed her arms and looked at him. 'How long is it since you've been out with a retrieval team, rather than just judging them at competitions?'

'Too long to remember,' Virgil answered with a shake of his head.

'Well, then, Dr Arterton.' Clara grinned up at him and winked. 'You might just learn something new.'

'Oh—my—goodness.' Clara said each word slowly as she straightened from looking over the side of the mountain. 'Is the car stable?'

The policeman, who had been the first at the accident site, nodded. 'We've managed to get a cable around the front axle, which will hold the front of the car quite firmly. Other cables have been attached to the driver's side and the rear of the car is wedged firmly into the ground.' He held out his hand to her and shook it briefly. 'I'm Senior Sergeant Edelstein and I'll be in charge up here.'

'Dr Clara Lewis. I'll be in charge of things down there.' She inclined her head to indicate the accident site.

The road had been closed off and the area was swarming with emergency personnel. Clara looked again at the car that was lit by two huge floodlamps that the Country Fire Service had set up.

The car had rolled a number of times and had finally come to rest on its side—passenger side down. As the policeman had informed her, the rear of the car had dug itself into the ground while the front was resting on an old gum tree.

As the CFS personnel had managed to secure some cables around the car, in case the tree branches gave way, the car would be suspended horizontally out from the side of the mountain. At least that was what they'd told her would happen.

Clara could feel her heart begin to pound in her ears. She'd told Virgil it was adrenaline that got them through these situations, and she realised she was going to need a heck of a lot to get through this one.

'What's the plan, Clara?' asked Geoff, her retrieval team buddy.

The rest of the team gathered around to hear what she had to say. Virgil was listening intently too. All of them were suited up with abseiling harnesses and ropes, ready to scale down the mountain to the accident site.

'The CFS have removed what was left of the front windscreen, which will make our job a little easier. They recommend getting the female passenger out first, and then the driver. He's being held in by his seatbelt and the steering wheel, so once we remove those obstacles gravity will naturally pull him downwards. If the passenger is out of the way we'll have more room to manoeuvre. These

CFS guys know what they're talking about and have already been down several times so we'll heed their advice.'

Everyone nodded and Clara continued.

'We need to have as little contact with the car as possible. They've said those cables will hold, but I don't want any unnecessary risks taken. If the danger is too great then we don't take the risk. Understood?'

'Yes,' everyone answered.

'Virgil, you go on the passenger side with the stretcher. You'll need to get down lower than the car, so that when Geoff and I lower her out she can go straight down on to the stretcher rather than being winched upwards.

'Geoff, you'll be with me, assisting with what I'll need.' She turned to one of the retrieval nurses. 'Amelia, get an area set up here, so when Virgil comes up with the female passenger everything he'll need will be ready.'

'On it,' Amelia stated.

'There has been no sign of consciousness yet, but when the CFS team checked, both patients were alive, their airways were clear and breathing was not compromised. We'll stabilise the injuries as best we can and then secure the harness around her. Once she's ready, we move her out. We'll have had a chance to assess the other patient, but will probably need the foot pedals and steering wheel to be cut away before we can remove him.'

She took a deep breath, knowing she needed to keep a cool, clear head. She couldn't look at Virgil too much because the last time she'd glanced his way, she'd seen a huge furrow on his brow—one of concern, not just for the patients, but for her as well. She couldn't think about that now. It was imperative she take things step by step and keep calm.

'Everyone knows their jobs. Let's do this.'

She had the CFS re-check her harness before she abseiled closer to the vehicle. The entire retrieval team were wearing headphone sets so they could easily talk to each other, as well as communicate with the rest of the emergency crew up top.

'To your right. Good. Now, slowly.'

Virgil was already in position, below and off to the side of the car. From where he hung, secured by his ropes, he could see everything.

'Geoff, stop your descent so Clara can get into position,' Virgil stated through his headset. 'Clara, a little more to your right.'

Clara was just passing the rear of the car, which was wedged into the ground. *Unbelievable*, she thought but kept her focus firmly on her work. As the car was still balancing on the strong gum tree branches, Clara needed Virgil's guidance to assist her through the maze.

'Watch that branch on your right. Good. Carefully find your way through.' Virgil's deep voice was clear and calm and she drew strength from it. 'Good,' he encouraged her as she moved just below the smashed front windscreen.

Securely held, Clara was ready to work.

The driver was hanging by his seatbelt, the steering wheel effectively jamming him firmly in place. The woman was pressed against the passenger window, her own seatbelt holding her securely. Thank goodness both had been wearing seatbelts, Clara thought, otherwise their services wouldn't have been required at all.

'Thanks, Virgil. Talk Geoff down while I take a look around.'

The light on her helmet illuminated the area, but she reached into her top pocket for a small medical torch. After taking the woman's pulse, which was faint, Clara quickly checked the pupils.

'Both pupils are constricting. Pulse is faint but present. There's a lot of blood,' Clara reported.

The woman was beginning to moan and Clara instantly tried to calm her.

'You're going to be fine. Help is here. I'm Clara—a doctor.' Clara's voice was firm but gentle.

'I feel…weak…' The woman's voice was a broken whisper.

'What's your name?' Clara asked as she waited for Geoff to get into position.

'Hmm…? G-Gale,' the woman answered after a moment.

'And your friend? What's his name?' Clara asked.

It looked as though Gale was ready to pass out again, but before she did she said softly, 'Dan.'

'Virgil, I'm going to need the largest compression bandage you have. I'll also need a neck brace to keep her head stable. Our patients' names are Gale and Dan. Gale has severe lacerations to the abdomen. Extensive bleeding. I couldn't even begin to guess what's been ruptured. It looks as though something has gashed her right across her stomach. Query fractured pelvis.'

Clara was hanging right beside the windscreen, almost parallel with it, and was therefore able to reach around to treat Gale's injuries.

'What about Dan?' Virgil asked as he manoeuvred himself into position to help.

'I can't get to him until we have Gale safely out of the way. I don't want to risk scrambling over the bonnet to check him out. The entire centre of gravity of the car would change.' She shook her head. 'He's unconscious at the moment, so until the situation changes we'll leave it at that.'

'Good call.'

Virgil continued to assist Clara as they treated Gale's injuries as best they could, needing to stabilise her before they could transfer her to the stretcher. When they were ready, Clara contacted Senior Sergeant Edelstein via her headset.

'Edelstein here,' the police sergeant at the top of the mountain replied tersely.

'Gale's medical harness is attached to the ropes. Have your team standing by. We're almost ready to move the patient to the stretcher below.'

'Will do.'

'Virgil, you'll need to come closer to help me support Gale. We need to keep her as horizontal as we possibly can. Sergeant Edelstein, get ready with the winch on the patient's ropes.'

'Standing by for your signal, Dr Lewis,' the police sergeant reported.

'Gale,' said Clara softly. 'We're going to move you now.'

Although Clara had administered pain relief, she hoped her patient remained unconscious until she was safely at the top.

'On three…' She waited for a moment while Virgil and Geoff came into position, so they could achieve this with as little fuss as possible. 'One. Two.' She held her breath and offered up a silent prayer. 'Three!'

The winch started moving and slowly Gale was hoisted from the car and lowered, through careful and meticulous instruction from Clara, to the waiting stretcher. Once she was there, Virgil's job began as he ensured Gale's safety and double-checked her bandages.

'All clear, Clara,' he reported. 'She's ready to go to the top.'

'Right. Sergeant Edelstein, the stretcher is ready, so

start easing her up slowly. Virgil, you accompany Gale while Geoff and I check Dan's situation.'

Soon Gale was halfway up the mountain, with Virgil rising steadily beside her.

'Geoff, I'd like to take a closer look at Dan and check him out.'

'Be careful, Clara.'

'I always am, mate.' She turned and smiled at the RN. 'Thankfully the car didn't shift when we moved Gale, and as I'm roughly the same size I should be fine.'

Gingerly, Clara pulled herself slightly up on her rope, so her feet were hanging level with the car's open windscreen. Keeping her body as still as possible, she began to lower herself through the opening and into the spot Gale had recently vacated.

'I'm in.' She exhaled slowly with relief.

Stretching upwards, Clara pressed two fingers to Dan's carotid pulse and found that it was slightly stronger than Gale's had been. She reported her findings into her headset. 'Pupils are constricting.'

Clara took a better look at the way Dan was jammed in and sighed resignedly.

'The steering wheel is all but sitting in his pelvis and his legs are well and truly jammed. Paraplegia would be my guess, but I sincerely hope I'm wrong. Sergeant Edelstein, I suggest we come up and the CFS crews come down to cut Dan free.'

'Roger that.'

Once she and Geoff were at the top, she headed over to where Virgil was pulling off a pair of bloodied gloves. 'How is she?'

'Almost everything is ruptured,' Virgil told Clara as Gale's stretcher was transferred to the ambulance. 'I found small splinters of wood. I'd say that a roadside fence pal-ing smashed through the windscreen as the car rolled and gashed Gale's abdomen.'

'Get to the hospital and do what you do best, Dr Arterton. Save a life.'

Clara held his gaze for a long moment before he climbed into the back of the ambulance. Virgil took the opportunity to put his hand on her arm, his eyes filled with fear and concern.

'You be careful when you go back down. Don't get into the vehicle. It's too unstable.'

'I'll make sure the CFS crews recheck the cables before I head down,' she stated.

'But—' He stopped, hesitating over whether or not to continue voicing his concerns. After staring into her eyes for a moment, he leaned forward and pressed a kiss to her lips. '*Please* be careful.'

Clara's heart fused with love for him. She could see he didn't want her going down, that he was concerned for her own safety, but he knew she had a job to do and he appreciated her skills.

She nodded, unable to find the words to reassure him as her throat had constricted with love for him.

CHAPTER TEN

CLARA AND THE rest of the retrieval team had extracted Dan from the car and got him back to the hospital. There had been one or two complications but they'd managed to prevail in the end. She checked with the theatre clerk and found that Virgil was still in Theatre with Gale. She handed over Dan's care to the orthopaedic registrar, then sat down to complete her reports, all the while just wanting to go home and sleep.

She was just finishing up the final report when Virgil sauntered towards her, still in scrubs and looking utterly exhausted. 'How's Gale?'

'Stable in Recovery. She'll need further surgery, but for now I can't do much more. I'm just waiting for the orthopaedic guys to call me in to do my bit on Dan.'

'He was in a bad way when we got him out, but I've seen worse and people have lived.'

'Like you?' Virgil sat beside her, wheeling his chair as close as possible, then leaning forward and pressing a brief kiss on her lips. 'I'm so glad you're OK.'

Clara pursed her lips and nodded, not wanting to talk about her accident, not wanting to open those flood doors on emotion, pain and anguish.

'You *are* OK, aren't you?' Virgil prompted when she didn't say anything.

'Yeah, I'm good.' She returned her attention to the computer.

'It's just that after seeing Gale's injuries, and still waiting to comprehend how bad Dan's are, it's made me realise I really don't know all that much about your accident except that you sustained a pelvic fracture and were in hospital and rehab for the better part of a year. For you to be incapacitated for such a long time can only mean your injuries really were extensive.'

Clara saved her work on the computer, then turned to face him, needing to ensure her professional mask was in place before she spoke. 'Yes, it was bad. No, I don't want to discuss it—especially not now.' She could feel her skin starting to get clammy and rubbed her hands together to combat it.

'Did tonight's retrieval bring back memories?'

'Retrievals always bring it back—especially when the team and I are trying to save a patient's life and I'm harnessed in and the only way to free the patient is to climb into the wreckage.'

'You went back in? I asked you not to.' Virgil straightened up and spread his arms wide.

'It was a judgement call. I discussed it with my team. Everyone was safe, and when the car shifted, all I sustained was a bruise on my arm—for which I've just finished filling out an incident report.'

'It *shifted*! Clara!' He stood and glared down at her. 'You could have been killed.'

'But I wasn't. Calm down.' She glanced around the ED and noticed that some of the staff were looking their way. 'Shh. You're making a scene and disturbing the patients.'

Virgil shoved his hands into his pockets and looked at

the ground, counting to ten. She'd seen him in this mood several times in the past, and even though she felt highly self-conscious right now, thanks to his outburst, she was impressed with the way he was really controlling that temper of his.

'Let me see your arm.'

'It's fine.'

'Please?'

Rolling her eyes, she showed him the enormous bruise on her upper arm, noting that it was already changing colour, dark purples starting to appear. 'There. Satisfied?'

The phone on the desk rang and Clara instantly snatched it up, eager to look away from Virgil's concerned eyes. 'Emergency Department.' She glanced across at Virgil. 'Yes, he's here. I'll tell him.' She hung up the receiver.

'Theatre?'

She nodded. 'Go work your magic and help save Dan's life.'

She smiled encouragingly but knew it wasn't a heartfelt smile. The strain of the night was starting to take its toll and all she wanted was to head home, take a shower and crawl into bed.

Virgil stood where he was, watching her closely. 'It'll probably be time for breakfast when I get out of Theatre. Mind if I pop round?'

'If you want to check up on me, then just say so.' She lifted her chin with defiance, calling his bluff.

'OK, then. I want to check up on you, to make sure you're all right, and that you don't have any physical or emotional repercussions from tonight's retrieval.'

'You don't have to, Virgil. I'm fi—'

'I want to, and I'm going to. I'll be round when I'm out of Theatre. Until then, try and get some sleep.' He leaned forward and pressed a concerned kiss to her lips. 'I love you, Clara.'

With that, he turned on his heel and headed off to do his job.

She was driving along. She was in a car and she didn't feel sick. This was a good thing. Wasn't it? But, wait, things around her were changing. She was now standing in the middle of Melbourne General's cafeteria and everyone was pointing and laughing at her.

'He left you.'

'He broke your heart and he doesn't care about you.'

'You'll never find love.'

Clara looked around at the people, some dressed in scrubs, some wearing white coats, some with stethoscopes around their necks.

'Why are you saying this?' she asked, but the only answer she received was a roaring round of people laughing.

Their laughing changed to shrieking, and then it wasn't laughter. It was the sound of tyres squealing on the bitumen road. It was the sound of crunching metal.

She was being spun around and around and around. She was back in the car, trying to clutch the steering wheel, trying to focus on the song on the radio, but the warbling noise made no sense. Nothing made any sense. Pain pierced her legs and metal seemed to fold in around her.

Clara tried to drag in a breath, tried to fill her lungs with air so she could scream, so she could alert the authorities to let them know that she'd been hurt. Where was the ambulance? Where were the doctors?

'Code Blue. Code Blue,' she kept trying to say, but her lungs refused to fill with air and she was unable to speak.

Gasping for breath, she felt a pulse of dread shoot through her, twisting her neck into a very uncomfortable angle.

She tried to look around her, but all she could see was the outside of the car she was in, hurtling through the darkened streets like a small ball in a pinball machine. The car went one way and hit a lamp post, the impact almost folding the metal giant in two. Then the car hurtled back the other way, smashing into some parked cars.

Clara blinked. She was still inside the car, but the large spacious inside cabin was now reduced to the side of a small cube, as though the car had been put through one of those giant compactors used in scrap metal yards. She needed to contort herself if she was going to fit, if she was going to survive this ordeal.

But did she want to survive?

Images of Virgil swam into her vision and once again she was back in the hospital cafeteria, with people pointing and laughing at her, telling her she'd never find true love ever again.

He'd left her.

He'd told her she wasn't important in his life, that his career would come first and he'd left her.

It was clear by his actions that she hadn't meant as much to him as he'd meant to her.

Virgil had been her one true love. Her friend for such a long time, her confidant, her study support. Now he wasn't here. He'd left her and he wouldn't be able to help her contort herself enough to fit into the tiny space which was now left inside the car.

Darkness threatened to engulf her—darkness at being all alone. She felt as though she were suspended in mid-air, in a sort of sling, trying to reach out to the people around her, trying to attract their attention, but no one seemed to be hearing her cries for help.

'It's because their careers are more important than you.'

Virgil's words swam into her mind and she looked around for him.

'Virgil? Virgil?'

She tried to call, but once again her lungs refused to fill with air and wouldn't co-operate with her vocal cords in making any sort of noise.

Why couldn't he hear her? Why had he left her? Why hadn't he loved her?

The next thing she knew she was sitting in a hospital bed, unable to move her lower limbs. Her pelvis was fractured in several places, her legs were broken, her toes crushed. Doctors were talking to her, telling her she'd been in Theatre for a long time and would still need several more operations, but they were hopeful she'd walk again.

'Unfortunately,' her doctors were saying, 'there was also a lot of damage to your internal organs. Your bladder was ruptured and your womb was damaged beyond repair.'

Damaged beyond repair.

They wanted to remove it, or they had removed it, or something else had happened. But her womb was gone. The bladder was fixed but she'd have to retrain it. One of her kidneys had also been damaged, but they were hopeful about that, too.

Clara looked behind the doctors to see her father holding her mother close, her mother weeping. Arthur stood next to his parents, patting his mother on the back, then he shifted and was standing next to the surgeons, nodding sadly and reading her charts as though he needed to recheck the information for himself.

Then everyone disappeared and she was left there. In traction. Unable to move. Suspended. Hanging there like a puppet whose strings were all tangled and its limbs in a mess.

She closed her eyes, wanting to have it all stop. She wanted it to stop. She wanted her world to just—*stop*!

Clara sat bolt upright in bed, her body bathed in sweat and trembling with fear. Gasping for air, she clutched a hand to her chest and stared unseeingly at her surroundings. The pictures on the wall. The light fixture on the ceiling. She was in her bedroom. She was safe. She was OK.

Slowly, she managed to calm her breathing as she climbed from the sheets and walked out into the kitchen to get a cool glass of water. The clock indicated it was almost six a.m. Sitting down at her kitchen table, she concentrated on deep breathing exercises. It had been years since she'd had a terrible nightmare about her car accident, but perhaps she shouldn't be surprised, considering the retrieval she'd just been through.

Clara had been trapped for almost seven hours before they'd finally managed to cut her free and transfer her to the Melbourne General Hospital emergency department—*her* department, at the place where she worked. Thankfully, the specialists had taken great care of her, but being a patient in the hospital where she had trained and worked had been an eye-opening experience.

Virgil had gone. Left her for his career. He'd left her and gone to start a new life for himself in Canada.

'Should I call him? Tell him?' Arthur had asked as he'd sat by her hospital bed in the intensive care unit.

Clara had been hooked up to several machines to monitor her vital signs, and she'd been in traction after several hours of surgery. Arthur, being the wonderful sibling he was, had told her she looked as though she'd gone several rounds against a champion boxer—and won!

Clara hadn't been sure she wanted Virgil knowing anything about her life now. *He* was the one who had chosen to leave, who had betrayed her. The real question which had nestled deep within her heart had been would he come back to be with her if he *did* know? Clara had been through too much heartbreak to risk him not bothering to return.

'Why?'

Her voice had been raspy and dry. Arthur had immediately given her a spoonful of ice chips.

'He clearly doesn't love me. If he did, he would have accepted me for who I am.'

To speak the words out loud had nearly caused as much emotional damage as the accident had caused physical damage.

Clara had had to come to terms with a lot in those first few days—especially the news that her womb and one of her ovaries had been removed.

'I'll never be able to have children, Mum,' Clara had wailed, and together she and her mother had wept, their tears somehow binding them closer together.

Her parents and Arthur had been wonderful, caring for her while she'd been an inpatient in hospital and looking after her life outside the hospital.

'The doctors say you're going to need a lot of rehabilitation once all your surgeries are done,' her father had said. 'And...er...' He'd looked across at her mother, who had nodded encouragingly. 'We wanted you to come and live with us when you get out.'

It was then that Clara had realised she was still paying rent on an empty apartment, and although she'd had accident insurance, there was only so far that would stretch. Her parents had helped her make some difficult decisions—namely breaking her lease and putting her furniture and belongings into storage.

Clara had been cut off from the outside world. Her new world had consisted of one medical appointment after another. Doctors, lawyers, physiotherapists, dieticians, psychologists—the list had gone on and on, and once Clara had been finally released from the rehabilitation hospital, nearly eight months later, she had gone home with her parents.

Her family had been incredible, and the accident had most definitely brought them all closer together.

'You're our miracle girl,' her mother had told Clara once. 'As hard as this year has been, you weren't taken from us, darling. That's all I care about.'

Eventually Clara had been able to think about working again, and Arthur had found her this apartment. Her parents had been more than happy to have her move out knowing her big brother was just downstairs.

Now, as she sat at the table, Clara sipped the cool water and shoved her hands through her hair, surprised to find she'd been perspiring. Given she often repressed a lot of those old emotions about that traumatic time of her life, and after tonight's emergency retrieval, was it any wonder her subconscious had burst open and given her the nightmare of the year?

Rising, Clara went to the cupboard where she stored her medical kit and took some paracetamol to help with the ache pounding in her head. No sooner had she swallowed them than she heard a soft knocking at her front door. Glancing down at her attire of comfortable pyjamas, and deciding she was decent enough for company, she opened the door.

'Hi.'

'Hi,' Virgil responded, and when she stepped back to allow him entry, he came in.

Clara shut the door behind him and noticed he was looking around the room, taking in the decor of her apartment.

'Nice place. Where's Juzzy?'

'Asleep on my bed.' She frowned. 'I think… Or she might be in her basket. Either way, it's too early for that princess to be out of bed.'

Virgil smiled, but it didn't last long as he studied her. 'How are you feeling?'

'OK.'

He glanced behind her, noticing the box of paracetamol and the half-drunk glass of water.

'Really?'

Without another word, he covered the distance between them and gathered her into his arms as though needing to share her pain.

'Is the headache bad?'

'It's just a mild one.'

'Liar.'

Her answer was to shrug one shoulder.

'Tonight's accident brought all your memories back, didn't it?' he asked softly. He eased back and looked deeply into her eyes before scanning her face. 'Have you had a nightmare?'

Clara nodded.

'Then why do you put yourself through doing retrievals if it brings back horrible memories?'

'Because I remember the people who were there when *I* was being cut out of the car.'

'You were cut out of the car!'

She nodded. 'A reckless drunk driver smashed into me. My car rolled, smashing its way through the streets, collecting a lamp-post and a few other cars on its way. I was trapped for seven hours, and during that time those people in the retrieval team were my lifeline. There were so many times when I really couldn't be bothered to fight. I wanted to *die*, Virgil.'

'Don't say that,' he implored.

'It's true.' She looked down at where his hand was still on top of hers, his fingers intertwined with her own. 'The accident happened two weeks after you left. When the hospital grapevine was working overtime with gossip about the way you'd left me—'

'Clara, I'm sorry.'

'I was crying non-stop, highly emotional, trying not to snap at the people around me and just wanting to finish my contract at the hospital and to be anywhere except where I was.'

Clara stopped, tears instantly springing to her eyes.

'I wanted to die that night, Virgil. I wanted it all to be over and done with. No more pain. No more problems. No more gossip. No more having to live my life without you.'

'Don't—just *don't*.'

She could hear the distraught sound of his voice but she continued. 'My body was as broken as my heart, and in a twisted, strange way it made me feel better. A lot of people can't see a broken heart, and I was able to hide mine—to lock it away while I focused on healing my body, going through surgery and then rehabilitation.'

Tears were slowly rolling down Clara's cheeks as she spoke, and when she'd finished Virgil gently wiped them away.

Leaning over, he claimed her lips, the touch tender and gentle. 'I'm sorry I broke your heart. I'm *so* sorry, Clara. If I had a time machine and could go back and slap some sense into my younger self, then I would. I would do that in a heartbeat. But I can't.'

He sniffed.

'All we can do now is to take what we've managed to salvage from the past and think of the fantastic things we've been sharing these past few weeks. We need to move forward with our lives.'

As he spoke Virgil started to yawn, and although he tried to hide it, it was to no avail.

'We need sleep.' Clara stood, but kept holding his hand. 'Come on.'

'Clara, if you're feeling amorous,' he stated as she led him towards the bedroom, switching off the lights as she went, 'you've chosen a terrible time, because I am *exhausted*.'

'Shh. I'm too tired and so are you. Just hold me, Virgil,' she whispered as the darkness of the room settled over them. 'Like you used to. Safe and secure. That's what I need tonight.'

'Your wish is my command,' he told her.

Clara climbed beneath the covers and waited for Virgil to join her. He kept his trousers on and she was grateful. He really did understand that, for tonight, all she needed was his arms, comforting and holding her. Washing away the past and the nightmares that lived there.

Snuggling deeper under the covers, Clara closed her eyes. Felt the warmth of Virgil's chest beneath her ear as she rested her head there, listening to his heart beating with its regular healthy rhythm.

This was where she truly belonged. This was where nothing bad could ever touch her. With Virgil at her side, Clara felt as though she could conquer the world.

But could she conquer the world if Virgil really knew all about her—warts and all?

CHAPTER ELEVEN

CLARA STIRRED LAZILY, slowly waking from the best sleep she could ever remember having. As she lay there with her eyes shut, trying to remember what day of the week it was, memories of the previous night came flooding back. The stress of the difficult retrieval, the nightmare as she'd relived her own accident, the way Virgil had comforted and supported her.

The last memory made her smile and she reached out a hand to the pillow beside her, expecting to touch his face or feel his body beside hers, but he wasn't there. Opening her eyes, she raised herself up onto her elbows. Whilst the covers were a little crumpled, and whilst she could most definitely smell his enticing scent on the sheets next to her, there was no sign of Virgil.

It was then she glanced at the clock and nearly levitated off the mattress.

'Half past twelve!'

She had a busy Monday morning clinic to attend to!

Clara threw back the covers and scrambled out. 'Virgil?' she called as she softly padded out to the kitchen. No answer. 'Virgil?' she called again, a little louder this time. Still no reply.

A quick tour of her apartment confirmed that Virgil wasn't anywhere to be found.

She checked her phone to see if he'd left her a message, and sure enough there was one text. It simply said:

You deserve a sleep-in. Your patients have been taken care of, so rest. Talk soon.

There were no little kisses, no emojis attached to the message. At the thought of Virgil sending her a message with emojis attached she grinned, because he really wasn't an emoji type of guy.

She quickly called the clinic, wondering if Jane had spent the better part of the morning cancelling her patients. When Jane answered, it was with a bright and easy air.

'Jane. It's Clara. I'm so sorry I didn't turn up this morning, but with the retrieval last night and—'

'Don't sweat it,' Jane remarked. 'Between Virgil and Arthur, all your patients have been seen. Mrs Holden was especially pleased to see the dashing Dr Arterton. She called him a "dish". Is that a compliment?'

'Virgil *and* Arthur saw my patients this morning?'

'Yep. Virgil did the first few hours and Arthur's just finishing off now.'

'But Arthur's supposed to be at the hospital!'

'Maybelle's covering for him there.' Jane chuckled. 'It's OK, Clara. We've all got your back and…well—' she giggled '—when Virgil gives you that smile and looks at you with those gorgeous blue eyes of his, how can you possibly say no!'

'Gosh, I hope he didn't use that trick on Arthur,' Clara mumbled, still confused as to how Virgil had managed to get Arthur to agree.

She rang off and decided that as her afternoon clinic didn't start for another hour, she could at least have some breakfast. As she made herself some coffee and patted her dog, she pondered Arthur's reaction to Virgil's request. When Clara had told her brother that she was seeing Virgil again, Arthur had been cautiously protective but not entirely surprised.

'I've been watching him around the hospital this past month—watching how he is with his patients, with the staff—and I have to say he has changed from the egocentric man of the past.'

'So you're OK with me seeing him?'

'Clara, you're a grown woman. You can make your own decisions.'

'But do you think it's a mistake?'

Arthur had hugged her close. 'Whether it is or not, I think you owe it to the two of you to find out.' He'd paused, then asked, 'Does he know about the accident?'

'He knows.'

'And about the extent of your injuries? That you can't carry a child?'

'Er…no.'

Arthur had let her go, but given her his best 'brother knows best' stare. 'You need to tell him, Clara. If you *are* going to end up together, he deserves to know.'

'I know, I know. I will—and soon.'

And yet as she finished her coffee and headed to her room to get dressed, she realised she still hadn't had that conversation with Virgil. After this morning, when he'd come by and stayed with her, holding her, letting her sleep, and then organising to cover her clinic…

She clutched her hands to her chest and sighed. It was the most romantic thing he'd ever done for her. She knew she owed him the truth—that if they were going to have any future together he needed to be aware that she could never give him a child.

With the way he loved Rosie, plus the few times he'd raised the topic of children, she instinctively knew he wanted more—and she couldn't give him any. Would that matter? Would he still want to be with her? He'd told her last night, before she'd left to come home, that he loved her. Why had he said that? All it had done was put more pressure on her. And whilst her exhausted heart had soared with happiness at the declaration, she'd also felt a band beginning to constrict around her heart.

The only way forward was to face the inevitable, and the sooner she did that, the sooner she would know where she stood.

She had to tell Virgil, and soon.

After her afternoon clinic had been completed, Clara headed over to the hospital for a debrief with the rest of the retrieval team from last night's accident. Before the debriefing, Clara went to check on Dan and Gale, and was pleased to discover that they were both off the critical list. Throughout the debriefing she found it difficult to keep her concentration on what she and the other emergency officials were saying, given that Virgil was standing close by her.

'You've got it bad,' her brother whispered in her ear once the briefing was done.

Virgil was chatting with Geoff on the other side of the room and Clara was simply standing there, watching him. Arthur's comments brought her back to reality. Several of the other staff members were heading out of the room, and soon it was just herself and Arthur, with Virgil and Geoff deep in discussion on the other side of the room.

'What?' She turned her back to Virgil and focused her attention on Arthur.

'Virgil. You really are in love with him.' It was a statement and Arthur shrugged a shoulder. 'Happens to the best of us.'

'You've changed your tune. You were telling me to be careful and—'

'And I still am, but I have to say I was very intrigued earlier this morning, when I opened my front door, to find him standing there asking me to help him cover your clinic so you could rest.' Arthur gave her a concerned look. 'He mentioned you'd had bad dreams about your accident. Are you OK?'

'Yeah. Often happens after car accident retrievals.'

'I know.' Arthur hugged her close for a moment. 'And where Virgil is concerned, I have to say I'm impressed. He really does love you, Clara.'

'Yeah?'

'And he wants to marry you.'

'Wait. What? How do you know?'

'Because when I asked him what his intentions were towards you, that's what he told me.'

Her eyes widened. 'He did?' Then her gaze turned worried. 'You didn't tell him about—?'

'No. That's your job. But whatever happens…'

He kissed her forehead, leaving the rest of the sentence unspoken because she knew what he was talking about. He would always be there for her, no matter what.

'Anyway, I'd best get back to work. Lots of paperwork to fill in and rosters to write. You still OK with your two shifts per month on a Saturday night?'

'Sure am, bro.'

'Good. That means you're working this Saturday and I get the night off to spend with my family.'

With that, Arthur headed out of the room. Clara turned to gather up her reports, but when she turned back it was to find Virgil walking towards her, grinning.

'Hi, there,' he stated. 'Did you have a nice sleep-in?'

'I did. I sent you a text, conveying my thanks, but I'll say it in person, too. Thank you for organising my clinic and my patients and people to help. I appreciate it.'

'Your family love you…as do I.'

'Virgil—' She stopped and looked down at the floor, unsure what to do or say next, because every time he said that he loved her, she felt the most glorious warmth and happiness wash over her before the hefty weight of guilt settled on her shoulders.

'Too soon? I can stop saying it.'

'No—it's not that. It's—' She glanced around the room, and although they were the last two people there she knew this wasn't the place to tell him what she needed to say. 'I need to talk to you.'

He was instantly concerned. 'Are you all right?'

'Yeah. I just need to share some things with you.'

'If you're not ready, I don't want to pry, Clara. You need to be ready.'

'I am.' She nodded for emphasis.

He smiled at her words and gazed into her eyes as though she'd just given him the moon. She hoped he still felt like that after he'd heard what she had to say.

'Do you have time now, or are you expected home for dinner? I wouldn't want you to miss putting Rosie to bed.'

'I was going to check on my patients in the ward, then head home. You could join me? Help me put Rosie to bed?'

'OK. Sounds good.'

His smile increased as he headed out of the room, leaving her clutching her reports to her chest and hoping against hope that she was doing the right thing.

Of *course* it was the right thing. If she was going to forge any sort of future with him, be able to put her trust in him once again, then she needed to address the past.

With a thread of determination running through her, Clara marched towards her future with her head held high and a heart full of hope.

When Virgil pulled into his driveway, his spirits were soaring. There was a spring in his step as he collected his briefcase and the flowers he'd stopped to buy on the way home. Clara was coming over to tell him something important, and if things went as well as he hoped then perhaps tonight they'd be celebrating her accepting his proposal.

He wanted to be with her—he'd made no secret of that. He'd declared his intentions to her several times, even though he'd felt a hint of reticence on her part, but whatever that part was, seemed to have been removed and she was ready to talk to him. She was starting to trust him again. This was good.

No sooner had he entered the house than a sudden ear-splitting scream pierced right through his heart.

'Rosie!' He dropped the flowers and his briefcase on the floor and rushed up the stairs. 'Rosie?'

There was no answer. Rosie knew that whenever he or Gwenda called her she must answer immediately. This time she did not respond.

Virgil hurried into her bedroom, his eyes scanning the floor. The bookshelves had fallen, trapping Rosie underneath. Virgil's heart hammered in his throat as he quickly bent and began tossing books out of the way before he could successfully remove the wooden shelves.

'Rosie?'

He heard Gwenda calling. 'In here,' he called back, and soon the housekeeper was by his side, helping to remove the debris.

'My goodness! Rosie! I was bringing in the washing,

then coming to get her ready for her bath, when I heard that crash.'

'She must have climbed up on the shelves and over-balanced,' he surmised as he was finally able to reach his daughter.

He stopped himself from instantly scooping her into his arms, even though that was exactly what he wanted to do. Instead he ran his hands gingerly over her bones, checking for breaks.

'Her leg feels broken. Get my medical bag from the car and I'll stabilise her before we move her.'

'Do you want me to call an ambulance?' Gwenda asked, wringing her hands in anguish.

'I'll be able to get her there faster. Just get my bag.'

Gwenda went off to do his bidding but he stopped her. 'Can you get me the children's paracetamol liquid first?'

'Of course.' Gwenda grabbed the medicine before going out to the car to get Virgil's medical bag.

Virgil brushed the hair from Rosie's eyes. 'Sweetheart? Rosie?' he soothed, but received no response.

He checked her pupils, took her pulse, made sure she didn't have any cuts or scratches.

'Blossom? It's Daddy,' he said, and this time her eyes flickered open for a brief second before closing again.

She started to whimper and Virgil's heart constricted in pain. He hated it when she suffered. Why hadn't he found the time to ensure those bookshelves had been secured to the wall? Why hadn't he taken better care of his girl? Because he'd been busy paying attention to Clara rather than doing the one thing he was meant to do—being a good father to his child.

'Where is it sore, baby? Does your head hurt?'

Virgil administered liquid paracetamol through a drop-per. Rosie was still whimpering.

'Shh. It's all right, darling. Daddy's here. Everything's going to be fine.'

Through the multitude of emotions Virgil was experiencing, uppermost in his mind was fear.

If anything happened to Rosie…he didn't know what he would do.

Being a father meant the world to him. Rosie was the most perfect thing he'd ever had in his life. Even though his marriage hadn't been the happiest, Rosie had been the little ray of sunshine which had brightened his existence.

He was angry at his daughter for attempting to climb up the shelves—especially when she'd been told not to do it. He was angry with himself for not ensuring the shelves were better stabilised. He was thankful he'd arrived home just at the right time—that he hadn't been delayed at the hospital. He was cross with himself for having dallied in buying flowers for Clara. If he hadn't, he'd have been home sooner and Rosie would have been playing with him, rather than making mischief in her bedroom.

When Gwenda returned, Virgil splinted Rosie's tiny little leg. It was ridiculous to realise just how small she really was. Once the splint was in place, he fashioned a small brace from a tea towel and the newspaper he'd asked Gwenda to fetch, so he could use it as a cervical splint.

'Just in case she has some injuries I don't know about,' he muttered to Gwenda as he carefully scooped his little girl into his arms. 'OK. Let's get her to the hospital.' His tone was brisk, his body rigid, his jaw set. 'You'll have to drive, Gwenda. Rosie may have a head injury and for the moment she's comfortable in my arms, so the less she's moved, the better.'

'OK.'

Just as they stepped outside he saw Clara's car just turning into his driveway.

'Never mind, Gwenda. We'll go in Clara's car.'

Gwenda was already opening the rear passenger door. 'I'll lock up the house. then meet you at the hospital,' the housekeeper told him.

Virgil only heard half of what Gwenda was saying as the majority of his attention was focused on Rosie. When Clara took in the situation, Virgil briefly registered the look of horror on her face.

'No, no, no! What's happened to Rosie?'

'Some bookshelves fell on her.' Virgil's words were clipped and direct.

'Right. Straight to the ED for us.'

As Clara drove, she had to stop herself from speeding, from taking unnecessary risks to get Rosie to the hospital sooner. Virgil simply sat there with his daughter in his arms, crooning over and over.

'Shh, baby. It's all right. Daddy's here. Daddy will fix everything.'

The anguish in his tone was veiled, but she heard it, and it broke her heart to see him in so much pain.

When they arrived at the hospital they were met by an orderly with a barouche. Clara had called ahead, with her hands-free phone, to let the hospital know of their imminent arrival.

'I need X-rays of her left femur and, more importantly, her head.' Virgil was giving orders. 'Clara, I've given her paracetamol but nothing else. Find out the correct dosage for a child of three and get her some analgesics.'

'Does she have any allergies?'

'No.' He paused for a second. 'At least none that I'm aware of. She's only three years old.' He shook his head, as though to clear it, then another round of instructions flowed from his mouth. 'Contact the children's hospital in Melbourne and organise for a paediatric orthopaedic surgeon to come here immediately. The less Rosie is moved, the better,' Virgil instructed as he walked with the barouche into the hospital and through to X-Ray.

Clara wanted to soothe him, to tell him that everything would be all right, that children were resilient, but she wasn't sure of anything right now. It was becoming increasingly difficult to hold on to her professionalism because she loved that little girl so very much, but she knew she needed to stay cool, calm and collected—especially as it appeared Virgil was in full parental panic mode.

She didn't blame him. Instead, she did as he'd suggested and checked on the analgesic dosage requirements for a three-year-old, estimating Rosie's weight. Next she placed a call to the children's hospital in Melbourne and spoke with the director of Orthopaedics. She related the particulars of the accident and enquired whether a surgeon would be able to come to Loggeen for review.

'I'm sorry, Dr Lewis. I can't possibly spare anyone today.'

'The patient is Rosie Arterton. Virgil Arterton's daughter,' she added hopefully.

She knew Virgil would have friends in high places and at the moment he needed every string that was available, pulled.

She heard the director groan with frustration. 'Is there any sign of head injury?' he asked.

'She's being X-rayed now and has been slipping in and out of consciousness.'

'I don't know what else I can do. I'm sorry, Dr Lewis, I can't possibly spare anyone to send to Loggeen. Believe me—if I could, I would. Best to get her flown here in the hospital's helicopter and we'll ensure she's seen immediately.'

Clara sighed and the director picked up on it.

'I know he's not going to like it, but it's the best I can do.'

'Thanks. I appreciate it.' She rang off, then set about organising the helicopter. Once the transfer details were taken care of, she called Gwenda.

'Oh, how is she?' Gwenda sounded distressed.

'She's in X-Ray. We'll know more soon. Have you left home yet?'

'Just about to get in the car.'

'Would you mind packing some clothes, please? One bag for Rosie—pyjamas and comfortable clothes—and also one for Virgil.'

'Why? Why? What's happened?' Gwenda choked back a sob.

'I can't get a specialist to come here so I've arranged a transfer for Rosie to the children's hospital in Melbourne.'

'Oh, no. *Oh, no.* I should have been watching her.'

'Gwenda, you can't be expected to watch her twenty-four hours a day. She'll be as right as rain.'

Even as she said the words Clara was trying to force herself to believe them. It all depended on the results of Rosie's head X-ray. If the little girl had suffered a concussion, or fractured her skull, things might take a turn for the worse.

'Oh, Clara, I hope so. How's Virgil?'

'Feeling helpless.'

'That's not good. OK, I'll go back inside and pack them both a bag.'

'Thanks. They'll be leaving in about half an hour, and at least the helicopter flight won't take too long.'

Clara rang off and reviewed her check-list to ensure she'd done everything that needed doing. She then called through to Radiology to check on Rosie's progress and was told that the little girl was being wheeled back to the Emergency Department.

Clara readied a treatment room and when she saw the orderly pushing the barouche, directed him into the room. She had analgesics ready for Rosie.

'What's the situation?' she asked quietly.

He turned and looked at her, his eyes wild. She'd never seen him looking so utterly helpless. He wasn't here as a surgeon in command—he was here as a father. There was nothing he could do medically to help his daughter and it was tearing him apart.

Seeing him standing outside his home with the small, limp girl in his arms had caused an instant panic to ripple through her. The two people she'd come to love and cherish were both hurting—one in physical pain and the other in emotional anguish. She wanted to do whatever she could to help.

'Head X-ray shows a small hairline fracture. I want a CT scan performed to rule out any further injury. I'm still waiting to see the X-rays of her legs. They said they'd email the scans as soon as possible.'

'I have an injection for her.'

Clara set down the sterile kidney dish she'd used to carry everything in. She opened the swab, unwrapped the needle and drew up the shot. Swabbing Rosie's right thigh, she injected it into the fatty tissue.

'There you are, darling.' Clara spoke softly once she'd finished. 'That will help with the pain.'

Rosie's eyes fluttered open at the sound of her voice. The child looked at her for a minute, quickly scanned the room until she saw Virgil, and then closed her eyes again. Clara felt a lump appear in her throat. Rosie was so vulnerable, so helpless. All Clara's suppressed maternal instincts came bursting out. 'Everything will be all right. Just sleep for now.'

Tears sprang to her eyes. So this was how a mother felt when her child was ill. It was devastating—heart-wrenching and unbearable. No wonder Virgil didn't want to leave her alone. After everything he'd been through, Rosie was his life. She looked at him, trying to convey the fact that she understood his feelings.

He was watching his daughter, his jaw clenched tight. 'When will the surgeon arrive?' he asked.

'She has to go to Melbourne, Virgil.'

'No.'

'I spoke with the director of Paediatric Orthopaedics. I told him it was your daughter but he can't spare anyone. He's asked for her to be transferred by helicopter and promises she'll be seen immediately upon arrival.'

'No,' he reiterated. 'I will not allow her to be moved again. She's in too much pain. She needs a CT scan.'

Clara counted to ten. 'Virgil,' she said firmly, 'I understand how you're feeling—'

'You have no *idea* how I'm feeling,' he responded vehemently. 'You're not a mother. You don't have children of your own. How could you *possibly* understand how I feel? This is my *daughter*, Clara. My own flesh and blood.' He pointed to where Rosie lay. 'My daughter is lying there with a head injury, broken bones and in pain and there's nothing I can do.'

He ground his teeth, having spoken his words with determination.

Clara tried to let his words wash over her—he was worried about his daughter, after all—but the way he looked, the way he was gesticulating with his hands, his whole manner was reminiscent of how he'd been all those years ago at the fundraising dinner, when he'd told her that nothing else mattered in life but his career.

She forced herself to breathe calmly. Although his mannerisms might be the same, this was a different situation. He was worried about his daughter.

Still, he had no idea of the anguish he was causing *her*, Clara. No, Rosie was not her own flesh and blood. Clara would never be able to have any children of her own. But she had taken heart in the knowledge that if she loved Rosie enough, that would be all that mattered. She loved the child, rejoiced in her, and needed those childish little smiles to make her life complete.

'I may not be a mother, Virgil, but that doesn't mean I don't understand this situation. I love Rosie as though she were my own. I, too, feel devastatingly helpless, but in this situation you have to do what is best for your daughter. A surgeon can't be spared from the children's hospital in Melbourne and therefore, Rosie must go there to be treated.'

'You have no right—' he replied coldly.

'I have *every* right,' she told him sternly. 'I'm the admitting doctor. Rosie is my patient. You're her parent—act like it.'

Clara held Virgil's piercing gaze, not allowing herself to be daunted by it. When he didn't immediately reply, she took that as a sign that he was now willing to cooperate with her.

'The helicopter leaves in twenty minutes. Gwenda is on her way here with clothes for you and Rosie. You'll no doubt be at least three to four days in Melbourne before Rosie can be transferred back here. I'll ensure your clinics and operating lists are postponed until you return.'

At the end of her speech she stared at him, holding his gaze, her chin raised in defiance, almost daring him to dispute her words. Virgil's answer surprised her. He stepped forward and pulled her into his arms, holding her tight for three seconds, burying his face in her neck. Then he let her go just as abruptly.

Was that his way of thanking her? Accepting that she was in charge? Being grateful for her support? She had no idea what was going on in that mind of his.

'Are you coming to Melbourne with us?'

'Just for the transfer.'

Virgil clenched his jaw. 'What about in Theatre?' he asked. 'If she needs surgery, will you stay for that? They'll let you in.'

Clara knew what he was getting at. She wasn't a blood relation to Rosie and could therefore be admitted into theatre as an observer.

'If they agree, I'll be there. I love her, Virgil.' Clara's words were soft and tears began to brim in her eyes. 'I love that little girl with all my heart, soul and mind.'

'I can see that.' Virgil sighed, and she hoped his previous panic was over. He looked over at his little girl and shook his head sadly. 'She's so helpless and I can't just snap my fingers and make it better. I hate it when she's not well. It's my worst nightmare coming true.'

'Let me check and see if those scans of her leg have come through,' Clara said, and walked to the nearest computer screen. Sure enough, the digital scans were there, and together they looked at them. 'Greenstick fracture. The bone's bent on one side and splintered on the other.' Clara clicked on a different file and looked at the X-rays of Rosie's cranium, where a small hairline fracture was visible. 'I've already booked a CT scan for her in Melbourne,' Clara remarked, after they'd reviewed all the different scans.

'So she *will* require surgery.' He exhaled slowly as the situation sank in.

'It's minor, Virgil, and the operation to realign the splintered part of the bone back into place, takes less than thirty minutes. Slap a plaster cast on her leg and she's done.'

'She's never had a general anaesthetic before.'

His tone was soft, and for the first time since he'd bundled himself and the small child into her car, Clara was talking to the real Virgil.

'I'm sure she'll be fine. Kids are resilient. It's the parents who end up going grey with all the worry and stress.'

Clara crossed to his side and brushed her fingertips through his hair, delighted that he wasn't pulling away from her any more. As though he sensed her need, he reached for her with his free hand, the other one still firmly holding his daughter's.

'Come closer,' he urged, and when she complied he pressed his lips firmly to hers, his kiss filled with apology. 'I'm sorry,' he whispered. 'I said some awful things to you. Forgive me?'

Clara sighed and brushed her fingers through his hair once more. 'I don't scare that easily any more,' she replied, and kissed him back, wanting to show him that she'd already forgiven him.

CHAPTER TWELVE

ROSIE WAS GIVEN a general anaesthetic for the CT scan. She needed to be absolutely still, and the machine was rather frightening—even for some adults. As Clara had predicted, everything was fine except for the small hairline fracture which had shown up on the X-rays.

She quickly reported the findings to Virgil, who visibly relaxed and sank into a chair. Gwenda had insisted upon coming with them to Melbourne, which meant Virgil wouldn't be left alone with his thoughts while Rosie was in Theatre.

After the CT scan, the next step was to realign Rosie's leg. Seeing Rosie's small body, limp with anaesthesia, almost made Clara want to weep. It was different when a child was sleeping—a natural, healthy sleep rather than being sedated. She'd seen it on countless occasions with other patients but this was *Rosie*.

Get a grip, Lewis, she instructed herself as the theatre staff prepared for the operation.

It proceeded without a hitch, and Clara managed to switch off her feelings and observe the techniques the orthopaedic surgeon used. Finally the cast was in place, and Rosie was being wheeled to Recovery. Clara went with her, holding her hand as they went.

'Clara.' Virgil came into Recovery and crossed to her side, his face anxious with worry.

'She's fine, Virgil. The procedure went well, with no complications, and she'll make a complete recovery.'

Clara released her hold on Rosie's hand and stepped back, allowing Virgil access to his daughter.

'She really is all right?'

The statement was made with astonishment, as though he'd expected something terrible to happen.

'She's fine.'

Clara took a few steps away from Rosie's bed and Virgil looked at her.

'Where do you think you're going? I want you here—with Rosie.'

Clara smiled, delighted to hear those words from him. 'You stay with her. I'll go tell Gwenda the good news.'

'OK, but don't be gone too long. Once Rosie comes round, I'm sure she'll want to see you.'

'"And then my heart with pleasure fills, and dances with the daffodils!"' She quoted Wordsworth to him and he smiled.

'Go and tell Gwenda our little girl is fine. I'll try and talk the recovery nurses into letting her come in.'

'I'm sure you will, Virgil.'

Clara laughed. He was back. Her lovable, caring and silver-tongued darling was back.

When she told Gwenda the good news the other woman's face instantly relaxed and she breathed out with relief.

'She's really OK?'

Clara chuckled and nodded. 'She really is.' Clara beckoned for Gwenda to follow her. 'Virgil is going to try and smuggle you into Recovery. After all, you're like another grandmother to her, and she'll want you close by.'

Sure enough Virgil had squared it with the nurses.

'But only for two minutes.'

'Two minutes is all I need to see that she really is OK.'

With Gwenda and Virgil by Rosie's side, Clara was starting to feel the area was a little crowded and, not wanting to make the Recovery nurses angry, she excused herself.

'I just need to check something,' she murmured before leaving Recovery.

She left Recovery and walked down a long corridor towards the front of the hospital. The late evening warmth surrounded her as she breathed in deeply, grateful that Rosie was all right. The sky was a blend of glorious colours and she forced her mind to settle down to a more normal pace. She stared at the sky, just absorbing the moment—something she'd learned to do during that long year of recovery—but knew she'd soon need to start making arrangements for her return to Loggeen.

'Hopefully,' Virgil said to her a while later as she bent to kiss Rosie's forehead, 'we can transfer her back to Loggeen tomorrow some time.'

Rosie had been moved out of Recovery and onto a ward. Gwenda was sitting in a nearby chair, passing the time by knitting, and Virgil was keeping a close watch on his daughter.

'Children do tend to recover so much quicker than adults, and if the doctors are happy with her progress then that's a definite possibility,' Clara agreed. 'But you take care, too, Virgil. Don't go skipping meals or sleep. You won't do Rosie any good if you do. Doctor's orders.' She pointed her index finger at him for emphasis.

'You're not my *doctor*,' he replied as he released his hold on Rosie's hand and placed his arm about Clara's waist, drawing her closer. 'You're my *fiancée*.'

Clara raised her eyebrows in surprise and then looked across at Gwenda, who had stopped her knitting.

'Did you hear that, Gwenda? I'm supposedly Virgil's fiancée.'

The older woman's lips twitched as she tried to hide a smile.

'Forgive me for pointing out one small flaw,' Clara continued, 'but you haven't actually *asked* me to marry you—ergo, I can't possibly be your fiancée.'

'A small oversight.' He shrugged. 'The fact remains, though, that I *do* want to marry you, Clara. So what do you say?'

She started at him, aghast. 'What? That's it? *That's* my proposal?' she asked incredulously.

'Well, it's not exactly the way I planned it,' Virgil responded, scratching the side of his head.

'Good—because I don't accept *that* proposal.'

His answer was to chuckle, and she sighed with relief. Seeing him less stressed was a good thing.

'Why don't I walk you to the helicopter and you can tell me what your answer might be when I *do* propose to you properly?'

'Checking to see I'm going to give you the answer you want?' she asked as they left Gwenda to keep an eye on Rosie.

'I may be impatient, Clara, but I'm not a complete fool. Of course I'm checking. What man proposes if he knows the answer is going to be no?'

As they got into the lift to head towards the helipad, Virgil slipped his arm around her waist, his tone soft as he spoke.

'I know we have a lot of things to discuss, but I'm sure we'll get there, Clara. You love me. I love you. Everything else is—irrelevant.'

'Virgil…' Her eyes were wide with concern. 'I hope that *is* the case because—'

'Shh.' He bent his head and placed his lips briefly on hers. 'It can wait. Everything will be fine—trust me.'

Once they stepped out, a cool breeze whisked around them. Now that the sun had set, the evening had become rather cool. Floodlights lit the area and the helicopter pilot gave Clara the thumbs-up when he saw her. He proceeded with his pre-flight check and she took the opportunity to say a proper goodbye to Virgil.

'Please keep me up to date with any changes, good or bad, in Rosie's condition?'

'Will do,' he promised, drawing her closer. 'You take care, Dr Lewis. We'll have that talk as soon as we can.'

Then, before she could say anything, he simply lowered his head and captured her lips with his.

The kiss was soft and gentle and yet filled with promise. The warm, masculine scent of him swirled throughout Clara's body and she sighed with relief. As the wind began to pick up slightly, Virgil gathered her closer, protecting and shielding her from its coolness.

Clara's heart pounded with love for him, and the knowledge that her feelings were reciprocated only intensified her own. Virgil loved her, and yet there was a niggling doubt in the back of her mind that refused to budge, and it was that which was causing her the most consternation.

'You love him. He loves you. I don't understand why the two of you aren't announcing plans for your future life together,' Arthur stated the following evening, when Clara and Juzzy went over for dinner.

'Arthur, things aren't always so cut and dried,' Maybelle said, her words pointed. 'Remember with us… We loved each other but there were other things to sort out first.'

Arthur sighed as he passed the salad bowl to his sister. Clara helped herself but then looked down at her plate, unsure she'd be able to eat the delicious meal her brother had cooked.

'What is the one thing that's really troubling you?' Maybelle asked, after watching Clara push her food around on her plate for a minute or two.

'The *one* thing?' Clara looked at her sister-in-law. 'I guess it was when Rosie was sick, and he looked at me with such disbelief that I could actually love her so much even though she wasn't my own flesh and blood. I *do* love that little girl.

Later, as Clara tucked Fuzzy-Juzzy into her doggy bed and went to brush her teeth, she started to count her blessings. She enjoyed good health, had a roof over her head, a good job, a loving dog and a family who stood beside her, no matter what.

But what she wanted was to have Virgil—her soul mate—in her life on a permanent basis. She wanted to adopt children so Rosie could know and understand the love of a sibling. She wanted Gwenda to enjoy being a grandmother to all those children, and she wanted to fill a house with love and make it a home. *Their* home. Hers and Virgil's.

Was it wrong to want so much?

Three days later, after sporadic short phone calls and many text messages, Virgil, Gwenda and Rosie were back home, the little girl apparently quite excited to have her leg in a purple plaster cast.

'She wants you to come over and write your name on it, and for Juzzy to put her pawprint on the cast,' Virgil said over the phone.

'That'll be…interesting. I can just imagine Juzzy stepping into a tray full of paint and then running around the place, leaving pawprints on everything *but* Rosie's cast.'

His answer was to chuckle, and the warm sound washed over her, causing the love she felt for him to burst forth within her again. No matter what his reaction might be to what she had to tell him, her heart would be his for ever. This was something she'd come to terms with over the past few days. She loved Virgil. One hundred per cent. And that meant she would either have a very happy life with him or a lonely one without him. For now, though, she was through living in limbo.

'Listen, are you free right now? My last patient has cancelled so I'm done for the day and, well… I need to talk to you.'

'I'm free,' he told her, but she thought she heard a note of concern in his tone.

Was he worried about what she might say? Or was Clara simply borrowing trouble yet again?

'Do you want to come to my place? See Rosie? Have dinner?'

'Actually, why don't you come to *my* apartment. We'll be less likely to be disturbed.'

'Fingers crossed no emergencies come in,' he stated. 'I'll be at your apartment in about twenty minutes. I just need to finish writing up some paperwork.'

'Sounds good. See you then.'

And she rang off before she could change her mind.

Twenty-five minutes later Clara was pacing around her apartment, wondering if something had happened to him.

'Where is he, Juzzy?' She opened the front door and checked the hallway again, but there was still no sign of him. Telling herself not to panic, she re-straightened the cushions and checked her phone for the hundredth time just in case Virgil had sent her a message. Nothing.

Thirty-five minutes later there was a knock at her door and she opened it, her eyes wild and filled with worry.

'Hi!' Virgil stood there, smiling at her, and all Clara could do was throw herself into his arms and press her mouth to his.

Given she hadn't seen him since she'd left Melbourne, he was most definitely a sight for sore eyes.

Their mouths knew exactly how to respond to each other, how to entice and excite. Clara shivered involuntarily and sighed as he continued the sweet torture, shifting them both slightly so they weren't standing in the doorway. Clara kicked the door closed with her foot before deepening the kiss. She loved him so much and wanted him to feel every ounce of that love. She wanted him to be secure in the knowledge that together they could accomplish anything.

Virgil's rough five o'clock shadow tingled lightly over Clara's face as he broke free and pressed small kisses all the way around to her ear. 'This is so right,' he murmured. 'We belong together. We've always belonged together.'

It was such an exact replica of her own thoughts that she marvelled at how in tune they were with each other's feelings.

She led him to the lounge, holding his hand in hers.

'Before you start, can I just say that I'm really happy you're trusting me with whatever it is you need to tell me?'

Clara nodded and let his hand go, her palms beginning to perspire with her increased anticipation. 'I have something to tell you. And I'd like you to remember while I tell you that I love you.'

'Clara?' He frowned at nervousness. 'This is *me* you're talking to. We've worked through so much. We can deal with whatever comes our way.'

'Oh, Virgil, I hope so.'

Clara swallowed a sob, trying to summon the courage to confess the truth. He went to envelop her in his arms but she held up a hand to stop him.

'No.'

She needed to see his face when she told him the news, to try and read his initial reaction. The best way was the most direct—just blurt it out. And blurt it out she did.

'Virgil, I can't have children.'

There—she'd told him. The millisecond of relief she felt was squashed by the immediate devastation that crossed his face.

'What? How?' he questioned. 'But I know you want children, Clara, and I know you love Rosie, so—'

'I do, Virgil.' She clasped her hands to her chest, covering her heart. 'More than anything in the world I would love to have a child to grow within me, but it's medically impossible.'

As though the penny had dropped, he stared at her for a moment. 'The car accident.'

'My pelvis was so drastically crushed that I had to have a hysterectomy and unilateral oophorectomy. The remaining ovary isn't in good shape either, and was only left so I didn't go directly into menopause at such a young age.'

She bit her lip, willing him to speak, to say something, but he remained silent, as though trying to take in everything she was saying.

Finally he cleared his throat. 'That evening when we went for the picnic—'

She nodded. 'I wanted to tell you but I didn't know how. I know you want more children, Virgil, but I... I... can't.' Clara choked on a sob. 'And I want you to know that even though I'm not Rosie's biological mother—I'll never be *anyone's* biological mother—I love her so very much, as though she really were my own. I *love* her, Virgil, and I hope that together you and I can raise her and love her and perhaps provide her with—with siblings in another way.'

'Adoption?'

She tried not to wince at the way he spoke the word, as though it were ludicrous.

'Or we could use a surrogate. Perhaps one of the reproductive specialists can find one good egg of mine and fertilise it and—'

'What?'

He was looking at her as though she'd grown an extra head. Clara wrapped her arms about her waist, glad she was sitting down, because the look on his face of utter disbelief at the realisation of what her words meant, was making her feel faint.

Virgil stood and walked over to the bookshelf, where there were several pictures of Clara and her family, but she could tell he wasn't seeing any of them. His mind was whirring, trying to compute what she'd told him.

Eventually the surrounding silence became too much for her to bear.

'Say something. Please?'

Virgil dragged in a breath and turned to look at her, raking his hands through his hair in agitation, as though he had no clue what to say or how to deal with the bomb she'd just dropped.

'I'll be honest with you, Clara. I'm stunned. Your injuries must have been utterly horrific. I mean, you told me you'd sustained a pelvic fracture as well as other trauma, but to have to deal with something like this as well…'

He trailed off, and Clara wasn't sure whether it was a good or bad thing that he was processing just how extensive her injuries had been. The question she needed an answer to was whether or not he'd be willing to try and have a family with her in the not so usual way.

He was looking at her now as though he was waiting for her to say more.

'Er…my accident… Right… Well, it was a good twelve months before my gait was back to almost normal, but my surgeons were happy with my progress.'

She wanted to add that it could have been worse—that she could have ended up in a wheelchair or even lost her life—but the physical trauma of her accident had been dealt with and she'd moved on. Hopefully Virgil would be able to move on with her.

He raked a hand through his hair once more, looking adorable and cute and so sexy and… And then she realised he was shaking his head in a negative way.

'I…er… I need to go.'

Clara closed her eyes, desperately trying to hold back the tears—tears which were only the tip of the iceberg when it came to the heartbreak she was presently feeling.

'I need to think,' he ventured, obviously feeling the need to twist the proverbial knife he'd just thrust into her heart.

He didn't make any attempt to hold her or kiss her or anything, but instead walked to her front door, opened it quietly and left.

Clara clamped both hands over her mouth in an effort to hold in the heartbreaking sobs which threatened to burst forth. She didn't want him to hear her crying. She didn't want him to see how his words, his actions, had ripped her to shreds once again.

She collapsed back onto the sofa, curling up into the foetal position and giving in to the pain. The old feelings of helplessness and heartbreak returned as the tears fell.

Juzzy—beautiful Juzzy—came and curled herself instantly in her mistress's arms. Clara held on to the dog as she sobbed. She had always yearned to be a mother, and with Rosie she'd been given that opportunity. Now it would all be taken away from her.

No friend in Gwenda.

No daughter in Rosie.

No soul mate in Virgil.

She was alone—again.

CHAPTER THIRTEEN

THE RINGING OF the phone pulled her from the deep sleep she was in and for a moment Clara had no idea where she was. The only thing she knew for sure was that she was very uncomfortable.

Opening her eyes, she realised she was still curled up on the sofa. Fuzzy-Juzzy had clearly decided to go and eat at some point, because she could hear the dog lapping from her water bowl.

The phone continued to ring. Sitting up, she groaned as her muscles protested at the position she'd contorted them into. Her mobile was on the coffee table in front of her.

'Hello?' she mumbled, her throat dry and scratchy. 'Dr Lewis.'

'Clara.'

Virgil's deep voice rumbled down the line and Clara almost dropped the phone.

'Virgil,' she whispered. All coherent thought left her as their discussion the previous evening, came flooding back.

'Clara—we need to talk.' He was direct and to the point. 'I know it's early, but can you come over before you head to work? Rosie would love to see you,' he added as an incentive.

Anger burst forth within her. 'Don't use Rosie as an excuse. I think it's best for Rosie if I don't see her again.'

'I can understand your anger—' Virgil ventured, but Clara interrupted.

'Oh, you can, can you? I don't think so, Virgil. Do you have *any* idea how hard it was for me to open up to you? To trust you? To tell you about something which has caused me years of distress? I saw a therapist for well over two years post-accident, because I wasn't able to deal with the fact that I might never become a mother, and then…and then you come back into my life and I think… Well, actually it doesn't matter what I thought, because all you've done is prove to me that you haven't changed at all. You're still that same man who put his own agenda in front of my happiness all those years ago.'

'Now, wait a second—' he started to say, but she cut him off.

'I have nothing more to say to you, Virgil.'

She was about to disconnect the call when his words tumbled out in a rush.

'Wait. I was an idiot. I love you, Clara. Please?' he implored. 'I handled everything badly. I'm sorry. I'm so sorry. Please, come over?'

Clara was silent. She'd never heard Virgil so worried, or so desperate.

'Please? Don't deny me the chance to explain.'

She looked at the clock. If she got ready for work and skipped breakfast she could make it to Virgil's, hear him out, and still make it to the clinic in time.

'I'll be there in an hour.'

'But—'

'An hour, Virgil.'

'An hour's time. See you then.'

His pleasant tone was forced and she rang off, her hands trembling with anxiety. Was she doing the right thing?

Clara dragged in a deep breath and stood, commanding her legs to hold her weight. She reminded herself that she was a strong, independent woman, and if she needed to live the rest of her life without Virgil Arterton, then she would.

'How much longer, Rosie?' Virgil was asking the little girl as they sat playing on the floor with some blocks. 'How much longer?'

Gwenda had let Clara into the house and told her that Virgil and Rosie were in Rosie's bedroom. Virgil had his back to her, playing intently with his daughter, mindful of the plaster cast on the little girl's leg.

Clara's heart swelled with love for him at seeing the caring and patient attitude he displayed with Rosie. He loved that little girl so much—surely he could extend that love to any other children they might have.

He built up a tower and Rosie knocked it down with her hand. Then her little blue eyes spied Clara in the doorway and her face radiated happiness.

'Clara!' she squealed, and instantly tried to stand, the cumbersome plaster cast making it difficult.

'Stay still, sweetheart,' Virgil told Rosie as Clara tiptoed her way through the toy debris scattered around the place.

She crouched down next to Rosie, wanting to keep a bit of distance between herself and Virgil.

'Hello, sweetie.' She gave Rosie a kiss. 'You're looking so much better.'

'You're here.' Virgil put out a hand to touch her. 'I'm not imagining it?'

The light touch on her upper arm caused a burst of

fiery awareness to flood through her. She did her best to ignore it. 'I'm really here, Virgil.' She tried not to put too much inflection into her tone.

Rosie clutched at Clara's hand. 'Let's have a special playtime with Daddy. Let's play with the blocks. I know the letters. That's an A,' Rosie announced, holding up the appropriate block. 'That's a G,' she told them earnestly.

'Can you build a tower?' Virgil asked. 'Get Clara to help you,' he decided. 'I bet she loves building towers.'

'I do,' Clara declared, and together she and Rosie built a big tower and let it fall to the ground. Blocks went everywhere and Clara started to gather them up again, delighting in the child's giggles.

That was when she realised what Virgil was doing.

He'd arranged some of the blocks to spell out a message.

Clara was immediately thankful that she was already sitting down.

There, in multi-coloured plastic blocks, he'd put the letters together to spell out WILL YOU MARRY ME?

Clara could only stare at the letters, her eyes beginning to blur with tears. She looked at him, and then at Rosie, who seemed oblivious to the adults, then back to Virgil again.

'I'm sorry, Clara,' he whispered, and took her hand in his. 'It came as a shock and I didn't handle it well. If we can't have any children, that's fine. We have Rosie but, more important, we have each other.

Clara appreciated what he was saying, but did he really grasp the concept? 'If we adopt a child,' she asked slowly, 'do you think you'll be able to love that child just like you love Rosie? A child that isn't biologically your own?'

Virgil instantly nodded. 'Yes.'

There was no hesitation in his answer, and that helped to alleviate some of Clara's tension.

'What I said to you when Rosie was in the hospital—that you couldn't know what I felt like because you weren't a mother—that was mean and cruel and I'm so incredibly sorry. My only defence is that I was beside myself with worry for—'

Clara leaned over and pressed a finger to his lips to stop him, tears brimming on her lashes. 'It's OK. I accept your apology.'

Virgil took her hand in his and gazed lovingly into her eyes. 'I have thought about what you've told me, and I've reflected on what you've been through and how, when you met Rosie, you simply accepted her and loved her. It was so natural and easy for you, and it made me realise that you deserve to be a mother. You and me, we deserve to be parents together. And Rosie...' He looked at his gorgeous girl. 'She deserves to be loved by both father *and* mother. Together—the three of us—we can make that happen, and if there are any other children who join our family then it will make us all richer in love.'

His words were heartfelt and sincere and Clara found it difficult to control her tear ducts.

'Please, Clara, marry me? We've been through so much and yet we've found each other again. It's meant to be. Please be my partner. Be Rosie's mother.'

Virgil tenderly wiped the tears from her eyes, a look of hope in his. Clara looked at the blocks, unable to believe this moment was finally here and that he was waiting... waiting for her answer.

'Clara?'

The word was filled with worry, and it was enough to help her to snap back to reality. Smiling, she reached out her free hand and gathered three of Rosie's blocks together, arranging them to spell her answer.

'Y… E… S…' Rosie read the letters out, then blended them together. 'Yes! It says yes!' Rosie clapped her hands with delight that she'd read a real word.

Clara looked at the little girl and kissed her. 'Yes. That's exactly what it says. It says yes.' She looked at Virgil. 'Yes, I'll marry you.'

A slow smile spread across Virgil's lips and his eyes were alight with love as edged closer, needing to kiss her immediately.

'Kiss Rosie, too, Daddy,' the little girl interrupted, and Virgil laughed.

Clara laughed too as he complied with the wish of the other female in his life. Clara felt incredible—on top of the world—and it was all because of the two people in front of her.

'Clara is going to come and live with us,' Virgil told Rosie.

'Yippee!' Rosie announced loudly.

'My sentiments exactly.' Virgil nodded.

EPILOGUE

'ROSALEEN CAIT ARTERTON...' Clara warned in a voice her daughter had come to learn and respect over the past three and a half years.

'Yes, Mummy?' the six-and-a-half-year-old asked innocently.

'You've been told countless times before not to climb up on your bookshelves. Thank goodness your father bolted them to the wall after your previous fall or there would have been another injury.'

'Sorry, Mummy.'

'All right. Go and tell the twins to pack up their toys and wash their hands for dinner.'

'Do we *have* to pack up? We love playing together. We'll be quiet. We won't wake the babies.'

Maybelle came into the dining room carrying a large bowl of salad. 'It's not a matter of waking the babies,' she told her niece. 'It's a matter of dinner being ready to eat. And if the girls don't listen to their big cousin, tell them their mummy will come and check on the state of the playroom and it had better be tidy.'

'Yes, Aunty Maybelle.' Rosie sighed again and headed off down the hallway, grumbling about how difficult it was to be the eldest.

Clara turned to Maybelle and both of them chuckled. 'Such a hard life.'

Clara walked over to where a large travel cot was set up in the corner of the room. Snuggled inside were two little babies. It had taken some time for the adoption process to happen, and when she and Virgil had been notified that there was a baby waiting for them in the Pacific Island nation of Tarparnii, they had been surprised to find the adoption was for twins.

'We know all about twins,' she'd said as they'd accepted the offer, thinking of Arthur's gorgeous girls. 'Double the blessing, double the love and—'

'Double the trouble,' Virgil had stated.

And so they'd been blessed with two baby boys.

That had been four months ago, and now both Eddie and Percy had finally settled into something of a routine.

'When I have baby number two,' Maybelle said, rubbing her enlarged abdomen, 'do you think Gwenda will help me?'

Clara laughed. 'I don't know how I would have coped without Gwenda. While Mum and Dad are more than happy to spend time with their grandchildren, they also like to travel. Besides, as far as everyone's concerned Gwenda's another grandmother.'

'And I love each and every one of my grandchildren,' Gwenda stated as she brought more food out to the table.

She came over to join Maybelle and Clara, watching the twins in their cot. The two boys, with their dark skin and big brown eyes, had captured everyone's heart.

'My cup really does run over,' Clara murmured.

'You and me both,' Maybelle added.

'I'll join that club,' Gwenda chimed in, and the three women embraced, knowing that even though they might not be biologically related they were family through and through.

'Right. Enough of this soppy stuff,' Gwenda said a moment later. 'I hope that Arthur and Virgil are done cooking on the barbecue outside. Why men persist in shooing women away from the barbecue, I don't know. I can cook on it much better than either of them.'

Gwenda headed off to check on Arthur and Virgil while Clara bent to pick up Eddie, who was starting to fuss.

'I'll go check on the progress of the crazy cousins,' Maybelle said.

'I might give Eddie his bottle before we eat.'

'Good idea.'

Maybelle headed off towards the playroom and Clara cuddled her son close. She'd just sat down with a warmed bottle, Eddie drinking hungrily, when Percy started to cry.

'*Ugh.* You boys. You always tag team.'

'I've got him.'

Virgil's deep voice washed over her as he came into the room.

'Dinner's ready, by the way, but I'll organise a plate of food for you and put it aside.'

'Thank you.' She smiled as she watched him pick up Percy, kissing the baby's head before holding him close. Percy instantly stopped grizzling as his father held him, as though glad he was finally getting some attention.

Virgil came and sat down next to Clara, watching Eddie drink his bottle of formula.

'I love our boys, Clara, and they are *our* boys. We've only had them a few months and yet I can't remember life without them.'

'They complete our family.'

'That they do.' He leaned over and kissed his wife's

lips. 'You, me, Rosie, Eddie, Percy, Gwenda, Fuzzy-Juzzy and Peachy the bird.'

'And in another four months—' Clara nodded to where Arthur was standing behind his wife, his hands resting on Maybelle's pregnant belly '—we'll add to that number again.'

'It doesn't bother you, seeing Maybelle pregnant?' Virgil asked softly.

Clara instantly shook her head. 'After everything Maybelle's endured, she deserves a world of happiness.'

'And that, Mrs Arterton, is what we all seem to have found.' He kissed her once more, as though he couldn't get enough of his wife.

'*Ugh!* Why do you always have to do that kissing thing?' Rosie asked as she looked across at them.

Their daughter was sitting up at the table next to her cousins.

'Yeah,' one of Arthur's daughters added. 'Our mum and dad do that too.'

'*Blech!*' the three of them said in unison, making all the adults laugh.

'If you eat your dinner quickly,' Clara told Rosie, 'you can feed Percy.'

'OK.' Rosie's attitude instantly changed as she started to spoon food onto her plate. She loved helping with her baby brothers.

'We're going to be big sisters too,' stated Samantha, one of Arthur's twins.

'And we're going to help Mummy and Daddy with our new baby,' added Kristen, the other twin.

'You bet you'll be helping,' Arthur agreed, winking at his daughters.

'We're all going to help each other,' Maybelle stated,

and raised her glass of apple juice in the air. 'I'd like to make a toast. Everyone get a glass.'

It took a good three minutes before everyone had a glass with something in it so they could make a toast.

'To family. Both here and those travelling. May we always support each other with unconditional love, never asking why but instead asking, What can I do to help? I've been so blessed since I came back into Arthur's life, and never in my wildest dreams did I think I could be this happy and this cherished.'

'And never in *my* wildest dreams,' Virgil added, tacking his own bit onto Maybelle's toast, 'did *I* ever think I would be married to the woman I love the most, and that we would have an incredible family.'

'To family,' Clara said, clinking her glass with Arthur's.

'To family!' everyone echoed.

'Can I eat now?' Rosie demanded, and they all laughed.

* * * * *

If you enjoyed this story, check out
these other great reads from
Lucy Clark

REUNITED WITH HIS RUNAWAY DOC
ENGLISH ROSE IN THE OUTBACK
A FAMILY FOR CHLOE
STILL MARRIED TO HER EX

All available now!

MILLS & BOON®

MEDICAL ROMANCE™

THE ULTIMATE IN ROMANTIC MEDICAL DRAMA

A sneak peek at next month's titles...

In stores from 2nd November 2017:

- **The Spanish Duke's Holiday Proposal** – Robin Gianna *and* **The Rescue Doc's Christmas Miracle** – Amalie Berlin

- **Christmas with Her Daredevil Doc** *and* **Their Pregnancy Gift** – Kate Hardy

- **A Family Made at Christmas** – Scarlet Wilson *and* **Their Mistletoe Baby** – Karin Baine

---

Just can't wait?
Buy our books online before they hit the shops!
www.millsandboon.co.uk

Also available as eBooks.

MILLS & BOON®

EXCLUSIVE EXTRACT

Dr Hayley Clark and Sam Price's holiday romance was unforgettable – and unrepeatable! Then risk-taking doc Sam arrives at her hospital… Could their fling become something more?

Read on for a sneak preview of
CHRISTMAS WITH HER DAREDEVIL DOC
the first book in the MIRACLES AT MUSWELL HILL HOSPITAL *duet*

'Hayley, meet your replacement, Samuel Price. Sam, Hayley's just been promoted to senior registrar and you've taken over from her. You'll be working together.'

Of all the places…

Sam hadn't told Hayley that he was about to start a new job in London, and she hadn't told him where she worked. London was a massive city with quite a few hospitals. What were the chances that they'd end up working together? The way her pupils expanded momentarily told him that she was just as shocked and surprised as he was.

This was going to make things awkward. They'd had a fling in Iceland, agreeing that it would be nothing more than that, and they'd said goodbye. What now? Would she want to see if their fling could be something more, something deeper? Or had he just been her transition person, the one who'd helped her to move on after her partner's death, so she wouldn't want to pick up where they'd left off?

The problem was, he didn't know what he wanted, either. He'd really liked the woman he'd started to get to know in Iceland. But then again he'd liked Lynda, too—and his ex-fiancée had let him down so badly. Could he even trust his judgement any more? Would he be making a huge mistake if he started seeing Hayley?

She recovered first, holding her hand out. 'Welcome to Muswell Hill Hospital, Dr Price.'

Don't miss
MIRACLES AT MUSWELL HILL HOSPITAL:
CHRISTMAS WITH HER DAREDEVIL DOC
THEIR PREGNANCY GIFT
by Kate Hardy
Available November 2017
www.millsandboon.co.uk

MILLS & BOON®